SPEAR
OF
HEAVEN

Tor Books by Judith Tarr

The Hound and the Falcon

AVARYAN RISING:

The Hall of the Mountain King
The Lady of Han-Gilen
A Fall of Princes
Arrows of the Sun
Spear of Heaven

Lord of the Two Lands

Throne of Isis

SPEAR
OF
HEAVEN

JUDITH TARR

TOR

A TOM DOHERTY ASSOCIATES BOOK
NEW YORK

This is a work of fiction. All the characters and events portrayed in this book are fictitious, and any resemblance to real people or events is purely coincidental.

SPEAR OF HEAVEN

This book is printed on acid-free paper.

A Tor Book
Published by Tom Doherty Associates, Inc.
175 Fifth Avenue
New York, N.Y. 10010

Tor® is a registered trademark of Tom Doherty Associates, Inc.

Library of Congress Cataloging-in-Publication Data

Tarr, Judith.
    Spear of heaven / Judith Tarr.
        p.   cm.
    "A Tom Doherty Associates book."
    ISBN 0-312-85543-5
    I. Title.
    PS3570.A655S67   1994
    813'.54—dc20   94-30174
                                                    CIP

First edition: November 1994

Printed in the United States of America

0 9 8 7 6 5 4 3 2 1

Rudyard Kipling would have known where this came from.
So would the lamas of Shangri-La.

THE CHILD SLEPT, and dreamed of Worldgates. In her dream she sat in front of one, right on the threshold, and watched the worlds shift and change. She liked the green ones, and the ones that were all sea-wash and blown spume, and the ones where it was always morning, with the sun just coming up, and birds—or things like birds—singing in the unchanging light. But the fire-worlds were splendid, and the worlds of ice, though they made her shiver, and the worlds that were always night, with torrents of stars.

They were always changing, never twice the same. A million worlds. Mother said it, and Great-Grandfather, and Vanyi who ought to know, since they were Vanyi's worlds, or Vanyi's Gates at least. Kimeri did not know what a million was, except that it was very many.

She dreamed of a million worlds, and of sitting as she would have liked to sit if there had not always been Guardians to chase her away: not quite touching the Gate, and feeling all the other Gates inside herself, and the worlds inside of them, millions and millions and millions. She made a song of it, because songs were what she liked to make, this cycle.

And as she sat and watched and sang, one of the Gates was gone. Like that. One moment there, like a bead on an endless string. The next moment, nothing. Except . . .

She would cry, she thought, when she woke up. But not until then. In her dream there was no one to notice, no one to hold her and pet her and tell her there was no need to cry.

She hugged her dream-knees to her dream-chest. The

dead Gate was hurting worse now. It had not hurt at first; it had been too different, and too surprising. She had not known what it was until she felt how it crumbled and fell in on itself like the dry husk of an insect that she had found on a windowsill, that Great-Grandfather had said was dead. Dead was gone, except for a smear of dust and a bit of a wing.

Not gone, said a voice that was not a voice, not really. It came from inside, from the place where Gates were. *Not gone. Not dead. I am. I am . . . I still . . . help me!*

Kimeri tried to answer, but the voice, whoever owned it, could not hear her. *Help me,* it begged. *The Gate—I can't—help me!*

"I can't," said Kimeri aloud, because maybe that would make the voice hear. "I'm too little. I can't do anything."

Help me, the voice said. *Help me.*

No matter if it was a dream. Kimeri hurt. The Gates hurt, because one of them was dead. And inside the dead Gate was—someone. A voice. A person who could only cry for help, and could not hear when Kimeri answered. She was too little, and she was only dreaming. She could do nothing at all.

She began to cry.

It was universal law, Vanyi thought. In time of crisis, everyone capable of contending with the disaster was either asleep, abroad, or overburdened. A Gate was broken, a Guardian lost, and the one Guardian who could be spared to watch over the inmost of the nine Gates in the Mage-hall of Starios was a silly chit of a boy with a horror of young children. Particularly young children who, he insisted, had appeared out of nowhere, sound asleep and weeping in it, on the threshold of his Gate.

The Master of mages in the Empire of Sun and Lion, Guardian of all the Gates, priestess of Avaryan, right hand of the emperor who sat the throne in Starios, went in her own person to the hall of the ninth Gate, and found the child as the boy had said, drawn into a knot almost within the Gate. In spite of herself, Vanyi caught her breath. Even a handbreadth more, and the Gate would have taken the child.

The young Guardian had fled. "Coward," Vanyi said to the space where he had been. The emperor's youngest heir—for it was she, the tangle of honey-amber hair was unmistakable—was deep asleep, and crying as if her heart would break.

Vanyi lowered herself stiffly to the floor, gathered the dreaming, sobbing child in her lap and rocked her, crooning, "There, little terror. There."

The little terror woke slowly, hiccoughing, choking on tears. Vanyi shook her to steady her breathing, and slapped her once, not too hard, to get her attention. Her eyes opened wide, amber-gold and quite beautiful, even bleared with weeping; and angry, too, and bright with stung pride. "I'm *not* a baby," she said fiercely.

"Did I ever say you were?" Vanyi asked in her driest tone.

That, as Vanyi had hoped, subdued the child's temper, if not her pride. But she could hardly help that, with the breeding she had.

"Now," said Vanyi, "suppose you tell me what you're doing here."

Kimeri looked about. She did not seem surprised, but then Vanyi had not expected her to. She would have crept in, of course, when the Guardian's back was turned, and fallen asleep watching the Gate. She had done it before. She would do it again, no doubt, as long as her keepers persisted in falling asleep at their posts.

"I was asleep," Kimeri said. "I didn't mean to be here. A Gate died, Vanyi. It hurts."

Vanyi told herself that that did not surprise her, either. Seeing that the child was who she was, and what she was. "A Gate died," Vanyi agreed somberly, "and you should have stayed home, where you would be safe."

"I'm safe here," Kimeri said. "Gates won't hurt me. Even Gates that die."

"O innocence," said Vanyi. Innocence stared at her with eyes the color of amber, in a face the color of old ivory. It was too young to understand. She smoothed the amber curls and sighed. "I had better return you to your keepers before they add their own panic to the rest."

"They don't know I'm gone," Kimeri said. "You won't tell them, will you? They'll carry on till nobody can think."

"You should have thought of that before you escaped," said Vanyi.

The golden eyes lowered. Vanyi knew better than to expect that the child was chastened. Quelled, yes. For the moment. It would have to do.

The Guildhall was rousing to uproar as awareness of the Gate's fall spread outward. Vanyi was needed in a dozen places at once, for a dozen different tasks, all of which only she could perform. No Gate had ever fallen except as the Guild willed it—not ever, not in a thousand years. The shock resonated from Gate to Gate, from Guildhall to Guildhall across this one of all the worlds.

It had not gone outward yet, she thought, affirming it as she knew how to do, from within. The worlds beyond this were quiet still, untroubled by the fall of a single Gate among the many. But that quiet would not hold. Her bones knew it, stiff with cold that was only in part born of the night's chill and her own advancing years.

All of that beset her; and she rose with the child in her arms, and said, "Come then. I'll take you home."

Home for Kimeri—ki-Merian, Merian of Asan-Gilen as she would be when she was older—was the palace that rose in the heart of the city as the Guildhall rose on its sunset edge. Vanyi brought her to it on the back of a mettlesome seneldi mare, riding without bridle or saddle, since fetching either would have meant waking the groom who slept in the back of the stable. Kimeri would have preferred a mount of her own, but Vanyi was in no mood for such nonsense.

The guards at the palace gate were awake and too well trained to ask questions. They barely widened eyes at the sight of the Master of mages mounted bareback and bridle-less with a small amber-gold child riding behind. They bowed low to the mage, a fraction lower to the child, and let them in without a word.

2

"I AM GOING."

"You are not."

There was a pause. It was not the first, nor was it likely to be the last in an argument that had gone on since the night was young. It had begun with the two of them sitting reasonably civilly face to face across a game of kings-and-cities. The game now was long forgotten, and they were on their feet, he by the window where his pacing had taken him, she by the table, stiffly still, with her fists clenched at her sides.

"I will go," she said. "You gave me leave."

"That was before the Gate fell. The Gate which, I should remind you—"

"Yet again," she muttered.

He ignored her. "—has just this night fallen, and none of us knows why, or how. I won't risk my heir in an expedition that has gone from mildly dangerous to outright deadly."

"Oh, and am I your only heir?" she demanded with bitterness that was as much a part of her as her golden lion-eyes. "I've done my dynastic duty, Grandfather. I've given you another royal object to protect until it stifles."

He turned his back on her and stared out of the window into the dark. He all but vanished against it, dark as he was, and dressed in plain dark clothes as he had come from a walk in the city. The only light in him was the frosting of silver in his hair, and little enough of that.

She was all light as he was all dark: all gold, golden skin, golden eyes, golden hair cut at the shoulders and held back from riot by a fillet of woven gold. But, as he turned to face her again, he had the same eyes, lion-colored, and much the same face, black-dark to her honey-gold: strong arched brows, strong arched nose, stubborn chin. His beard was greyer than his hair, but not overmuch.

"Daruya," he said a little wearily, "no one ever forgets that you have given the empire an heir. It's still a remark-able scandal."

"What, that I wouldn't name her father, let alone marry him? Believe me, Grandfather, you wouldn't want him playing consort to my imperial majesty, when I come to it, which pray god and goddess won't be for long years yet. He's a beautiful, brilliant political idiot."

"And married," said the emperor, "to a woman older than he, much wealthier, and possessed of considerable power in the western courts." Her eyes had widened. He smiled. It was not a gentle smile, though there was affection in it, and a degree of amusement. "Yes, I know his name. You thought I wouldn't learn it? I've had four years to hunt him down."

She sucked in a breath. "You haven't killed him."

"Of course not," the emperor said. "What do you take me for?"

"Ruthless," she answered.

He laughed with a tinge of pain. "Well, and so I am, when I have to be. The man's an idiot, as you say. And you knew it when you bedded him?"

"I knew that he was fertile, though even if he hadn't been, I was sure the god would find a way to alter it. I wanted his looks and his intelligence for my child."

"And you didn't want a man who could bind you with the name of wife." He came back to the table, studied the pieces laid out on the board, shifted the black king to face the golden warrior. "I could have forced you to marry a man whom I chose, to cover the shame of a child born without a father."

"There's no such shame," she said, "in the tribes of the north."

"Then it's a pity you aren't a tribesman, isn't it?" He looked into her furious face and sighed. "We're all rebellious in our youth. My rebellion was to refuse to rule the western half of my empire, then to insist on ruling only there, and nearly breaking the whole with my stubbornness. My son's was to hunt aurochs at a gallop in country too rough for speed, and to break his neck doing it. Yours is mild to either of those. You gave us a scandal, no more, and an heir of your body. No breaking of necks or empires; merely of strict propriety."

She snatched the warrior from the board and flung it at him. He caught it in a hand that flashed gold—like her own, like her daughter's. Like that of every heir to the throne of the Sun. They carried gold in their right hands like a burning brand, born there—set there by the god, the priests said. She did not know. It burned, that she knew, and worse, the more she fought it.

"I'm going with the mages," she said. "They'll go still, you'll see. They have to find out what broke their Gate. I can help them. I have a gift for Gates, and for that kind of magery."

"So do they," he said, "and they aren't heir to the empire."

"You promised me," said Daruya. "When you refused me the right of Journey, when I became a priestess—you promised that I would have one later."

"As I recall," he said, "what I refused you was permission to run away to sea when you were pregnant with ki-Merian. I very nearly had to chain you in the temple then."

"But you didn't," she said. "I stayed home. I did my duties like a proper humble heir to the throne. I delivered my daughter, I nursed her myself, I raised her and weaned her and taught her what I could. Now she's old enough to be separated from me. I'll leave her here, I'll surrender her to you. But I'm going with the mages."

"No," said the emperor, impervious to her sacrifice. "Not since the Worldgate broke."

Daruya heard a sound behind her. She whipped about.

Vanyi smiled thinly at her. Daruya flung up her hands, the one that was simple human flesh, the one that flashed gold. "You too, Guildmaster? And what did he pay you to keep me in my cage?"

She gave Vanyi no chance to answer. Some time after she was gone, while the storm of her passing was still rumbling on the edge of awareness, Vanyi said, "Well. I presume you've told her she can't go."

"You always were unusually perceptive," said the emperor. He was not angry, nor particularly bitter. Wry, that was all, and a little sad. "I can't let her, of course. Whether or not she's been so generous as to leave an heir to come after me."

"Which, from the look of you, won't happen for another forty years at least." Vanyi spoke without envy. She had not grown old with excessive grace. Her hair, once the color of sea-moors in autumn, red and brown and gold intermingled, was winter-grey. Her pale skin was gone paler with age, the lines of laughter and of care drawn deep. She looked her threescore years and more.

He, who was but a little younger, seemed a man still in his prime. He made a gesture as if to deny her, but she stopped him. "No, don't say it. We're what our breeding makes us. I like to see how little you've changed, except to grow into yourself. It comforts me."

She left the door and came into the room, and sat in the chair that Daruya had long since vacated. He stood with his hands on the back of his own chair, staring down at her from his not inconsiderable height. "You think she should go?"

"No," said Vanyi. "Not in the least. While the way was open, while it was a simple expedition to the other side of the world, what better ambassador than the heir to the empire? But now . . . we don't know what we're going into. We don't even know what broke the Gate."

"And yet you'll go?"

"You can't forbid me," she said calmly.

"I wouldn't try," he said. "That was our pact from long ago. The empire for me. The Mageguild for you, and the mastery of Gates. Alliance wherever we could. But where we could not . . . well. We've never been enemies, have we?"

"Once or twice," she said, "we did disagree on policy."

His lips twitched. "Rather more often than that, I recall. But enmity—we never came to that."

"No," said Vanyi. She sat back in the tall chair and sighed. "I shouldn't even be here. The Guild is in an utter taking. You'd think it had never seen a crisis before."

"It's got used to having you in command," he said.

"Don't flatter me," she said with an edge of annoyance. "I'm running out on responsibility, much as your granddaughter would love to. Did you know that your great-granddaughter spent the night in the Guildhall, on the threshold of the ninth Gate?"

She had taken him completely by surprise. He looked so startled that she laughed; and that roused his temper, which only made her laugh the harder.

He shook her into some semblance of quiet. She looked up into his face, suddenly so close. He would kiss her, she thought. It was a fugitive thought, from nowhere that she could discern. It fled as swift as it had come, as he let her go and stepped back. She could not see that it cost him any effort.

Forty years, she thought. Forty years since she last shared his bed, and lovers enough in between, and she could still go all to bits when he laid hands on her.

He seemed long since cured of her. There had never been any hope in it to begin with, a fisherman's daughter from Seiun Isle dreaming that she could wed as well as bed the Lord of Sun and Lion. They had parted long ago, and properly enough. He had taken nine concubines in Asanion, half in obedience to the custom of that ancient empire, half in defiance of it.

The obedience was in the taking. The defiance was in the setting free, in giving them to choose whether to marry or to go where they would. In their own western country they would have had no choice but to remain in his harem; but in his eastern realm they could take the freedom he gave and do as they pleased with it.

Most had chosen to marry among the lords and princelings of the east. Vanyi had reason to suspect that not all of them had gone maiden to the marriage bed; but none of the husbands had objected that Vanyi ever knew of.

One of the royal concubines had desired no husband. She had gone away to rule a princedom in the east of the world, had prospered and grown old and adopted a daughter to rule after her.

Only one had remained with the emperor, and that was exactly as he wished it. She had borne his son and heir, and held in great honor the name and the title of empress. She was aging sadly now in the way of her people, but she was still alive and still hale, and he was devoted to her. Of that, Vanyi had no doubt at all. She had only to read it in his eyes.

He took no notice of her abstraction. "Where is the child now?"

She had to stop and remember Kimeri and the Gate, and the nurses' snoring as the child crept through the door into her own chambers. "I brought her back," said Vanyi, "and put her to bed, none the worse for her night's wandering.

There's a binding on her now, and I called one of the palace ul-cats to enforce it. She won't go anywhere again until morning."

"God and goddess," said the emperor. "She's as bad as her mother."

"I wouldn't say that," Vanyi said. "She was sleepwalking, it seems. She doesn't remember coming to the Guildhall. The Gate's fall brought her, I think—she's got Gate-sense."

"All the Sun's brood do," he said. He sounded faintly angry, though not at Vanyi.

"Poor Estarion," she said with rough sympathy. "It always ends in your lap, no matter where it begins. It's your doom, I think: to be the one who holds it all together."

He shrugged. Self-pity, Vanyi knew, was an indulgence he had given up long ago. He had been emperor since he was twelve years old, when he saw his father dead of poison in the palace of what had been the western empire, when western Asanion and eastern Keruvarion were united only by force and by ancient enmity. He had spent his youth and all his manhood uniting those two hostile realms into one empire, building his city on the border between them, bringing their courts together, making their disparate peoples one people. Now he had his reward. For five whole years he had had no call to war; for three seasons, no assassin had tried to take his life.

Strange how little he showed of all that. He had scars in plenty, but his coat and trousers hid them. His face was still more young than old. He kept from his youth a kind of innocence, a resilience that never seemed to fail or to harden, no matter how sorely he was tested.

If he was aware of her thoughts, he gave no sign of it. He sighed and said, "She's punishing me, you know. For letting her father die and her mother go away as soon as she was born. So she had an heir without a father, and meant to leave the heir as she was left, but I was cruel: I wouldn't let her."

"That was brutal, yes," said Vanyi, dry as winter grass. "You left Varuyan to find his own way as all sons must, even princes. If that was into marriage with a pretty fool, and into an aurochs' horns while that fool was pregnant with his daughter, that was his fault. Not yours."

"I know that," he said a little sharply. "Not that Salida was—or is—as much a fool as you insist. She's Asanian; she's practical. She didn't have the will or the strength to raise a Sunborn daughter. She knew it. She also knew that if she stayed in the palace, she'd be immured there, condemned to be nothing more than a dowager princess. If she gave up the child, surrendered her rank and her dowry, went back to her kin, she could marry again; she could have children that honestly were her own, and not the get of a god."

"Granted," said Vanyi. "But she could have spared something of herself for her firstborn: a word, a letter, some intimation that she remembers the girl's existence."

"We decided, she and I," said Estarion, "that it were best if she did no such thing. Less pain for her. Less difficulty for the child whom she so wisely gave up."

"That wasn't wise," Vanyi said.

He said nothing. She could not tell if he agreed, or if he was being stubborn, or if he had simply tired of the subject. He wandered back to the window. There was something of the caged beast in the way he stood, but a beast resigned to its captivity, its yearning shrunk to a dull ache.

"You were all the father she ever needed," Vanyi said, not to comfort him, but because it was the truth. "Haliya has always been a mother to her. But that's never enough for the young. They're the strictest traditionalists of all."

She could not see his face, only the broad line of his shoulders, and the heavy braid that fell between them. His mood to the touch of her magery was surprisingly calm. He said, "If Haliya loses the child of her heart, I don't know that she'll recover."

It was calm, then, over grief. No use to say that he had known it when he married. His line lived long, if sudden death did not take them, and he had taken an Asanian wife, of a people who blossomed early and died young. It had been necessary, one of the many necessities that bound two empires into one.

Vanyi gentled her voice as much as she might. "Is she so frail?"

"You should know as well as I. You saw her yesterday."

She ignored the snap in his voice. "She's grown old, to be sure, and I'm sorry for it. But I think she's stronger than you imagine."

"Strong enough to withstand the cruelty of a child?"

"That's what mothers are for. Grandmothers, too."

He carefully did not observe that Vanyi had never been either. She would have borne his son, if she had not miscarried. There had been no children after, of any of her lovers. Her choice. Her grief, when she had leisure for it. Which mostly she did not. The Gates were her children, the mages her kin.

"And I should go back to them," she said. He was a mage, if not of the Guild. She did not need to speak aloud the thoughts that were clear for him to read.

He turned in the window. "You will go?"

She almost smiled. "O persistent. Of course I'll go. I've watched my mages girdle the world with Gates, walking or riding or sailing from each to the one that must be built after. Now I want to see for myself what's on the other side of the world."

"And what broke the Gate there." He spread his hands, the dark and the golden. "I have no power to stop you."

"Of course you do," she said. "But you won't use it."

"Because I promised," he said, a little wearily, a little wryly. "I'm cursed with honesty: I keep my word."

"There are worse things to be cursed with," she said. She rose from the chair, creaking a little.

"Thank you," he said.

She blinked.

"For bringing ki-Merian home," he explained—not even a hint of rebuke that she, the mages' Master, should fail to read a simple thought. "She'll have better nurses after this. More wakeful."

"Less susceptible to her sleep-spelling." Vanyi caught the flash of his glance; she smiled. "Yes, I know they're all mageborn, and those that aren't, are ul-cats, with magic in their blood. Maybe she needs a simpler guardian: one too mindblind to notice when she's working her magics."

"I'll think on that," he said.

He would, too. That was the great virtue of the emperor Estarion. He listened to advice. He might not take it—but he did listen.

3

ONCE DARUYA'S TEMPER had carried her out of her grandfather's sight, she calmed as she always did, into a kind of sullen embarrassment. She went to lair in her safe place, the stable that housed her own seneldi, the herd that she had bred. There in the dark and the hay-scented quiet, she slipped into the dun mare's stall and sat on the manger, elbows propped on knees, chin on fists. The mare, accustomed to Daruya's presence at odd hours, chewed peacefully on the remains of her supper.

Daruya let the mare's peace seep into her mind, blunting the sharp edges of anger. "I don't know what it is," she said. The mare flicked an ear, listening. "Whenever I stand in front of my grandfather, I shrink till I'm no bigger than Kimeri, and no wiser, either. And then we fight. Or I fight. He just smiles in that way he has, and lets me howl, till he decides it's time to shut me up."

The mare nosed in the corner of her manger. Daruya stroked the black-barred neck, ruffling the mane with its stripes of black and gold. This was a queen mare: unlike the bulk of her kind she had horns, though not the ell-long spears of a stallion; hers were a delicate handspan, straight and sharply pointed. Daruya brushed one with a finger, pricking herself lightly on the tip. "I wish," she said, "that he could see anything of me but my worst. He thinks I'm an utter child, spoiled and irresponsible."

"And aren't you?"

Daruya flicked a glance at the stall door. A shadow leaned on it, regarding her with golden eyes. He was faceless else—veiled, hooded, black-robed from head to foot. He inspired no fear in her at all, and no surprise. "Chakan," she said. "What are you doing up at this hour?"

"Much the same as you are, I suspect," he said. His voice behind the veils was light, even laughing. "Let me guess. He won't let you go to the other side of the world."

"Worse than that," said Daruya. "The Gate we were to pass through is broken, and the mages don't know how, or why. Vanyi and the others are still going, but to the Gate before the one that broke. I'm to stay home. Just as I always do."

"I wouldn't say that," said Chakan, folding his arms on the half-door and resting his shrouded chin on them. "You're not kept a prisoner. Not even close."

She glowered at him. Chakan the Olenyas was a cheerful soul, for all his black veils and his face that none but another Olenyas or a heart's friend might see, his robes and his twin swords and his long bitter training. She knew that he grinned at her behind those veils—his eyes were dancing.

"But there," he said. "I cry your pardon. I'm supposed to indulge your temper, and here I persist in being reasonable."

"I hate you," she said.

"Of course you do." He straightened, stretched, yawned audibly. "Are you contemplating a suitable punishment for his majesty? An aurochs hunt, maybe? I'd rather a boar, myself, it being spring and all, and the aurochs not in rut until the fall. They're dreadfully peaceable at this time of year. A boar, now—a boar will rip you to pieces no matter what the season."

She never could help it with Chakan—he always made her laugh, even when she wanted to kill him.

He knew it, too. "There now," he said. "It's almost dawn. If you won't hunt boar, and I think you shouldn't, seeing as to how we'd have to rouse out the whole hunt, and they're all sleeping off their night's carouse—shall we ride instead? I've a fancy to see the sun come up from the Golden Wall."

"If you wanted that," said Daruya, "you should have left at a gallop an hour ago."

"Bet on it?" he asked.

Hells take him. He knew exactly how to twist her to his will. "Six suns, gold, that we don't reach the top before the sun is up."

"Done," said Chakan.

Daruya took the striped mare. Chakan had his own gelding saddled already, waiting in the stableyard and sneering at the stallion in his run. The stallion, who knew the cranky little beast, ignored him as a king should.

It was very dark, but the stars were brilliant, and Bright-moon rode the zenith. They rode down from the palace hill through a city already awake, the markets rousing and set-ting up, the bakers baking the day's bread, the smiths work-ing the bellows in their forges. Asan-Gilen, city of the two empires, which everyone called Starios—Estarion's city—was properly said never to sleep. Rather, it changed guards. Even as the merchants set about opening their stalls, the nightfolk drifted yawning to bed.

Some of them knew Daruya and greeted her, either with silence in the western fashion or with a word and a dip of the head in the way of the east. By the courtesy of Starios, none detained her, nor was she ever beset with crowds. Un-less of course she wanted them.

Spoiled, Chakan would say to that, and arrogant, too. Odd, she thought, that he could say such things and barely ruffle her temper, but if her grandfather even hinted at them, she flew into a rage.

She shut down the thought. The processional way, wide

and all but empty in the not-quite-dawn, ended in the Sunrise Gate, the gate that looked on Keruvarion. That was shut still, but the lesser gate beside the great one opened to let them through, with a grin and a salute from the guard. She found herself grinning back. The wind blew straight out of the east, full in her face. It smelled of morning, and of green things, and of open places.

Chakan's gelding was already out, already stretching into a gallop on the grass that verged the emperor's road. Daruya's mare tossed her unbitted head and snorted, and launched herself in pursuit.

East out of Starios they ran, across the fields new sown with spring, through the arm of forest that stretched out toward the city, and then up, veering off the great way to a narrower path. It wound upward through the trees, till the trees gave up the pursuit. The land here was stony, the way steep, tussocked with grass. Once, and then again, the seneldi leaped streams that crossed the track.

The sky, that had been all dark and stars and bright arc of moon, greyed as they rode, till it was silver, and the stars were gone, and the moon a pallid glimmer. Chakan's gelding stumbled in landing, after the second stream; but he steadied it, and it went on undismayed, racing the sun.

Daruya let the other take the lead, narrow as the way was, and difficult. Her mare was reasonably content to settle to the smaller senel's pace, flattening her ears and threatening his rump with her teeth only when he seemed to slacken. Daruya, after all, was not trying to win the race.

This steep rock that they climbed was the Golden Wall, not for its color, which was green in spring and brown in summer and white with snow in the winter, but for that it marked the border between Keruvarion in the east and the old Golden Empire in the west. Estarion had set his city just beyond the shadow of it, where it sank into a rolling land of field and forest, athwart the traders' road from east to west. There was a little river running through it, tributary in time to Suvien the mighty that was the lifeblood of Keruvarion, opening westward of the city to a lake on which the people fished and the high ones kept their summer villas.

All that, Daruya could see as she reached the summit of the ridge. Her mare snorted and danced. Chakan laughed aloud. The sun, just rising, shot a shaft of light straight into his eyes.

Daruya slid from the saddle and let the mare go in search of grass. She was breathing hard, and all her black mood was gone. She spread her arms to the sun. The morning hymn poured out of her, pure white song.

When the last note had rung sweet and high up to heaven, she stood still with her arms out, head flung back, drinking light. It had a taste like wine.

Awareness came back slowly. Chakan was sitting cross-legged on a stone, watching her in Asanian fashion, side-long. His eyes were the same color as the sunlight. "Sometimes," he said as if to himself, "one . . . forgets . . . exactly what you are."

The exultation of light gave way to a more familiar irritation. "Oh, not you, too. I get enough of that from my grandfather."

"You do not," he said, and he sounded like Chakan again, immune to the awe of her rank. "He is utterly matter-of-fact about anything to do with being a mage or being a Sunchild. It drives some people wild. He should be a figure of awe and terror—not a quiet-spoken man in a plain coat, who can drink light like water, and make the stars sing."

"That's just magery," she said.

"No," he said. "Mages can work great wonders, I'll never deny it. Sunlords are different. The god speaks to them directly."

"Not in words," said Daruya.

"Does he need them?"

That silenced her. She paced the rough level of the summit, turning slowly as she went. Away eastward stretched forest and plain, the wide reaches of the Hundred Realms. West was a broader level, forest that gave way quickly to tilled fields and clustered towns. Below on its own hill and on the level about, was Starios beside its lake.

The sun had reached all she could see, turned it to gold, melted mist that clung to hollows. She could if she wished gather the light in her hands. She knotted them behind her. The right hand with its golden brand was burning fiercely; she shut her mind to it. Chakan, if he knew, would say that the god was talking.

And did she not want to be what she was?

With a sudden movement she pulled off the fillet that bound her brows, worked fingers into tangled curls. Priests and royalty did not cut their hair. She had cropped hers short not long after Kimeri was weaned—chiefly, Chakan had opined, out of petulance that the child's birth had not been more of a scandal. People expected Daruya to do outrageous things. Often they forgave her, because she was their princess, and beautiful: the Beauty of Starios.

It was quite maddening. "Sometimes I think," she said to the wind, "that all royal heirs should be brought up far from court, in ignorance of their rank, until they're old enough to bear the weight of it."

"It's too late to try that with Kimeri," said Chakan.

"Yes, and I was going to leave her with the burdens while I ran away. Is that what you were thinking?"

"No," he said.

He did not point out that she could read his thoughts if she tried. In fact she could not. Olenyai were protected against magery; and Chakan, like some few of his kind, was born shielded, unreadable even if he had wished to be read. It could be disconcerting, if one heard his steps, saw him approaching, but sensed nothing in the mind at all, not even the shadow of presence that marked the rest of the Olenyai.

Daruya found it restful. He asked nothing of her as mage or woman—he had never wished to bed her, that she knew of, nor been anything but friend and, as much as anyone could be, brother. She had brothers in blood, or so she was told, sons of her mother and her mother's husband, but none of them had ever come forward to claim the kinship. Chakan was more truly kin, Olenyas though he was, bred and shaped to serve his emperor.

She, bred and shaped to be empress in her turn, said less bitterly than wearily, "All priests, even royal priests, are given a little freedom, a bit of Journey to teach them the ways of the world. I've not been allowed it. Yes, I know it wasn't safe before—there were still wars, rebellions, assassins coming right into the palace and dying on Olenyai swords. But that's over. After forty years of war, we have peace. We've had festivals from end to end of the empire, to celebrate the wars' ending. It's time now, if it will ever be—time for me to have the rest of my training."

"It's not," mused Chakan, "as if you'd never had training elsewhere. You've ridden to war with your grandfather. You've accompanied him on all his progresses since you were old enough to sit a senel, and sat in his councils and attended his courts. You've done your year in the temple in Endros Avaryan, and gone up to the Tower at the end of it, and come into your power before the bier where the Sunborn sleeps."

"But that's not everything," she said. "It's not complete. You know how a smith makes a sword—how he forges the blade over and over, and shapes it, and makes it into an image of what it will be. But it's only a bar of steel until it's tempered. Then, and only then, is it a sword."

"You don't call all that tempering?" He went on before she could answer. "No, maybe it wasn't. You know enough for a whole college of mages, and a court of lords, too. But you haven't turned that knowledge to use. You need to grow yourself up, I think."

"That's what *he* says," said Daruya. "He doesn't understand that I can't do it here. He's here, do you see? He'll pick me up if I stumble. He'll smile if I make a mistake, and be oh so forbearing, but I'll always know that he could do it better and faster and stronger. I need to be somewhere where he can't meddle."

"Does it have to be the other side of the world? You could ask for a princedom anywhere in the empire. He'd give it."

"He gave me this embassy," she said. "Now he's taken it away."

"He's only being sensible," said Chakan. "Whoever's broken a Gate isn't likely to balk at killing an emperor's heir."

"Does it need to be the act of an enemy? It could have been the Gate itself that was flawed."

"All the more reason to be cautious, then, if as I'm told the expedition goes to the Gate nearest the one that fell, and goes overland from there. That Gate could fall, too, and with the heir to the empire in it."

Daruya shivered in her bones, but fear was a little thing to this yearning of hers to be out, off, away. "And if that happened, would it be any worse than my getting killed in battle, or being stabbed in my bed by an assassin, or breaking my mind in entering the Tower of Endros? My grandfather *led* me to battle and the Tower. What's the difference in this, except that he won't be there to pick me up if I fall?"

"The difference could be exactly that," said Chakan. "Or that you want it so badly. That much wanting is dangerous. It closes off sense."

"Maybe it's something I have to do," said Daruya. "Have you thought of that? Maybe I'm called to it."

"If so, then you just realized it."

Daruya walked to the edge where the Wall fell sheer, down and down to the plain of Keruvarion. She poised there, rocked lightly by the wind. Chakan said nothing, made no move to pull her back.

He knew her too well. She would never leap unless she knew she could fly. Death was not what she yearned for. Not at all. Life—she wanted life, great gleaming handfuls of it. More than she could ever have under the emperor's loving tyranny, his light hand that weighed more than the world.

"I need to do this," she said. "I *need* it, Chakan. I don't feel death in it. Only necessity. And I think the expedition needs me, now more than ever. The place it goes to is all strange to us, and its people are afraid of magic. Or, no, maybe not afraid, but wary of it; inclined to hate it, because they don't trust it. If something happened to the Guardian because of that, and broke the Gate, then it may be that I can use what I am for once, use it to teach these strangers that magic is nothing to fear or hate."

Once she had said it, it sounded hollow, bombastic, a child's arrogance. Chakan said nothing of that. He said, "What can you do that the Master of mages can't?"

"Be my grandfather's heir," she answered without even thinking. "Speak for him with the authority of his own blood."

"So you won't escape him even on the other side of the world."

Daruya hissed at him. "I'm not trying to run away from my inheritance! I just want to stand on my own feet."

"And make your own mistakes." He lay back on his flat stone. After a moment he slipped the fastenings of his veils and let them fall free, baring his face to the wind and the sun. It was a handsome face, beautiful in fact, as Asanians of pure blood and long, close breeding could be: smoothly oval, white as new ivory, nose straight and finely carved, lips full, chin as sweetly rounded as a girl's. And yet it was not a girlish face, not at all. The right cheek bore healed scars, four thin parallel lines running from cheekbone to jaw; and a fifth, matched to the rest, so new that it still bled a little.

Daruya caught her breath at that. "You didn't tell me you were being raised to the fifth rank."

He slanted a glance at her. "I didn't know. My Master called me in in the middle of the night, ordered me to unveil, and marked me as soon as he saw my face."

"He didn't by any chance say why?" she said.

"Eventually," said Chakan. "I'm to take ten Olenyai to the other side of the world, to guard the mages."

Daruya's fury was so perfect that it did not even blur her senses. "Mages don't need guarding."

"For this they might," he said. He laced his fingers beneath his head, raised a knee, looked utterly off guard. That, she knew, was a complete deception. She was fast, and Olenyai-trained—but if she leaped, he would meet her in the air, and give her a ferocious fight.

She might have welcomed it. But she was stalking other prey. "Tell me why they chose you."

"Because I'm very good at what I do," he said honestly. "And because I'm used to mages."

"And," she said, "because they can't get at you with magic. That's it, isn't it? That shield of yours—they want it. Maybe need it, if it's mages they fight."

"They also want my skill with the swords, and the ten bred-warriors I can lead. I'm going to ask for Rahai. He's so good with his hands, he never has to use his swords."

He was happy, hells take him—full to bursting with his good fortune.

She sprang. To her startlement, he did not meet her in midair. When she struck the rock with bruising force, he was gone.

She lay winded, gasping for air. His voice sounded

above her head. "I was thinking. You can't wear the robes and the veils—you're too tall. But there's another way."

She rolled onto her back, still wheezing. "What—in hells—"

"It is a pity you overtop the tallest of us by a head," he said, maddeningly roundabout as Asanians were when one most wanted them to be direct. "Your eyes would do. Your skin is darker than most, but in veils that's less noticeable. Do you think your daughter will be another long tall creature? She's shaping for it already, poor thing."

"You babble like a flutterbird," said Daruya. She could breathe again, if shallowly. Her ribs hurt. "I can't play the Olenyas. It would cost you your honor at least."

"It would cost me my life," he said with no perceptible apprehension. "It might be worth it, mind, for the splendor of the trick. But not unless you're mage enough to make yourself smaller."

She cut through his nonsense with a voice like a blade. "You said there was another way."

"There might be," he said. "It would cost, too, seeing as to how I'm sworn in service to the emperor, and the emperor has forbidden you to go."

"Swear yourself in service to me," she said.

"I can't do that," said Chakan. He said it lightly, but there was no yielding in it.

She sat up carefully, glaring at him. "You'd sacrifice your honor to dress me in Olenyai robes, but you won't honorably swear yourself to the heir of the blood royal?"

"Robes are the outer garments of honor. Oaths are its heart. I'm sworn to the throne, and through it to the emperor. When you are empress," he said reasonably, "I'll serve you till death, with all my heart."

"But you'll break your oath if you help me escape the emperor."

"I will not," he said. "You'll serve the emperor on this

embassy, though he may think, at the moment, that you won't."

Daruya's head was spinning. It might, to be sure, be the shock of her fall. But one did not have to plunge middle first onto a rock to reel before Asanian logic.

He held her and patted her while she emptied her stomach on the stones. "There," he said. "Next time you attack me, do it somewhere where you can land soft."

She snarled at him. He smiled sweetly, sadly, and buried the evidence of her foolishness, producing from the depths of his robes what looked for all the world like a gardener's trowel. Probably it was. Olenyai robes could conceal anything, and often did.

When he was done, he crouched in front of her, arms resting on knees. "You do want to go, and he did give you leave, though he rescinded it. I'm thinking he might be overcautious as you say—emperor or not, he's a grandfather, too, and he dotes on you. I'm also thinking you may have the right of it; they'll need you out there, your Sunblood and your training, and your power to speak for the emperor in the emperor's absence."

"You think too much," muttered Daruya.

He grinned at that. "Yes, don't I? I never learned to shut myself off and be simple muscle. It's a flaw in a warrior. It's rather useful in a commander."

"If he lives long enough to become one." She leaned forward, no matter what it did to her ribs and her uncertain stomach. "Are you going to roll me up in a blanket and hide me in the baggage?"

"Very near," he answered. "I'm not visible to mages, yes? One told me once—unwisely, I'm sure—that I cast a kind of shadow; when someone stands in it, he vanishes, too. Suppose you dressed in black, not Olenyai, not exactly, but cloaked and hooded, and rode one of my remounts. You can become a shadow, yes? If you blur the eyes and I blur the mind, what will anyone see but a troop of Olenyai and their seneldi, and nothing more?"

Daruya wanted it to be so easy—wanted it with all that was in her. But she had learned to be wary. Yes, even she, with her name for recklessness. "If I'm caught, there's hells to pay."

"Don't be caught," he said with grand assurance.

"It's not sensible," she said.

"Of course it is," said Chakan. "Not that I don't think your grandfather is perfectly right, as far as he goes. You should stay safe where he can protect you. But that's no way to fly a hawk. You have to let it off the fist, or it never learns to hunt."

"Asanian logic," she said. "And I've nothing left in my stomach, to cast at your feet."

"I'll survive the lack," said Chakan. He sat on his heels, comfortable, quite clearly pleased with himself. "The Guildmaster means to leave as soon as may be—before sunset today, I'm told. You'll have to be quick if you're to do it; and clever, too, to make your farewells without being caught."

"I can mask my face and my thoughts," she said. "I was trained to rule an empire."

He was impervious to irony as to the weapons of mages: it sank into the shadow of his self and vanished. "Well and good. We meet in the Guildhall in the hour of the sixth prayer. You'll be a shadow, remember. A whisper in the air."

She stood. It was amazing how elation could kill pain, even of ribs that, she suspected, were cracked. She met his grin with one at least as wide. Hers had edges in it, the sharpness of teeth. "You could have told me this before you let me play the ranting fool."

"But you needed to rant," he said. "And who knew? You might see sense. This isn't sense that we're up to."

"No. It's necessity." She reached out a hand for him to grasp, pulled him up. In the moment of unbalance he shifted, treacherous, seeking to pull her down. But she was ready for him. She set her feet, made herself a rock in the earth.

He laughed up at her, for, standing, she was much taller than he. "No, it won't be as splendid as if you were one of my Olenyai, but riding as my shadow—yes, that will do. We'll sing it when we're done, like the song of the prince and the beggar's daughter. She was dead, you see, but he loved her withal."

"I don't intend to die on this journey," said Daruya, "or for a long time after. I'll live to take your oath from the Throne of the Sun, Olenyas. You have my word on it."

"And the word of a Sunchild," he said, half laughing, half deadly earnest, "is unalterable law."

4

THE HALL OF the ninth Gate was quiet. With its Gate hidden behind a veil, a curtain of white silk no paler than the walls, it seemed but an empty chamber, the hall of a temple, perhaps. Its floor of inlaid tiles made a map of the world as mages knew it. Half was wrought in intricate detail, with cities marked in colored stones. One that was gold, heart of the west, was Kundri'j Asan. One that was a firestone, heart of the east, was Endros Avaryan that the first of the Sunlords had built. Between them lay a great jewel like a star: Asan-Gilen, Estarion's city, that had brought together the realms of Sun and Lion, and given them a place where neither claimed the sovereignty.

The other half of the map was vaguer, its shape less clearly defined. Its cities were few. Crystals marked the Gates, a thin line across the broad mass of the land. Mages had traveled to each place, the first sailing in ships across the wide and terrible sea, coming to land and building the first Gate. New mages had come through the Gate, traveling on foot across a vast plain, and at each Brightmoon-cycle's journey, building a new Gate through which yet newer mages could come.

The eighth Gate was set on the knees of mountains that to its builders had seemed mighty. But those who followed discovered that the mountains were but foothills, and low at that. They climbed to the summit of the world, and nearly died in doing it; but when they would have turned back, too feeble to build their Gate, strangers found them and led them to safety.

There in the mountains that touched the sky, they found a valley, and in the valley a kingdom: the Kingdom of Heaven, its people called it. There was the ninth Gate, the Gate that had fallen. On the map it was unharmed, a crystal of amethyst—the color, said the mages who came back, of the sky above the mountains' peaks.

Vanyi stood pondering the color of the sky and the integrity of a crystal and other such inconsequentialities, while the others came together near the veil of the Gate. They were not many as expeditions went; dangerously few, if they were to be an army. Six mages, three of the light and their twinned mages of the dark. Ten black-robed Olenyai with their commander. Mounts and remounts for them all, since there were no seneldi on that side of the world, laden with such baggage as they could not live without; the Guardian of the eighth Gate would provide what more was needed for the ascent into the mountains.

All together they crowded that end of the hall, with much clattering and snorting. One senel in particular, a handsome dun mare, was being difficult. The Olenyai commander took her in hand, gentling her with soft words.

Vanyi recognized his voice and, as she came out of her reverie, his hands, strong for their smallness and beautifully shaped. Her brows rose. She had hoped that the Master of Olenyai would send his best, but she had not expected him to send Chakan.

Chakan the prince, some called him, because he was so free of the emperor's courts and counsels. He had been raised with the princess-heir, and was as close to her as a brother. He managed somehow to avoid the malice and the envy of courts, to be both foster-brother and perfect servant. His only flaw, in Vanyi's estimation, was that no mage could read him.

He made Vanyi think of another who had worn the veils and the swords, who also had been born with shields against magic. But that had been no Olenyas, for all the purity of his blood and the strictness of his training. He as much as duty and empire and her own obstinacy had taken Estarion from her.

That one was long dead. Estarion had killed him, killed the last descendant—save only himself—of the Golden Emperors. This was no long-lost Son of the Lion. The eyes in the veil were yellow gold, to be sure, but they were not lion-eyes, not so great-irised that they seemed to have no whites at all unless they opened wide; nor did they bear such a weight of bitterness as Koru-Asan had borne. Chakan of the Olenyai, for all his gifts and his skill, was an innocent, and devoted to his emperor.

Which, no doubt, was precisely why the Master had sent him. Vanyi liked him. She even trusted him—as long as he was not called on to do anything that would run counter to his emperor's purposes.

Vanyi met eyes that were true eyes of the Lion, set in the face of a black king from the north. Estarion regarded her unsmiling. She had not seen him come in. He could walk like a shadow when it suited him, even before the Master of the mages.

"Did you lock your granddaughter in her rooms?" Vanyi asked him. "I thought I'd see her by now, trying to beg or cajole or threaten me into taking her in spite of you."

"I left her in an imperial sulk," he said, "but I didn't think it necessary to lock the door. She understands her duty, however much she may resist it."

"I hope so," said Vanyi. She held out her hands. He took them without constraint, and set a kiss in each palm. Her breath caught. She turned it into a flicker of laughter. "I'm going to miss you. Who'd have thought it?"

"Maybe you'll find someone there who'll give you grand arguments, and slap you down when you get above yourself."

"*I* get above myself!" She mimed mighty indignation. "You, sir, were arrogant in the womb."

"Well," he said, "it's an honest arrogance." He went somber all at once, as he could do; looking suddenly much older, though never as old as he was. "Guard yourself, Vanyi. Whatever breaks Gates can break mages, too. Even Masters of mages."

"Oh, I'm too mean to die," she said; but she too sobered, gripping his hands tightly and then letting them go. "We have to know what broke the Gate, before it breaks another. If it's a weakness, you see—if we're doing something amiss in the building—we have to know, before there's too much passing back and forth of mages, and we lose more than a single Gate, or a single Guardian."

"And well before those who aren't mages begin to cross," he said, agreeing with her. "I've a pack of merchants already clamoring to explore this whole new country. They don't care that it takes a mage to direct a Gate, and a mage to guide the crossing. They're drunk on dreams of profit."

"They'll dream for yet a while," she said dryly. "You too, my lord emperor. I'll come back, I give you my word."

"Alive?"

"What, afraid of windy ghosts?" He looked so stark that she patted his cheek, a touch that stopped just sort of a caress. "Yes, I'll come back alive, or close enough to make no difference. Don't wait about for me. I'll be taking my time at it."

"Not too much," he said. "And send me word when you can."

"That I can do," said Vanyi. She stepped away from him. It was an odd sensation, not quite like pain. Well, she thought; they had been apart often enough, and once for a whole hand of years, while he fought his wars in the far west of Asanion, and she ruled mages in the raw new city that would be Asan-Gilen. But that had come after a quarrel, and they had parted with bitter words. Parting in amity, when god and goddess knew when they might meet again—that was harder.

Best get it over. Mages were drawing back the veil that hid the Gate. It was sleeping, showing no passage of worlds, only a grey nothingness.

As she approached, it began to wake. She felt it in her bones.

Likewise she felt a wrench, a little like envy, a little like grief, that after a moment she recognized as not her own. It came from Estarion, standing on the map, with his foot beside the broken Gate. There was a shadow just behind him, a cat as large as a small senel, as dark and golden-eyed as he was himself: one of his ul-cats, the king of them from its size and its air of lazy power. It blinked at Vanyi and yawned, baring fangs as long as her hand.

Estarion took no notice, seemed to be aware of little apart from Vanyi and the Gate and his own solitude. He did not look like a king or a conqueror. He looked like a man who must remain behind while his friend journeys to the other side of the world.

Looks were deceptive, she thought, drawing nearer to the Gate. Meruvan Estarion was emperor to the marrow of his bones. As she was mage and master of Gates. She raised her hands. The Gate woke to the touch of her power, woke and began to sing.

Daruya thought silence, thought shadows, thought nothingness. It was a delicate balance, a sensation not a little like the moment before one was disastrously sick—a dissonance between the fact of her existence and the illusion that she was not there at all. She was cloaked for further safety, wrapped in black, with her face shrouded, though not in an Olenyai veil. Her one indulgence and indiscretion, the mare she rode, seemed to have attracted no attention even when she indulged herself in a flurry of temper. Striped duns were not uncommon, and Olenyai were fond of them. One of the bred-warriors even had a rarity, a silver dun, grey bars on white.

For all her care and caution, she nearly forgot herself when she realized that the emperor was there. He must have come in under the same sort of protection that concealed her. She strained her ears to hear what he said; relaxed in every muscle when he spoke of her being safely shut up in her rooms. She thrust aside the niggling of guilt. He trusted her—he had not locked her in.

No. He trusted his own vanity, his conviction that she would yield to him simply because he asked. By the time he found out that she was gone, it would be too late to call her back. Then she could prove how groundless his fears had been, and how much he needed her where she was going.

The Guildmaster had left the emperor standing alone and come to wake the Gate. Daruya, divided between watching Vanyi and sustaining her deception, still kept her eyes on the emperor. He was watching Vanyi. He always did. A blind man could see that they had been lovers, could still be if either one of them were even a fraction less stiff-necked.

Her grandmother the empress was excuse, not obstacle. Haliya, great lady and queen, knew perfectly well how it was between her husband and her husband's friend and frequent rival. It had never troubled her. Little to do with men and women did. She had not even blinked when Daruya came to her first, pregnant and defiant and scared, because her plan had worked and now she was not so sure she wanted to face the consequences. Without Haliya's quiet good sense, those consequences might have been even less pleasant than they were.

Daruya had visited the empress before she came to the Guildhall. She did so every day and at much the same time: after the daymeal was done, when the emperor was occupied with matters of state, but before the empress held her own court. Today Daruya had thought of turning coward and staying away, but she found her courage and her cunning. If she did not go to see her grandmother, people would wonder, and perhaps be suspicious.

Haliya was lying on a couch in her day-room as she too often was of late, fully and properly dressed in the Asanian manner, except for the threefold outer robe that she would assume when she held her audience. She seemed tiny in the swathing of robes, shrunken, bleached to the color of old ivory. All but her eyes, which were the true Asanian gold, bright and vivid still in the withered face.

She had grown so old so suddenly. Her hair had been white for as long as Daruya remembered, but as late as Autumn Firstday she had been riding with the emperor's hunt, keeping pace with him through the wild coverts, and shooting a fine big buck for the evening's feast. Somehow, in the winter, the life had drained out of her.

They did not say anything of consequence. Daruya did not confess what she was about to do, nor did she hint at it. Sitting her senel on the threshold of the Gate, feeling the Gate-music that throbbed in her center, she remembered the softness of her grandmother's cheek as she kissed it, the sweet husky sound of the voice that like the eyes was still perversely young, the scent of *ailith*-blossoms that the empress had always loved.

Daruya would not be there in full spring, to fill the empress' rooms with flowering branches. But in the autumn, when the fruit was heavy and sweet—then, she promised herself and the memory of her grandmother, she would come back. She was not going away forever. Only for a while, because she must.

The Gate sang its deep pure song. Vanyi matched the measure of her power to it. She felt the resonance that rang six-fold from the mages who would cross with her, the quiver of discord that was the company of Olenyai with their beasts and baggage.

A strong sweet note rose through the dissonance, smoothed it, shaped it into harmony. She started a little in the working, but caught herself. Estarion had made himself a part of the Gate-magic. He was no mage of the Guild, nor could ever be; that was forbidden him as emperor. But he was mage and master.

She was wise enough not to resent the help he gave, though it stung her pride. Six mages and a Master should have been enough to open this Gate. Still, his strength was welcome. It made her task simpler, spared her power for when she would need it most, past the Gate's threshold on the worldroad.

The grey blankness of the Gate had shifted, transmuted, come alive. As with all Gates, it strove ever to change through the turning of the worlds. But she had set her will on it. It fixed on the eighth Gate of that other half of this world, holding pace like twin seneldi in a race, each desirous of outrunning the other, but held level by their riders' compulsion.

The Guardians on the other side were holding likewise, their task the less because their Gate was lesser, bound in servitude to this one. Any who passed that Gate could only come here, although from here he could pass anywhere in the worlds, even to the Heart of the World itself, which was master of all Gates.

In the moment when the two Gates matched, Vanyi brought them all together with a word. Two mages passed first, and then the Olenyai and the animals, and after them the rest of the mages. She was last of all, and Estarion who would not pass the Gate.

They did not speak, even when, briefly, they were alone. He was holding the whole force of the Gate in the hands of his power, even that part which she could well have held. It was by no means the limit of his capacity, but he showed the strain a little: a tightness about the nostrils, a rim of white about the eyes. It did not prevent him from smiling his old, white smile. She took the memory with her into the Gate.

5

THE STORM STRUCK as Vanyi crossed the threshold. She knew a moment of calm, a vision of the worldroad as it should be: grey road, grey land, grey sky, and before them the glimmer of the Gate to which they traveled. Then the sky shattered.

All Gates were present in her awareness, no more or less to it than the parts of her own body. But as a body convulses with pain of a blow, now the Gates reeled. The whole great chain of them, from world to world, shivered and cracked and began to break.

The road heaved under her feet. She staggered. Shadows milled ahead of her, men, beasts, the glimmering shapes of mages with their power laid bare. She started toward them, wavered, turned back.

The Gate through which she had come was there still, though its lintel sagged. Estarion stood in it, arms braced, holding it up. His power surged toward her like a tide of light. "The chain!" he cried, faint amid the howl of the storm. "The Gates—let me—"

Her own power reared up like a wall. The tide crashed against it and recoiled. As it rolled back upon Estarion, she thrust the wall behind it. It struck the Gate with the clap of stone on stone, locked and barred and sealed it until she should open it again.

Estarion would suffer for that. But he would not die— and die he would have done, if he had done what he was setting out to do, and tried to restore the chain of Gates with his sole and unaided power. No one man, even the Lord of Sun and Lion, was strong enough to do such a thing alone.

All such thoughts encompassed but a moment of the worlds' time. Even as she thought them, Vanyi was wheeling away from the sealed Gate, back to the tumult upon the worldroad. One at least of the seneldi was down—dead, and its rider beneath it, unnaturally still. Shadows beset the rest, driving them together. Mages fought with bolts of power. Olenyai fought with swords, useless against shadows—far better for them were the amulets they wore, that protected them against magic.

The watchers of the road were nowhere to be perceived. She called them, received no answer. If they had come, they could have driven off the shadows, the dark things without substance and yet with deadly strength. Even as she fought through a road turned to clinging mire, catching her feet and causing her to stumble, a shadow enfolded a lightmage, Jian who was youngest of all.

In desperation Vanyi formed and aimed a dart of power. But she was too far, too weak, and the shadow too swift. She felt, they all felt, the mage's fear, her resolve to be strong, to resist pain; pain mounting to agony, till nothing was in the world but that, and agony beyond agony, and abruptly, without warning or transition, nothing.

Jian was gone. Her darkmage cried out, a raw, anguished sound, and flung himself at the shadows. They slipped away from him, eluded his grasp, his power, the maddened stabbing of his dagger. They seemed to mock him. With a spring like a cat's, one of them fell on the darkmage who was farthest from him, who had stopped to stare aghast, and was too slow to escape. His lightmage, leaping to his defense, fell into the shadow's maw.

A blaze like the sun blinded them all, even Vanyi in the raising of her power. Shadows withered and died. The road's heaving steadied. The chain of Gates, at the point of rending asunder, subsided into a kind of quiet.

In the center of it, soft and calm but rather strained, a

voice said, "I can't hold this for long. Do you think you could all stop goggling and get a move on?"

"God and goddess," said Vanyi, astonished that she had any voice at all, let alone one that could be heard in this place. The road was solid underfoot. She forced her creaking knees to drive her forward. "You heard her. *Move!*"

They were deadly slow, but once they had begun, they gained speed. Those who were mounted pulled those on foot up behind, even the one who struggled and fought and tried to fling himself back to the place where his lightmage had died.

A tiger-patterned gelding—no, it was a mare, a horned queen mare, and a black shadow on her back—wheeled in front of Vanyi. Its rider thrust out a hand. Vanyi caught it, let it and the mare's movement swing her up. Even as she settled on the crupper, strong muscles bunched beneath her and surged toward the glimmer of the Gate.

The light was dying behind them, the road breaking apart. The mare's hind feet found purchase in the last of it before it melted into nothingness, and thrust them through the wavering Gate.

Light. Solidity. A waft of scent, pungent and strange.

They had come through. The Gate was fallen: its posts were broken, its lintel shattered. But they were on the other side, in a place so strange that Vanyi could find no thing to rest her eyes upon, except a pair of Guardians, mute and still: one on her feet and looking whitely shocked, one sitting up as if he had fallen and just now come to his senses.

Her arms, she discovered, were locked in a deathgrip about the rider's waist. Grimly she pried them free. She slid from the back of the motionless senel. No one else was moving, not even the animals.

She counted. All seneldi present and safe except for the one that had died early in the battle. One Olenyas lying too still across a saddle. Three mages—she bit back a cry. Of six that had left the Guildhall, only three had come through the Gate: darkmage and lightmage, slender elegant Miyaz and quiet-eyed Aledi, and one lone stark-faced darkmage, young Kadin who had lost his lightmage to the shadow.

Her eyes returned to the rider who had brought her out of the Gate, the rider whose light had kept them alive to come this far. Now that there was no way back, all concealment was gone, hood and veil thrust aside, golden lion-eyes holding hers with remarkably little defiance. "You did need me," said Daruya.

"I'll tan your hide," said Vanyi.

She turned slowly. The place was beginning to make sense. It was a temple, she knew that already: safest, her mages had said, for the raising of a Gate, and least likely to attract attention with its comings and goings. Ah, but such a temple. Every level surface was carved and painted and glittering with gilt. She could, if she struggled, recognize the shapes of leaves and flowers, birds, beasts, men, things that were all of them and none and everything between.

At the end of the hall opposite the broken Gate stood the greatest monstrosity of all. It was supposed to be a god, she supposed. Its shape was manlike, but it had—she counted—a full score of arms, each hand clasping a different object: a sword, a flower, a bow, a basket of fruit. Its face was fully human and yet profoundly alien, a smooth mask of beaten bronze, high-cheeked, proud-nosed, thin-mouthed. Its eyes were black and quiet. Its lips were smiling.

It indeed. The full breasts were a woman's, but the organ below, vastly and proudly erect, was indubitably a man's.

She stared at it. She had never, she thought in a dim corner of her mind, been so purely aware that she had come to a foreign place. No, not even when, fresh from the boats and the fish and the peasant simplicity of the Isles, she came to Endros Avaryan that the Sunborn had built, and came face to face on the public street with a young man who happened to be the emperor. And she had thought him strange, with his face like a northern tribesman's and his startling eyes.

Estarion had been as common as seawrack compared to this. And yet it was all part of her own world. The same sun shone through louvers in the roof, catching fire in the gilding. The same moons would rise in the same sky. No sun like an orb of blood, or twin suns, or triple, or more. She could have traveled here, given a year or five and a ship and a herd of strong seneldi.

She was in shock. Gates were broken, mages dead. Her power had strained itself to the utmost in doing what little she had done. Estarion had done more, before she trapped him on the other side of the Gate; and Daruya, rebellious, reckless fool, but for whom they would all have died.

It dawned on her, slowly, that Daruya was receiving a shock of her own. One of the packs in the baggage stirred, shook itself, sat up on its senel's back. "Mama," said ki-Merian fretfully, "my head hurts."

6

CHAKAN SWORE BY all the Asanian gods that he had had nothing to do with this second shadow among his baggage. Vanyi was inclined to believe him. He confessed without shame to the concealment of the princess-heir, but the princess-heir's daughter had come entirely of her own volition.

Kimeri said as much when Vanyi pressed her. "I had to come," she said. "The Gate's crying. Can't you hear it?"

And that was all she would say, except to burst into tears herself, wailing, *"Mama!* My head *hurts!"*

It was nothing, Vanyi assured herself, but a headache— the child had taken no harm, by the god's mercy. Once Kimeri was put to bed in the elder Guardian's own chamber, with a warm posset in her and a cool cloth on her brow, they held their council there, speaking soft so as not to wake the sleeping child.

There were four of them: Daruya, Vanyi, Chakan, and the elder Guardian looking worn and haggard. The younger had insisted on standing watch though the Gate was broken. The rest, mages and Olenyai both, slept as they could in rooms that had been prepared for them, or tended the seneldi in the stable, or mourned their dead in quiet corners of the temple.

None of those here suggested that they move elsewhere, even to the outer chamber. Daruya, who had never struck Vanyi as the most attentive of mothers, stayed fiercely close to her daughter, with a look about her that defied any force of hells or heaven to harm a hair of that head. "Not," she said, "that I fear anything here. All threats to us are in the empire or on the worldroad."

"I'm not so sure of that," Vanyi said. "Something here is breaking Gates. Did you feel it? It was coming from outside—but not from the Gates in Starios."

"Then," said Daruya, "it's only this chain of Gates—only the ones bound to the Gate we departed from."

Vanyi opened her mouth to correct her again, but paused. She had felt all Gates from the worldroad, she was sure of it, and all had felt the blow. And yet . . .

"It was strongest on this road," she said. "So strong that maybe it deceived us into thinking it was greater than it was. If it's only the Gates on this continent, the ones that we built and bound to the ninth Gate in Starios, then—"

"Then we're safer than we thought," said Daruya. "And so are the rest of the Gates, and the Heart of the World."

"Certainly," said Chakan, "no one will be assailing us from within the Gate. Nor will we be running back to Starios through it."

How like him, thought Vanyi, to say what none of the others would say. They were trapped here. Oh, they could go back, take the year and more, journey overland, find a ship, journey overland again. But the few moments' walk from Gate to Gate—that was ended, for who knew how long.

"Estarion will be beside himself," she said. "Both of his heirs fled to the far end of the world, and no quick way back."

Daruya shot her a lambent glance. "You don't think he'll just walk through the gate of his *Kasar* and drag us all back home?"

"You know I don't," Vanyi said levelly, "or you'd be doing it yourself."

"I can't," said Daruya, too shocked with the discovery even to be angry about it. "It's all bound together somehow. When I came through, I felt it close behind me—everything. Every Gate and every road. There's no way back. Except the simple human way." She glared, though Vanyi had not said anything, nor changed expression. "I didn't plan this!"

"Certainly not," said Vanyi. "You're only an idiot when it comes to yourself. We were all fools for not expecting that the child would try to follow us. She's always had a fascination with Gates."

"She was under guard," said Daruya. "I saw to it myself—set priest-mages over her and commanded them not to let her out of their sight. I hope Grandfather rends them all limb from limb."

Chakan sat softly on the end of the bed and tucked up his feet. "It is interesting," he mused, "that she eluded priest-mages. You can do that. Your grandfather certainly can. Would you be willing to wager that your daughter is as strong as either of you?"

"She's so young," said Daruya. It was not a denial, not of what he said. She smoothed her daughter's curls, gently. Kimeri smiled in her sleep. Daruya's face set. "Wherever the fault lies, both of us are here. I may choose to think that the god wanted it so. Why else would he have allowed it?"

Maybe he did not care. Vanyi was too circumspect to say it. "Well then," she said. "Here we all are, and here we stay until we know it's safe to raise a new Gate. I'm going to go on as I intended, into the Kingdom of Heaven. The source of the trouble is there, by all the evidence I've seen, and we're expected there."

"Maybe not now," said Daruya. "Maybe that's why the Gates were broken."

Vanyi grinned ferally. "Then we'll surprise them. They don't know us if they think a little matter of fallen Gates will keep us away from the expedition we've been planning since the first Gate went up."

"We are a tenacious people," observed Chakan. His glance took in them all: the white-skinned Island woman with her sea-colored eyes, the wizened brown Guardian from the Nine Cities, the tall princess-heir of both Keruva-rion and Asanion, and even himself, the Asanian bred-war-rior. "And we are that, do you notice? All these years of fighting, and now we're entirely *we*, and those out there are *they*."

"Even the worst of warring clans will unite against a common enemy." Vanyi sat back in the chair that she had chosen, and rubbed her weary eyes. "Faliad, have you have word from the other Guardians?"

"Not since before you came," the Guardian said. He looked as tired as she felt, but his voice was strong enough. "They were well enough then, except for the Guardian in Shurakan—what we call the Kingdom of Heaven."

"Only the one Guardian?" Vanyi asked sharply. "There were to be more."

Faliad lowered his eyes. "Yes, Guildmaster. There were. But we had lost one to a fever, and another was recalled to Starios. Before any others could be sent for, the Gate fell. There was only Uruan to guard it, and he died in the break-ing."

Kimeri stirred in her sleep. Faliad fell silent, but she was only dreaming. She pressed close against her mother, sighed, and was still.

"It seems," said Vanyi after a while, "that we made mis-takes. Maybe building these Gates was a mistake. No mage ever built them in chains as we did, with intent to open them to those who weren't mages. Nor were lesser chains bound to greater Gates. It may be that in making so many, and interweaving them in such complexity, we weakened the fabric of the whole."

"No," said Daruya with such certainty that Vanyi shot her a look. But she was oblivious. "Somebody did this. I felt the thrust of will on the Gates, just before they started to fall. Somebody wanted them down."

"Can you prove that?" Vanyi demanded.

"Not if you didn't sense it for yourself."

Vanyi stiffened. She was Master of the Gates. How dared this haughty child tell her that she knew nothing of them?

She caught herself before she spoke in anger, knocked down the anger and sat on it. When she was sure that she could speak reasonably, she said, "Maybe you saw what I was too preoccupied to see."

Daruya accepted the concession with surprising grace. "I was slower than you were to understand what was happening, and much slower to act. Too slow, or people wouldn't have died." That was grief; she caught it and hid it as soon as it escaped. "I had time to look, and to see what came at us. There was human will behind it. I know the taste and the smell of it. It was human, have no doubt. And it hates us."

"Us?" asked Chakan. "Foreigners? Gates? Mages?"

"All of them," Daruya answered.

"Yes," said Faliad slowly. "Yes, there is hate for us here. It's not so strong in this place, where all the traders' caravans come through, and strangers are a common thing. Out on the plains, in Merukarion—Su-Akar is their name for that country—strangers are mistrusted, and keep to their own places, apart from good native folk. They call us demons, in particular our Asanians, since demons here have yellow eyes. Our northerners they call gods, because the dark gods look so, taller than mortal men, and black as night without stars. Me they endure: I look like some of them. The rest recall the people of the Hundred Realms, with their bronze faces and their narrow eyes. Some are red-headed, did you know? like red Gileni."

Daruya, who was kin to the Red Princes of Han-Gilen, inspected her hand. It was long and narrow, with tapering fingers, the color of pale honey. She turned it palm up. The gold in it caught the lamplight and blazed. "The Guild would have done better," she said, "to appoint only Guardians who were plainsmen."

"We considered that," said Vanyi, "long ago. We decided not to hide ourselves. They'd find out in the end, whether we wanted it or no; best that we be honest from the beginning, and be as foreign as in fact we are."

"So they think that we're all in league with demons and dark gods. Wait till they see our emperor. They'll want to sweep us from the earth."

"They already do," said Chakan. "Or if not us, then our Gates at least. You will go on, lady? In spite of that?"

He was addressing Vanyi, his eyes on her—demon-eyes, she thought. They seemed very human to her, for all that they were as yellow as a cat's. "Yes," she answered him. "We go on, and the sooner the better. For now I think it best if we sleep. We'll want to be awake and thinking clearly when Estarion cames roaring down the mindways. He's going to be in a right rage."

"With the grandmother of headaches," said Chakan. His voice was light, but his eyes were wide with alarm. "Ai! I won't want to live, by the time he gets done with me."

"He won't have time for you," Daruya said. "He'll be too busy tearing into me."

"You both should have thought of that before you colluded in this escapade," said Vanyi coldly. Neither had the grace to look abashed.

She pushed herself to her feet. "Well. Enough. Faliad, come with me. Olenyas, you got her into this, you guard her till she gets out of it. Me, I'm going to bed. I might even manage to sleep."

"Sleep well," they said together. She looked sharply at them, but neither showed any sign of mockery.

She sighed, considered another spate of advice, left them instead, without another word. When she glanced back, Daruya was sitting as she had been for much of their council, cradling her daughter. The Olenyas lay across the door with his swords clasped to his breast.

"They'll do," she said. She was reasonably content, all things considered.

Faliad, poor man, looked ready to drop. She sent him to bed and made sure that he obeyed her. He took the younger Guardian's cell as the Sunchildren had taken his own; Vanyi plied him with wine that she found there, until he fell asleep.

She was weary to exhaustion, but there was no sleep in her. She wandered through the temple, peering at its strange-nesses until they palled on her. By the time she found the door and opened it on a narrow street, it was dawn.

No, she thought. Dusk, with the lamps just lit in sconces along the walls that lined the street. This was the other side of the world, where day was night, and night, day. There was still light in the sky, but it faded fast.

The people walking by were not so strange. They were, as Faliad had said and she knew from her mages' accounts of their travels in this land of Merukarion, as much like plainsmen of the Hundred Realms as made no matter. There were differences, but those were small: shorter stat-ure, broader build, lighter skin—and yes, one or two even of the few she saw here had hair the color of copper. The rest were dark, of course, or grey with age.

They were like Asanians in that they did not stare, ex-cept sidelong, under lowered eyelids. She was not dressed as they were, and her skin was white—white as a bone, they said in the empire. Her hair had been red once, but not the red of copper; a darker color by far, like moors in autumn, with brown lights and gold. Now it was all gone to ash.

She leaned against the doorpost and watched the people pass. No hatred touched her, and no fear. Wariness, that was all, and a veiled curiosity, a whisper of thought: *There's*

*another strange one in Shakryan's temple. I wonder how they con-
jured it up? Is it a ghost? A ghoul?* A shiver at that, but of the
more pleasant sort. But then, as the thinker came level, dis-
appointment. *Only an old woman. Poor thing, she has a disease.
It took all the color out of her.*

Vanyi laughed at that, but silently, drawing back into
the shadow of the doorway lest she alarm the passersby.
Northerners used to think that of her, too, even when she
was young. Even Estarion had, at first: Estarion with his
black-velvet skin and his black-velvet voice and his astonishing eyes.

"Damn," she said aloud, as she always did when she
could not get him out of her head.

And there he was in it, as if she had invoked him: spit-
ting mad, she noted, and yes, as the Olenyas had predicted,
he had a glorious headache. Not one bit of him was muted
by coming from half around the world.

She let him rage himself to a standstill. She could, if she
put her mind to it, see him where he was, still in the Guildhall, with the sun shining through the high windows of her
own morning-room. They must have taken him there after
the Gate collapsed: he was sitting on the couch she liked to
nap on, stripped to breeches, his hair worked out of its plait,
and a gaggle of mages and priests hovering, looking frantic.

He took no notice of them at all. His eyes glared straight
into hers. She heard his voice as if he stood in front of her.
"Damn you," he said. His tone by now was almost reasonable. "*Damn* you, Vanyi. You've got both my heirs on your
side of the world. And I can't get there. My way is no more
open than yours is." He flung up his hand, a flash of gold.
"It's locked tight shut."

"I know," said Vanyi. "Your elder heir said as much.
Eloquently."

His eyes glittered. "And the younger? What did she
say?

"No," he said quickly, before Vanyi could answer, "don't bother. I don't want to know."

"Believe me," Vanyi said after a pause, "if I could send them back, I would. Were you the one who taught them the shadow-trick? Even the baby's mastered it."

"*No!*" That much vehemence was too much for him: he winced and clutched his head. "God," he said much more softly. "Goddess. What a ghastly mess this is."

"It would be worse," she said, "if Daruya hadn't been there to keep the road steady till we could all get past it. She's worthy of her training, Starion."

"If her training had been adequate, she wouldn't have gone at all."

"Granted," said Vanyi, silencing him before he could go off in another rage. "I'll undertake to complete it as I can."

"Has she left anyone a choice in the matter?"

He was wry, which was reassuring: it meant that he was getting his temper back in hand. He ran shaking fingers through his hair, pulling out the last of the plait.

Vanyi regarded him in something resembling sympathy. "We can still talk," she said. "That's not so ill."

"But I can't *be* there." He leaped to his feet, scattering priests and mages, and paced out his frustration. "If we muster all our power, ward it with all our strength, then raise another Gate—this time let me go through it. If the Gate alone isn't enough, the *Kasar* may be—"

She stopped him before he could go any further. "You will not! I don't even dare raise one here. It's deadly, Starion. And don't tell me how strong you are," she said, as he opened his mouth. "I know it to the last drop of power. It might be enough. But it might not. We can't have the emperor dead, no matter where his heirs are, or how long it will take them to get back unless we raise the Gates again."

He was looking fully as rebellious as Daruya, and about as young. But he had more sense, or more cynicism. The rebellion faded from his face. He raised his hands, sighed. "Hells take you for being right. I'll go mad here, waiting."

"Of course you won't," she said briskly. "You'll be too busy. Isn't today your judgment-day? You must be late already."

"I put it off," he snapped. Good, she thought: he was thinking, even with his temper as chancy as it was. "See here, Vanyi. We've got to do something."

"And so I shall," she said. "I'm going over the mountains, just as I planned to. Do think, next time you want to talk to me. The people here are sure I'm a lunatic, or a god's plaything."

"Wise people," said Estarion. "Vanyi, you're not—"

"I have to go," she said.

Even as he began his protests, she cut him off, raised the shields about her mind, withdrew into the temple, in the dimness and the strangeness and the scent of incense. Someone was chanting. The younger Guardian? Or did they keep a priest or two here, to preserve their pretense of holiness?

She was too tired to hunt down the voice and ask. She could, in fact, have slept where she stood. Speaking across the world was harder than it looked while one did it.

She found a bed, it little mattered where, and fell into it, clothes and all. Not even fear could keep her awake, nor her creaking bones, nor grief for the mages whom she had lost. She laid them all on the breast of Lady Night, and herself with them. If she had dreams, she remembered none of them, till it was morning again, and fear and pain and grief were locked once more about her neck.

7

VANYI THRUST ASIDE the remnants of breakfast, unrolling the map that Faliad had brought for her, anchoring it with cups and bowls and a jug half-full of the local ale. The others—all of them, mages and Olenyai and Sunchildren—craned as best they could, to see what was drawn on the fine parchment.

She ignored them. "So," she said. "Here we are, out on the western edge of Merukarion—Su-Akar, we should be calling it, I suppose. This is the town called Kianat, and here are the mountains that are only foothills. What's this?" She peered. " 'Here be demons'?"

The younger Guardian of the fallen Gate, whose name was Talian, spoke quickly. "There are, truly. The mountains are full of them. They haunt the peaks, and lure travelers astray."

Vanyi shot her a glance. She was flushing under the sallow bronze of her skin and wishing transparently that Faliad were here to spare her the ordeal. But the elder Guardian, having slept little if at all, was standing watch in the outer temple.

Vanyi decided to have mercy on this younger fool. "Ah well, we're mages. We'll raise the wards and chant the spells and keep the demons at bay."

"Lady," said Talian with shaky determination, "you may smile, but this isn't our own country. It shares a world and a sun with us, yes—but it's as alien as any world on the far side of Gates."

"That's well enough put," said Vanyi, unperturbed by

the girl's presumption. She turned back to the map. "So. Demons in the mountains. There's a pass, this says, that seneldi can cross. Yes?"

"In this season," Talian said with a little less trepidation, "lady, yes. You won't want to delay too long, or go too slow. The snows close in early at those heights."

"There really are no seneldi here?" asked one of the Olenyai.

"Really," said Talian. "They have a kind of ox that draws their wagons, but no swift riding animal."

"Then how do they wage their wars?"

"On foot," Chakan answered for the Guardian, "and well enough for that, I'm sure. Our traders, once it's safe for them to come here, should make a great profit from the sale of seneldi. A whole new realm, empty of them. Remarkable."

"It is strange," Talian agreed, "like everything else here. They don't have mages, either."

"Everyone has mages," said Vanyi. "How can they help it? Even where there's no Guild to teach the spells, mages are born, and grow up to wield the lightnings."

"There are none here," said Talian.

"None that anyone will admit to, you're saying." Vanyi frowned at the map. "Suppression, then. Witch-hunts, I'd wager. Children disposed of when they begin to show the gifts."

"It could be, lady," Talian said. "They are afraid of magic; they won't talk about it, or let it be mentioned."

"It took mages to break the Gates," said Vanyi.

"But need they have been native mages?" Chakan met her glare with limpid eyes. "Consider, lady. Between the Mageguild and the priesthood of god and goddess, our part of the world has made magery a known and regimented thing. We take it for granted. Here in Merukarion, how do we know what's common and what's not? The gift might not appear here, for whatever reason. If there are mages, who's to say they're not renegades of our own country, who hate the Guild and mean to break it as they can?"

"Possible," said Vanyi. "But my bones don't think so. They tell me it's something else, something that comes out of here." Her finger tapped the map where it marked the kingdom of Shurakan. "Tell me about the Kingdom of Heaven."

The Guardian looked briefly rebellious, as if she wanted to remind the Guildmaster that she had been told everything that anyone knew. But she controlled herself. Maybe she reflected that everyone here might not have shared the counsels of the Guild, and that they should know what they confronted before they went out to face it.

"The Kingdom of Heaven," she said after a pause, in the tone of one teaching a lesson to a circle of intelligent children, "is called Su-Shaklan in their language. Our tongues are more comfortable calling it Shurakan. It keeps to itself, people say here, to the point that while it permits foreigners to pass its guarded gates, it does so only on sufferance, and never allows them to stay past a certain fixed term. That varies according to the purpose for which the strangers come. Ambassadors may linger a season; two, if they come too near the winter, when the passes are shut and the mountains impenetrable till spring."

"Why are they so wary?" asked Chakan. "Have they had enemies so bitter that they fear all strangers?"

"I think not," Vanyi said. "Consider where they are. Here are the mountains, so high they touch the sky—there's no air to breathe, it's said, and anyone who climbs so high, unless he's a mage and spell-guarded, will die. And they have no mages, we're told. And here's their kingdom, a valley no larger than a barony in our empire, and a small one at that. It's green, warm, rich, everything that's blessed, and more so after the barrenness of the mountains. They've made themselves a haven, difficult to reach, small enough to crowd quickly. Strangers would be rare there, but when they came, they'd threaten to strain the little space, and drive its people out by simple force of numbers."

"And," said Talian, "their minds are walled as high as their country. They're afraid of new things, strange things. Their kingdom is old—ancient, they say—and set in its ways. And they fear and hate magic. Their first rulers were a god's children, king and queen, brother and sister, who fled some calamity that had to do with magic, and led their people to the valley, and set up a kingdom that would be forever free of the taint. The word for magic in their language is the word for evil, and for the excrement of their oxen."

The mages were appalled. Chakan laughed.

He caught Vanyi's eye and sobered, if only a little. "Well, Guildmaster. There's your reason for the breaking of Gates, however they went about it. How in the million worlds did they let one be set up there at all?"

"There is a faction in their court," Vanyi said, "that wants to be sensible, not to mention practical, about the existence and practice of magic. It's a heresy, I suppose, but it's strong, and it's been ruling Shurakan. Its leaders welcomed our mages and allowed them to raise the Gate."

"Ah," said Chakan slowly. "So. This, you didn't tell the emperor."

"Or me," said Daruya, startling them all. They had forgotten her, as quiet as she had been, sitting in a corner with her daughter playing at her feet. "If you had, my grandfather would never have let me come here even before the Gate fell. He wouldn't have given you a company of his Olenyai, either."

"No," said Vanyi. "He would have wanted to come himself with an army at his back, and whole temples full of priest-mages to bring the Shurakani round to the error of their religion."

"He is not as bad as that," Daruya said stiffly. "A company of cavalry, yes, he would have wanted that, and more Olenyai. And a priest-mage or two, such as he is himself, in case you forget."

"And himself," said Vanyi. "There's the trouble, child. He'd have insisted that he was the only right and proper ambassador to such a benighted people, and run right over me, too, because he is strong enough to do that. He'd want to conquer these people as he conquered the whole of our half of the world, because it's in his blood to do exactly that. How not? He's the god's child. He was born to rule the world."

"And I wasn't?"

Vanyi faced her full on. "You, I think, for all your crotchets and your persistent conviction that you have to be a scandal in order to be noticed, are at heart a more reasonable creature than he is. And if you aren't, you'll refuse to conquer Shurakan simply because your grandfather *would* conquer it—purely for its own good, of course, and because he's the god's however-many great-grandson, supposing that you accept the dogma that Mirain An-Sh'Endor was the god's son in truth and not the bastard-born offspring of a northern priestess and the Red Prince of Han-Gilen."

"They still repeat that slander?" Daruya was surprisingly calm about it. "Ah well. You explain this"—she flashed her golden hand, dazzling Vanyi briefly—"and then we consider who sowed the seed of the Sunborn. Meanwhile, what if I decide that I can't resist the urge to be a conqueror, either?"

"I doubt that," said Vanyi. "Men conquer by force of arms. Women have other methods. Some of which I hope you'll see fit to use."

Daruya eyed her narrowly. She gave nothing back to that stare but a bland expression and a faint smile.

"He can't come now," said Daruya, "even to drag me back home in disgrace. By the time we have the Gates back up, we'll have had time, I should think, to fend him off. Unless you're going to give him a new war to fight, somewhere in his own empire?"

"I should hope not," Vanyi said tartly. "He can find his own war. His own places to meddle in, too."

"And a new heir?"

The girl was trying to goad her into an indiscretion. Vanyi gave her smile a little more rein. "I suppose, if he had to, he could see to that for himself. With as many females as he has, flinging themselves at his feet—"

"He does not!"

Vanyi laughed aloud. "Oh, there's nothing like a sinner for outraged virtue! Of course he does, silly child. I suppose he looks horribly old and decrepit to you, but to any woman who's not his granddaughter, he's a big beautiful panther of a man—and he brings with him a promise of empire. Many's the woman who'd leap at the chance to bear a Sunlord's heir. She'd have to wait to share the throne, but share it she certainly would, with the empress growing so frail."

For a moment Vanyi wondered if Daruya would spring. But she had more control than that, if not much more—not enough to find words that would suffice. Vanyi hoped that she had made the child think. It would do her good.

In the barbed silence, Chakan said, "So. We're to have guides through these mountains?"

Talian answered him with evident relief. "Certainly. Pack animals, too—some of their hairy oxen."

Chakan raised a brow. "You found men here who would endure the company of demons and dark gods?"

"Some men," said Talian stiffly, "are less superstitious than others. Even here. And greed is as potent an encouragement here as anywhere."

"Greed for gold?"

"Gold isn't what they crave," said Talian.

If Chakan found the Guardian's coyness annoying, he

showed no sign. His face of course was never to be seen by anybody but his brothers and, Vanyi was reasonably certain, Daruya, but his eyes were limpidly clear, betraying nothing but calm curiosity. "Oh? What do they value above gold?"

"Silk," said Talian. "Silk of Asanion, in the most gaudy colors imaginable. One bolt of it can buy a princedom here. Or a troop of guides through the mountains, with oxen and provisions."

"Remarkable," said Chakan. "Silk, so precious? I wish I'd known that. I'd have brought a bolt or three to do my own trading with."

"Warriors will stoop to trade?" Talian asked, shocked out of discretion.

Chakan's eyes laughed. "Warriors do whatever they must do to win their wars. If the weapon of choice is silk— why, so be it."

Talian clearly did not know what to say to that. Vanyi found the silence blessed, but doubted that it could endure for long. She broke it herself before anyone else could be minded to try. "We leave as soon as we can be ready. The guards are waiting, I hope?"

"They have been sent for," said Talian.

Poor child. She had not found any of them comfortable guests. Vanyi had a brief, wicked thought of commanding the girl to accompany her. But although she could be ruthless, she was not needlessly cruel. Talian was only a child, just past her making as a mage, when she gained no twinned power, became neither darkmage nor light, but showed herself for a Guardian of Gates. It was a false belief among the young mages that Guardians were weaker than twinned mages, lesser powers, mere servants of the Gates; but from the look of this one, she believed it. The Olenyai alarmed her. The Guildmaster rendered her near witless with terror.

Vanyi took pity on her, after a fashion. "Fetch the guides here. If they're to lead us where we want to go, it's best they know now what we are—all of us at once."

"Demons, dark gods, and all," said Chakan, impervious to her withering stare.

He, with his Olenyai, had eaten before they came in, when they could do it without the hindrance of veils. They had no breakfast to abandon. None of them was obvious about it, but now that Vanyi took the time to notice, they were standing idly, comfortably, casually, in a circle that encompassed both herself and the emperor's heirs. There was a placid deadliness in the way they stood, hands well away from swordhilts, faces hidden behind the black veils, yellow eyes calm, fixed on nothing in particular.

All but Chakan, who took an easy stance beside and just behind Daruya's chair. Kimeri looked up from playing with what looked like a ball of string, and smiled. He did not do anything that Vanyi perceived, but the child got to her feet, dusted herself off conscientiously, and held up her hands. The Olenyas swung her whooping to his shoulders, where she sat like an empress on a throne.

Vanyi wondered very briefly if there was more to that than anyone would admit—if the child had been fathered by the Olenyas. But her bones said not. If Olenyas and princess-heir had been lovers, it was utterly discreet and long over. They were guard and princess, friend and dear friend, or Vanyi was no judge. But nothing more than that.

Pity, rather. An Olenyas in Daruya's bed might be better protection than an army of mages.

No one spoke while they waited for the Guardian to come back. The mages were still stunned by the Gate's fall. Miyaz and Aledi seemed to cling together. Kadin, who had lost his lightmage, sat with them and yet irrevocably alone. He had eaten nothing, drunk little. His fine dark face was grey about the lips. His long fingers trembled as he picked up his cup, paused, set it back down again.

Vanyi watched him but did not speak to him. It was too early yet. A mage who lost the half of himself died as often as not, either from grief or by his own hand. She did not think that this one would do that. He was a northerner, from Ianon itself that had been the Sunborn's first kingdom. He had pride, and strength of spirit.

The mark of his clan was painted fresh on his forehead—a good sign, even if it were no more than habit. His beard, that had been chest-long and plaited with gold, was cut short, his hair cropped to the skull in mourning. Again, good enough. He could have turned the blade against himself.

They would all suffer if he did. Six mages and a master had been ample for the embassy that Vanyi had in mind. Three of them dead left the rest overburdened, even if Kadin came through this grief intact. If he did not . . .

She would think of that when she had to. She let her eyes return to the map, tracing and retracing the ways they must take. Guides they might and must have, but she never trusted to one expedient if several would do.

"Daruya," she said abruptly. "Come here."

Daruya came, for a wonder; what was more, she seemed inclined to pay attention as Vanyi set about teaching her the map and the journey. But, thought Vanyi, this mattered to the girl. It touched her pride.

Pride was useful in swaying kings, and kings' heirs.

8

THE GUIDES WERE a woman and her three husbands. Daruya at first would not believe what her magery told her she was hearing; surely her gift of tongues was failing or turning antic. But the woman's mind quite clearly perceived the three men with her as husbands—men who shared her bed and stood father to her children. They were brothers, sturdy-built middling-tall men like heavyset plainsmen, with bronze skin seared dark by sun and wind, and narrow black eyes, and black hair worn in cloth-wrapped plaits. Their wife was much like them, near as tall as they and quite as solid.

She did the speaking for them all. Her name was Aku, which meant Flower; she named her husbands, but Daruya paid little attention. Names were not what they were. They were stolid, at least to look at, but there were festoons of amulets about their necks, and they eyed the Olenyai in what they fancied was well-concealed terror. The Olenyai, without the mages' gift of tongues, had leisure to observe, and to be amused. Daruya hoped that one of them would not take it into his head to do or say something appropriately demonic, and lose them their guides before they even started.

The woman seemed fearless enough. She was brusque, striking a hard bargain with Vanyi, whom she had singled out without prompting as the leader of the expedition. That spoke well for her perception, since Vanyi had not been trying to look conspicuous. The other mages in their robes— lightmage silver, darkmage violet—were far more impressive than she was in her plain coat and trousers and boots; and the Olenyai were alarming, faceless black shadow-men with golden demon-eyes. Vanyi could have been a servant, an old woman of no particular height or distinction apart from a certain air of whipcord toughness.

But Aku knew, and for that, Vanyi let herself be haggled with. Daruya might have done it herself, for the matter of that, if she had had occasion. At the moment she seemed to have been included with the Olenyai in the class of demons, in the minds of the men, and as young and therefore insignificant in the mind of the woman.

Old age held great power here. Daruya made note of that.

At length the bargaining was concluded, the guides given half a bolt of scarlet silk in payment, the rest to follow at the end of the journey. Daruya rose in relief and gathered up Kimeri, who had fallen asleep in Chakan's lap. Kimeri murmured, burrowed into Daruya's shoulder, and went back to sleep again.

"Poor baby," said Chakan. "She hardly knows where or when she is."

"She knows it very well," Daruya said. "She wore herself out, that's all, creeping through the storm in the Gate."

He looked as if he would have said more, but he did not. She was glad. It frightened her that ki-Merian of all people was so docile and sleeping so much. She could find no wound in the child, of mind or body, nothing but tiredness and a desire to be near her mother. But that was disturbing enough. Kimeri was the least clinging of children, and the least inclined to sleep when she could be up and doing.

Daruya did not want to say anything of that, even to Chakan whom she trusted. She busied herself with the flurry of departure—a last meal eaten in haste, farewells said to the Guardians, gathering and mounting and forming their caravan in the temple's inner court. The seneldi were snorting and rolling their eyes at strangers, hairy oxen as Talian had called them: great shaggy beasts, taller than a tall senel, with broad curving sweeps of horns, and feet as broad as banquet-platters.

There were four of them in the court, wearing harnesses that translated into saddles and bridles of a sort, as each guide approached his beast and mounted by climbing its harness like a ladder. He had only one rein, and a stick that he used to turn his massive mount and to drive it forward.

Daruya, fascinated, almost forgot to mount her own fretting, head-tossing mare. Chakan passed Kimeri up to ride on her saddlebow, still asleep and dreaming peacefully of riding her pony in the empress' perfume-garden. Once the mare felt the twofold weight she settled, though she still snorted at the oxen.

Vanyi was speaking, not loudly but clear enough to be heard over the stamping and snorting of the animals. "We're shadow-passing through the town for convenience's sake—this many seneldi appearing from nowhere would raise a frightful riot. Daruya, will you anchor the casting?"

That meant riding in the rear and securing the edge of the working. It also meant great trust, and a degree of concession that she had not expected so soon. She sat her mare nonplussed, until she found her tongue somewhere and put it to use. "I'll ride anchor. Chakan, you too. I can use you."

Vanyi's approval was quick, sharp, and surprisingly warm. Daruya began to wonder exactly how surprised the Guildmaster had been to find her with them in the Gate— and exactly how unwelcome she had been. Not at all, maybe. Vanyi did not share the emperor's concern for his heirs; or at least not his concern that they be kept close, and therefore safe. Vanyi in fact cared little for royalty at all, that Daruya could discern. She was a commoner, and an Islander into the bargain. Kings to her were a blasted nuisance, no good at all for mending nets or catching fish or sailing a boat in the teeth of a gale.

Daruya, who had learned from Vanyi herself to do all three, caught the thread of power as it spun toward her, and drew it taut. On it she strung a web of shadow. It was the same working she had used to conceal herself on the way through the Gate, and she used Chakan's shield as she had then, but this was wider, stronger. Anyone not a mage who looked at the passing of their company would see four oxen with their riders, the train of pack-oxen that waited outside the temple, and a confused image of guards, riders, caravanners, but no clear faces and no certainty as to their numbers.

With five of them working the concealment, it was a simple enough thing, and no great effort. Daruya was able to see the town as they rode through it, to be startled at its earthen plainness. After the wild extravagance of the temple, she had expected the rest to be as gaudy.

The temples were eye-searing spectacles, to be sure, and there were a great number of them, but in among them the houses of the people, large and small, were simple blocky shapes of mud brick, unadorned even by a scrap of gilding over a lintel. The people were of like mold: dressed in grey or brown or at most a deep blue, hung with amulets but boasting no other adornment—until she saw a procession of what must be priests. They marched in a long undulating line, matching pace to the deep clang of a bell, chanting in a slow drone. Their heads were shaven and painted like the carvings in the temple. Their bodies were bare in what to her was a wintry chill, but for the simplest of robes, a length of cloth, saffron or scarlet or a searing green, falling to the ground before and behind, open else, and hung about with a clashing array of gold, silver, copper, great lumps of amber, river pearls, firestones cut and uncut, strung together without art or distinction. They made an astonishing spectacle, the more astonishing for that passersby seemed to take no notice of them except to move out of their way.

The caravan bade fair to run afoul of the procession, but just before the two collided, the priests swayed aside down another road. The caravan paused, waited for the rest of the procession to pass.

Daruya, forced to leisure, took in as much of the town as she could see. It was built on level ground, but beyond it reared the wall of a mountain, so sheer and so high that it seemed to crown the sky. Snow gleamed on its summit and far down its slopes—small wonder the air was so cold here. There seemed no way over or past it.

She was warmly dressed in gleanings from the temple's stores, her coat lined with fur and a cloak over that, and a hat on her head, but still she shivered. Kimeri, cradled in her arms, nuzzled toward her breast. It ached as if in answer, though the child had been weaned since her second year. Daruya brushed the warm smooth forehead with a kiss, and swayed as the mare started forward again.

They left Kianat unseen and took the caravans' road to the north and west. It was steep, and in places it was very narrow, but it found the pass that went over the mountain and climbed it, higher than Daruya had ever been in her life.

And when they came to the top, the second day out of Kianat, all unshielded now and riding openly as they were, demons and dark gods and all, Daruya caught her breath. What she had fancied to be a lofty mountain was, indeed, but a slave and a servant to the peaks that marched away before her, wave on jagged snow-white wave of them, mounting up and up into the pitiless sky.

It was beyond imagining. She was ant-small, mote-small, crushed under the immensity of mountains and sky. But the sun that rode over them, casting fire on the snow, was her own, the face of her forefather. Its fire burned in her hand. Her blood was full of it.

That raised her head before it bowed too low, and straightened her back. She bore the weight of the sky. She faced the mountains' vastness and gave it tribute, but no fear; no submission.

"Here," said Chakan, "be demons."

They had made camp just below the top of the pass, where the land dropped away to a brief level. That this was a frequent resort of caravans, Daruya could well see. There was grazing for beasts, with a well-cropped look, and stone hearths to build fires in, with walls about them that kept out the wind. The guides unloaded a heap of tanned hides that, sewn together swiftly with strips of leather and secured to the walls, made roofs for a cluster of huts about the yard in which the beasts would be penned. They were not to graze all night, it seemed, for the reason Chakan had hinted at.

"Just until sundown," he said, "and then they come in, no matter how hungry they still are. Demons eat oxen, we're told, and would discover a taste for senelflesh if given the opportunity."

"You were told all that?" Daruya asked, prodding at the fire she had built of dried ox-dung and dried grass and a flash of magery. "You don't speak their language at all."

"No, and I'm not turning mage, either, to know what their babble means." He squatted on his heels, warming his hands at the blaze. "Still and all, signs are clear enough, and the three husbands seem to think that when a demon wants to know something about his cousins of the peaks, the demon should get an answer however he may. Besides," he added, "I asked a mage to translate for me. We're judged not to be the man-eating kind of demon, did you know that? The Old Woman—that's what they call the Guildmaster— has us enslaved, and we're condemned to live and eat like mortals until she lets us go."

"Including me?" Daruya asked with lifted brows.

His eyes danced. He was grinning behind the veil. "Why, of course. You're the chief of us. We're your husbands, so hideous that our faces must never be seen lest they drive men mad; but you're merely mortally ugly, so you don't hide yourself or your little demon, who they think was conceived of the night wind and suckled on milk of the snow-cat. They're not far off, are they?"

She bit her tongue. He would laugh if she said what she wanted to say, which was that if she was ugly, then what in the world did they reckon beautiful?

Vanity. It stung her nonetheless. She had been the Beauty of Starios for as long as she could remember. It could be a nuisance when men young and not so young, and not a few women, flung themselves at her feet; but she took no displeasure in what her mirror showed her, all honey and amber, and queenly proud.

Chakan read her much too easily for a man with no magery at all. "Beauty's an odd thing. Changeable. Madam Aku's a great beauty here."

"She's built like a brick," said Daruya, with a snap in it.

"Maybe a brick is beautiful," said Chakan serenely, "where they don't value gold. Silly of them, but there you are. It could be worse. They could have decided that it would be an act of virtue to murder us in our beds."

"They may yet," said Vanyi, lowering herself to sit beside the fire. She had a flask in her hand, which she passed to Daruya.

Daruya sniffed, then tasted. Wine, and good wine too. She drank a swallow, then two, and handed the flask to Chakan. He did not hesitate, but slipped it under his veils and drank with practiced ease.

"Dinner's coming when it's had time to cook," Vanyi said. She looked about, drawing Daruya to do the same. This was the largest of the huts, with room enough for a good half-dozen people. Through the open side, the one that faced the yard, she saw the beasts being herded in, in dusk that had fallen with startling suddenness. The seneldi did not like to be crowded together with the oxen, but they were getting better about it. There was only a little squealing and kicking, and only one bellow as Daruya's mare gored a dilatory ox.

It was a shallow gore, and little blood shed through that shaggy pelt and thick hide. The mare looked very pleased with herself. With the contrariness of her sex and her kind, she settled to share a heap of fodder with the offending ox, as peaceful as if the beast had been a herdmate, and one she honored, at that.

Daruya sensed nothing beyond the circle of huts but empty spaces, height and cold and raw wind. Her head ached vaguely with the thinness of the air, and her breath came shorter than it should, but that was nothing to take particular notice of. If there were demons, they avoided this place.

Even so, she ate with little appetite and slept ill. Heightsickness again. One or two of the Olenyai and both the elder mages were in worse state than she. She fretted for Kimeri, but the child was no more and no less well than she had been since the journey began.

Kimeri kept wanting to fall asleep. She did not like it, and at first she thought it was something her mother or Vanyi was doing to keep her quiet. But they were worried. They tried to hide it, but she knew. She could not think of anything to say that would make them feel better. Certainly not that she kept seeing Gates and feeling them inside of her, broken and hurting, and a Guardian who thought he was dead.

Something happened when they went over the pass. She stopped being so terribly sleepy. She still saw Gates, but the mountains were stronger, a little. She could look at them, at their sharp white teeth against the purple sky, and even, almost, forget about the Guardian. But only almost. The Guardian was inside of her too, now, like the Gates.

The mountains outside of her were stubborn. They tried to make her think that they were the only thing that mattered, but she knew better. "There are people like you at home," she said to them while everybody was making camp for another cold restless night, but nobody was paying much attention to her.

She was too wise to wander out of sight, too restless to stay where she was put. She climbed on top of one of the big patient oxen, the way she had seen its rider do, up its side with the harness like a ladder, and sat on its back that was as broad as a table. The mountains stood all around the place where they were, a high valley full of new green grass, with bits of snow in the hollows, and a spring that bubbled out of a tree-root and filled a bowl of rock; stood and stared.

The seneldi had decided after a great deal of fuss that the oxen were sort of distant cousins. The oxen thought the seneldi very silly. They got on well enough, and Daruya's mare had made friends with the ox that Kimeri was sitting on, the big queen ox who told the others what to do.

Now as they grazed side by side the mare threw up her head and snorted. The ox kept on grazing peacefully, but it was awake inside its armor of horns and shaggy hair. Kimeri looked where they were looking.

Something sat in the branches of the tree that overhung the spring. It looked a little like a bird and a little like a man and a great deal like neither. It had feathers, white and grey and silver and faint grassy green, and a wide round face with wide round yellow eyes, and very sharp, very pointed teeth. It showed them to her, and flexed curved claws like a cat's, and hissed.

The senel was ready to bolt, but the ox sighed and yawned and chewed its cud. Kimeri decided that if the ox was not afraid, then neither would she be. It took some deciding. This was a demon. She had heard the guides talking about them, especially their yellow eyes and their long fangs. The guides thought the Olenyai wore veils to hide fangs just like these, though of course Olenyai were only men, with plain Asanian faces and ordinary Asanian eyes, yellow and gold and amber and ocher-brown.

This was not a man at all. It did not have a babble of thoughts like a man, but neither was it the wordless nowness of an animal. It felt most of all like a mage when he worked his magic—a singing presence, a flicker like a fire on the skin. But it was not as strong as a mage, not as solid on the earth. She thought of ice, that was like stone but very different.

She must be careful, she thought. She was Sun-blood— she burned too fierce sometimes for magical things to bear. Things like spirits of air, or fetches on their masters' errands, or demons of the mountains come to see what trespassed in their country.

The demon was surprised that she did not shriek and run away. She was supposed to do that, all the earthborn did. Even earthborn who were demon-eyed. She stayed where she was. The demon tried jumping up and down on its branch. It had no weight: the branch never moved. That was interesting. The demon started to chitter and gnash its teeth.

"Why do you do all that?" she asked it. "You can't hurt me."

The demon stopped. Its big yellow eyes blinked. It filled her mouth with the taste of blood, like iron but strangely sweet. That was the blood of an earthborn man, fresh from his throat that the demon had torn.

"That was because he was afraid," Kimeri said. "He let you eat him. I'm not afraid of you."

Her great-grandfather would know what to say to that. It was a long word. Arrogance, that was it.

"But it's true," she said. "You don't need to drink blood. You have the air up here, and the wind off the snow."

Blood was sweet, the demon told her. It was warm.

"Mine would burn you," she said. She clambered down off the ox's back, holding on to harness and pelt, and went to stand under the tree. The demon stared down at her. She stared up. "You won't be drinking any blood here. If you do I'll tell my mother. She's much stronger than I am. Her blood is like the sun."

The demon shut its big round eyes. When it opened them, they were all of the demon that was left; then they were gone, and so was the demon. But it was near—she felt it, it and its brothers and sisters and cousins.

"Remember," she said to them. "No bad tricks. I'll know it was you, and I'll do something about it."

9

THERE WERE PEOPLE in this country. What seemed inhospitable beyond believing and beautiful in the coldest way imaginable, a jagged landscape of peaks and lofty valleys, snowfields and icefields and sudden plunges into green oases, had its own thin tough populace. Villages clung to the sides of crags or huddled round the warmth of a valley. There were fortresses on peaks that should have been too steep for any creature to climb, inhabited often by wind and dust and sky, but often again by a dirty scrabble of people whose only pride seemed to be in the sharpness of their weapons.

The people were like the land they lived in, harsh, stark, often cruel, but showing flashes of sudden beauty. In a town so steep it had no streets, only ladders from house to stone-built house, and no open space but the level in its center, where its market was set up and doing a brisk trade, Daruya heard a singer whose voice could have called the stars out the sky. The singer was blind, and therefore oblivious to Daruya's strangeness; he sang on even when the rest of the listeners drew back, giving her demon-eyes a wide space.

She heard a hiss and a scuffle behind her, where Chakan was insisting on guarding her back. She glanced over her shoulder. The Olenyas had a wizened townsman by the throat. He shook the man as a hound shakes a rat. Something fell tinkling: a fistful of coins that wore familiar faces.

"Right out of my purse," said Chakan, almost too amused to be angry. "It's no defense to be a demon, it seems. Not against thieves."

The thief struggled in his grip. He laid the point of a dagger against the man's throat, just under the chin, and hissed. The man went grey. Chakan laughed and let him go. He bolted.

"That should warn off the rest," said Chakan.

Daruya had her doubts. She had observed that demons in this country were as fair game as any other travelers. She has also noticed that they seemed to have no fear of theft among themselves. It was only dishonor, she supposed, to steal from one's own kind.

Her own valuables were wrapped in silk and hung between her breasts. A thief would have to pass a heavy coat and a leather tunic and a pair of shirts to reach the treasure. She wished him well of it if he came that far; he would have earned it.

The singer's song ended on a wailing note. It wound up and up, spiraled down, and faded. She plucked a coin or two from Chakan's hand and tossed them into the bowl at the singer's feet. They would be safe there, since the singer was not a foreigner.

Daruya was still pondering thieves and honor and the relation of foreigners to both, as their caravan scrambled up yet another steep and stony pass. The town on the crag was far behind. Shurakan, the guides said, was far ahead: at least half a Brightmoon-month of journeying, as much time as lay behind them since they left Kianat. It went slow; it always went slow in this country of endless up and down and very little level.

This pass was like a knife-cut in the earth, a thin slash in the mountain's side. Steep as it was, its walls nearly sheer, closing in on them as they went on, it seemed likely to narrow to nothing and so trap them, and leave them at the mountain's mercy.

She let out her breath at long last as the narrow wall—

barely wide enough for the oxen to scrape by—began to widen again, and the slope to soften slightly. The caravan, with her in the middle, kept on at its plodding pace; no wall in front of it yet, and light still in the gap. Echoes ran up and down the walls: snort of senel, grunt of ox, thud of hoofs, low mutter of voices as Vanyi, up ahead, conferred with Aku the guide.

There was no getting closer. The way was too narrow. Daruya tried stretching her ears to more than simple human keenness, but Vanyi was too canny a mage for that; she and her companion rode as if globed in glass. Daruya had to content herself with straining to catch the odd word, and praying for the walls to open before she went out of her wits—the more so for that the one word she caught was *ambush*.

Her eyes ran up the walls of the cleft. Too steep surely for any man to come down, and too high to leap. If she were a bandit or mountain lord, she would close off the ends of the cleft and trap her prey within. But no one had done that. Her magery, seeking, found nothing. The way was open behind as in front.

She did not ease for that. Eyes were on them, unseen, not truly hostile but not friendly, either. The beasts were quiet, which was well. She combed her mare's mane with her fingers, shifted in the saddle, stretched a kink out of her shoulder. A glance found Kimeri riding on Chakan's crupper. The child had wanted a mount of her own this morning—sure sign that she had come back to herself. Maybe tomorrow, Daruya thought, she would have one of the remounts saddled and let Kimeri ride it for at least a part of the day.

The walls of the cleft opened slowly and sank by degrees into the land beyond, until they rode through a stony valley, steep-sided, with grass growing amid the remnants of winter's snow. They paused to drink from a stream, found it clean and bitter cold: snow-water. The sun was high enough to reach beyond the walls of the valley, and warm enough that the guides took off their coats and their furred hats and rode in their shirts.

Daruya, less hardy, still pulled off her hat and let the wind run fingers through her hair. A gust blew it in her face, a heavy curtain of amber-gold curls. She laughed for no reason that she could name, and shook it back.

Her laughter ran its course. There were smiles about her, in Olenyai eyes or mages' faces. But she was watching the summit of the ridge, where sunlight dazzled and shadows seemed to dance. Shadows born of living bodies, and within them a glitter of metal, and awareness keen and sharply pointed and very clear.

She said to Chakan, very calmly, "Look up. No, not there. Up. East wall."

The soft hiss of sword from sheath was his answer, and his voice, as calm as hers, and no louder. "Eyes up, Olenyai. We have company."

It was not a good place to be at the bottom of. The east slope was too steep for a senel, but not for a man with the surefootedness of the mountain born. There were men and weapons ahead, too, and behind. They were nicely trapped.

Daruya caught Vanyi's eye. The Guildmaster raised a brow. Daruya tilted her hand till gold caught the sun and flashed. Vanyi smiled a cold white smile.

Briefly Daruya considered the guides, and the lack of magic and mages in Su-Akar. *Let them learn,* she thought. She had not called in her power in long and long, not since the Gate. It came gladly, swift as a hawk to the fist. The sun fed it.

She was aware of Vanyi calling her own magic, a weaving of dark and light, shadow and sun; and the mages summoning each his own, even Kadin who never spoke, never sang, rode always mute and wrapped in grief.

His gladness was a dark thing, tinged with blood. He

wanted to take life, to kill as his lightmage had been killed. She brushed him with a finger of power, bright Sun-gold to his black dark. He recoiled in startlement. She gentled him with patience, pressing no harder than she must with raiders closing in on every side. *Softly,* she willed him. *Be calm. You'll have revenge—but not now. These fools are unworthy of you.*

He begged to differ, but she was stronger. He subsided, sullen but obedient, letting her direct him as she judged best. She was not his lightmage, yet the familiar force of matched yet opposing power comforted him, filled a fraction of his emptiness, muted his grief.

Instinct had taken her to him, as if even she, priestess-mage and Sunchild, had need of the dark one, the power that lay in shadows. Yet she could not bond with it; could not be his lightmage. That was forbidden her.

She would ponder that later, when there was leisure. For now she took it as it offered itself, and used it as it asked to be used. Hilt to her blade of light, haft to her spear of the sun, bow to the arrow of power that flew flame-bright from her hand.

It was beautiful and terrible. Mere earthly arrows shot down from above flared to ash and vanished. Swords melted in a fire hotter than any forge. Men shrieked—pain, in those who found themselves clutching white-hot hilts, and fear in archers whose bows crumbled in their hands, whose arrows were ash in the quivers. What they saw, Daruya saw through them: a small odd caravan trapped in the valley that was so perfectly suited for ambush, mounted on strange beasts, and guards in black ringed about a towering shape of light.

Back of the light was shadow. It waited to take what the light left, to drown souls that held no more substance than a moth's flutter. Seductive thought, alluring prospect, to be rid of these bandits with no fear of reprisal.

But Daruya's training was too strong. One did not slay with power. Above all, one did not destroy the soul, even of an enemy. The price for that was the power that had destroyed so much, but not—cruelly—the life of the mage.

The shadow struggled, resisting. She reined and bound it and loosed a last, blinding blaze of light. There was no harm in it, only terror. The bandits broke and fled.

"Well done," said Vanyi dryly.

Daruya quelled a hot retort. She had done it again: swept in and done what needed doing without regard for the Guildmaster's precedence. In the Gates it would have been death to wait. Here, she should have yielded; should have waited upon the rest.

Vanyi did not say any of that. She did not think it, either, that Daruya could discern. She simply nudged her senel forward past the still and staring guides. The others, mages first, then Olenyai, followed slowly.

Only Daruya did not move; and the guides. The men had a look she had seen in battle, in warriors who had seen too much, whose minds had stopped, leaving them blankly still. The woman was stronger, or more resilient. She flinched at the brush of Daruya's glance, but she steadied herself, lifted her eyes, met Daruya's.

Daruya was prey to both arrogance and impatience, as her elders never wearied of telling her. But she was not a fool. She spoke very carefully, choosing her words as meticulously as if she had been addressing the emperor of a nation with which she could be, if she failed of diplomacy, at war. "I swear to you by all that I hold holy, that I have harmed not a hair of their heads, nor done aught but win us free of ambush."

Aku's eyes narrowed. "You did it? Only you?"

Daruya felt the flush climb her cheeks. "If there is blame, yes, it is mine alone."

"But the other could," said Aku. "Could have done the same."

She meant Vanyi. Daruya hesitated. To lie, to prevaricate, to tell the truth . . . "She did nothing."

"She would have," Aku said. Perceptive, for a woman who had no magic. She was no longer quite so afraid. "I see that you're very foreign."

"Very," said Daruya, a little at a loss. She thought she understood what the woman was getting at. But she could not be certain—even knowing what thoughts ran through that brain, both the spoken and the unspoken. "We're still mortal," she said. "Still human. We're not gods, nor demons either."

"So you say," said Aku. She struck her ox with the goad, urging it forward onto the track the caravan had taken. Her husbands, stirring at last, fell in behind her.

Daruya, left alone, baffled, a little angry, had the presence of mind to sweep the land round about. Nothing threatened. The bandits were still running. Already the tale had grown, the caravan swelled into an army of devils armed with thunderbolts. By the time it passed into rumor, it would be a battle of gods, into which the bandits had fallen by accident and barely escaped alive.

None of which mattered now, with guides who could turn traitor and lead them all into a crevasse. What dishonor would there be in that? Not only were they foreigners; they were mages.

Fear would be enough, Daruya hoped. And common sense. Aku had that. She would want her payment, her scarlet silk. And maybe she would see the profit in seeing this journey to its end, the tales she could tell, the travelers who would pay high to pass through the mountains with a woman who had guided a caravan of demons safely into Shurakan.

* * *

And they were safe. Whether word spread swifter than they could travel, or whether they were simply blessed with good fortune, they met no further ambush. No one tried to rob them in the villages, nor were they fallen on in camp and forced to give up their valuables. The snows that were not uncommon even at this time of year veiled the upper peaks from day's end to day's end, but never came down upon their track. All their passes were open, the ways unblocked by snow or rockfall or avalanche.

The luck was with them. Kimeri heard the Olenyai saying that to one another, in whispers so as not to frighten it away.

They could not see the demons who followed, spying on them, or clustered round their camp at night, round-eyed as owls, staring and wondering. The mages, who should have been able to see, were not looking. The guides had made themselves blind, because seeing made them so afraid.

Demons kept bandits away, though her mother's magic helped. The one whom she had come to think of as her demon, the white-feathered one that she had met at the spring, actually chased off a ragged man who was too desperately hungry to care about the rumor of fire and terror. Kimeri was angry at the demon for that. She made sure there was food for the man to steal, left some of her supper and some of her breakfast behind, and hoped he found them and was not too frightened to eat.

The demon understood anger, but its memory was very short. It was like the wind: changeable. But its fascination for her went on and on, and made it as solid as it could be, almost solid enough to touch.

Other demons came and went. There were different kinds. The ones with feathers were actually not common. Most had a great quantity of horns and teeth and claws, and scales and tails and leathery wings, and always the yellow eyes. The ones that drank blood looked at the men and the seneldi and thought hunger, but Kimeri's demon warned them off with growls and teeth-gnashings. It was not the largest demon and certainly not the most terrible to look at, but the others seemed to listen to it. Maybe, she thought, it was like her: royal born.

When her mother actually let her have a senel to ride all by herself, the demon came to sit on her crupper. The bay gelding did not like that at all. Kimeri calmed it down, shaking for fear her mother would think it was too much for her and make her ride like a baby again, the way the demon wanted to ride. But it was a good senel, sweet-tempered and quiet, just not prepared to carry a thing that had substance but no weight, and looked so odd besides. Once she had explained, it pinned its ears and fretted but gave in, and put up with the demon. The demon helped by being quiet and not moving around too much, except when it forgot and stood up on the senel's rump and made faces at demons that peered down from the sides of mountains.

It was a very happy demon, riding behind Kimeri, being invisible to everybody else. Sometimes she thought Vanyi might know it was there, but Vanyi said nothing. Kimeri was careful not to talk to it aloud, and when she talked to it in her head to make sure nobody else could listen. It took a little thinking to manage that, but it was not hard once she began.

At first the demon never thought in words, but the longer they went on, the clearer the demon's thoughts became, until they were having conversations, long hours of them, as the senel climbed up and climbed down and scrambled from mountaintop to mountaintop along the roof of the world. Demons had been there always, like the rocks and the snow and the sky—"From forever," the demon said. It liked the thought of forever, played often with it, turned it around in its head like a bright and shining toy. "Forever and ever and ever. We fly in the air, we swim through the earth, we dance on the waters that come out of the dark. We are here always. Always."

"Do you go anywhere else?" Kimeri asked it once in her head, after they had ridden through a valley with a waterfall. The demon had shown her how it danced on water. She had set out to try it, too, but her mother had caught her just as she began, and scolded her for getting wet, and made her change all her clothes, even the ones that were dry. "Do you only live in the mountains?"

"Where else is there to live?" the demon asked.

"Why," said Kimeri, "everywhere. There's a whole world beyond the mountains."

"The mountains are the world," the demon said.

"No," said Kimeri patiently. "The mountains are the roof of the world. The world is much larger than they are. There's the plain out past them, and the ocean, and more mountains, though not so high, and more plains, and rivers, and forests, and home, where I come from."

"You come from the mountains," the demon said. "You come from the thick places—the low mountains, the ones on the edge of the world, where air is heavy and easy to ride on."

"That's not the edge of the world," Kimeri said. "That's only the edge of the mountains."

"The edge of the world," the demon said.

It was a stubborn demon. She tried to show it home, the palace, the plain and the forest, even the Gate. But it insisted that home was the mountains, and the palace was like the palace in the place she was going to, which the demon thought of with a shudder. "The walled place," it said. "The place that burns." It meant wards, she thought, because it said the mages' wards burned, too, but only a little, and once she let it ride with her, it could ignore them completely.

But the wards that made it so afraid were Great Wards,

or something like them—wards stronger than any few mages could raise. It scared itself right off the senel and into nothingness, scaring her so much that she thought she had killed it. But it came back a long time later, after they stopped to camp, and it acted as if it could not remember what had scared it away. It would not talk about the walled place again; she did not ask, for fear that it really would go away and not come back.

10

"THE BURNING PLACE is near," the demon said. It was almost as hard to see as it had been the first time Kimeri saw it. Quivers ran through it, ripples of fear, but it clung stubbornly to the back of her saddle.

She would be afraid of the place herself if she had not heard her mother and Vanyi talking about it. To them it was a human place, that was all, and maybe it was dangerous, but it was nothing to frighten a mage. Demons, who were mostly air, had more to fear, and more to be wary of.

Her demon stood up on the senel's rump. "Stay here," it said.

It was not talking to the senel. It caught at her hair with claws like a brush of wind. "Stay in the mountains," it said. "Don't go down to the burning place."

"But," she said, in her head as always, "what would I do here?"

"Be," the demon answered. "Be with me."

"I'm not going to get hurt in the burning place," she said, trying to comfort it. "I have my own burning inside of me, that keeps me safe."

"Stay in the mountains," said the demon. "We can fly. We can play with the wind. You can sing, and I can dance. Stay."

She was usually careful not to act as if there was anyone with her, but now she turned and looked at the demon. It looked like a shadow on glass, with eyes that glowed like yellow moons. Its whole self was a wanting.

She remembered that some of its kind drank blood, and

some had claws that could rip an ox to pieces. But not her demon. It wanted her to stay, that was all, and keep it company.

"I learned words from you," the demon said. "Who will talk with me, if you go away?"

Kimeri's throat started to hurt. Her eyes were blurry. "I have to go."

"You can stay," said the demon.

"No," said Kimeri. An idea struck her. "You can teach the others words. Then they can talk to you."

"I want you," the demon said.

"I have to go," Kimeri said. "I have something to do. I can't not do it. Even to talk with you, and play on the wind."

The demon's claws tightened in her hair. They were more solid now, but still no stronger than the wind. Gently, because she did not want to hurt it, she let out a flicker of magery. The demon tried to cling, but the burning, even as little of it as there was, was too much for it. It wailed and let go.

"I'm sorry," said Kimeri, "but I can't stay. I'll try to come back."

"That is not now," the demon said.

There was nothing that Kimeri could say to that. She had more than a demon to think of, a Gate and a Guardian and a place where they both were, as terrible in its way as the burning place. She could not stop her throat from hurting and her eyes from filling up, but she could not do what the demon wanted, either.

It was too much for a very young person, even a princess with a Sun in her hand. The wind whipped the tears from her eyes, and kept the others from asking questions and being awkward. But her senel's saddle was too cold a comfort, its mane too rough to bury her face in. She made her way to where her mother was riding, talking to Chakan;

pulled herself over behind her mother's saddle and wrapped her arms about that narrow middle and clung.

Kimeri was acting strangely again, clinging and refusing to let go. Daruya worried, but magery found nothing wrong except a sourceless grief. Homesick, she decided, and afraid of this bleak steep country that seemed to go on and on without end. It was disturbing enough for a grown mage; for a child it must be terrifying.

She gave what comfort she could, and it seemed to be enough. Kimeri grew calmer, though she still did not ask to go back to her own saddle. Daruya let her stay where she was, glad of her warmth and her presence.

It seemed that they had been traveling for whole lives of men, ascending each mountain only to find another beyond, crossing each pass into a new and higher country. The air blew thin and bitter cold. Spring lagged behind, then vanished in endless fields of snow.

This was the summit of the world, as high as any simple man could go and live. Mages could have gone higher, but even Vanyi was not moved to that degree of curiosity, not with what she faced, ahead in Shurakan. There were peaks above her, white jagged teeth, and sky the color of evening although it was midday. Both moons were up, Brightmoon a white shadow of the sun, Greatmoon like a shield of ruddy copper, hanging above the crenellations of the Worldwall.

Those who needed mages' help to breathe, had that help and welcome. That was most of them now, all but the guides, who were born to this country. They kept formation as they had from the beginning, Aku leading, the men bringing up the rear. Their expressions were unreadable. Since Daruya disposed of the bandits to such spectacular effect, the ease that had been growing between Vanyi and Aku had vanished.

Aku was still civil, would still converse with Vanyi, answer her questions, perform her duty well and fully. But there was no warmth in it. A mage, like demons, like foreigners, was nothing that Aku wished to call friend.

It was not even hostile, that withdrawal. It was, that was all, like the language Aku spoke, the clothes she wore, the way she harnessed and rode her ox. Vanyi, speaking Aku's tongue through a trick of magery, wearing the winter garments of the Hundred Realms, riding a senel, was no more kin to her than one of the animals.

Vanyi was stubborn. She did not take refuge in aloofness, did not sequester herself with her mages and let the guides do as they pleased. She kept on riding beside Aku, kept on asking her questions, kept on pushing against the barrier that Aku had raised. It never moved, but neither would she desist.

She was as bad as Estarion, she supposed. She did not want to conquer, only to know and to understand. But she wanted that understanding. She fought for it, even against such determined resistance. There were hatreds enough in the realms of Sun and Lion, tribe fearing tribe, nation despising nation. But never minds closed and locked as these were. Never such perfect refusal to accept a stranger, still less a stranger who was a mage.

If Shurakan was as bad as this, she thought more than once, it might kill them out of hand, lest their alien presence pollute the land's purity.

And now as they crept across the roof of the world, Shurakan was close at last. Vanyi sensed nothing but rock and snow and cold, but Aku pointed to a peak like a spearhead, leaf-shaped, clean and hard and white against the sky. "That is Shakabundur," she said, "the Spear of Heaven, that stands guard on Su-Shaklan."

Aku's face was unreadable. Her mind offered nothing to the reading but a deep relief. The journey had been no joy to her, even with the prospect of riches in return for it.

Vanyi suppressed a sigh. It was tempting to pay the guides off now and go on alone, with their destination in sight. But she was not that great a fool. There were leagues yet to go, she judged; two days at least, and likely more, before they came to the valley—and who knew what between. One bridgeless chasm could set them back days, as they tried to find a way round.

She urged her senel forward. The gelding's ribs were beginning to show, what with long marching and short commons, but he was healthy enough. They had not lost any of their seneldi, even on the steepest tracks. That was good fortune. God and goddess approved of the journey, the priests would say—though not Estarion, who was lord of them all. Estarion did not approve in the least.

There was no warning at all. One moment they were scrambling along a precipice. The next, they found themselves on the very edge of it, and the mountain dropping down and down and down into a vision of misty green. After white snow, black rock, sky so blue it was near black, the mist and the greenness seemed utterly alien.

"Su-Shaklan," said Aku beside Vanyi. Vanyi raised her eyes from the vision of green to the white spearhead of the mountain that stood guard over its northern flank, then let them fall again into the country called the Kingdom of Heaven.

And no wonder, if it struck all travelers so. It was beautiful beyond comprehension.

"You must go there," said Aku, pointing. Vanyi followed the line of her hand to the cliff. For a moment she saw nothing but sheer drop; but slowly she perceived the line of the track, twisting back and forth down the precipice, shored with ledges. The bottom was out of sight, obscured by mist and distance.

Vanyi brought herself sternly to order, and faced the guide and what she had said. "You're not coming down with us."

"You have no need of us," Aku said, "and we are not of that country, nor welcome in it. We agreed to bring you here. We've done that. We'll take our payment and go."

And if Vanyi refused to pay, she made it clear, it would be simple enough to arrange a fall over the precipice. The three husbands were sitting their oxen with perfect casualness, just near enough to separate Vanyi from the rest, just far enough away to maintain their unthreatening air. She considered that they were sixteen to the guides' four, but the guides had the advantage, at the moment, of position. She shrugged. She had never intended to play the guides false, whatever they might think.

"Chakan," she said. "Pay them as they ask. Half the bolt of scarlet, on the whitefoot ox."

"We're taking the oxen," said Aku calmly. "We'll leave you what's yours."

"Oh, no," said Vanyi, just as calm, with a hint of a smile. "We bought and paid for those oxen. And those packs. And those provisions. We'll keep them, if you don't mind. We may have need of them."

Daruya, bless her intelligence, had spoken a word to the Olenyai. They were as casual as the husbands, hands not too blatantly near to swordhilts, sitting their seneldi in a loose, easy, and quite impenetrable formation around the huddle of oxen.

Aku inclined her head slightly. "We need to eat," she observed, as if to the air.

"You have your own ox," Vanyi said, "and I notice that his pack is remarkably large and heavy." She smiled again, a fraction wider. "My thanks for a journey well guided. May your gods prosper you."

Aku understood the dismissal. She shrugged slightly, spreading her hands in a gesture half of resignation, half of respect. "Prosper well," she said, "if the gods allow."

THE DESCENT INTO the Kingdom of Heaven was heart-stoppingly steep. They dismounted to begin it, dropping one by one over the side of the mountain and picking their way along a narrow thread of a track, with a wall of stone on one side and empty air on the other. Daruya at least was aware that the guides were left behind and in no friendly mood. But no great stones rolled down from the summit to sweep them aside, and no arrows flew. They were as safe as they could be on so steep a slope, with seneldi that, though surefooted, were not mountain oxen.

Kimeri had been notably reluctant to begin the descent. She kept lagging behind, looking back at the summit. There was nothing there; the guides were gone, heart-glad to be rid of their charges.

Chakan, in the rear, met Daruya's glance. His own was watchful, his pace just quick enough to keep the child from stopping. He would guard Kimeri and see that she was not lost or fallen. Daruya sighed and fixed her mind on the track.

Climbing could be exhausting, but going down was worse. One had to brace constantly, even where the track pretended to be more or less level, running sidewise along the cliff-face. And one could see where one was going—downward a league and more, and god and goddess knew whether they could reach the bottom before night caught them all and pinned them to the precipice.

It had been morning when they began, not long after sunrise. At noon they halted. There had been halts before, too many of them in Daruya's mind, but necessary. Even the Olenyai could not go on without pausing, not on such a road as this.

This pause was longer, with time to eat leathery dried oxmeat and still more leathery dried fruit, and drink water that still tasted faintly of snow though it had been carried in leather waterskins since last night's camp. The beasts had a handful of corn each, which finished out the store of fodder. If there was no grass below, only green illusion, they would starve.

It occurred to Daruya as she sat on the stony ground and tried to chew a strip of meat somewhat tougher than the sole of her boot, that they should long since have seen what they descended to. Morning's mists should have lifted. The valley should have opened below them. Yet it was still hidden; still featureless, an expanse of misty green with the Spear rising out of it.

"Wards," said Vanyi beside her, rubbing legs that must have ached as fiercely as Daruya's, grimacing as her fingers found a knot. "And Great Wards, at that. Do you feel how strong they are, and how old? They're anchored in mountains, with the Spear for a capstone."

"So they do have mages," Daruya said.

"Not necessarily. Mages could have been here long ago, set the wards, and died or gone away. The people who live here now might not even be aware of what protects them."

"How do we get in, then?" Daruya demanded.

"We knock on the door," said Vanyi, unperturbed.

"Are you sure there is one?"

"I'm assuming it. Our mages got in, after all. It can't be closed to people who come peacefully—just to invaders with weapons."

Daruya's eyes slid to the Olenyai, each with his two swords, his bow and quiver, and his other, carefully concealed armament.

"We'll get in," said Vanyi. "Swords or no swords."

* * *

The air grew warmer as they descended, until they had all packed their hats away, and their coats. The Olenyai kept their robes and veils, but the others were down to tunics and trousers or mages' robes when at last they came to the bottom of the cliff. It was a broad shelf of rock, bare of grass, and beyond that only air. A bridge stretched across it. Of what lay on the other side they could see nothing but mist.

The bridge was no solid work of stone such as they built in the empire. This was a wavering makeshift of wood and rope, swaying in the wind that swept down off the mountain. It was wide enough for an ox, more than wide enough for a senel. Whether it was sturdy enough . . .

Daruya's stomach ached with clenching. Her eyes burned. She should be able to see across the chasm. She could see perfectly well to the bottom of it: a long, long fall, and a tumble of rocks, and a river, its roar muted with distance. The drop was much deeper than the bridge was long; it had to be. And yet the bridge seemed to vanish into infinity.

She turned her face to the sky. It seemed very far away and very pale. The sun hovered on the rim of the precipice, as if it hesitated to abandon her in the trackless dark.

No one else was moving, either. Chakan had Kimeri on his shoulders and was calming his fretful senel with strokings and soft words. Vanyi stood on the first plank of the bridge. She stamped. The bridge echoed. "Solid enough," she said through the echoes. "We'll have to make sure none of the seneldi puts a foot through."

Or shied and leaped over the utterly inadequate rail of stretched rope and fell to its death. Daruya swallowed. Her throat was dry. She stroked the dun mare's neck. The mare was quiet enough, slick with sweat from the descent, and mildly annoyed that there was nothing to forage.

"Come then," Daruya said to her. "Let's get it over."

She rode past Vanyi, deliberately closing ears and mind

to objections. The mare hesitated as her hoof touched the bridge, but she had always been valiant. Daruya urged her gently forward. She snorted, lowered her head to examine this oddity to which she must trust her weight, and advanced gingerly upon it. The echo made her stiffen, but she did not halt.

Daruya kept her eyes on the road directly ahead of her and tried not to think of the fact that the rails, chest-high on a short man, were knee-high on a rider mounted on a tall senel. If she fell, she would keep them both alive and bring them safely to earth. Her magery was strong enough for that. But it would be less trouble if she forbore to fall.

Nobody had followed her yet. They were all waiting to see if the bridge would hold her. She could not hear them breathing.

The mist ahead seemed impenetrable, but it came to her slowly that there was something in it. A shape—shapes. One on either side of the bridge. Massive, looming figures, narrow and tall. Men? Giants? Demons?

The mare was unafraid of what lay ahead. All her tension was for the unsteadiness of the bridge and the hollow booming of her hoofs and the sough of wind in the ropes. Daruya supposed she should have walked, but riding seemed more queenly somehow—more like the act of a Sunchild entering a new country.

The tall shapes grew slowly clearer. The faint maddening humming in her skull was the warding, she realized. She had never felt one so strong before, or so removed from human source. It might have been a power in the earth, for all the sense she had of the mages who had raised it.

She was glad suddenly that she had not yielded to temptation and flown on wings of magery, avoiding the bridge altogether. The wards would have armed themselves against her. But because she came quietly, riding as any woman could ride, they did no more than rattle her teeth in her skull. Even that muted with the raising of her shields.

It was not a warding against mages, then. Only against magery.

The mist was thin now, revealing glimpses: green of grass and tree, white of—was it roof? Tower? And directly before her, vast shapes of men, stone-stiff and stone-still, tall pillars that seemed to hold up the sky. Their faces were weathered and worn. Their hands were rigid at their sides. They stared blankly, eternally, across the bridge and the chasm.

They had been painted once—brilliantly, from the look of them. Under the paint was grey stone, bones of the mountains. All their power was in their stillness, and in their height even above one who rode on senelback. The Great Wards were not in them; they signified them, no more.

At first she did not see the men who stood beyond the pillars, dwarfed by them. But she heard them: the song of metal on metal in the armor that they wore, and the ring of armed feet on stone as they advanced. She halted her mare between the pillars and waited for them.

Fear was a dim and feeble thing. Curiosity was stronger by far. The armor that these men wore was as fantastical as the temples in Su-Akar. Every edge of it was flared and fluted. Its surfaces were carved, gilded, colored in eye-searing patterns. It covered them from head to foot. On their heads were helmets like temple towers, some visored with scowling demon-faces, a few open. Those she stared at. Plainsmen again, she thought, high-cheeked, narrow-eyed, bronze-skinned; taller than the men in Su-Akar, as tall as in the Hundred Realms, and while not slender, not nearly so broad and thick. They grew beards here, the first that she had seen in this part of the world: a thin straggle by northern standards, confining itself to chin and upper lip. They looked only vaguely ridiculous, and very stern.

Behind her the bridge boomed. The others had decided at last to cross it, more slowly than she had, but determined once they began. She stayed where she was. The guards would have to shoot past her to strike any of the rest.

"Greetings," she said in the language that her magery had taught her, "and well met, men of Su-Shaklan."

"Greetings," said the guard in the center, whose thin beard and mustaches brushed his breastplate. His armor was even more ornate than the others', his helmet higher, with a winged golden thing on the crest: dragonel, perhaps, or dragon proper. He did not say that she was well met. "You will give me your weapons if you wish to pass this gate."

Haughty man. She gave him in return the hauteur of an empress born. "I am unarmed, as you should see." All but the magery that she could not use, not here, and the small dagger in her boot, which she used for cutting meat. She lifted her chin a fraction higher. "Now may I pass?"

"Not alone," said the captain of the guard. His eyes slid past her to what she was already aware of, the knotting of people and animals at her back and on the bridge.

She nudged the mare aside. Vanyi's mean-eyed gelding pranced past her, snorting and tossing his horns. The mages followed, and the Olenyai, and Kimeri riding beside Chakan. Daruya remained where she was.

"If you would enter Su-Shaklan," said the captain of the guards, "you will give to us your weapons. None but a man of the kingdom may go about armed."

Daruya held her breath. Olenyai swords were more than edged blades; they held the honor of their master. They were not to be parted from, even in sleep.

And yet, one by one and following their commander's lead, the Olenyai surrendered their swords, their bows, their knives and such other weapons as they could be seen to carry. That there were more, and many, hidden in the black robes, Daruya knew for a certainty. Either the guards did not know, or they did not care what weapons a stranger concealed.

She suspected the former. No one judged an Olenyas rightly at first. The robes and the veils were alarming enough, but the men in them were small, more often slender than not, and little given to posturing. They never saw the need.

They had given up their swords for the emperor's sake, for this embassy that he had sent. They would not forget the sacrifice. Nor would they hesitate to exact a price, if they could.

For the moment they were quiet, keeping their demoneyes lowered, playing the humble strangers. It was not ill played. The guards ignored them, speaking to Daruya. "These animals of yours. They are clean?"

As clean as they could be after such a journey, she almost answered; but they were speaking of ritual. While she wondered how to reply, Vanyi said, "They are clean in the eyes of our gods. I speak for them as for the men who follow me."

The guards accepted that. Like the guides, they saw her grey age and reckoned her wise. The captain even inclined his head to her, mighty concession to a foreigner in this of all places in Shurakan. "And the woman, too? And the child?"

"All who are with me," said Vanyi, no sign of a smile in her voice, but Daruya sensed her amusement even through her shields and the hum of the wards.

The captain turned abruptly on his heel. "You will come," he said.

12

FROM THE OTHER side of the Great Wards, Shurakan showed itself clear, unveiled and unconcealed. The pillars of its gate stood on the rim of a valley like a goblet, slopes and terraces descending half a league and more to a lake like a blue jewel with a broad rim of green. Beside the lake was a city of dark roofs and white towers. Other, smaller cities and towns and villages scattered through the valley and up the slopes of its sides. On the terrace just below and northward of the pillars, under the Spear of Heaven, rose a second city. Its towers were airier than those of the city in the valley, its walls higher, broader, running along the edge of the terrace. Between terrace and walls, the city stood nigh half a league high; only a bird would wish to fall from that wall.

Vanyi's mages of the Gates had named both cities to her, and she to Daruya a few evenings since beside a fire in the mountains. That in the valley was the Winter City, that on the height its companion of the Summer. The high ones, the lords and princes, court and king and queen and all their followers and dependents, traveled from one to the other in the long round of the year. Winter saw them below in the green warmth of the valley, drinking sweet water from the lake and hunting on the forested slopes to south and west. Summer brought sullen heat and pestilence and stinging flies, and sent the court fleeing up the mountain to cool airs and clean stone amid which they set their gardens. Only the poor remained below, and the holy men and women in their temples, and the folk who tilled the rich land beside the lake, preparing for the harvest and the winter and the lords' return. Then the Summer City was silent in its mantle of snow, and only the hardy remained, and the holy ones in the temples, and those commanded for their sins to hold the city until summer came round again.

It was summer now—the very day of High Summer, Daruya realized with a start, the greatest of festivals in the empire, and she had forgotten it. The Summer City was full of princes. On this longest day of the year, with the sun sinking fast below the mountains but light lingering in the pellucid sky, the streets were thronged with people, in the music of bells and drums. They all wore the faces of plainsmen as she knew them in the Hundred Realms, familiar and yet subtly strange: features both stronger and finer, hair dark but often with a ruddy sheen, men as tall as she and broad with it, women walking proud in long coats and wide-legged trousers. Many wore the open-sided robes of temples, men and women shaven-headed alike, bare alike beneath the robes, and no more shame in them than she might have seen in kilted tribesmen of Keruvarion's own mountains.

They had no fear. It was an odd thing to think as she rode among them walled in guards, but it was true. They stared at the strangers, commented openly on demon-eyes and shadow-gods and foreign horrors, seemed not to care if they were understood, or if the strangers might take revenge for what was said of them. They looked on what to them was superstition and terror, and they shrugged at it. They were the people of the Kingdom of Heaven. Their gods defended them. Nothing could touch them or do them harm.

And yet a Gate had fallen here. They knew fear of that, surely, and hate. She did not find it in the faces that she passed. Even the poor seemed decently fed and reasonably content.

They had entered the city through its eastern gate, the gate of the dawn that looked upon the pillars and the mountain wall. Once past the gate they turned northward and made their way up a road not much wider than a cart-track in Asanion. Here it was a broad thoroughfare. Blank walls lined it, set with elaborate gates. Those that were open looked in on the jeweled extravagance of temples, or on gardens full of flowers, lit with lamps in the dusk.

Ahead of them rose a greater wall than any, strung with lights like a necklace of firestones. Its gate was of bronze, the pillars like those of the kingdom's gate, mighty man-shapes in postures of guard. These were freshly painted, their armor gilded, their helmets ornamented with lamps.

As with all gates once the sun had set, this one did not open for them, but one lesser, to the side of the great gate, where new guards waited to relieve the old. The guardians of the pillars turned without speaking and went back to their duty, unmindful of the dark or the hour. The guardians of the palace—for it could be nothing else—took them in hand with as little ceremony.

First they wished to separate the strangers from their animals. Daruya would have protested that people who had never seen a senel could not know how to care for a herd of them, but Vanyi was before her. "Kadin, go with them. Show them what to do."

Daruya could hardly quarrel with that. Kadin surveyed the persons waiting to take charge of the beasts, and was surveyed in turn. He was by head and shoulders the tallest there, and dark to invisibility outside the light of torches, but for the gleam of his eyes. After a long moment a man in a coat that swept the ground, which seemed to indicate rank here, held up his hand and said, "Show us."

The others eased at that, as if at a master's command. Kadin went away with them, with seneldi and oxen following. Vanyi and Daruya and Kimeri, the two remaining mages and the Olenyai, went onward on foot into the lamp-lit palace.

Daruya would remember little of that first sight of the Ushala, the palace of the brother-king and sister-queen in the Summer City of Shurakan. Lamps, she remembered those, burning perfumed fat and faintly rancid oil. Corridors that went on and on. Courtyards walled in darkness. Expectation that, tired and filthy and road-weary as she was, she must face the king and the queen and be as royal as they.

But she was not asked to suffer that. She was taken through the heart of the palace and out into its gardens and thence to the walls, where stood a row of houses. Guest-houses, the guards said, with an intonation that made her think *pesthouses,* houses set apart for the victims of a plague. All but one were dark. That one was waiting, ready for them, and it was surprisingly pleasant. Its rooms were not large but airy and clean, clustered round a courtyard in which was a fountain, and flowers sending sweet scents into the night. There were servants, soft-footed quiet people who offered baths, food, drink, rest.

Daruya took them all, one after the other. Vanyi stayed with her, and Kimeri. The others went away with most of the servants to baths and food and rest of their own. Chakan would have stayed, but the servants were persuasive, and Daruya commanded him. "You're dropping on your feet. Go and sleep, and come back to nursemaid me in the morning."

Vanyi she could not compel so, nor did she overmuch wish to. There were great basins full of steaming water for both the women, and a smaller one for Kimeri, who for once was too tired to object. The servants were quiet and skilled. Daruya fell asleep under their hands; woke with a start to find herself lying on soft cloths, having the aches stroked out of her.

Vanyi lay almost within reach, much wider awake than she, and palpably on guard. Daruya knew a moment of shame—she should have been as wary, she who had her daughter to think of. But there was no danger here. All her senses assured her of it.

They were still assuring her of it when she woke to a dazzling-bright morning and Kimeri bouncing on her stomach, caroling, "Mama, see! See where we are!"

Daruya barely had time to scrub the sleep out of her eyes before Kimeri was dragging her to the window through which all the light was coming. It dazzled her; and yet it was not sunlight. That was away out of sight to the eastward. She was receiving the full force of it reflected from the Spear of Heaven, blinding white and seeming to hang directly before her, with a brief dip of valley between.

The house, she realized with the sluggishness of the barely awake, was built into the palace wall. There was nothing below her window but eventually—very eventually—the valley's floor.

Kimeri scrambled up onto the window's broad sill, laughing with delight. "Mama, isn't it wonderful? We're as high up as birds!"

"We were higher in the mountains," Daruya said. "And on the bridge."

"But we couldn't *fly* there." Kimeri leaned out as if she intended to do just that.

Daruya barred her with a stiffened arm. She had not been this animated since Starios, nor this openly inclined toward mischief. It was a relief in its way, but Daruya found herself wishing that the child could have clung to her unwonted docility for a day or two longer. "You won't be flying here," Daruya said sternly. "You'll scare people. They don't have any magic, and they don't know about people who do."

"I can teach them," said Kimeri.

"Not today," Daruya said. That quelled her, for a won-der. She let herself be swung back into the room and in-spected. Rather to Daruya's surprise, she was clean, combed, and dressed, and yes, fed. The servants were mar-vels indeed, if they could accomplish that much with this young imp.

Kimeri wriggled, impatient with motherly fussing. "May I go now, mama? Chakan says I can play in the gar-den with Hunin if you say yes."

"I say yes," said Daruya. "But only the garden, and only as long as Hunin says you may."

"Yes, mama," said Kimeri meekly.

Her tone warned of disobedience, but not for the mo-ment. Daruya decided to let it suffice. Hunin was the eldest of Chakan's Olenyai, sober and sensible. He would keep Kimeri in hand, nor hesitate to call on a mage if there was need.

With Kimeri there probably would be.

Daruya sighed and let her go. Time enough to worry when the child lost patience with her limits and went about testing them. For now Daruya would see what could be had in the way of bath and breakfast—another bath, yes indeed; after so long with nothing to bathe in but icy streams and water in waterskins, she meant to be clean from morning till morning, and every moment between.

Vanyi's waking was easier and somewhat earlier, her bath simple and brief, her breakfast likewise. Once she had dis-posed of both, she said to the servant who attended her, "I would speak with the queen. Whom shall I send with the message, and when may I be granted audience?"

The servant did not change expression, nor ask why Vanyi wished only to speak with the queen. He had been expecting the question, then, and he had an answer ready.

"Madam should speak with the Minister of Protocol, since it is he who determines who shall and shall not address the children of heaven. This unworthy person may send one yet more unworthy with a message, if madam wishes."

"Madam does wish," said Vanyi. "Madam is called Guildmaster, or lady, or if one is suitably familiar, Vanyi."

"Lady," said the servant, bowing in the manner of this country: hands folded on breast, head bent low. She doubted that it was proper to bow in return.

The message went out as promised, but the answer was slow to come back. While Vanyi waited, she discovered that none of them was being held prisoner. They could come and go as they wished, not only in the palace but in the city. The guards who had brought them to this house had left them in the care of the servants, none of whom showed inclination to be a warrior or a jailer. They made no objection to Vanyi's ordering the house as she pleased, with Olenyai on guard, mages established in an inner room to set up wards and begin their search for the destroyers of Gates, and seneldi stabled, after some negotiation, in the house next door. Pastures they could not have, but they were given ample grain and fodder, and the courtyard was large enough for them to run in, two and three at a time.

It would do, Kadin conceded; he kept his position as groom and guard. He was avoiding the other mages. Naturally enough, Vanyi thought, though it grieved her. It would throb like a raw wound to see Miyaz and Aledi together, weaving their powers of dark and light. He made no effort to enter their sanctum, slept in a room in the house that he had made a stable, devoted himself to the care of the seneldi. He had even, since he came to the city, put off his violet robe and put on the kilt of his people. He wore it with an air that defied his Guildmaster to challenge it.

She did no such thing. When it was time for him to be a

mage again, she would see that he did so. Now he would mourn as he must, without her to meddle. Jian had been lover and wife as well as lightmage. He was entitled to a certain extravagance of grief.

"A visitor, lady," said the servant whom, by the time the sun reached zenith and sank slowly westward, Vanyi thought of as her own. She was sitting in the room she had been given, watching the play of light over the valley and testing the strength of the Great Ward. It had no weaknesses that she could find.

When the servant spoke, she started out of a half-dream. "A messenger?" she asked.

"A visitor, lady," the servant repeated. "A guest who bids you welcome to Su-Shaklan. We have given him the cakes of welcome, and the tea. Will the lady receive him in the room that is proper for such things?"

The lady would, and with alacrity, no matter what the servant thought of that. Vanyi was not noble born, to care for such silliness—unless of course it suited her.

The visitor was waiting for her in a room that faced the garden, nibbling the last of a plateful of cakes and sipping a tiny cup filled with the hot herb-brew of Shurakan. He was not, as she had still dared to hope, an emissary of the queen, not openly or obviously. He was a priest in a saffron robe, with a pattern of flowers painted on his shaven skull.

It took a moment to see the face between the robe and the paint. It was not a young face, wizened and weathered, but its eyes were bright, its smile sweet, showing an expanse of toothless gums as he rose and bowed. He did not bow as low as the servant did, Vanyi noted—there were degrees of reverence, then. This seemed to indicate respect but not servility, and a measure of equality.

His voice was sweet and rather high. It was not a eunuch's voice. There were eunuchs here, her Guardians had said, and all of them were priests, unmanned in the service of one of their bloodier goddesses. But he was not of that sect. His voice had a trained purity, as if he were a singer.

"Lady," he said, "it is well you are come, and well that I see you, come at last to Su-Shaklan. I greet you in the name of the gods and the gods' children, and all who are in this kingdom they make blessed."

It took Vanyi a moment to understand him. Magery could teach a language, but not its odder nuances. Some of these were very odd. She did not try to rival them, but said, "Greetings to you also, priest of the gods. My name is Vanyi, master of the Guild of Mages in the empire of Sun and Lion."

The priest's eyes narrowed a fraction. He was wincing, she realized, and in the most delicate manner possible. "Lady. Ah, lady. We do not use such words here, if we are most properly polite. I am named Esakai, priest of Ushala temple, where the children of heaven pay their devotions."

He was telling her something, subtly. That she must not speak of mages here, yes, she had expected that. He had responded as a courtier might in requesting an outland barbarian not to relieve himself on the palace floor. The same delicate revulsion; the same careful consideration for the stranger's ignorance.

But that was not all he was getting at. "Are you a messenger of the queen?" Vanyi asked him.

The tilt of his head and the lift of his brow reminded her that they were both standing, and he was old, and his feet were no longer as sturdy as they had once been. She chose not to ignore him. Rudeness was not what the occasion called for; and if he meant to divert her, then he had misjudged his target. She sat in the chair opposite the one he had occupied, thus allowing him to sink back into it with a barely audible sigh of relief.

Which too was subtlety. She countered it again with blunt directness. "The queen sent you, then?"

"Oh," he said. "Oh, no, lady. Of course not. The daughter of heaven needs no unworthy mortal to speak for her."

"Then how does a mere mortal gain audience with her?"

"Why, lady," said the priest in limpid innocence, "he does not. Mortals are unworthy to gain the attention of the gods' own children."

"In my country," said Vanyi, "our ruler also is descended from a god, but he never shuns the company of his people. He walks among them as one of their own, and they love him for it."

"So do our people love the children of heaven," said the priest, unruffled, "but the children of heaven would never lessen themselves by walking on common earth."

"That was so once," Vanyi said, "in part of our empire. Its emperors, as they were then, became so rarefied that they had to take the earth to themselves or perish. The last of them mated with the sun-god's child and begot a new world in which the gods walk with men, and men give the gods their power to rule."

"How strange," said the priest. "How . . . unusual."

"That may be," Vanyi said. "But surely people do speak to the queen? She condescends, I'm told, when need demands."

"Ah," said the priest as if she had explained a matter that puzzled him sorely. "Ah, lady. The queen speaks, yes, for herself and in the times that she chooses. She never sends messengers or begs mortals to attend her. They come when the Minister of Protocol bids them come, and she comes as she wishes, or not."

Slowly Vanyi worked her way through the tangle of alien logic. "The queen chooses when and to whom she speaks. The Minister of Protocol decides who will speak to her, if she chooses to speak, which is her right and her decision. Therefore the queen sends no messengers. The Minister of Protocol, however . . . "

"The Minister of Protocol abides by the will of heaven. The queen and the king her brother may speak or not speak. That too is the will of heaven."

"I think," said Vanyi dryly, "that the Minister of Protocol has a great deal of power. Has he sent you to instruct me?"

"I came by the will of heaven," said the priest, "and of my own curiosity, to see what manner of people you are. The lowly mortals name you demons. I'm thinking that you are no such thing. But you are very strange—and your shadows most of all."

"What, my blackrobes?" Vanyi allowed herself to smile. "They're warriors of that empire which had to wed itself with the Sun or die. No demons; no creatures of terror. Merely men, bred and trained to defend their emperor."

"Very strange men," the priest said. "Were their mothers bred to demons, to make them strong?"

"We have no demons in Asanion," Vanyi said, "which is the name of their country. Nor in Keruvarion, which is the name of mine."

"There are demons everywhere," said the priest, "except in Su-Shaklan. Our prayers keep them out."

Their Great Wards kept them out, Vanyi thought. She did not say it. "Still, in Asanion, men look as these men do, as the lady does who rode with us, though she's taller than any of them. Their faces are like hers. They veil them for honor and for custom."

The priest shuddered delicately. "Ah, poor things, to be so ugly. Maybe they do descend from demons, though they deny it. Demons are very strong."

"Daruya is reckoned beautiful in our country," Vanyi said with a hint of sharpness, catching herself a moment too late, suppressing rueful laughter. She was as vain as that girlchild, and on her behalf, too.

"Ah," said the priest, mildly nonplussed. "You are strange."

"But human," said Vanyi, "and desirous of addressing the queen. Might the Minister of Protocol be persuaded to grant me a few moments of his time?"

"This mere mortal could hardly say, lady," said the priest.

"Venture a guess," Vanyi said with a flash of teeth.

The priest blinked. "Oh, that is beyond me, lady. It has been a great pleasure to speak with you. May I return, if your charity permits? I should like very much to hear more of this empire of yours, where demons call themselves men, and kings walk in the dust without fear of soiling their feet."

Vanyi inclined her head. She could keep him there if she tried, but she was not minded to do that. He would go back to his Minister of Protocol, she was sure, and report every word that they had said. Then, with any luck at all, the Minister himself would be curious enough to summon her—or to send a messenger with a better head for the heights.

She could wait. For a while. Then, with or without the mighty Minister, she would do as she had meant to do since she conceived this expedition.

13

Daruya was bored.

Everyone else had things to do. Vanyi was pressing for an audience with the queen. The mages had raised their wards and begun a working to discover what had broken the Gates. The Olenyai took turns on guard. Even Kimeri had occupation in plenty, what with the garden, the stable, and the discovery that Kadin the mage had no objection to the presence of a small girlchild as he went about his business with the animals.

Daruya was the odd one, the one who had no duty and no occupation. Vanyi did not need her to assist in the campaign for an audience with the queen—if anything she was a hindrance, what with the need to explain who she was and what she was and why she had come, and the delicacy of balancing her rank as princess-heir with the queen's rank as ruler of Shurakan. Kimeri needed her only to be there and to offer praise of the flowers she brought in great untidy armfuls, or the spotted cat-kit she retrieved from the straw of the dun mare's stall, or the bit of harness she had mended all by herself. The mages certainly did not need her; she had proved already, too often, that she overwhelmed their subtle workings with her great blaze of power. And when she went into the city, to the house where the Gate had been, to see what was there, she found Kadin in the empty echoing place with no need or want of her, and a shrinking from the light of her power that made her blind angry and inexplicably inclined to weep. She had nothing to do and no purpose here but to wait, and to hope that when Vanyi won through at last to the queen, Daruya would be permitted to speak in the emperor's name.

There was only so much she could do to occupy herself in the house they had been given. The servants needed no assistance, and looked askance at any offer of it. Kadin was not displeased to let her help with the seneldi, but she could not spend every moment of every day in their company. The Olenyai neither needed nor wanted her to take a turn on guard.

For a full hand of days she kept her patience reined in. She wandered about the palace, finding no obstacle to passage, merely polite stares and respectful bows. People spoke when spoken to. Some even addressed her before she addressed them, greeting her, inquiring as to her health and the health of her companions. They all seemed to know a great deal about the embassy, even to understand that it was an embassy and not an invasion of demons from beyond the Worldwall. It was not a matter of importance, they indicated with glance and gesture and inclination of the head, but it was pleasant to see strangers here where strangers came so seldom.

"You'll take back the tale of us, I'm sure," said one exquisite courtier in a coat that trailed behind him, from beneath what had at first seemed a towering helmet but revealed itself to be an edifice built of his long lacquered hair. "Your empire would wish to know how we order the world in Su-Shaklan."

"It is curious, yes," Daruya replied with careful courtesy. "It's always eager to learn the ways of strangers."

"It will learn much from ours," said the courtier. "Why, it might even become civilized, and your emperor be judged worthy to address our children of heaven."

Daruya stared at him. It dawned on her with the slowness of incredulity that he was calling her a barbarian and her emperor an inferior monarch, unfit to stand in the presence of Shurakan's divine rulers. Her first impulse was to laugh; her second, to box this idiot's ears. She suppressed both. "My emperor is the son of a god," she said stiffly.

"Ah," said the courtier, polite. "How pleasant. Is it a god we know?"

"We call him the sun," she said more stiffly still.

"Ah," the courtier said again with an expression of mounting ennui. "A great god, yes. Very great. But not one of ours."

They were not interested. That was the maddening thing, the thing that Daruya would never have credited if she had not seen and heard it. This little sipping-bowl of a kingdom fancied itself great; looked on the mighty realm of Sun and Lion, and smiled as at the fancy of a child; called its lords mere barbarians, and disparaged its god with a shrug of sheerest indifference.

How tiny this realm was, how minute the concerns of its people, how very narrow their minds. She would have been happy to open their smug little skulls with an axe.

The palace was too small for her grand fit of temper. She walked right out of it, with an Olenyas to keep her shadow safe: Yrias, who was young and diffident and too shy to stop her. He would be her protection against Chakan's wrath when the captain of Olenyai discovered that she had ventured the streets of the Summer City without him.

They were as steep as ever and as narrow, and as straitly walled. It was like walking between cliffs in the mountains, except for the gates that opened here and there, and the people who went back and forth in a jostling crowd. No one rode here, even on an ox; they were all afoot, many laden down with mountainous packs or trotting between the shafts of a wheeled cart in which sat a toplofty noble or a painted-faced lady or a mound of roots and greens for the market.

Common people, she had come to realize, dressed as she

did, in trousers and hip-long coat. People of rank wore coats of increasing length, until the princes swept about in elaborate garments that trailed behind them, worn over the same simple shirt and wide-legged trousers as that affected by the lowest urchin—though of cut and color befitting their station. Her good plain clothes, which in Starios would have marked her for what she was, here made her seem a commoner, and not a wealthy one at that.

The distinction was not as sharp as it might have been. She saw a princeling give place to a man in a coat that hung only to his knees, because the latter was larger and older and walking with ponderous dignity. The prince acted as if he were doing the man a favor; the man acted as if he had expected that favor and would have been shocked not to receive it.

Age mattered, she had already observed. Size did, too, it seemed. And dignity. But a prince was still a prince. The queen and the king still were thought of as equal to the gods. Everyone bowed to divinity and yielded place to it, but when priests walked past, unless they marched in procession, they had no more precedence than anyone else. It all seemed very complicated and very hard to make sense of.

There were temples everywhere. Asanion's thousand gods seemed to be mirrored here in Shurakan, if not doubled and trebled. Every god had his priesthood, too, and every family gave at least one child to a temple. She saw a gaggle of such children in the care of an erect, stern woman, being herded toward a sweetseller's stall. They were reciting as they ran, in eerie unison: "The gods are all. The gods are one. We are all one in the eyes of the gods."

Priests all wore the same robe, although its color might change with the god and the temple. Children of princes stood equal there to children of beggars. She stopped to ask the woman who herded the children, waiting till each had been given its fistful of sweetness and squatted in a line to eat it, perched like birds on the low wall that ran from the sweetseller's stall to that of a maker of shoes. "You *are* all one?" Daruya asked. "Truly?"

The priestess stared at her, curious but not hostile, and unafraid of her yellow eyes. "All of us," she said, "yes. Hush now, Kai-Kai, you know you like the redspice buns better than the honeytits."

The child sulked but ate her bun, reminding Daruya forcibly of Kimeri in a similar fit of indecision. Daruya smiled at her. She would not smile back, though she stared as hard as the priestess had. "So everyone is the same in the gods' eyes. And yet you have divisions; you have princes and you have beggars."

"Of course," said the priestess. "That's how the gods ordered the world. But we're all the same in the end. We all die."

"Even your children of heaven?"

The priestess' lips thinned. "You are a foreigner. You don't understand."

"But I would like to."

"No," said the priestess. "You only think so." She gathered her charges together abruptly and swept them onward, most still eating, and all sticky-fingered.

Daruya stayed where she was. She had meant to discomfit the priestess, there was no denying it, but she had not intended to feel guilty about it. It was time these smug self-satisfied fools had a comeuppance.

On the other side of the street, between a goldsmith and the extravagantly gilded gate of a temple, was a place that looked interesting. Its gate opened on a courtyard, which was a garden as they often were here. Low tables were set in and about the garden, so low that they had no need of chairs, and people sat at them on silken rugs, sipping from little cups or nibbling what looked like rarefied examples of the sweetseller's wares. Nearly all of the people were men, and few of them were priests. The coats that she could see trailed in long sweeps on the clipped grass or the patterned stones of pavement.

This, she saw as she drew closer, was a teahouse—tea being what people drank here when they did not drink gaggingly sweet wine or, even worse, the milk of oxen. It was a poor excuse for a quencher of thirst, being but hot water poured over a handful of mildly bitter herbs, but they made a great fuss over it, with ceremonies devoted to it, and whole houses that served nothing but tea and sweet cakes.

In Starios this would have been a tavern frequented by the lordly sort. Daruya had spent many an evening in such a place, drinking and gaming and seeing what trouble she could get into without incurring her grandfather's wrath. It was to the upper room of one that she had taken a certain gold-and-ivory beauty of a lordling, and conceived an heir without the complication of a husband.

Shurakani teahouses were quieter places, from the look of this one. Her arrival caused a mild flutter—very mild. She was not asked to leave. When she sat at a table, a soft-footed servant glided up, deposited on the table a delicate night-blue pot and an even more delicate gilt-rimmed cup, and glided away.

The pot was almost too hot to touch. The cup was cool, no larger or more substantial than an eggshell. The scent that wound with steam from the spigot of the pot was as delicate as the rest, with a suggestion of flowers.

She thought of calling for ale, and raising a tumult until she got it. But she was too well trained to do that. Pity. She was bored, and growing more bored by the heartbeat. She poured tea into the cup, found it an exquisite shade of golden amber. Its flavor was subtly bitter and subtly sweet. It was like the tea of ceremony, somewhat, but darker, stronger: more fit for use.

Conversations that had paused with her presence had resumed. They were not all as quiet as she might have expected, considering the elegance of the teahouse and its servitors. One table crowded with young elegants was discussing in detail the wares of a certain house of pleasure on a street called the Path of the White Blossoms. At another, three or four grey-mustached men discoursed lengthily on the nature, number, and kind of the gods.

"Incalculable, innumerable, and ineffable," said a man who sat alone near Daruya. He had been watching her for a while; she had been undertaking to ignore him. That was rather difficult, as it happened. He was not as young as the young elegants, not nearly as old as the grey philosophers. His hair was black with ruddy lights, worn in a club at his nape. His mustaches hung just below the line of his shaven jaw. His shoulders were broad beneath his coat, which was long enough to gather in folds on either side of him as he sat cross-legged on the grass. She thought he might be tall: he sat eye to eye with her, and she sat higher than most of the men round about.

He met her stare with one as frank, and grinned at her frown. "What, stranger, do I offend you? Don't people take one another's measure in your country?"

"How do you know what country I come from?" she demanded.

He laughed and gestured in a graceful sweep: her hair that escaped all bonds she set on it, her eyes, her face, her height that was rather extraordinary here. He had long hands, she noticed, and tapering fingers; but they were not either weak or effeminate. They looked, in fact, quite strong. "You would be one of the people from beyond the Wall," he said. "The demon's daughter, I'd suppose—and is that one of your husbands behind you?"

Yrias' indignation was so sharp that Daruya started. It was on her behalf, of course—it always was. She wanted to slap him. Instead she said to the man who spoke so boldly, "None of them is my husband. They're my guards. And I am not a demon's get!"

"Oh, surely," said the man with no evidence of contrition. "You are human, yes, the priests say that you say so. Pardon me for needing to confirm it."

"I suppose," she said with acid precision, "that it's only to be expected. You know no race but your own."

"What, there are others?"

He was laughing at her. People who laughed at Daruya never escaped unscathed. Yet, because he was an innocent in such matters, she said sweetly enough, "Ah, but you people have never seen any faces but your own. I have kin who look like you. And kin who look like my warriors, or like me. And kin who are taller than I, and black from head to foot. All bow to the Lord of Sun and Lion, who rules from the city in which I was born."

"Truly?" The man swept up his pot of tea and his cup and a basket fragrant of sweetness and spices, and established himself boldly and shamelessly at her table, facing her across it, favoring her with what no doubt he reckoned an enchanting smile. "Tell me more of all these people who sound like men and demons and dark gods all mixed in together."

"They're all men," Daruya said, snappish. "And you are presumptuous. Did I invite you to share my table?"

"You answer when I ask questions," the man said as if that countered her objection. He dipped cooled tea from her cup into the roots of a blossoming tree and filled it again, and held it out to her till she had perforce to take it. He smiled as she sipped, transparently approving. "My name is Bundur of House Janabundur."

She raised her brows. Was she supposed to be awed? "My name," she said, "is Daruya of House Avaryan."

His brows rose in echo of hers. "That is a proud house?"

"That is the royal house," she said. "Is yours?"

He shrugged, nonchalant. "I'm not the king, and not likely to be, for which I praise the gods. Are you likely to be queen?"

"If I outlive my grandfather," she said, "yes."

"And he let you come here. That was generous of him."

She felt the slow flush climb her cheeks. He saw it—she traced it in the gleam of his eyes. Narrow black eyes above proud cheekbones. He did look remarkably like a plainsman. A very handsome, very presumptuous plainsman. Sharply, angrily, she said, "I am my grandfather's envoy."

"You, and not the woman who is said to lead your embassy?"

Oh, he was a clever man, and he knew it, too. "Vanyi leads. I speak for the emperor when the time comes."

"Emperor," he said, musing, downing a cup of his own tea and a cake from the basket as he did it. "That is a king, yes? But more than a king?"

"A king of kings."

"How can there be more than one king?"

"In the same way that there can be more than one god. Kings are common in the world. Emperors are rarer. There were two, for a while. Now there is one."

"One killed the other?"

"One died. His son married the daughter of the other. Their son was emperor. And so it continued."

"Ah," said Bundur. "An emperor is only a king after all."

"He is not," Daruya said. "Kings bow to him. He rules kings. Your whole kingdom would fit into a minor barony, with room left to graze whole herds of oxen."

"Our kingdom is the heart of the world," said Bundur, "its model and its pattern. Your emperor should have let his sister rule also, as the gods decreed."

"Our emperors have no sisters. Or brothers. The god

gives each royal descendant one child, and one child only. That child rules."

Bundur tossed his head. "No! You don't say it? What did your first king do to offend the gods?"

"Rather a great deal," said Daruya with sudden wryness. "But that was supposed to be a gift."

"I think he cursed you." Bundur had to drink another cup of tea and devour another cake to calm himself. "What if your child dies?"

"Your child's child inherits."

"And if there is none?"

"The god provides," said Daruya. She found herself running her hand along her thigh. Her right hand, with its burning brand. She was not tempted to turn it palm upward to show him what she carried, the god's seal and his promise that her line would not perish from the earth. It was no secret in the empire, but neither was it for every eye to goggle at.

All the more so here. Her tea had cooled, but she drank it. It was wet; it quenched thirst after a fashion.

"Do you have sisters?" she asked Bundur abruptly.

"Seven of them," he answered with some complacence. "Three gave themselves to temples. Two married into families of distinction. One is still unbound by either husband or god. One was our sacrifice."

Daruya frowned.

He saw fit, at that, to explain. "You don't have that? When sickness comes, or the gods' displeasure, one child takes it all on herself. If she lives, the plague or the curse is ended. If she dies, likewise. The rest of her family is safe."

"That is barbaric," said Daruya.

"It's great honor," he said, unoffended, "and great courage. It increases the distinction of the house. I would have been the sacrifice myself, but I had no brothers. I wasn't allowed."

"If she had had no sisters, would it have been allowed?"

"Of course not," said Bundur. "There must always be one sister and one brother. The gods decreed it."

"Even if only one child is born?"

"Then," he said, "the master of the house takes another wife. Or the mistress another husband. Or they adopt a child, if those expedients fail."

"How utterly strange."

He regarded her in mild surprise. "You don't do that? Ah—but of course. Your gods allow one child. What do you do when none is born at all?"

"In our line that never happens. In other lines, the lord takes another wife. Or adopts an heir."

"See, then? We're more alike than you think."

"Our women don't marry more than once at a time."

"Yet your men take many wives?"

"Only in Asanion," she said, "where the people look like your demons."

"Ah," said Bundur. "Demons. They do as they please."

He seemed to think that that explained everything. She drew breath to set him right, sighed instead, let it go.

"You have no husband," he said, "and yet you have a daughter."

She stiffened. Her hand, reaching for the pot to fill her cup again, stopped short of pouring tea over the table and into his lap. "I have a daughter," she said, tight-lipped. "Is that a sin in your country?"

"Only if you bear no son to keep her company."

"There will be no son," said Daruya, "whether I marry or no."

"Do you know that?"

"I know that." She filled the cup. Her hand was steady. She was proud of it. "Women of my country are not in the habit of discussing intimate matters with strangers in tea-houses."

"Ah, so you are different. I thought so."

Her glare should have shattered him where he sat. He only smiled. "If this were my own city," she said deliberately, "and you had said such things as you have said to me, you would be whipped and cast out."

"But this is my city," he said, still smiling, "and I speak as I reckon it proper to speak. You're sadly ugly, lady of the yellow eyes, but supremely interesting. May I speak with you again?"

She could not speak at all, for outrage.

He rose and bowed as low as she had ever seen a man bow in this country. He must wash his teeth in his own piss, she thought viciously, to keep them so white and to display them so freely. "I'll visit you," he said.

She lunged. But he was gone, deceptively swift. She found herself on her knees, trembling with rage, in a circle of silence. All the eyes that had been fixed on her were now fixed scrupulously elsewhere. The voices began again after the faintest of pauses.

She set hands to the table to hurl it in the nearest politely averted face. A brawl would be splendid, would be glorious.

Would be most inadvisable in this country where her rank mattered nothing and her lineage met with massive indifference. If, that is, she could have started one at all. Teahouses did not seem given to the wilder extremes of conduct. One needed wine for that, or bad ale—the worse, the better.

Carefully, meticulously, she gathered herself together and rose to her feet. It did nothing for her temper to discover that Bundur, damn him to the lowest of the hells, had paid her reckoning, or that, if he had not, the teahouse would not have accepted her good imperial gold.

"You will want to change that," said the polite personage in charge of the proceedings, from her seat under the tallest of the flowering trees. "The Street of the Moneyers takes gold sometimes, to melt down for the goldsmiths. One of them can give you proper coinage of our kingdom."

Daruya could have overturned that table, too, and the woman with it. But she was still in command of herself, still mindful of her position, although she would have given all her despised gold to have been able to forget. She said something not too rude—the personage did not bridle, and did not call for the watch, or whatever did duty for that here—and got herself out before she said or did something truly inadvisable.

14

WHILE DARUYA WAS discovering the extent of her self-control, Vanyi was testing her own against a master of obstruction.

It had taken her five days to reach the Minister of Protocol. Five days of incessant campaigning, intriguing, and outright threats, against a phalanx of functionaries who made the Golden Palace in Asanion seem a haven of simplicity. But she had ruled the Mageguild for forty years, and she had learned to cut through obstruction with a sword of purest obstinacy. If a functionary would not pass her to the next highest of his kind, she did it herself, got up and walked to the office that she saw in the functionary's mind. If the one above him, growing wise, sought to prevent her by slipping out the back door, he found her waiting there. If he set guards on her, she called her shadows forward. Olenyai, even swordless, were dangerous fighters. No one in Shurakan could match them. Shurakan, after all, had never known war, nor had occasion to make an art of it.

And so, step by step, she won her way to the gate, as it were: to the Minister of Protocol, who alone barred her way to the queen. There she found herself halted.

The Minister of Protocol did not affect the trappings of power. He wore a coat that fell discreetly to his ankles, the color of clouds, with the merest suggestion of embroidery about the hem. His shirt was simple, his trousers undistinguished by excessive width or richness of fabric. He wore his hair in a severe knot at his nape, and his thin beard and greying mustaches at an unassuming length, barely past the collar of his coat.

She, who had mastered the art of discretion for herself long since, regarded him in jaundiced approval. He offered her tea. She accepted it and the cakes that came with it, ritual welcome everywhere in Shurakan. One could judge the degree of one's welcome, she had been told, by the quality of the tea and the kind and quantity of the cakes.

If so, then she was barely welcome here. The tea was simple, without adornment of flowers or sweetness. The cakes were plain redspice buns just touched with honey, and there were only two for each of them. But, considering the Minister of Protocol and his studied simplicity, she suspected that the frugal refreshment was a statement not of her insignificance but of his desire to be thought a harmless fool.

That was a game she too could play. She drank her tea and ate both of her buns and sat waiting for him to begin, wearing an expression of mindless amiability.

He might be the most powerful man in Shurakan, but he lacked one thing that Vanyi had a world's worth of: time. Her whole duty at the moment was to speak to the queen. His was manifold, and not all of it could wait for him to conquer her with superior patience.

It was he, then, who spoke first, after the pot had been emptied and the basket of buns stripped bare. He chose the weapon of directness, as she had expected. The subtle never understood how predictable they could be when they tried to take Vanyi off guard. "Tell me why it is so urgent that you speak with the queen."

"Surely," said Vanyi, still wearing her amiably vague expression, "her majesty is accustomed to greeting embassies from outland royalty. It's a frequent duty of our imperial house."

"Surely," he responded with a thin smile, "their celestial majesties are both accustomed to receive strangers in audience, when the press of their duties permits. You can be received . . . " He consulted a book that lay on his work-table, not the rolled and cord-bound books of Vanyi's part of the world but a strange thing, plaques of horn as long as a man's arm and as wide as his hand, hinged and jointed together. His finger ran down the long closely written columns. "Their majesties will admit you to their presence on the fourth day of the eighth round of the bright moon."

Even with magery Vanyi needed a moment to render that into the reckoning she knew. When she did, she heaved a mighty sigh. "Oh, come, don't be ridiculous. That's five rounds of the moon from now. I'll confer with her majesty within this round, and sooner if possible."

"Their majesties," said the Minister of Protocol, "have many matters of import to occupy them. You are fortunate that they can see you before the new year."

Or, his tone implied, that they would see her at all.

He was a subtle man, enclosed within himself, but he let her see what passed behind his bland face. He loathed magic, despised mages. He believed that foreigners should summarily be cast from the kingdom. But for deep-grained courtesy and a not entirely illogical suspicion that Vanyi might prove useful to him or to the rulers he served, he would have refused to contend with her at all.

She sat back in her chair, rather thoroughly at ease. "Very well then. Tell me why I shouldn't just walk past you and hunt out the queen for myself."

"Tell me why you refuse to speak to the king."

Vanyi raised a brow. "Rhetoric for rhetoric, is it? Would the king allow me to pollute his presence?"

"The son of heaven is no friend to what you are," said the Minister of Protocol, "but he knows the value of circumspection. He would admit you. As he will, on the fourth day of the eighth round of the moon."

"By which time," said Vanyi, "with any luck at all, our embassy will be finished and we'll be gone. Don't you want to hurry us through and be rid of us?"

Clearly the Minister of Protocol would not have minded that. Equally clearly, his duty required that he impede her in any way he could. "You may not address the daughter of heaven alone in the absence of her brother. That is never done."

"No?" Vanyi inquired. "That's odd. I distinctly heard one of your underlings granting a party of priests an audience with her majesty at the same time that same underling arranged for his majesty to participate in a rite of purification for a temple."

"Those were minor matters," said the Minister of Protocol, unruffled. "Embassies are of greater import, and involve both children of heaven inseparably."

"But ours is a minor embassy, you've all been careful to make that clear to us. Our empire is as nothing to your celestial kingdom. Our emperor can never be equal to your queen and her king. Our gods bow at the feet of your myriad divinities. All of which," said Vanyi, smiling sweetly, "is so self-evident that surely even you can't deny we're insignificant enough to speak to the queen alone."

"That is not done," said the Minister of Protocol.

"Why? Are you afraid she'll let us corrupt her?"

"The children of heaven are incorruptible."

"Therefore you have nothing to fear."

"What is there to fear?" asked the Minister of Protocol. "What haste compels you to press for an audience before the time their majesties have allotted?"

Vanyi kept her smile, though it hurt. "I don't suppose," she said, "you know what became of the man we lost here, or the Gate he guarded."

"One of your people has died? Please accept my condolences."

Vanyi met his blandness with blandness. "Let's suppose you do know, since I've been assured that all knowledge in Shurakan comes to you before it reaches their majesties' ears. You don't think that would have ended it, did you, to break our Gate and kill our Guardian?"

"No rumor of such has come to me," said the Minister of Protocol. His mind was as blank as his face, and as smoothly innocent. "You speak of . . . that, yes? That art of yours." His nostrils thinned. "It was suffered here by the grace of the daughter of heaven and by the silence of her brother. If it failed, or if its servant proved too weak for his task, that is no concern of ours. So it was agreed when her majesty permitted the building of the temple that housed your Gate."

"Oh, I'm not blaming you," Vanyi said. "But if you do know anything of it, or if the queen does, we'd welcome the knowledge. The man we lost was dear to us."

"And his Gate," said the Minister of Protocol, "dearer still."

That was false, but Vanyi saw no profit in saying so. "You do understand why I should speak to the queen. What would destroy a Gate and a Guardian, might not hesitate to destroy a kingdom."

"If that kingdom were such as the Gate was, perhaps. Ours is clean of such taint."

"Is it?" Vanyi asked. "Su-Shaklan is warded by magic. How else do you think it's kept itself so safe for so long?" She stood, bowed slightly: an inclination of the head. "I'll speak with you again. And then, I'm sure, with the queen."

"And you left him? Just like that?" Aledi the lightmage was not surprised, not as well as she knew Vanyi, but she was amply bemused.

Vanyi rubbed her aching eyes and thought of asking for a cool cloth to cover them. It was brutal work, waging war with ministers of protocol. "I launched my bolt and got out, yes. I thought I was being clever—showing him who was master. Probably I was a coward, not to mention a fool. If he believes me, I've talked myself out of a rather valuable weapon on our behalf."

"I doubt he will," Miyaz said. He looked tired himself. The room in which they were sitting, the inner one in which the two mages had drawn their circle and set up their magics, had already acquired a faint reek, somewhat of sulfur, somewhat of flowers, that spoke of power wielded often and strongly.

"They don't believe in magic here," he said. "They curse it and they fear it, and yet in their hearts they know there's no such thing. It's profoundly disconcerting."

Aledi rose from her cushion and knelt behind him, working the knots out of his shoulders. He rolled his head back onto her breast and sighed. She kissed the yellow-curled crown, just where the hair was thinning. "It's worse than disconcerting, at least to me," she said. "It's frightening. Kadin goes out, you know, and prowls—poor boy, he's all broken inside since Jian was lost. We found him in the house of the Gate. He was sitting in the middle of it, in dust and cobwebs that looked as if they'd been there for years and not for Brightmoon-cycles. He said what we were all feeling. 'People say it's haunted. But there's nothing here. There might never have been a Gate at all.' "

"Is he still there?" Vanyi asked a little sharply.

"Oh, no," said Aledi. "We made him come back with us. It wasn't the first time he'd been in that house. He went there the first morning after we came to the city. It's always the same, he says. Always empty."

"I sent him," said Vanyi, "that first day."

The two mages stared at her. Aledi looked mildly hurt. Miyaz was only weary. "I rather thought so," he said. "Why did you send us today?"

"To see if you felt what he's been feeling," Vanyi said.

Aledi bent her head, hiding her face in Miyaz's hair. Her voice came muffled, ashamed. "I was afraid to go before you commanded me. It was so much easier to stay here and make the circle, and not think about what we made it for."

"Today you were ready to think about that," said Vanyi. "Would you be willing or able to raise a circle in the house of the Gate itself, to see what you could find?"

Aledi shivered. Miyaz looked pale. "We'll do whatever you bid us do, Guildmaster," he said.

Vanyi considered them through the pounding in her skull. She had to make herself remember why she had brought these of all possible mages. The three who had died, Kadin who lived broken and grieving, had been stronger, wiser, bolder in the wielding of their power. These two were to have given her the graces of courtiers, well-bred as they were and raised to the Asanian High Court; they were to have been ambassadors more than mages, fellow warriors against the Minister of Protocol rather than against the less-than-shadow that had broken the Gate in Shurakan.

But she needed mages now, when she must be ambassador and win through to the queen by proper channels. Forcing her way with magery would only prove to the Shurakani that mages were to be feared and hated.

While she wasted her strength on the Minister of Protocol, these two had to be strong enough to raise and sustain wards about this house and to bolster Kadin in his watch on the house of the Gate. They were mages of great skill—she would hardly have chosen them otherwise—but she wondered, looking at them, if that skill would be enough. She said to them, "For now, rest easy. I won't ask you to do anything but what I've had you doing here. But be ready to help Kadin if he needs you—whether he asks you or no."

Asanians had one virtue, preserved even in the melding of their empire into Keruvarion. They took orders, and if they asked questions they did not press for answers. Miyaz closed his eyes and to all appearances went to sleep. Aledi clung to him and kept silent.

Vanyi levered herself up. The circle of power was quiet, the lamps that marked its wards burning steady. She could sleep, she thought, if no one interfered. Sleep would be a pleasure.

Her mind reached to the limits of its wards and found no danger. It touched Daruya—in a snit as usual, but not in trouble that Vanyi could discern—and Kimeri playing contentedly with a companion or two. Nothing to fear there, either. The other children meant her no harm beyond a small, shivery, delightful conviction that they had made friends with a demon-child. Only Kadin was cause for anxiety: he had gone back to the house of the Gate, to sit in the dimness and the empty silence that matched the condition of his heart.

He was not thinking of death, not at the moment. He was not thinking of anything at all.

Better nothing than death. Vanyi could not help him; he was not ready for that yet, if he would ever be. She left him alone, drew in the boundaries of her power, became simply herself again, and a bone-tired self at that.

Vanyi.

She started out of a drowse. A moment longer and she would have been asleep.

The voice spoke again, soft round the edges of her shields. *Vanyi, let me in.*

Temper would have refused, but habit opened a gate in the wall of her mind. He entered as he had so often before, fresh and morning-bright—it was that on the other side of the world, and for an instant her yearning to be there was as sharp as pain.

"Estarion," she said without voice. "You woke me up."

He did not look remarkably contrite. "Oh, it's night there again, isn't it? Everything's backwards. Do people have their faces in their bellies or on the backs of their heads?"

"Don't be silly," she snapped, but he had lightened her mood. Eased her headache, too, without her even being aware of it: a touch like a cool hand, a fading of pain. He never asked permission, never thought he needed to.

He looked about this room that was her mind's conception of itself, noted what had changed and what had not, and said, "I dislike this Minister of Protocol. What a fish-faced fool!"

"So he would like us to think," said Vanyi.

"He reckons himself clever and subtle and wise, and I suppose he is, by his lights. He's still a fool." Estarion leaned against a wall, insouciant as any young bravo in a tavern. His mind-self was much as his bodily self was; he did not affect the image of youth, nor feign more beauty than he had. That was rare, but it was also Estarion.

Vanyi resigned herself to his presence. She was not entirely displeased by it, though she would have welcomed the sleep that he had put to flight. He was a fairly restful guest. With her headache he had taken some of the dragging tiredness, smoothing it away as easily as he breathed.

"Do you know," he said, "you've done a great deal for so short a time in this place. I doubt a stranger would get so close to me in a hand of days."

"A stranger from the other side of the world would find you in her sitting room before she was well settled in it, pouring out wine and besetting her with questions."

"Well," he said, shrugging. "I suppose so. I've never been particularly careful of my station. Perhaps I should get myself a Minister of Protocol?"

"You already have one," said Vanyi. "He's sweet, elderly, and erudite, and you drive him to distraction."

"What? Who? Rezad? Is that what a Minister of Protocol is—a chancellor of the palace? Well then. Rezad definitely won't keep the filthy commons from my presence, and I'd have his liver for breakfast if he tried. He knows it, too. He's very wise, is Rezad."

"And very long-suffering."

"Rezad is Asanian. He expects to suffer for his emperor. If he didn't, he'd think there was something wrong."

Vanyi sighed. "This Minister of Protocol is no Rezad. He's going to give me what I ask—but I'll have to fight for it."

"Which is precisely why I call him a fool. It may be his duty to protect his queen and her king from importunate strangers, but an ambassador deserves greater consideration."

"An ambassador from you in particular?"

He flashed his white smile. "Oh, but I'm nothing on this side of the world! It's courtesy, that's all. Not to mention common sense. If I'm as terrible a monster of a mage as he must think, I could be mounting armies of dragons and preparing to descend on his kingdom."

"Are you telling me you aren't?" He grinned at her. She resisted the urge to slap him—too common an urge, and too easy to gratify. "Estarion, I need to sleep. Are you going to get to the point or will you go away and let me rest?"

He looked briefly guilty. Too briefly. "I wanted to see that you were well."

"And your heirs? Both of them?"

It was difficult to catch him off guard. He regarded her calmly, arms folded. "I see that they're well. Have you tanned their hides yet?"

"No," said Vanyi. "And I won't, unless they try something like that again. Daruya got us through the Gate. We'd have died without her. Did you know she was that strong?"

"She's Sun-bred and priestess-trained. All appearances to the contrary, she has remarkable discipline—when it suits her to remember it."

There, thought Vanyi. He was colder than he needed to be. Irked, and afraid, too. His heirs had abandoned him; that pricked his pride, at the very least, and roused him to the fact that if he lost them both, he was an emperor without an heir.

She did not soften her voice for that, or treat him more gently. "I know what Daruya is. I helped to train her. I'll tell you what worries me more. Ki-Merian. She hid herself from us all, and survived a Gatestorm that should have killed a child so young and so untrained."

"The god protected her," Estarion said. "And her own power, too." He drew a long shaking breath. "God and goddess. What I wouldn't give for an ordinary, common, simple, mischievous child without a drop of magery in its blood . . . "

"You'd be bored silly before the hour was out," said Vanyi. "Live with it, Estarion. You're a mage and the father of mages. They do what it suits them to do, and they make fools of us all when they're minded, and if they outlive us, why, it's a miracle, and the god's own mercy. We have nothing to do with it."

"That's a lesson I've never been able to learn." He straightened, unfolding his arms. "I'll let you sleep. I only wanted to know—"

"I know," said Vanyi. She said it more softly than she might have, after all. "Go on. I'll do what I can to keep your descendants alive and sane. If it will console you, I think they do that very well for themselves, all things considered."

He was consoled, perhaps. His farewell was like a brush of a hand, a flicker of a smile. She took them both down with her into sleep.

15

KIMERI IN SHURAKAN missed the demon of the mountains very much at first. But it was out there beyond the wards that were so little really to a mage with any power at all; and she was here, where it could never come. Someday she would find it again. She did not think that would be very soon.

She dreamed about it now and then. She saw it teaching words to the other demons of the mountains. None of them was as quick of wit as it was, and most of them still ate travelers for dinner, but it seemed content after its fashion.

It never did try to pass the wards into Shurakan. That, it was sure and Kimeri supposed, would shake its poor airy self to pieces.

She, who was fire and earth and water too, was happy in Shurakan. That was a little surprising. She still had her other dreams, the ones about Gates, and the Guardian was still caught in the broken Gate. She tried more than once to go where the Gate was, but an Olenyas always caught her.

Once it was even Vanyi who was standing on the other side of the door Kimeri was going out of. Vanyi was coming in: she had her clothes on that she wore when she went to the palace and tried to talk to the queen. Kimeri should have been more careful, but she was looking for Olenyai and not finding any; she forgot to look for a mage.

Vanyi herded her straight back in, saying something about mothers who let children run wild in enemy territory. Kimeri had heard that before. When she could stop, which was all the way in and most of the way to Vanyi's rooms, she said in complete exasperation, "You have *got* to let me go out."

Vanyi's brows went up. "Have I, your highness?" she asked. "And why is that?"

She was being nasty and sweet at the same time. Kimeri was aggravated enough to tell her the truth. "Because the Gate isn't dead, and neither is the Guardian. He's trapped inside it. I've got to get him out."

"You've been having dreams, haven't you?" said Vanyi. But before Kimeri could say yes, she had them every night, and they were horrible, Vanyi went on, "There now. When people die, especially if they've been killed, we always want them to be alive again. We dream about it, we wish for it. But it doesn't bring them back."

"He *is* alive," Kimeri insisted. "I know he is. I hear him. He's trapped in the Gate. He doesn't know how to get out. If I went there, I could—"

"Maybe you could," said Vanyi, "someday, when you're older. If there's anyone to rescue from a Gate that's broken. But not now. It's not safe."

"He's trapped," said Kimeri. "He hates it. He wants to get out."

She was almost in tears. That was never a wise thing with grownfolk. It just convinced them that she was a baby, and too young to know anything.

Vanyi said things that she meant to be soothing, and handed Kimeri over to the servants and told them to feed her a posset and put her to bed. And never mind that the sun was only halfway down from noon. Nothing Kimeri said made any difference to her at all. She simply was not listening.

Kimeri thought about a shrieking fit, but that was the sort of thing babies did. She set her teeth and did what she was told. "Grownfolk never listen," she said to the walls when she was finally alone.

But it was not all like that. Vanyi was out most of the time, and so was Kimeri's mother. Kimeri could not go out in the city, and all she could do to help the Guardian was tell him in her dream that she was trying, and she would keep on trying. And yet, in everything else, she had more freedom here than she had ever had at home.

It started with being able to spend as much time as she liked in the stable with Kadin, which no one had ever allowed before. It got better when she found out that there were children round about, and what was better yet, none of them had nurses to make their lives miserable.

They did have nurses, that was true, but those were indulgent when they were not outright lazy. Children here could do much as they pleased, provided they were sensible about it and kept out of grownfolk's way. When they grew very big—seven whole summers' worth—they had to go to the temples to school, and many never came out of the temples again. But before then they were as free as birds.

Kimeri, who had always had armies of nurses hovering and fretting, found it wildly exciting to slip away from the stable, where Kadin never took much notice of her anyway, and find the places where the children liked to gather. Those were usually places where grownfolk never came, odd corners or dusty passages or rooms full of things that no one knew the names of, the makings of games that could range from one end of the palace to the other.

The first time Kimeri went to a gathering place, she had a friend to speak for her. His name was Hani; he was older, almost old enough for a temple, but he was not as tall as she was. She found him straddling the wall of the stable the day after she came to the city, staring at the seneldi. He was much too curious to be afraid, and he was not shy at all. As soon as Kimeri saw him he grinned, showing a mouthful of more gaps than teeth, and said, "You were our protect-us-against at prayers this morning. What are you really?"

"Kimeri," she answered, not knowing what else to say. Then because he was thinking that she did not know his language: "That's my name. I'm a person. What are you?"

"But what *kind* of person are you?" he asked her.

"A Kimeri person," she said. "Me. Myself. I'm not a demon. That's stupid."

"All right," said Hani, sliding down from the wall and landing neatly on his feet. He had straight black hair cut staight across his forehead and straight around his head just below his ears, and he was wearing a coat and a pair of trousers much like the ones she was wearing, and altogether he looked like a perfectly ordinary person from the Hundred Realms. But so did everybody here. There was nobody who looked like an Asanian, as Kimeri did, or like a northerner, which was what Kadin was.

Hani stood in front of her, and he looked and sounded older but he was definitely smaller. He looked her up and down. After a moment's thought, he stretched out a hand and tugged at one of her curls. She let him. He was curious. He had never seen curly hair before, or hair the color of yellow amber. "You're very funny-looking," he said. "What did they do to you to make you look like this?"

"I was born this way," she said. "You don't look funny to me. Lots of people where I come from look like you."

"Of course they do," said Hani. "People look like that."

Out in the courtyard, where Daruya's mare was loose with two of the Olenyai geldings, the mare decided that the geldings had been taking too many liberties, and went after them with teeth and horns. Hani watched them with his narrow eyes gone wide. "They're going to kill each other!"

"Of course they're not," said Kimeri, feeling superior. "The striped one is a mare. She's telling the other two to stop thinking they're as good as she is. Mares," she explained, "are the center of the world."

"Why?"

"Because they are," said Kimeri. "There, see? They're all quiet again, and the geldings are behaving themselves. They know how they're supposed to be."

"They look like mountain deer," Hani said, "except that they're so much bigger, and they have manes, and long tails with tassels on the end. And their horns are straight instead of branched, and much shorter than the stags'."

"That's because they're geldings, and mares don't usually have horns at all. You should see the stallions. They have horns two ells long, and sharp as spears."

"Do they kill people with the horns?" Hani wanted to know.

He was not particularly bloody-minded, she noticed. Just curious. "Sometimes," she said. "When people get in their way, or are cruel to them. You don't whip a senel, my mother says. Seneldi are our hoofed brothers. We treat them like people, and they carry us because they love us."

"Would one carry me?"

"Why, of course," said Kimeri.

And one of the geldings did, because Kimeri asked; and Kadin came to see what they were doing, but said nothing, which was much better than Kimeri would have got from a nurse. Kadin was a mage, and a northerner besides. He saw nothing alarming in riding seneldi around a perfectly safe and completely closed-in yard, even if they did leave off the bridles and saddles.

Hani found Kadin terrifying, but he put on a brave face for Kimeri. She let him think he convinced her. Northerners were so very tall and so very dark. Even Asanians were a little afraid of them, and Asanians were used to them.

After that, Hani was her friend. He took her to the palace, and got in trouble for it too, what with the other children being sure he had taken up with a demon. But he was one of the oldest, and while he was far from the biggest, he could knock down and hammer on anyone who argued with him. He did that to a boy or two, and she did it to another boy and one of the girls, and when the two of them were finished, they all decided to forget what Kimeri looked like and treat her like a person.

The others never quite came close enough to be friends. Hani was different. He found her much more interesting than anyone else he knew, and even if he did not believe most of her stories of what the world was like outside of Shurakan, he liked to listen to them. He had his own stories to tell, too, and he knew all the fascinating places to play.

One of his favorites was one of the hardest to get to. First of all it was in the part of the palace where the most people were, though they only gathered in that particular place once in a Brightmoon-cycle. The rest of the time there were people muddling about, cleaning the floors, feeding the incense burners, braiding flowers into garlands to hang from everything a garland could hang from.

But once one got past those and slipped through a heavy curtain like chainmail, one was in the best place. A lamp was always lit in it, to honor the god whose house it was. The god himself stood on a plinth, all carved of wood and set with glittery stones and painted and gilded and dazzling in his gaudiness. His robe came off at every cycle, and priests put a new one on.

The day Hani took Kimeri to see the god, he was wearing cloth of gold. "That's a good omen," Hani whispered, being very careful not to wake any echoes. "His robe is the same color as your hair, see?"

Kimeri stood in a shadow in that shadowy place and smelled the incense, and felt rather strange. She felt that way in temples in Starios, too. "There are gods here," she murmured.

Hani blanched, but he kept his chin up. "Why, of course there are. This is their place. Are you going to come and see the best part, or are you afraid?"

Kimeri, who was not afraid at all, gave him a disgusted look and walked across the patterned floor. She walked the way she had been taught to hunt, very, very quietly, putting each foot down from the toes backward. Hani, tiptoeing behind her, made a great racket. *He* was scared, but he was excited too, and a little irked with her for being so much braver than anybody else. She could have told him that gods' children would hardly be frightened of gods, but he had already refused to believe that she was the sun-god's child.

It was very quiet in the room, which was actually a tall, wide alcove in a much larger space. The lamp flickered in a draft, making the shadows leap and dance. Hani's heart was thudding—Kimeri could hear it. Her own beat as it always did, maybe a little faster because she was excited, that was all.

They reached the wooden god and stared up. He was a terrifying thing to look at, with his four sets of arms and his scowling face, but Kimeri rather suspected the scowl was a mask. He felt stern to her, but not unwelcoming. The flowers he was festooned with were almost too sweet-scented. She stopped a sneeze before it burst out and betrayed them.

Hani, heart still thudding but perfectly in control of his courage, led her by the hand around the plinth on which the god stood. The shadows were very black there, but when she sharpened her eyes and used a little magery, she saw how the god stood in a niche, and the niche was a hollow half-circle. Hani set hand to wall and felt his way around behind the god. It was dusty in there, and it smelled of old wood and new paint and something sharply pungent that came from the god's robe, and of course flowers everywhere. But there was plenty of space, plenty of air to breathe. Kimeri noticed the shape of a door in the very back, and just across from it, in the god's leg, another door.

Hani, blind in the dark, groped for the catch that Kimeri

could see perfectly clearly. He was thinking that he could be quiet and keep from letting her guess what he did. He did not know mages, she thought a little smugly. The catch made a distinct click, and then the door was open, with a ladder leading up into the god's body.

He tugged her in. The scent of old wood here was overpowering. "Climb," he whispered, hardly to be heard if she had not been a mage's child. He thought he was helping her by setting her hands on the rungs of the ladder and nudging her feet toward the wall that was the inside of the god.

She climbed. Hani was behind her, panting so loud she wondered how anyone could keep from hearing him.

It was not a long climb. The god was not terribly tall, merely tall enough to be imposing. The top of him was almost big enough to be a room—his head, and there were windows, long and narrow like Shurakani eyes. Someone long ago had spread cushions underneath them to lie on, dusty but comfortable.

Kimeri looked out of one eye, Hani out of the other. The floor was surprisingly far below. The light of the lamp was hurtfully bright after the dark inside the god. Kimeri shut down her magesight and let herself see with ordinary eyes.

Hani nudged her with his elbow. "See this?" he whispered.

She looked at what he was holding. It looked like a trumpet, except that it was soft, made of cloth. Its bell was bronze.

"That's a speaking trumpet," Hani said. "A person sitting here can talk into it, and his voice comes out of the god's mouth and sounds like the voice of heaven. That's how they make prophecies here when the priests think it's time."

She was supposed to be shocked and amazed, but she did not see why she had to be. "We don't need to pretend at home," she said. "Our prophets are real. They make prophecies in their own voices, and priests write them down."

"So do the priests do here," said Hani, a little annoyed. "The prophecies are real. The god inspires them. But the people believe them better if they come from his mouth, instead of from somebody who might look like you or me and be somebody's brother, or his cousin."

"How silly," said Kimeri. "Prophets *are* one's brother or sister or cousin. What else would they be?"

Hani opened his mouth to reply, but froze. The curtain of the god's shrine was sliding back with a great rasping of metal and grunting of men who heaved away at it. When it was drawn about half aside, it stopped, and people came through. What they were up to was clear enough to see: they were carrying enormous sheaves of flowers, baskets and baskets of them.

"Oh, dear," breathed Hani.

Kimeri would have agreed with him, except that she remembered the door behind the god. She tried to tell him about it, but he clapped a hand over her mouth. "Don't move," he whispered. "Don't breathe. If they find out we're up here ... "

His visions of dire fates were clear enough to shut her up. The least of them showed him being whipped while she got a royal spanking.

The people with the flowers were in no hurry at all. They brought lamps with them till the space beyond the curtain was blazing with light. They settled down to weave garlands and gossip and pass round skins of something that made them warm and giggly. The lamps gleamed on their heads, which were all shaved bare, and in their eyes, and on the flowers they were weaving and the flowers that others were taking down from the rafters and the plinth and everywhere between, including the god's hands.

Once or twice Kimeri was sure that one of the garland-takers had looked straight up into her eyes, but the man turned away without saying anything. She crouched down a little lower and tried not to breathe.

All the dead and dying flowers being moved meant a great deal of dust and a scent so strong it made her sick. She did her best to keep her stomach where it belonged. She needed to go to the privy, too. But worst of all she needed to sneeze. She needed it so badly that her eyes itched and watered and her nose hurt, and her throat felt as if she had swallowed a bone sideways. She held her nose, but that meant breathing through her mouth, and that was noisy. And the sneeze kept on fighting to come out.

The inside of the god exploded.

She was still holding her nose, but the sneeze had shocked itself to death without ever coming out. Hani crouched with streaming eyes, yellow-grey with shock. The people outside were gaping and goggling. Some of them had fallen over. Hani's sneeze had gone through the speaking trumpet and come out like the god's own.

He grabbed her before she could say anything, and nearly threw her down the ladder, scrambling so fast to follow that he trod on her fingers. Outside she heard people yelling, arguing—"The god spoke!" "No, he didn't. Someone got inside." "What? If it's a demon—" "We *have* demons in the palace. Haven't you seen them?"

Sooner or later one of them would remember how to get inside the god, and come running to look. Kimeri shut her eyes and woke up her magery and dropped.

She landed light, with Hani almost on top of her, too scared to notice what she had done. He was still holding on to her hand. He half pulled her arm out of its socket, yanking her through the door—and then stopping cold as he remembered that he had nowhere to go.

The door in front of them had a perfectly visible catch, if one had magesight. Kimeri opened it and dragged him through and shut it tight.

They were in a passage like a dozen others, narrow and dim-lit and dusty. Hani was blind in it, but there was light farther on. Kimeri pulled him toward it.

"Do you know where we are?"

Kimeri looked around her. They had gone through a great many passages, because Hani was sure there were people running after them, and would not hear Kimeri when she tried to tell him that the priests had never even found the door behind the god. People never listened to her. She looked at him sullenly and set her chin. "You're the one who knows everything. Where do you think we are?"

"I don't know."

It cost a great deal of pride for him to say so. She was glad. "I thought you knew every crack and cranny of the palace."

Since he had said so in the same exact words, he could hardly call her a liar. He glared at her instead. "I don't know *every* one. Just the ones that are important."

"This one is very important. We're in it."

"Then why don't you get us out of it?"

Kimeri was ready to burst into tears, but she was not going to let any nit of a boy see her cry. "I can't find my way, either. I haven't learned to do that yet. I get all twisty when I try."

He thought she was talking about being a girl and being too silly to tell where she was. He did not know anything about being a mage and being too young. If she told him, he would not believe her. Nobody believed in mages here.

That made her angry, and anger made her walk, she did not care where. Forward was good enough. He could follow or not. She did not care.

He did follow, of course. Being lost made him scared. Being scared made him angry, but not as angry as Kimeri was at him for getting them into this in the first place. She stalked ahead and he stalked behind, and neither of them said a word.

They walked for a long time. Sometimes they took turns because Kimeri got tired of going straight. They were going in circles, she thought. Not the way they would in the woods, the way people got lost when they went hunting, back to the same place over and over, but the way walls could turn and twist and bend in on themselves and keep people from ever finding the way out.

Once she thought they had found it, but when they looked out at the blessed light it was coming in through a high window in the wall, and the room they were in was as empty as the rest, and there was no door but the one they had used to get in.

Hani stamped his foot and flung himself down on the floor. "We've got a curse on us! The god's punishing us for climbing inside his statue."

"He never punished you before, did he?" Kimeri asked reasonably.

The last thing he wanted was for her to be reasonable. "I never climbed inside him with anybody else before."

"You mean I'm the curse," said Kimeri. "Because I'm a foreigner and I look funny. I'm *not!* We're lost because you don't know as much about the palace as you thought you did."

"We're cursed," he repeated. His face looked pinched and nasty. His eyes were slits. "Cursed, cursed, cursed."

"We are not!"

"Are."

"Are not." Kimeri started to hit him. He spat at her. She whirled and ran away.

She did not care where she ran or how fast she did it. She careened around corners and through doorways. She heard him behind her—running and calling and trying to apologize, but she would not listen. He was only scared to be left alone.

There was furniture, suddenly, to dodge around, and instead of stone underfoot there were carpets. There were still no people. People were all somewhere else.

Except for the one she fetched up gasping against, who had come out of nowhere and stepped right in front of her. It was a tall narrow person with strong arms that caught her and held her even when she struggled. She was not thinking about that; once she did, she stopped.

The arms stayed strong, and kept holding her. She looked up. A woman looked down. She was not old like Vanyi but she was not quite as young as Daruya either, and she had a way of looking older than she was. Her face was narrow and her lips were thin and she looked very severe, particularly when she frowned.

Kimeri burst into tears. It was not anything she thought about doing. It just happened.

The woman did not push her away, but held her and let her cry. When she was almost cried out, the woman said in a voice that was both rough and sweet, "There. That's enough, I think."

Kimeri sniffled hugely and swallowed the rest of her tears. The woman gave her a cloth to wipe her face. She used it. Her face had been very dirty: the white cloth was quite black when she tried to hand it back.

"No," the woman said. "Keep it. Give it back to me later."

And clean, she meant. Kimeri sniffled again, but that was the last of it. "Lady," she said huskily, "can you tell me where I am?"

"Do you have a particular need to know?" the woman asked.

"I got lost," said Kimeri. "I can't find my way out."

The woman's face was no less stern, but her eyes were a little warmer. "I know how that feels. I've been lost here often myself. Have you been about it long?"

"Forever," said Kimeri, fighting back the tears again.

This was not a person to cry much in front of. She was like Vanyi that way, and about as sharp in the tongue, too.

"It's always forever," the woman said. No: she was not quite as sharp as Vanyi. But almost. "Here, I'll show you the way. Does your friend need help, too?"

But Hani was gone. Coward—he had recognized the room and known how to get out of it and run while Kimeri was getting the front of the woman's coat wet. "I hate him," she said. "I just hate him."

"That's often how we women feel about men," the woman said. "We never can stop living with them, for all of that. He'll come creeping back, you'll see, and worm his way into your heart again."

"He won't," said Kimeri. "He hates me."

"I think he likes you and is afraid of me." The woman looked bemused at that. "People often are. It's a puzzlement."

"I suppose it's because you're so tall," Kimeri said, "and so narrow. And you look so severe. But you aren't really, are you? If he's so afraid of you and he's still my friend, he should be trying to rescue me from you."

"He's a rarity in a male: he's wise. Do forgive him for it. It's a virtue we see too little of."

"I hate him," said Kimeri.

"Of course," the woman said. She was laughing inside, which made Kimeri hate her, too. A little. Before she took Kimeri's hand and led her out of the room and down a passage and across the corner of a garden and up a stair and to a door. "And past that," she said, "is the court of the strangers where your house is."

Kimeri knew that it was. She could feel her mother near, and Vanyi, and the others all together. None of them even knew that she was missing.

The woman started to draw her hand out of Kimeri's, but Kimeri stopped her. "What's your name?" she asked.

She could see it in the woman's mind, as clear as everything else that she might ask, such as what the woman was and what she was doing here, but it was not polite to say so. Polite mages asked, and let people tell them.

The woman's brows quirked. "My name is Borti. What is yours?"

"Merian," Kimeri answered, "but they call me Kimeri— ki-Merian, because I'm little. But I'll grow."

"That," said the woman, looking her up and down, "you will."

"May I see you again?" Kimeri asked.

Borti smiled. She did not look severe at all then, or even very old. "Yes, you may. Come to this door and take the way I showed you, and if I'm free I'll be in the room where you met me first. I'm often there at this time of day, and usually alone."

Kimeri knew about alone-times. She needed them herself. She gave Borti her best smile and let her hand slip free. By the time she opened the door she was running. But she paused to look over her shoulder at Borti, who stood where Kimeri had left her, watching. She lifted a hand, the one that burned sun-hot, and ran through the door.

16

NOT LONG AFTER her foray into the teahouses of the Summer City, Daruya began to make a habit of going to the stable in the mornings and riding whichever of the seneldi seemed to need it most. It was dull enough work when she thought about it, riding in circles within the same four walls, but there was an art to it, like a dance of rider and mount. Her mare in particular had a talent for it.

It took the edge off boredom, certainly, and filled the mornings. She was close to happy, one bright cool morning, trying something new with the mare: a flying trot, legs flashing straight out, reined in by degrees until all the mare's swiftness and fire contained itself into a powerfully cadenced trot in place. The mare was amenable to a degree, but found it much more enjoyable, once contained, to lighten her forehand until she sat on her haunches. If Daruya urged her forward then, she reared up and sprang on her hindlegs. If Daruya sat through it, she came back lightly to a standstill, enormously pleased with herself.

At last, after considerable negotiation, Daruya coaxed the mare to permit half a dozen strides of trot-in-place. The mare bestowed them with the air of a lady granting an enormous favor. Daruya praised her lavishly, which she felt was no more than her due, and sprang from her back, and nearly jumped out of her skin.

A stranger, a Shurakani, stood watching, grinning at her. After the first shock she recognized him: the man from the teahouse, whose name right at the moment was emptied out of her skull. But not the eyes. Not the clear strong presence of him. He was larger than she remembered, broader in the shoulders, and he was quite as tall as she.

"That's a splendid display," he said without even taking the time to greet her. "You should offer it as an entertainment for princes. They'd give silk to see such a rarity."

"I am not a hired entertainer," Daruya said stiffly. The mare snorted and rubbed an itching ear on Daruya's shoulder. She turned her back on the intruder and tended the senel, taking her time about it.

He was not at all dismayed by her rudeness. He watched with perfect goodwill, and had the sense not to offer to help. She took off the mare's saddle and bridle; he stood by, curious. She walked the mare to cool her; he followed. She sponged the mare with water from the fountain; he watched. She led the mare into the house that had been made into a barn; he strolled after, with a moment's hesitation as he realized that all the walls had been taken down and partitions set up, and the house filled with strange horned beasts.

Daruya was used to it. She led the mare to her stall, fed her a bit of fruit, and stood smoothing the damp neck, ignoring the watcher with strenuous concentration.

She was still aware of him. It was impossible not to be. He regarded the seneldi warily but without fear, walking down the lines of stalls. The first nose that thrust inquisitively toward him, he shied at, but he came back bravely enough and stroked it. He was prepared for the next, and for the one after that.

The seneldi approved of him. He found the itchy places behind ears and at the bases of horns, and he was respectful of flattened ears and snapping teeth. He had brought nothing sweet for them to eat, which was a count against him, but they made allowances for ignorance.

He made a circuit of the stalls, coming to a halt at last outside of the one in which Daruya was standing. "These are marvelous animals," he said. "And the way you ride them—astonishing! Would you teach me?"

"Everyone asks that," said Daruya, addressing the mare's mane, which she was combing and smoothing with unnecessary precision. "It's easiest if you learn as a child."

"But not impossible to learn as a man grown?"

He sounded plaintive. She refused to be swayed by it. "It would take years to learn to ride as I ride. Just to stay on—that's possible, I suppose."

"It would make a beginning," he said.

She shot him a glance. "Right now?"

He was startled—his eyes went wide. But he laughed and spread his hands. "Why not?"

He had not the faintest conception of what he was getting into. She thought briefly, nastily, of setting him on Vanyi's gelding and letting him loose, but it would hardly do to kill or maim a man of high house in Shurakan, simply because he was presumptuous. She fetched the starbrowed bay instead, a plain, sweet-tempered, imperturbable animal who made no objection to being saddled and bridled and subjected to the weight of a large and substantial man who had never sat a senel before.

He had, however, sat an ox—and not badly, either, Daruya had to admit. There was no finesse in the way he scrambled into the saddle, but he balanced well, he took quickly to the commands to start and stop and turn, and he could ride the gelding on a circle and keep it there. He might, with time, come to have a decent seat on a senel.

He knew it, too. His expression reminded Daruya forcibly of the mare after her most impressive leap on her haunches: pure self-satisfaction. Daruya felt much less charitable toward the man than she had toward the mare. "You have talent," she said, because she could not lie about that, "but you have no art."

"No? Then will you teach me?"

She did not want to. It would take time to do it properly, far more than she had or meant to have in Shurakan, and she could not for pride do it otherwise than properly. But he annoyed her. "I'll teach you," she said, "if you can be taught. Beginning here." She slapped his back. He stiffened in outrage. She showed him the count of her teeth. "You're slouching. Sit up straight. No, not as if you had a rod for a spine. Softly, flowing with the movement of your mount. Now let your legs fall as they want to, softly, always softly. Ankles, too. Let them follow as he moves. Yes, like that."

She worked him to a rag. It was only a brief span by the sun's ascent, and it was a bare few moments' exercise for the bay, but the man slid from his back and nearly fell as his knees buckled. "By the gods! I'm destroyed."

"You've barely begun," said Daruya. "And you still have to cool him and unsaddle him and take him to his stall."

"You are merciless," said Bundur.

"You asked for it," she said.

But she lent him a hand, not out of pity for him, of course not, but out of concern for the senel. He gained back much of his strength as he worked, which was the object of the exercise—and a curse on his cleverness, he saw that, too. When he was done, he had most of his arrogance back. Enough to say, "Tomorrow, again?"

"You won't want to," she said.

"Yes, I will. Tomorrow?"

She wondered if the Shurakani had a god who protected fools and innocents. "Tomorrow, then. If you can walk this far."

As it turned out, he could. Just. And once he had pulled and hauled and heaved himself onto the senel's back, and gasped as he perceived the full and painful extent of his folly, he rode creditably enough. "My muscles are so insulted, they've expired in protest," he said from the saddle.

"Sit up," said Daruya. "You're slouching again."

"O cruel," he sighed, but he obeyed.

He came back the next morning. And the next. Sometimes early enough to watch her ride—and to mourn his own ineptitude. Sometimes so late that she feared—hoped, she corrected herself in considerable irritation—that he was not coming at all, until she saw him striding through the door. Then she was snappish, because her heart had leaped so suddenly, startling her. He never seemed to notice.

What he thought of her, he did not tell, and she did not try to read as a mage could. Because it mattered too little, she told herself; because, her heart muttered to itself, it could all too easily matter too much.

He never stayed longer than it took to saddle, ride, and put his mount away. He talked freely enough and most engagingly, but he never said a word that was not perfectly proper. However bold his eyes might be, his tongue was as circumspect as any woman could wish. He never offered to accompany her wherever she might be going afterward—to the house, usually, or to wander in the city. He did not, ever, bring a friend and ask her to increase the number of her pupils. That rather surprised her. Most ambitious princelings would have been flaunting their new accomplishment all over the court.

For all she knew, he was doing that—but keeping the rest from besetting her. She was not invited to court, nor was she courted by various of the palace functionaries as Vanyi was. She was quite the isolate, quite perfectly the nobody, and she was determined to be happy in it.

Chakan did not approve at all. She took her time in telling him all that she was doing in the stable from sunrise till nearly noon, which was an error. He came to her, half a dozen days after Bundur first appeared in the stable, and set himself in front of her as she debated between a jar of honeyed wine and one of Shurakani ale to go with her day-meal of flat bread and softened cheese. She chose the ale, filled a cup, held it out.

He refused it with a snap of the hand. "What is this I hear," he demanded, "of your entertaining a Shurakani noble in the stable every morning?"

Daruya found that her mouth was open. She closed it. "What in the worlds—" Her temper caught up with her tongue. "You of all people are concerned for my virtue?"

He dropped his veil. His face was white and set. "Do you know who that man is? We've been following him when he leaves here. He goes directly to the king's apartments, as often as not. And when he doesn't go to the king, he goes to other notables of the king's faction."

"Why shouldn't he visit the king?" Daruya demanded. "He's a prince here, even I can see that. Princes keep company with kings."

"Did you know that his mother is the king's half-sister?"

Daruya stiffened. No, he had not told her. But she had not asked. "Well then. Why shouldn't he visit his uncle, if he's so minded?"

"His beloved uncle," said Chakan, "has shown himself to be a powerful opponent of foreigners in Shurakan, and a devoted hater of mages. If he had his way and were not restrained by the queen's moderation, we would all be flayed and our skins spiked to the walls."

"Oh, come," said Daruya. "Now you're talking nonsense."

"I am not. You may think that this city is a haven of innocent goodwill, but there are powerful factions in the court that would kill us as soon as hear our names spoken."

"And how do you know that?"

"We listen," he said. "We watch. We stand guard. You're watched from sunrise to sunrise, and not only by us.

Everywhere you go, you have at least two shadows: your
Olenyas and a king's spy. You'd be dead now if it hadn't
been for Yrias. He's driven off more than one attack on you
while you meander happily through the city."

"Those were footpads," said Daruya, "or simply the curious, trying to see how easy it would be to steal from me."

"They were not," said Chakan. "They were in the pay of
the king's faction. As you can be sure this princeling of
yours is. What better way to keep you in hand than to occupy you all morning, every morning?"

"God and goddess! I'm not tumbling him in the hay. I'm
teaching him to a ride a senel." Daruya came desperately
close to flinging her ale in his face. But she was stronger
than that; and he looked as if he was expecting it, which
made it worse. "If he really were under orders to keep me
busy, don't you think he'd outright seduce me, and stay
with me all day into the bargain? He doesn't even try to
coax secrets out of me, except the ones that have to do with
riding."

"He hasn't had time to do more," Chakan said. "He
will, you can be sure of it."

"I say he won't. He wants to learn an art that no one else
here knows. What's reprehensible about that?"

"Nothing," said Chakan, "if he were not the king's sister's son."

"He is also," Daruya pointed out, "the queen's sister's
son."

"No," said Chakan. "They're children of the old king,
both. But the queen's mother, who was also queen, died
bearing her. The king married again to beget the canonical
second child, who was the king. His wife had been married
before, and had a daughter. The daughter was this man's
mother."

"How complicated," said Daruya. "But he's the queen's
kin, one way and another."

"Half-kin," said Chakan. "Children of different wives seldom love one another. And this man is the king's sister-son."

"He means me no harm," Daruya said stubbornly. "I'd know if he did."

"Would you? They have arts here. They don't call them magery, but what's a name? Who's to say he isn't concealing his mind from you?"

"I can read a great deal more of him than I can of you."

He hissed in disgust. "Yes, and his face is open for anyone to see, too. There's a Great Ward on this kingdom that reckons itself free of mages' taint. Gods alone know what else it's lying about to our faces—even to yours, my lady of Sun and Lion."

"He's not lying to me," she said through gritted teeth.

"No? And you had no idea he was the king's nephew."

"I didn't ask."

"You shouldn't have had to."

"I didn't need to. He's not my enemy."

"You know that?" Chakan asked, viciously sweet. "You know that for an incontrovertible fact?"

Daruya could be as vicious as he was, and as nastily reasonable. "So come and watch his lessons. Look as deadly as you please. See if it makes any difference."

"Oh, I will," he said. "I promise you I will."

Daruya hated to quarrel with Chakan. He never fought fair, and he always turned and swept out before she could flatten him with a final blow. He was properly rattled this time: he forgot to veil his face again with the flourish that temper put in it. It was a victory, but a small one.

Maybe he was right. She was sure that he was not—but doubt had a way of creeping in and gnawing at the roots of one's surety. Mages' courtesy kept her from reading the mind of every man she met, but she did not go about blind, either, least of all with strangers who might be enemies. Bundur was not an enemy. Truly, she would know. Other motives he might have had for visiting her that first time, but he had come back because he wanted to learn to ride a senel.

Maybe too because he wanted to observe her. Why not? She was a foreigner. She had no easily visible function in the embassy. He would have wanted to assure himself that she was no danger to his kingdom.

And maybe he wanted to see what kind of creature she was. There was nothing like her in his world. Maybe he kept coming back because he found her interesting. A man might do that, even with a woman of respectable virtue.

A little more of this and she would be getting aggravated because he had not ventured anything improper. She had thought about it more than once. He was a very handsome man. But he thought her ugly; he had made that very clear. Interesting, but ugly.

Goddess, she thought. Men were such maddening creatures. How did any sensible woman stand them?

Chakan was there the next morning, standing like a stone beside the wall of the riding-yard. Daruya ignored him as she put the mare through her paces. She kept on ignoring him as she took first the brown gelding, then the whitefoot black, and rode them.

Bundur was late. Very late. It was nearly noon, and no sign of him.

Chakan had an air of grim satisfaction. She almost screamed at him: "How could he know you were going to be here?"

But she knew the answer before he spoke. "They see everything we do."

She had been going to visit the city. There was a festival, she had been told, with music and dancing and a procession. She went back to the house instead, had a bath so long she was shriveled and sodden when she came out, and thought about cutting her hair again. In the end she let it be but had the servant twist it into a myriad small plaits, each tipped with a bead of lapis or malachite or carnelian. They swung to her shoulders, brushing them when she turned her head to consider her reflection.

Odd, by the lights of Shurakan, but becoming. It was a fashion of the north of Keruvarion; in its honor she put on what went with it, the kilt and the gauds. The servant was scandalized. Women did not bare their breasts here.

How backward, she thought. It was a warm day for Shurakan, almost hot. She was not going anywhere, or at least no farther than the garden, where she intended to lie in the sun and brood on the faces of treachery. Vanyi was gone, waging her war among the functionaries. Kimeri was out playing somewhere in the palace—safe, and annoyed when her mother brushed her with a finger of magery; Daruya would have something to say to Chakan, when she could bring herself to speak to him again, of how he let the daughter run wild while he overprotected the mother. The Olenyai were either guarding Daruya or occupying themselves. The mages were inside their circle, discovering the usual nothing at all about the breaking of the Gates.

The sun was hot and blissful on her skin. She had been starved for it these past days, what with skulking in the house and riding within walls, or wandering about a city that left little space for the sun to get in. She lay on the cropped grass, basking in light. She slept a little, lightly, dreaming of gold and of lions.

She woke suddenly. Two shadows stretched over her. One was Olenyas, barring the second, much taller and broader. That one was taking little notice of the obstacle.

Still half asleep, she slid behind those bright black eyes

and saw what he saw: golden body all but bare, glittering with gold, in a pool of light as solid as water.

Malice sparked, fed by the light in his eyes. She stretched luxuriously, as a cat will, muscle by muscle.

Ugly, did he think her? But interesting, he had said at that first meeting. Most interesting, lying with arms stretched above her head, grinning ferally at him.

"Go away, Yrias," she said. "This man is safe enough."

The Olenyas' eyes were narrow, mistrustful. But he was an obedient guardsman. He withdrew to the edge of the grass—near enough to leap if he was needed, far enough not to intrude.

Daruya rolled onto her side, propped on her elbow. "You didn't come for your instruction this morning."

Bundur's breath was coming just a fraction fast. She watched him take himself in hand. He did it very well, she thought. "It's festival day," he said. "I had duties I couldn't escape."

"Marching in procession? Waiting on the king?"

He did not start at that or look guilty. "Standing in court, too, while the children of heaven bestowed gifts of the season on an endless parade of worthy recipients. Your chief ambassador was there. She caused a stir—foreigners have never appeared at such a function before."

"And how did she manage it?" Daruya inquired. She hoped she sounded casual. She was seething. Vanyi had plotted such a coup, and not brought the rest of them into it?

"She did it on the spur of the moment, I gather," he said, pricking her bubble of temper rather thoroughly: "heard about the event, decided to observe it, and walked in as calm as you please. The Minister of Protocol was beside himself."

"I can imagine," Daruya said. "Was she thrown out on her ear?"

"Of course not," said Bundur. "We're not barbarians. Somebody found a gift for her, and she had it from the queen's hand—but the Minister of Protocol got her out before she could make any speeches."

"Maybe she wasn't going to deliver any," Daruya said. "She'd made her point, hadn't she? That would be enough for her. The queen's seen her, knows she's here—the queen can do with the knowledge as she best pleases."

"Which could be nothing," said Bundur.

"That's the queen's right," Daruya said with the certainty of one who had been raised to be an empress. She sat up and clasped her knees. Bundur looked faintly disappointed. He had been enjoying the sight of her with rather too much pleasure, once he had got over the first shock. She let a bit of edge into her voice, to call him back to himself. "I suppose you came to beg for a late lesson?"

"Well," he said, "no. I'll be there tomorrow, never fear. Today I wondered—" He looked unwontedly diffident, even embarrassed. "I should have come much earlier, but I was being an idiot about it, I suppose. I wondered—on festival night we have a dinner, which we prepare according to very old custom. It's eaten with one's family, and a friend or two, no more." He stopped. She did not help him with word or glance. He let it all out in a rush. "Would you share dinner with us in House Janabundur?"

"Just me?" she asked. She caught Yrias' eye. "I can't do that."

"No, no," he said hastily. "You and your kin who are here, and your captain of guards—he's your friend, yes?"

"How do you know that?"

He was blushing: his skin was darker than usual, more ruddy than bronze. "It's known. One is like a brother to you. He, your daughter, your lady ambassador—they're welcome, and should come."

"It's short notice," she said.

"My fault for that. But festival shouldn't be spent alone."

"I was going to go to the city," she said, "and watch the processions."

"That's done, too, after the dinner is over. Everybody takes lanterns and puts on a mask and goes out, and dances till dawn."

That was tempting. More than tempting.

And to dine in the house of the king's sister-son on the night when people dined only with friends and close kin— what magnitude of coup might that be?

Maybe it was a trick. Chakan would say so. But if Vanyi was with her, and Chakan himself, and Kimeri who was a weapon of remarkable potency, surely they could protect themselves against any danger Shurakan might offer.

She looked up into Bundur's face. It was empty of guile. Which could of course be a sleight in itself, and probably was. But she saw no enmity there. What she did see . . .

Ah, she thought: the power of northern fashion in a country that reckoned women's breasts a secret to be kept for the inner room. She was too wise to flaunt them any more than she already had. She tilted her head, beads on braid-ends sliding on bare shoulders, and feigned deep reflection.

Just as a shadow began to cross his face, she said, "Very well. One dines at sunset, yes?"

"At sunset, on festival night," said Bundur.

"Does one do anything in particular? Bring a gift? Offer flowers? A prayer?"

"A gift isn't necessary." Which meant that it was. "Flowers are welcome, and prayers, always."

"I see," she said. "At sunset, then."

"At sunset." His voice was a little strange—thick. He was excited. Not, she hoped in the depths of her stomach, because she had fallen into a trap and would be dead by midnight.

* * *

Chakan was sure that it was a trap. Vanyi, most strangely, was not. She had made her point indeed, let the queen see her and left the woman to make the next move in the long game. When she came home to a near-war in the dining-room between Daruya and Chakan, she ascertained its cause at once and stopped it with a pair of words. "We'll go."

Chakan rounded on her in such fury that Daruya flinched. Vanyi did no such thing. "Down, young lion," she said. "Draw in your claws. You don't have the faintest understanding of what this means."

"I know that it lures us all to the house of strangers, shuts us therein, and leaves us easy prey to the king's assassins."

"So it might," said Vanyi, "if it were any other night and any other festival. This the festival of the summer moon. It's for kin; for heart's friends; for lovers. Enemies are never hunted on festival day. No wars are fought, no feuds pursued. If a man meets his brother's murderer in the street on festival night, he smiles and wishes him joy and goes on. In the morning they go back to killing one another—but while the festival's peace is in force, no man ever breaks it."

"What better chance," demanded Chakan, "to destroy the unsuspecting with the semblance of perfect peace?"

"Not during the festival," said Vanyi.

"In the mountains," he said, "no one steals from anyone else. But foreigners are fair prey. Theft from them is no dishonor. How can it fail to be the same here? We're outlanders. We don't keep festival. We can be killed, and no one will look askance."

"This isn't the mountains," Vanyi said. "Honor is truly honor here. We've been bidden to keep festival in the highest house in Shurakan short of the royal house itself. If it's the house most closely connected with the king, then so much the better. The queen is at least not disposed to murder us out of hand. The king would happily see us dead and burned. Let his sister see us, know us, learn that we're not monsters, and maybe she'll talk to him, and maybe, for a miracle, he'll listen."

"Minds like that never open," said Chakan. "They're locked shut."

"Maybe," Vanyi said. "Maybe it doesn't matter, if we can get a foothold in the king's faction. It's not just a matter of finding out who broke the Gate here, Olenyas. When we do that, when we've got the Gate up and working again, then we'll want to use it. And we'll need friends here, to keep us from being attacked all over again. Those friends may be in House Janabundur."

"Or they may not," said Chakan.

"We can't know that till we go there, can we?" Vanyi dismissed him with a wave of the hand. "Go. Get ready to guard us tonight. I need to talk to Daruya."

He snarled, but he went.

Daruya rather wished he had not. Once he was gone, the door shut and an Olenyas on the other side of it, Vanyi fixed her with a profoundly disconcerting stare. "Well?" Daruya snapped after it had gone on for quite long enough. "Are you thinking what everybody else seems to be thinking? No, I haven't been tumbling the master of House Janabundur in a senel's stall."

"I don't doubt it," said Vanyi imperturbably. "He's a handsome buck, isn't he?"

"I can't say I ever noticed," Daruya said. But she felt the heat in her cheeks. She had never been a good liar.

Vanyi saw it, raised a brow at it. "Maybe you didn't know you were noticing. He'd be old to you, I suppose. He must be thirty winters old, give or take a few."

"He has twenty-seven summers," Daruya said stiffly, "and that is hardly old at all. He rides a senel very well for someone who was never on one before this past Brightmoon-cycle. But then he's ridden oxen since he was Kimeri's age. The skills do translate."

"As do a few other things," Vanyi observed. She inspected the daymeal that had been laid on the table some untold number of hours ago, picked out a fruit that was still fresh and a loaf that was not too dry, and ate each in alternating bites. In between she said, "Consider this. When our mages first came to Shurakan, a faction in the court welcomed them, admitted them to the kingdom, gave them a house for the Gate, and gave them leave to come and go as they pleased. Through the Guardian of the Gate they invited an embassy from the guild in Starios, and promised to receive that embassy with honor and respect.

"Then the Gate fell. The faction fell, too, it seems, either just before the Gate or just after. Certainly I've seen no evidence of it. We've been admitted, yes, and given a place to dwell in, and freedom of the city. But no one comes to us with any direct purpose except curiosity. I got at the queen today, but only because I'm a brash foreigner and I seized a chance. They won't let me loose to do that again. To all appearances we came here on our own, uninvited by any person or persons in Shurakan, and we're being treated as humble petitioners to their celestial majesties, not as invited ambassadors." She finished the loaf, deposited the fruit-pit in a fine bronze bowl, poured a cup of the inevitable tea. "I haven't said any of that to the Minister of Protocol, you know. It isn't something I'll say to someone whom I'm not sure I trust.

"And in any case," she said, "if this faction is indeed discredited, its members, if they live, are lying low. They aren't letting themselves be seen to speak with us or approach us. Unless one of them, their leader even, is the man who will be our host."

"I don't think he's that subtle," said Daruya.

"Does he need to be?" Vanyi asked. She paused, as if she

needed to ponder what she said next. "I think you ought to know what it means when a man comes in his own person, without a messenger, and bids a woman and her kin to dine with his kin on festival night."

Daruya could well guess. The catch in her throat was temper. Of course. "It's a dreadfully public way to ask her to bed with him, isn't it?"

"Not if it's marriage he has in mind."

"That's preposterous," said Daruya. "I'm a foreigner. I'm nobody that his benighted people will acknowledge: no family, no kin, no power in the kingdom. And if that isn't enough, I'm hideously ugly."

"None of that would matter," said Vanyi, "if he thought he had something to gain. Or if he could persuade his enemies to think exactly that. Is there a better way to blind them to what he's really doing, if he's leading his faction back to power and using us as his weapons?"

"That's supposing there's a faction at all, and he's part of it. He's the king's sister-son. Could he turn traitor to his own kin?"

"He might not think of it that way. His faction—if it is his—believes that Shurakan can't be forever shut within its walls, and has to learn to contend with foreigners on their own ground. Even foreigners who are mages."

Daruya could not see it. She tried; she battered her brain with it. But she could only see Bundur riding the star-browed bay, trying to sit gracefully in a jouncing trot.

Vanyi broke in on the vision. "I'm thinking that we've been kept here in careful isolation, handled at arm's length, and ignored as much as possible. Someone is keeping us from being cast out altogether. That someone may have sent us a message through your Bundur—or may be that gentleman, as innocuous as he seems. No nobleman of his age in Shurakan is a complete innocent. I'd say none could be completely honorable, either, but I haven't seen all of them yet, to be sure. He's up to something, if it's only a campaign to get you in his bed."

"That's all it probably is," said Daruya. "I'll tell him he doesn't need to make a grand performance of that—I'll bed him happily enough, and never mind the priests and the words."

"What if he wants those? For honor's sake?"

Daruya laughed a little shrilly. "Then he's a fool. I didn't marry the man who sired Kimeri. I haven't married any man I've bedded since—and many's the one who's hoped for it. It's not greatly likely I'll marry this one, either. Who is he at all but a petty princeling of a kingdom on the other side of the world?"

"And you will be empress of all the realms of Sun and Lion," said Vanyi. Her tone was perfectly flat. "Which, if your grandfather has his way, will include Shurakan and the lands between. With armies to hold them. And Gates to march the armies through."

"Then maybe," said Daruya with sudden bitterness, "it's as well the Gates fell when they did, and they should never be raised again."

"What, you don't want to conquer the world?"

"I don't want to make a fool of myself," snapped Daruya. "My grandfather never troubled his head with such nonsense. I'm vainer than he is, and weaker, too."

"Which," said Vanyi, "may be your great strength." And while Daruya stared at her, for once emptied of words: "Go get dressed. It's getting late."

She sounded exactly like a mother. Daruya bristled, but as Chakan had done long since, she obeyed. There was, she told herself, no great profit in refusing; and yes, the sun was low, slanting through the windows and pouring gold upon the floor. She took a handful of it, part for defiance of Shurakani propriety, part for warmth in a world that could grow too quickly cold.

17

House Janabundur stood on a promontory of the city westward of the palace, sharing its eminence with an assortment of temples, one or two other lordly houses, and untold warrens of common folk. It was very like the kingdom it was built in, Daruya thought, waiting at the gate in the last rays of sunlight for her company to be recognized and let in.

They had done their best to look like the ambassadors of a mighty empire. Chakan had brought half his Olenyai and left the others to guard the house by the palace walls; they could show no weapons, but their robes were impeccable, their veils raised and fastened just so, their baldrics oiled and polished and crossed exactly. Vanyi had put on the robes of the Mageguild's Master, as she almost never did. They were cut in the Asanian fashion of robes within robes within robes, seven in all, grey and violet interleaved, and the outermost was of silk and woven in both violet and grey, a subtle play of color and no-color that shimmered in the long light. Her hair was plaited and knotted at her nape, bound with a circlet of silver; she wore no other jewel but the torque of the priestess that she had been from her youth, plain twisted gold about her throat. Kimeri, clinging to her mother's hand, wore a gold-embroidered coat and silken trousers, with a jeweled cap on her head and rings of gold and amber in her ears.

Daruya had caused the servants an hour's panic, but the result, she rather thought, was worth the trouble. She had traveled light perforce, and brought nothing suitable for a state occasion. By dint of ransacking the embassy's stores and taking the market by storm, the servants had made do handsomely. The shirt and trousers were her own, of fine white linen woven in Starios; and the boots were made in Shurakan, white leather golden-heeled. The coat over them, like Kimeri's, was new-made of silk from Vanyi's stores, a shimmer of fallow gold brocaded with suns and lions, gold on gold on gold. Along its hem and sleeves ran a wandering line of firestones. Her hair was in its braids still, but its beads were amber and gold. There were rings in her ears and about her wrists, plates of amber set in gold. Her belt was gold, its clasp of amber. But lest the eye weary of so much white and amber and gold, she wore a necklace of amber beads interwoven with firestones, shimmering red and blue and green.

She smoothed the long coat with the hand that did not hold Kimeri's, a nervous gesture, quickly suppressed. Chakan had struck the gong that hung in front of the gate; its reverberations sang through her bones. Kimeri fidgeted. "Mama, can I take my boots off, please? My feet hurt."

Daruya swallowed a sigh. The boots were new, of necessity, and made for the child, with room to grow in—and they were stiff, and she had walked half across the city in them. "When you get inside," said Daruya, "we'll ask if it's not too unpardonably rude for you to go barefoot to a festival dinner."

"Why would it be rude?" Kimeri wanted to know. "My feet *hurt*."

Daruya was spared the effort of a reply by the scraping of bolts within and the opening of the gate. An aged but still burly porter scowled at them all impartially, but said nothing, merely stepped back and bowed, hands clasped to breast.

Vanyi interpreted the gesture as an invitation. She entered in a sweep of robes. The others followed a little raggedly, Olenyai last and darting wary glances at the walls that closed in beyond the gate.

That was only the entryway. The wonted court opened beyond, lamplit, with the inevitable fountain. A servant waited there, elderly and august, to lead them up a stair to a wide airy hall full of sunset light.

Daruya saw nothing of it at first but the light, which poured through a long bank of windows framed in a tracery of carved wood and molded iron. Slowly she accustomed her eyes to the splendor. The room was long and high but not particularly wide, stone-vaulted, with slender pillars holding up the roof. The floor was of the patterned tiles that were so common here, the walls hung with embroideries, too bright and many-figured to make sense of in a swift glance. At one end of the hall, near a broad stone hearth, a table was set.

No one sat there, although the plates and cups and bowls were all laid in their places. There was no one in the room but themselves and the servant who had brought them, and that one was retreating, bowing, saying nothing.

Chakan hissed and flashed a glance at Daruya. She refused to indulge him. None of them knew the custom here. In Starios the host would have been standing at the table, the family seated, awaiting the guests. Shurakan might well do otherwise; leave guests alone in an empty room while the family mustered outside and entered in a body.

They emerged from a door at the far end of the hall, as the guests had entered in the middle. Bundur led the procession. Daruya told her heart to stop beating so hard. It would never have been such an idiot if Vanyi had not vexed it with her tale of festival dinners and offers of marriage.

He was not at all ill to look at. As if to counter her white and gold, he wore shirt and trousers of the shimmering black near-silk that they wove here from the floss of a seed-pod, and a coat of scarlet embroidered with black and bronze. His head was crowned with scarlet flowers. They should have been incongruous; they were merely splendid.

A group of women walked behind him. The eldest, with her silvered hair, must be his mother. She looked like him, with the same proud cheekbones and robust figure; her garments too were black, her coat the color of bronze. Two younger women accompanied her, one with the free hair of a maiden, the other wearing the shortened coat and severe plaits of a new widow and leading a child by the hand. It was a boychild as far as Daruya could tell, not as tall as Kimeri but seeming older, with a thin, clever face.

Bundur spoke words of greeting, which Vanyi answered. She gave him the gift she carried, a length of gold-green silk; he received it with open admiration and an honest gleam of greed, and passed it to the eldest of the women. She was his mother, yes, the Lady Nandi, and the younger women were his sisters: Kati who had not yet chosen a husband, and Maru whose husband had died in the spring of a fever. The child's name was Hani; he was not Maru's son but Bundur's. Daruya stiffened at that.

"His mother chose not to keep him," Bundur was saying to Vanyi, ostentatiously ignoring Daruya, "and left him to me."

"The mother lives? You're married to her?" Vanyi asked.

"The mother is a priest of the Blood Goddess, who forbids her devotees to marry. I wouldn't have married her in any case," said Bundur: "we weren't mated except in the flesh. And since no priest may keep a child in the temple, I took this one to raise as was only proper. He'll go to a temple himself, come winter solstice."

"I don't suppose you've asked him if he wants to go," Daruya heard herself say.

It was the child who answered. "Of course I'll go, lady. I want to learn everything a priest can learn."

"Will you be a priest?" asked Daruya.

He shrugged. "I don't know. I don't think so."

"My mother is a priestess," Kimeri said in a clear voice, rather cold. "Ours can marry and keep their children if they want to. I'm going to be a priestess when I grow up, and have a daughter, and keep her, no matter what her father says."

"Her father might say no," said Hani.

It dawned on Daruya that these two knew each other, and not happily, either. They were as stiff as children could be who had had a quarrel, and Kimeri was itching for a fight. "*You* won't be the father," she said nastily, "so what would you know?"

"Children," said Lady Nandi, "this is festival, when all enmities are laid aside."

Neither looked particularly contrite, but they subsided, shooting occasional, baleful glances at one another. Kimeri was thinking openly at Hani. *Coward, coward, coward.* Daruya had a vision of some outrageous prank in the palace, and Kimeri left alone to face the consequences while Hani bolted for safety.

Hani saw it differently. He had run for help but found none, and when he came back Kimeri was gone. He was too stiffly proud to say so. Kimeri was too angry to read him properly.

Daruya bit her tongue and kept out of it. She had not even known that Kimeri was playing in the palace. Of course the child had to have been; she was never home, and Daruya had yet to see her in the stable in the mornings.

That would stop, Daruya resolved to herself. An Olenyas would accompany the imp hereafter, and keep her out of trouble if he could. An Olenyas should have been doing so from the beginning.

Another weapon in her war against Chakan. She stored it away and focused on the festival, which after all was a feast of amity.

Bundur held out his hand. She found herself taking it and being led to the table and seated in the center, with Vanyi on her right hand and Chakan—too startled to resist—beyond her, and Bundur on her left, and his mother and his sisters beyond. The children had their own place at the table's foot, with a feast suited to their taste, and bright boxes set in front of them that proved to be full of games and toys and manifold amusements. They seemed to arrive at a truce, however temporary: when Daruya looked toward them they were playing together, arguing softly but without perceptible rancor over the untangling of a puzzle.

"Children are good fortune," Lady Nandi said in her strong sweet voice. "Don't you think?"

She was addressing Daruya, showing no particular revulsion at either her ugliness or her foreignness. Daruya blessed her long and often bitter training for vouchsafing her a harmless answer. "A child is the hope of its house."

Lady Nandi greeted that ancient banality as if it were priceless wisdom. "Truly! And yet my son tells me that you intend to have but the one?"

She wasted no time in getting to the point. Daruya rather liked her for it. "It's not a matter of intention," she said. "The god so far has given one child to each of his descendants, one heir and one only. I don't expect that I'll be any different."

"Our gods are kinder," said Lady Nandi.

"I don't doubt it," said Daruya.

There was a pause while servants brought the first course: platter after platter, bowl after bowl of fragrant and often cloying delicacies. Daruya watched in dismay as her bowl was heaped with the pick of them. Bundur selected with his own hands the roasted wing of a bird, and a slender pinkish object that was, he said with relish, a bird's tongue, and something shapeless that he promised would give her a taste of heaven. It gave her a taste of salt and mud and peculiar spices. It was, Bundur told her while she struggled to keep a courteous face, the nest of a bird that dwelt in cliffs above the city.

There were words to speak as they began, a chant from one of their sacred books, which Bundur led and the women responded to in chorus. It had something to do with war in heaven, and with an army of birds, and a goddess' two children fleeing the field of battle.

For all the quantity of food that filled her bowl, she discovered, watching the Shurakani, that no one ate more than a bite of each offering. The bowls were taken away almost full. "For the poor," Bundur said, as if she had asked.

Odd custom, but not unappealing. The second course was the same, and the third. The first had been devoted to creatures of the air. The second was comprised of creatures of water: fish broiled and spiced, fishes' eggs, the legs of a fen-leaper. The blessing-chant took up the tale of the goddess' children, who fled from the realm of air through river and fen to the protection of the waterfolk, and there were kept alive while all their people perished. In the third round of the feast, over the fruits of the hunt, mountain deer and boar and the strong flesh of the cave-bear, Bundur sang of the deer that led the children of heaven to the secret place in the mountains, and the sow who gave her piglets to feed them, and the bear that sheltered them in its cave until they gathered a new people and founded the kingdom of Su-Shaklan.

Last of all came a mountain of sweet cakes and a palace of spices, and the delicate flowery tea of ceremony, neither given nor shared lightly. Over it the Lady Nandi spoke the blessing, the words that formed the center of the festival: " 'Rule in joy,' the goddess said to her children, 'and rule in memory of sorrow. Do not fight, nor give yourselves up to hatred, nor take the life of any living thing but to feed your bodies or to defend your souls. Remember; and keep this festival in the name of peace.' "

"In peace," the others echoed, Bundur's deep voice, the women's lighter, the children's lightest of all. Vanyi's too, Daruya noticed, and Kimeri's. But not Chakan's. And not her own. By the time she thought of the courtesy, it was too late. The prayer was ended. The cakes were going round, and the tea, and Bundur was smiling at her.

"So," he said, "what do you think of our festival?"

"We have nothing quite like it," she answered. "There's High Summer, when we celebrate the birth of the Sunborn, and Autumn Firstday, when children come of age and heirs come into their inheritance, and Dark of the Year, when we all do penance for our wrongdoings. But no festival like this, when every year people try to remember to love one another."

"You're a warlike nation, then?"

"No," she said. She was aware that the others were listening; that she was being judged by what she said. But then she always had, who had been born the emperor's heir. "We've had wars, and many—there's no help for it in a realm as vast as ours. But we've had peace, too; long years of it. I remember the Feast of the Peace, when my grandfather ended the last of the wars, and all enemies were brought together in one place and made into one people. They weren't all happy about it, but they came, and they swore not to fight again. Nor have they."

"How long has that been?" Bundur asked.

"Five years," said Daruya. "It looks like lasting, too, though there've been small skirmishes here and there. Some people never do understand when a war is over."

"We haven't had a war in a dozen generations," Bundur said.

Daruya smiled thinly. "Yes, and whom would you fight with? Your mountains protect you. We don't have such mountains where I come from. It's mostly open plain. Armies have fought across it for a thousand years."

"You must feel naked," said Bundur, "and defenseless."

"Not any longer," she said. "We're all one empire. You could begin walking by the western sea, and by the time you came to the shores of the east, you'd have been traveling for half a year. And safely, too. Bandits don't hunt the emperor's roads."

"Do they infest the lesser ones?"

"Not if he can help it."

"He must be a very busy man, to look after so vast a realm."

Bundur did not believe any empire could be that large— he was indulging her, and transparently too. "The emperor has lords and servants in plenty. And someday," she said, "I'm going to take you there and show you how wide it is, you who can't imagine anything larger than your tiny goblet of a kingdom."

His face lit from within. "You would do that? You would show me the world beyond the Wall?"

She was a little surprised. She had been threatening him, she thought; but he acted as if she offered him a great gift. "You actually *want* to see the world?"

"You thought I didn't?"

She lowered her eyes. Her cheeks were warm. Damn him, he did that to her much too often. "You all seem so smug. Self-satisfied. Content to think that Su-Shaklan is all the world you need to know."

"Oh, no," he said. "Su-Shaklan is the heart and soul of the world, yes, but some of us do want to know what else there is."

"You might not like it," she said. "It's very wide. And in places very flat. And no one there has ever heard of Su-Shaklan."

"No one here has heard of your empire, and you do rather well despite it," he pointed out.

"You think so?" she asked.

"I think," he said, "that you are like the sun in a dark place. You gleam, do you know that? All gold, even in the shadows."

"That's the god in me," she said. "No god of yours, as everyone is so careful to remind me."

"Maybe we can be taught," he said.

She laughed, short and cold. "Do you want to be? You might be corrupted."

She was aware of his mother, listening, and his sisters. They offered no objection, betrayed no disapproval. She might have been a player on a stage, performing for their pleasure.

He spoke as if they had been alone. "If I can be corrupted by a single foreign woman, however fascinating, then I deserve whatever fate I suffer for it."

"What do they do to heretics here? Burn them? Flay them? Spike them to the walls?"

"That depends on the heresy."

"They flay mages, don't they? And bathe them in salt, and keep them alive and in agony, till the gods have mercy and take them."

"Not in this age of the world," he said. "We have none of that kind." Ah, she thought: even he could not say the word. "But some of us lack the ancient animus against them. Not all of them are evil, we believe, and not all of what they do is foul."

"I'm glad to find you so enlightened," she said levelly, "considering that I am a mage of a line of mages, and all my blood is afire with magery."

"We call that the gods' fire here," he said.

"It's the same," said Daruya, "no matter what name you set on it."

He lifted a shoulder, flicked a hand: shrug, dismissal of the uncomfortable truth. "You're a priest, yes? You're consecrated to your god."

"All the Sun-blood are," she said.

"So," said Bundur. "Your god lives in you. That's a heresy in some sects here, but not in all. Not in ours."

"Are you saying," she said slowly, "that you can sweeten what we are to your people by calling us priests and our power the gods' power?"

"Isn't it the truth?"

"Well," she said, "yes. But—"

Vanyi intervened, and none too soon, either. "We used that expedient in Su-Akar. We were told it wasn't necessary here."

Bundur turned his attention to the Guildmaster, apparently unruffled by her meddling. "Once, it wasn't. Things have changed."

"So I see," she said.

He smiled. His teeth were white, and just uneven enough to be interesting. "We'll speak of that. But this is festival night, when we should forget our troubles. Will you come into the city with us?"

Vanyi looked as if she might have pressed him for more, now that he had begun. But she was no less wise than Daruya. She let be, for a while. "We were intending to see the dancing."

"With us," he said laughing, "you can do better. You can join in it."

"Well now," she said, "I don't think—"

"Come," he said, sweeping her up, and Daruya too, and whirling them out of the hall. "Masks, cloaks, festival purses—come! We'll revel the night away."

It was a mad, glad night, night of masks and laughter, sudden lights, sudden shadows, dancing and singing and long laughing skeins of people winding through the city. Daruya was swept right out of herself, whether she would or no. With her alien face hidden behind a mask, her alien mane concealed by the black hood of a reveller, she was no stranger at all. No one stared at her; no one whispered, or called others to come and see the demon walking free in the streets of the Summer City.

For all the wildness of the festival, her companions clung close together. Bundur's hand was strong in hers, fingers wound together, inextricable. When she danced, she danced with him. When she ran, he ran with her, and the others behind.

She had no wish to be free of him. He seemed like a part of her, the moon to her sun, whirling ever opposite, ever joined, but never touching save at arms' length. More than once some stranger tried to pull her loose; Bundur laughed and spun her away and shouted something that she could not make sense of, something about festival right. It always sent the other spinning off to a new quarry.

The music was all bells and drums, with once in a while the moaning of a great horn. It sounded odd, but after a time it seemed fitting—particularly after she had drunk a beaker or two of another wine than she had had in Shurakan before. This was strong, heady, and not sweet at all. If anything it was sour, like the yellow wine of Asanion. What color it was, she could not clearly see. Pale, she thought, not red, not blood-colored. Gold like sunlight. It burned going down, and warmed her to her fingers' ends, and made her feet light in the dance.

Bundur drank off a whole jar of it, dancing round a fire that leaped and capered in a square. There were masks all around it, laughing, clapping their hands, beating on drums. It came to Daruya with a shock of cold that she was standing alone and he was far away, across the fire. He whirled on the other side, arms wide, singing in his deep voice.

She ran, lifted, sprang through the fire. It reached for her as she flew. She laughed at it. "Cousin," she said to it.

"Soul's kin." It warmed her but could not burn. It was never as hot as the fire in her blood.

She landed lightly, reaching for Bundur. Their hands clasped. The fire leaped out of her and wrapped him about.

He gasped. He was burning—but he was not. The fire filled him and did not consume him.

"Mageborn," she said, but in her own tongue, the language of princes in Starios. "Fireborn, Sun's blood. You—too—"

He understood, but in his bones, where he refused to listen. In himself he knew only that there had been fire coming out of her, and it was gone. They stood on cold paving, with the dance going on around them, and the fire—simple mortal flames again—casting ruddy light upon them all.

No fear, she thought. Even in the refusal of knowledge, no fear.

He pulled her away from the flames, but not back into the dance. She tried to twist away. The others were gone. She could not find them. The fire—

But he was too strong, and he was running, dragging her whether she would or no. This was the trap, her mind gibbered. Now he had her alone. He would take her away, hold her hostage, demand an empire's worth of ransom. Chakan would be gratified.

Stupidity. He was running away from the fire and the knowledge it held. He dragged her because he lacked the sense to let her go. He was lordly drunk, pure mazed with wine, and still too much the gentleman to throw her down and rape her as many a self-respecting princeling might have done.

Although, at that, he might not be so drunk that he thought she would allow such a thing. She would have gelded him if he had tried.

He ran, and she ran with him, weaving through the crowds. There was a giddy pleasure in it, once she gave herself up to it. Running, darting, dancing when they fell into a skein of dancers, running loose again, from end to end of the city and back, from fire to fire, dance to dance, sunset-side to sunrise-side, till movement was all there was and all there need be. So was the sun in its dance with the moons. So were the stars, wheeling in their courses. Such was the festival, this feast of the peace in the Summer City of Shura-kan.

18

IT HAD NOT been a pleasant morning. Festival wine was stronger than it looked, and hit harder; and Vanyi, having fallen into bed just as dawn paled the eastward sky, was roused much too soon after sunup to greet a guest. Esakai of Ushala temple, fresh and bright-eyed as if he had slept the night through, wanted to wish her a bright morning and was disposed to linger. He was curious as always, questioning yet again the preposterous belief the mages shared with Asanion, that there was no war in heaven between the light and dark, between good and evil; that the worlds hung in a balance, and that both light and dark were faces of the same power.

She was never completely averse to debating theology, but in the morning after a night of revelry it was more difficult than usual. She trapped herself, one way and another, into inviting her guest to breakfast. He might have stayed till noon if Daruya had not come to her rescue.

Daruya, trained in a harder school than Vanyi had been, got rid of the man in the most amiable way possible, but with admirable dispatch. He seemed hardly aware of the speed of his dismissal; he was still smiling when Daruya thrust him out the door, and still trying to persuade Vanyi that perhaps balance was not the way of the worlds.

Once he was gone, Vanyi found herself wishing for a less taxing escape. Daruya shut the door and barred it with an air of ominous purpose, dropped into the chair that Esakai had vacated and filled an empty bowl, tasting as she went, with a young thing's ravenous hunger. She had come to bed later than Vanyi, if in fact she had slept at all. Her hair was out of its myriad plaits, new-washed and curling more exuberantly than ever; she was back to the plain trousers and the worn coat that she wore among the seneldi, her only ornament the torque of Avaryan's priesthood. She looked stunningly beautiful, and completely unaware of it.

She filled a cup with tea, grimaced but drank it. "This has to be the most vile excuse for a tipple that man ever thought of," she said. "I even find myself missing Nine Cities ale."

"You aren't either," Vanyi said. "That stuff is undrinkable by human creature. This is rather pleasant once you get used to it. It's subtle."

"I'm not." Daruya spread a round of bread with herbed cheese, folded it over, devoured it in three bites. "You were wrong after all."

"What?" Vanyi asked. "About tea?"

Daruya's glance was disgusted. "Of course not. About that man."

Vanyi opened her mouth to play the idiot again, and to ask if the child meant Esakai; but that would press her temper too far. "What did he do, try to bed you?"

"No!" Daruya snatched up a fruit, hacked it open, scooped a handful of blood-red seeds. She ate them one by one, frowning. "No, he didn't. We danced, that was all. And I had to carry him home and help his servants put him to bed. He was drunk to insensibility."

"Mean drunk?"

"Charming," said Daruya. "Full of delightful nonsense. And never, even once, trying to lay his hands on anything he shouldn't."

"Ah," said Vanyi. "You're insulted."

That won her a molten glare, but Daruya's tone was mild. "From all you said, I thought he'd at least offer a proposal of marriage."

"Oh, no," Vanyi said. "That's not how it's done. The young man and the young woman keep company, and dance round the festival fires. The families discuss the colder aspects of the arrangement."

Even through her wine-caused headache, Vanyi was tempted to laugh. Daruya looked suddenly horrified. "You didn't—they didn't—"

"As a matter of fact they did," said Vanyi. "His mother took me back to the house—over my objections, I should add, and in spite of the fact that she was right, the children did need to get to bed. She brought out much too much of that damnable wine, and showed herself for a master negotiator. If their majesties ever send an embassy to your grandfather, I'll wager they send the Lady Nandi. She's as deadly as any courtier in the empire."

"I hope," said Daruya, thin and tight, "that you told her to take her wine and her fever-dreams and vanish."

"I thought of it," Vanyi admitted. "But she's persuasive. It's not, as she says, that her son can't find a wife in Shurakan. Many's the noble family that would give silk to buy him for their daughter."

"Then I wish her well of him, whoever she is," said Daruya. She sounded defiant. Vanyi, studying her, began inwardly to smile.

She kept the smile from her face. "He wants you," she said. "It's peculiar and considerably awkward, her ladyship and I agree, but they have a belief here, a doctrine that rather reminds me of some of our own. You know how their rulers are paired, king and queen, brother and sister; and they shudder at the thought of a single child. In their philosophy, souls are twinned, too, and for each man there is another matched to him. Sometimes it's a man—did you know they allow that here, and don't frown on man wedded to man or woman to woman?"

"That is strange," said Daruya, but not as if she paid much attention.

"It would explain your grandfather," Vanyi mused, "and his Olenyas with the lion-eyes, all those years ago. And Sarevadin the empress and her Asanian prince. And—" She shook herself fiercely. "In any case, my lord Bundur is convinced that you are the other half of his soul. He insists that he felt it the moment he saw you, and he's been adamant that he won't consider any other woman for his wife."

"He's out of his mind," said Daruya. "And if that's his doctrine, why in the world do women take handfuls of husbands here, and men marry only once but take women to their beds as often as they need to, to get themselves their pair of children?"

"I asked that," Vanyi said. "Nandi replied that the soul-bond is precious rare, and good sense does dictate that people marry for practicality's sake."

"Then let him be sensible," Daruya said, "and marry one of those nice respectable ladies. Even if I wanted to be his wife, it would be impossible. I'm a foreigner, I'm a mage, I look like a demon's get—and I'm the heir to an empire he's barely even heard of. I can't stay here and be the next matriarch of House Janabundur."

"He knows all of that," Vanyi said. "So does his mother. It doesn't matter."

"It might matter when my grandfather hears about it. He'll be livid."

"I should think that would be an incitement to do it," Vanyi said dryly.

Daruya bared her teeth. "Shouldn't it? But this time I think I'll actually be the obedient granddaughter." She raised her voice slightly, and the voice of her mind very much indeed. "Grandfather!"

Vanyi should have expected the young chit to do that. The ringing note of the mind-call nearly shattered her skull, but then, paradoxically, mended it. It was like being tempered in a forge.

There was no mercy in Sun-blood. But she had always known that. She felt the call reach the one it sought, felt the shifting of that powerful mind, wheeling like a dance of worlds, fixing itself on this place, this room, the two of them in it.

With an effort of will she brought him into his wonted focus. Not the great mage and emperor on his god-wrought throne; not the terrible warrior at the head of his armies. Simply Estarion, that dark man with his golden eyes, saying to his granddaughter as if they stood in the room together, "Good evening, grandchild. Is this important? If not, you have some explaining to do."

Daruya did not even blush. "Oh, and is she angry, Grandfather?"

"Rather," he said. In this meeting of minds he put on a garment, a robe like woven sunlight, and divided himself briefly to soothe the woman in his bed. Quite a lovely woman, and amenable enough once she had had the circumstance explained to her—she was a priestess-mage, and not so young as to be jealous of a man's grandchild.

"She sends her regards," he said to Daruya, "and asks if you're still willing to put your stallion to her Suvieni mare."

"By all means," said Daruya with remarkable grace. "My regards to her, too, and, Grandfather, do you know that people here are trying to marry me off?"

He barely reeled with the shift; his eyes widened, and then, to Daruya's visible outrage, he laughed. "Are they, now? And is he worth it?"

"Is any man worth it?" she shot back.

"Most people would think so," he said mildly. He sat in a chair as if he were a solid presence in that room, and investigated the remains of breakfast. He pointed to one of the fruits in the basket, the blue-green one with the thorny rind. "What in the hells is that?"

"Fen-apple," Vanyi answered. "It looks poisonous,

doesn't it? It doesn't taste bad. A bit tart, is all. They slice it and dip it in honey."

"They're going to marry me to a man in this kingdom-in-miniature," Daruya said sharply, "and you waste your time making faces at fen-apples?"

"I don't call it time wasted," he said, "if it gives me time to think. Who is this man, and why is he aspiring to your hand?"

"His name is Bundur," said Daruya, still with a snap in her voice, "and his mother is the king's half-sister. He thinks that our souls are mated, or some such nonsense, and he insists that he'll have no wife but me. He also thinks that I'm ugly, but because I'm interesting, it doesn't matter."

"How unusual," said Estarion. He might, for the matter of that, be speaking of the fen-apple, which he was examining from all sides. He had tried to pick it up, but his ghost-presence was not solid enough for that. "Is he ugly by our reckoning?"

"He looks like a Gileni nobleman," Daruya said. "In a word, no."

"Ah," said Estarion. "You have too much nose, then. And are too tall and too narrow. And much too oddly colored."

"And I have a demon's eyes." She shut them, drew a breath. "Grandfather, if you forbid it, he'll leave me alone."

"I never noticed that that made any difference to a determined lover," he said. "Particularly if, as I've been told, nobody here has the least regard for our lineage or our power."

"They do have regard for age," she said, "and for authority in a family. Even if I pretend that I have to send to you for permission—that would take years—"

"You should have thought of it before you summoned me," he said. "Now you'll have to lie about it."

She gaped at him.

"If Vanyi approves of this man," he said, "and if he comes of a decent family, and means you well, I can't see that I have any objection to his marrying you. It would give Kimeri a father, for one thing. For another, it would be useful for the embassy to have one of its members married to the king's kinsman."

"But you've never even seen him," she said with growing desperation.

"Vanyi has," he said. "I trust her judgment." He slanted a glance at Vanyi. "Do you like him?"

"He'll do," Vanyi answered. "He's good-looking, he's clever, and he can play politics—but he's honest about it. And he dotes on your granddaughter. Can't take his eyes off her."

"He can't believe any woman can be so hideous," Daruya said. She looked as if she would have liked to seize her grandfather and shake him. "Grandfather! You can't allow this."

"Granddaughter," he said, "you won't take anyone in my empire. If this man will do, then take him with my blessing. It will be a very pretty scandal that you had to marry a barbarian from the other side of the world, and wouldn't take any man, lord or commoner, in your own realm."

"Oh, no," she said. "I won't let you sway me with that. I don't want to marry anybody."

"You should," said Estarion. He stretched, yawned. "Ah me. I'm tired. They're trying to start a rebellion in Markad again, would you believe it? People are laughing in the rebels' faces, and the rebels are getting progressively more rebellious. All six of them. Maybe I should marry them off to ladies in Ianon, who will keep them nicely occupied and beat them soundly when they get out of hand."

"I think you should, at that," said Vanyi. "Unfortunately I don't think this man will beat our princess when she needs it. He's too much in love with her."

"I'd kill him, of course, if he laid a hand on her," said Estarion, as amiable as ever. "I wish you joy of the wedding."

He was gone before Daruya could say a word. Vanyi laughed at her expression. "Well, child. I'd say you were fairly effectively outflanked."

"You did this," Daruya said with sudden venom. "You colluded with him. You *told* him."

"No, I didn't," Vanyi said. "By my honor as a mage. I never said a word to him, or asked him to help. Though I admit I was less confident than you that he'd see your side of it. He wants you well matched, and with a man who will love you as well as keep you sensible."

"He doesn't know the first thing about Bundur."

"But I do," said Vanyi. "I like him. I think you do, too."

"What does that have to do with it?"

"When it comes to wedding and bedding," Vanyi said, "rather a great deal." She levered herself to her feet. "I'll leave you to think about it. But do bear in mind that this is a prince, and a power in the kingdom—and he favors our embassy. If you refuse him, you've insulted him terribly."

19

DARUYA THOUGHT BEST when she was in motion. Motion that, this time, took her to House Janabundur and halted her in front of its gate. She had not intended to come here, still less to let the porter admit her, but once it was done, it was done. Lady Nandi was not at home, the servant told her with careful courtesy, but the master of the house could be summoned if she wished.

She did not wish. She heard herself say, "I'll see him."

"Lady," the servant said, bowing her into a room she had not seen before, and leaving her there.

It was a receiving-room. She knew the look. Cushions to sit on, a low table, tea in a pot, the inevitable cakes that every house kept on hand for welcoming guests. The walls were hung with figured rugs, some of which looked very old, and all of which were as intricate as everything seemed to be in this country. Each told a story, sometimes simple, sometimes fantastic. She liked the small purse-mouthed man with the long mustaches, engaging in combat with an extravagantly streamered and barbeled dragon-creature. It was a most peculiar combat: it ended with the man and the dragon in a cavern, drinking tea and eating cakes in delightful amity.

She was smiling when Bundur made his entrance. It took him aback, which made her laugh.

"Lady!" he cried. "You devastate me. No howl of rage at the very least? No rampant display of temper?"

"I'm saving that for a larger audience," she said.

"Intelligent." He poured tea, handed her a cup. She

sighed and sipped from it. It was the flowery tea of ceremony, of course. He said, watching her face, "You don't like
tea."

"I'm getting used to it." She tilted her head toward the
dragon tapestry. "What does this mean?"

"Why, whatever you want it to mean." But before she
could frown: "It's an allegory, or so I'm told, about the folly
of war. Personally I prefer the literal interpretation, that a
warrior went to destroy a dragon of the heights, and they
fought a mighty battle, but in the end, when neither could
overcome the other, they declared a truce. Then after they
had had a long and satisfying conversation, they decided
that enmity was foolish, and became friends."

" 'Know your enemy, find a friend.' " Daruya shrugged.
"We have that story, too, though we don't put a dragon in
it."

"Wisdom is the same wherever you go." He emptied his
cup and set it down. He looked well, she thought, considering the condition in which he had been put to bed. "So,
then. Are you going to say yes?"

"Aren't you being a little bit precipitous?" she asked
him. "You're supposed to circle all around it, yes? And wait
for our elders to conclude the agreement."

"No," he said. "Not once everyone's been told."

"I'm not going to say yes," she said.

He betrayed no surprise, and no sign of hurt, either.
"But of course you are. You just don't know it yet."

"No," she said.

"Yes," said Bundur. "What concerns you? That I'm a
prince in this kingdom, and you're a nobody? That you're a
queen in yours, and I'm a nobody? That's a perfect balance,
I should think. Or is it that I'm older than you? Eight years
is nothing—or is it nine?"

"Eight," she said. "Closer to seven. I'm not a child."

"Of course not. If you were, I wouldn't be asking for

you. So that's not what troubles you. Your daughter? I balance her with my son. Each has need of a sibling. Marry me and they can be brother and sister forever after."

"I don't want to marry anybody," said Daruya.

"Of course you don't want to marry just anybody. You want to marry me."

"You," she said in mounting incredulity, "are the most arrogant, cocksure, headstrong, stubborn, obstinate—"

He was grinning, and wider, the longer the catalogue grew. "Surely," he said when she ran out of names to call him. "And you love me for it. I'm exactly the man for you. Else why did you refuse all those men in your own country, which you say is so vast and has so many people? You were waiting for me."

"Oh!" said Daruya in frustrated rage, flinging the cup at him. He caught it deftly, avoided the spray of tea that came with it, set it down with the care due its fragility.

"You see?" he said. "We match. You fling my mother's best cup, which is a hundred years old, last work of a master. I catch it. A perfect pairing."

"Why?" she shouted at him. "Why do you insist on this travesty?"

"No travesty," he said, as calm as ever. "Destiny. I argued with it too, you know. I had a long discussion with several of the gods. They all told me what I knew already, which was that you were meant for me. I saw that the first time I looked on your face, there in the teahouse, and reflected that ugliness can be its own kind of beauty."

"I am *not* ugly," she gritted.

"No," he admitted freely. "You aren't. It was only that first time, before I learned to see you as you are, and not as something out of nature. Now I think you quite beautiful. In your strange way."

"I'm not flattered," she said. "I'm not going to marry you."

"Of course you are."

He smiled. His eyes were limpid, amiable. He was no more yielding than the mountain he was named for, Shaka-bundur that was rooted in the deeps of the earth and clove the sky. He did not care what she said or how she said it. He was going to have her.

Why then, she wondered with a shock, did she not feel more truly trapped? She was angry, yes. Furious. She wanted to knock him down and slap the smile from his face. But she felt as she had in the festival, without even the excuse of wine and the dance. As if they were supposed to be here, face to face, bound and in opposition. She had not even the luxury of rebellion. As easily rebel against the color of her eyes, or the shape of her hand.

Her hand. She raised it. There was pain in it, but not as it had been before. The burning was muted, the throbbing dulled almost to painlessness.

The brand was still there, the *Kasar* with its glitter of gold in the pale honey of her skin. Its power was not gone; she felt it like the weight of the sun in her palm. But the pain that had been with her since her earliest memory, that she had been taught would never leave her, was sunk so low that it might not have been there at all.

Bundur was staring at it. Had he seen it before? She could not recall. She did not flaunt it. A man, seeing flashes of it, might think he imagined them, or she was carrying a coin in her hand, or wearing an odd fashion of ornament.

She answered him before he could ask. "Yes, you see what you think you see. I was born with it. All of my line are. It's the god's brand."

"It's splendid," he said.

"Do your kings carry such a thing?" she asked. She meant to mock, but not entirely.

If he caught the mockery, he disregarded it. "No. Our kings and queens are known for what they are, but the god doesn't mark them, except in the soul."

"I carry two brands, for my two empires," she said.

"Sun in the hand, for Keruvarion, and eyes of the Lion, for Asanion, which was the Golden Empire. Our gods are given to displays, I suppose. It makes it easy to tell who's meant to rule and who is not."

"But it makes it difficult to get away from it when you need to."

She stared at him, surprised. No one had ever understood that before.

He smiled and laid his palm against hers, unafraid, unaware that the brand could burn. His hand was broader, stronger, the color of bronze. It was warm. His fingers wound with hers. His face behind its smile was austere, proud, with its sharp planes.

"Your people," she said, "must be kin to our plainsmen. Did they come across the sea long ago and settle here, or did they begin here? How old is this world of yours?"

"Old," he said. "Ancient beyond telling. And yours?"

"Maybe older than that. Maybe younger." She clenched her fist. It wound their fingers tighter. "I'll bed you if you want it. Happily."

"I don't want that," he said. "Not for a night or a season. I want it with honor, in the marriage bed."

"Why?"

"Because it should be so. Because you are worthy of it."

"I the outlander. I the ugly one. I the mage."

"All of that. And worthy. Do you not want me because I'm ugly to you, too?"

"No. I don't want to marry."

"Why?"

Her own question, returned with that ceaseless smile. "I don't. That's all. Someday I'll have to, to get myself a consort—then it had better be someone suitable, who can share the throne and the duties, and rule in my name when I can't be everywhere at once. How would you do that? You know nothing but Shurakan."

"I could learn," he said.

"And leave Shurakan?"

"Even that," he said steadily, "I could do if I must."

She wrenched free in sudden disgust. "You don't have the faintest conception of what you mean when you say that. You're not getting a wife if you get me, you lovestruck fool. You're getting the heir to an empire, and the whole empire with her. If you were ambitious I'd understand it. But you don't even know what my empire is. Nor do you care."

"I said," he said, "I can learn. And if we're talking of politics, be politic now and think. I may not understand your empire, but I understand Su-Shaklan—and Su-Shaklan is about to become rather more than dangerous for you and your embassy. Do you know that there are many who hate and fear foreigners, and you above all? They're growing in numbers, and they're growing powerful. The king has been resisting their persuasions, but he's weakening fast. The least he'll do, once he gives in, is lock you in prison. His counselors are begging him to kill you outright."

"I know that," she said impatiently. "I've known it since we came here."

"You don't know how close the king is to the edge." Bundur took both her hands, though she resisted, and held them. "Listen to me. I visit the king often—he's my mother's brother, it's expected. We're fond of one another. But he's immovably convinced that foreigners mean nothing but harm to Su-Shaklan, and foreigners of your ilk more than any other. This morning he told me that if I want to keep you safe, I had best marry you soon, and bring you all under the protection of Janabundur. Otherwise he can't promise that any of you will escape this place alive."

Daruya's lip curled. "Oh, do tell me another. Why in the hells would the king tell you that, if he hates us so much?

He'd be locking you up for a madman, for wanting to marry me at all."

"He understands the soul-bond," Bundur said. "He doesn't like it, he doesn't approve of it, but he can't deny it. 'Marry her,' he said, 'and seal it for all to see. Or see her hunted down and killed with all the rest of her kind.' " His hands tightened, bruising-hard. "Lady, Daruya, he's not an evil man, but he's a righteous one. And he's beat upon day and night by those who hunger for your blood and the blood of all mages. It's an old, old hate, from the beginning of the kingdom. He fights it, but he can't fight it much longer."

"Then how come you can?"

"Maybe," he said, "because I'm not the king. My mind is my own. I can use it to think, and my eyes to see. You're no more evil than any other child of men."

"If no less." Damn, thought Daruya. Her fingers were locked with his again. They seemed to think that that was the way of nature.

This must be what Vanyi felt when she was with Estarion—and forty years had done nothing to ease it, either. What Estarion felt with Vanyi, Daruya could not presume to know. He loved his empress, of that she was certain. He had refused an Asanian harem for her, but as she grew old but he did not, he had taken other lovers, with the empress' knowledge and consent.

The first one or two, Daruya had reason to suspect, had been of the empress' choosing. The empress was Asanian. She would have been perturbed, even offended, if he had forsaken all the pleasures of the bedchamber, simply because she was not herself able to share them.

But none of those lovers had been Vanyi. With Vanyi it would have mattered too much.

Getting with child had been simple compared to this. Daruya chose the man, she found him willing, she took what she needed and bade him farewell, and that was that.

He went back to his doting wife. She went back to her grandfather, and to the splendor of a scandal.

This would be a scandal only insofar as the man was a foreigner. Her grandfather approved it, the more fool he. The Master of the Guild wanted it—pressed her to do it. They all saw the advantage in it, the embassy saved, and their lives too if Bundur spoke the truth. None of them seemed to comprehend that when a woman married, she married, one could hope, until she died.

Or she might not. She might leave her husband. Daruya might leave Shurakan when their embassy had done what it set out to do; leave him, go back to Starios, be princess-heir again without the pressure of urging that she marry and be respectable. Her child would have a father-in-name. The man who held that name . . .

"This is impossible," she said. "We can't do it."

"We can," he said, as she had known he would.

"Then why," she inquired acidly, "don't you marry Vanyi instead? She'd do anything to further this embassy. She's not bound to any one place, she's not heir to any empire, she's not young, either, but she's strong; she'll live another thirty years, and keep you well satisfied, too."

"The Lady Vanyi is not soulbound to me," said Bundur, "or I might consider it."

"If I said the words with you," said Daruya through clenched teeth, "I could not promise to stay with you, or even to stay married to you for longer than necessity requires."

"I could take that risk," he said.

"You don't know what you're saying."

"On the contrary," said Bundur, and for the first time she saw a hint of temper, "I do. Give me credit for a little wit, my lady. I understand all the arguments against this— I've had them from my kin, too. None of them matters. Nothing matters but that my soul bids me take you."

"And that we're in danger if I don't."

"Well," he said. "If you weren't, I wouldn't push so hard or so fast. Too fast for you, I know. But the king never cries the alarm without excellent reason."

"I'll think about it," said Daruya, pulling free as she always seemed to be doing, and leaving him before he could call her back.

20

KIMERI DECIDED THAT she did not hate Hani after all, even if he was a coward. He kept saying that he had been going to get help, but she went away before he could come back—very well, she would say she believed him. It was true that he was afraid of the tall woman, though why he should be, she could not imagine. The woman was of high rank, but then so was Kimeri; and Kimeri's mother was as tall as most men, and quite terrifying too when she was in a temper. Kimeri would be that tall someday, everybody said she would. She was looking forward to it. Then Hani would be afraid of her, and she would show him what an idiot he was.

They had called truce for the festival, and had a splendid time, even if Hani's grandmother had dragged them back home much too early and put them to bed in the same room. They were going to be sister and brother, Hani's grandmother was thinking, because Kimeri's mother was going to marry Hani's father. Kimeri had her doubts about that. Hani's father was big and handsome, and he made the room brighter when he came into it, but Kimeri's mother was very clever about escaping from people who wanted to marry her.

Kimeri had the same dream as always, the same dark place, the same presence that she knew was the Guardian in the Gate. As always, she was glad to wake up, but sorry too; the Guardian's sorrow, because while she dreamed he had company, but while she was awake he was all alone. It was hurting more, the longer he stayed in the Gate, but at the same time it was hurting less, as if he had stopped caring about being alive again.

She was surprised to wake up and find the walls all wrong, and the bed not the bed she had got used to. She was in Hani's house, and Hani was sound asleep in the bed next to hers. Kimeri thought about waking him up, but if he stayed asleep she could have all of the tea with honey in it that a servant brought as soon as she got out of bed, and most of the redspice buns. She ended up leaving him some of each, because she was not as selfish as she might be.

There was an Olenyas sitting in a shadow the way they liked to do, waiting for her. It was a different one than had been there when she went to sleep. "Rahai," she said, touching his shoulder. His eyes were dark for an Olenyas', almost brown. They smiled at her. He got to his feet in the way she tried to copy but never could, as if he had no bones at all, and followed her when she walked out of the room and the house.

He knew where to go once they were outside, which saved her trouble, because she wanted to dawdle and not pay attention to where she was going. The city was all quiet and rather tired, with bits of festival garland scattered everywhere, and sleepy-eyed people sweeping it up. Nearly everybody was still asleep, or just awake with a pounding headache. Grownfolk woke up like that when they had had too much wine the night before.

She wandered a bit, because she needed to think. She thought about going to the house where the Gate was, since she was outside the palace anyway, and Rahai might not stop her. But something said, *Not yet. Soon, but not yet.*

She thought of arguing, but the *soon* was very soon; she felt it. She kept on walking, then, without Rahai saying anything. He had no headache. He had been asleep while everybody danced and played. She felt a little sorry for him, but not too much. Olenyai had their own games and their own festivals, and those kept them as happy as men could be; and meanwhile he was wide awake and pleased to be guarding her on this fine summer's morning. Bits of thought trickled through the protection all Olenyai had: right-here-nowness, high clear sky with a cloud here and there, mountain walls, air like wine chilled in snow. Shadows that were people, people-harmless, people-who-might-harm. Those latter he watched, ready to defend if there was need, but there never was.

They came to the palace eventually and went inside. The guards on the gates looked blurry-eyed and headachy. Kimeri gave them a festival gift, a touch that took the ache away. None of them knew where it came from, but that was the way it should be.

Rahai tried to lead her straight through to where the house was, but she was not ready to go there yet. Vanyi was there, just about to wake up. Her mother was just coming in, thinking about Bundur and not knowing she was doing it, nor wanting to if she had known. She was all in a tangle about him, wanting and not wanting, being part of him and not wanting to be a part of him at all.

Maybe she *would* marry him, Kimeri thought. She had never been like this about a man before, especially one who wanted to marry her. If she liked a man, she bedded him; if not, she told him to lose himself, and shut the door in his face. Kimeri had never seen her in a such a confusion of wanting-not-wanting.

She did not want Kimeri to see her that way, either. Kimeri got out of her mind before she noticed the intruder, and went looking for somewhere to go that would not get in Daruya's way.

The palace children were still asleep, like Hani, or being fussed over by their parents or their aunts or their cousins. Servants were up and working, but none of them would speak to Kimeri unless she spoke first, and they certainly would not play with her.

But there was someone who might be glad to see her.

Whom she felt she might talk to, and maybe, finally, be listened to. That someone was awake and had no headache, and was mildly bored herself. She was in the room she had told Kimeri to come to, reading a book she had read too many times before, and thinking about too many things at once. How Hani could be afraid of her, Kimeri could not imagine. Even if she was the queen.

She thought Kimeri did not know. She still thought it when Kimeri slipped through the back door, the one that was not supposed to open on anything at all, and Kimeri did not like to tell her she was wrong. She might be insulted.

She smiled, not knowing what Kimeri was thinking, and Kimeri was glad of that. "Good morning, child," she said. "Good morning, shadow-man."

Rahai bowed. He did not understand Borti's language, since he had no magery to teach it to him, but he could tell when he was being spoken to. He was wary, his eyes watching everything at once. Kimeri tried to tell him silently that he had nothing to be afraid of, but his protections kept him from hearing magewords. He stayed close, on guard.

Kimeri ignored him. Borti, studying her, did the same. "Good morning," said Kimeri. "Did you have a good festival?"

Borti's smile stayed the same, but the thoughts in the front of her mind were full of sad things: a fight with a man who must be the king, a great number of people smiling but looking as if they had fangs, fear she could not put a name to. Kimeri tried not to listen, but when a person thought so loudly, it was very hard to shut one's ears inside.

Borti's thoughts were deeply troubling, but aloud she said, "I had a pleasant festival, I suppose. And you?"

"Very pleasant," Kimeri said more honestly than Borti had. "My friend is my friend again—you know, the boy who ran away. He's a coward, but I can forgive him that. He's only a boy."

"Wisely said," said Borti. She reached for the box on the table next to her and opened it. A great odor of sweetness and spices wafted out. "These were a festival gift. Would you like to share them with me?"

Rahai slipped in before Kimeri could, and tasted one. Kimeri frowned at his rudeness, but Borti seemed to understand, and even to approve. After an endless while he got out of the way and let Kimeri sit down and try the sweets. They were odd but wonderful, like Shurakan.

"You didn't have a shadow-man before," Borti said. "Did your mother give him to you for the festival?"

"Oh, he's not a slave," said Kimeri quickly. Rahai could hardly be insulted, since he did not speak Borti's language, but she did not want Borti to think the wrong thing, either. "He's a bred-warrior. He serves the emperor, and my mother since she'll be empress someday, and me since I'll be empress after her. He thinks we all need guarding."

"And you didn't before?"

"I slipped away then," Kimeri confessed. "This time I didn't. Everyone's getting more afraid instead of less, the longer we stay here."

"Do you know why that is?" Borti asked.

She did want to know, not the why, but whether Kimeri knew it. Kimeri supposed she should be clever and pretend not to know, but she hated to tell lies. "Because we have enemies, and they hate us. They're going to do something soon, aren't they?"

"They might," Borti said, meaning they would.

"Something like breaking the Gate," Kimeri said. "That's what they did before."

"Gate?" asked Borti. "Which Gate is that?"

She was testing again. Kimeri hated it when people played the testing game, but she decided not to get angry yet. "The Worldgate, the Gate the mages made. But mage is a dirty word here, isn't it?"

"Some people think so," Borti said. Thinking louder

than ever: that it was foolish, but who knew what mages really were, or what they could do? Except raise their Gates. She had seen the one in Shurakan. It was strange, but it had not felt evil. It looked like a door, but on the other side of it was a place that could not be as close as it was—a place on the other side of the world.

She came back to what Kimeri said. "The Gate is broken, you say?"

"You didn't know it?" Kimeri asked her. "I thought everybody knew. That's why we came here the way we did. We didn't have a Gate to come through. Vanyi has been trying to get to y—to the queen and tell her, and ask her to help find out who did it. Her mages can't find anything at all."

Borti's eyes narrowed. She looked frightening then, if Kimeri had been the kind of person to be scared by a face. "Is it so? Has the Gate broken and no one has told me? How did it break? Do you know that?"

"Something broke it," said Kimeri. "I don't know what. Nobody does. But nobody knows what happened inside it, either. Except me. The mage who was Guardian—they think he's dead. Even he does. But he's not. He's trapped inside the Gate."

"How do you know that?"

Kimeri swallowed the bit of sweet she had been chewing. It was too sweet suddenly, and too sticky. It gagged her going down. But once it was down, it stayed there.

Nobody ever listened to her, or paid attention when she talked about Gates. But Borti did—Borti was fixed on her without the least doubt in the world that she knew what she was talking about. That was so strange that for a moment Kimeri had no words in her, and no way to speak them if she had.

Her voice came back all at once, and her wits with it. "I know because I'm a mage, too. I felt the Gate break. I saw it trap Uruan. He's still in it. I dream about him all the time, about how he's in there, and he thinks he's dead. He's scared, when he remembers to be."

"Why haven't you tried to get him out?"

"I don't know how," said Kimeri. "Vanyi won't even let me talk about it. The other mages pat me on the head and say 'Yes, yes' and don't hear a word. Even Kadin—he says maybe so, but what difference does it make? Dead is dead."

"And yet you leave him there. Surely there must be something you can do."

"They won't let me go outside the palace," Kimeri said. "Except for the festival, and then they watched me every minute. I did try. I did." She was almost in tears. "He doesn't feel anything, not really. He just dreams, and makes me dream, too. I try to help him then. I try to make him feel better."

Borti was not the kind of person to melt when a young person cried, or even to pay much attention to it unless it flung itself into her arms. Which Kimeri was deliberately not doing. "Can you show me?" Borti asked.

Kimeri blinked at her, shaking away tears. "Now?"

"No," said Borti a little too quickly. "I mean, can you show me where the Gate was?"

"I don't know if I can get out," Kimeri said.

"Can you come here?"

"I think so," said Kimeri slowly. "I did before. If it's night—if you don't mind that people say the house is haunted—"

"Ah, and so it would be," said Borti. She was amused, but scared too. "Tonight? Before the bright moon rises?"

"I can try," said Kimeri.

The voice inside of her was singing. *Soon. Yes, soon.* She told it to be quiet, before somebody heard, and unmade it all.

21

TONIGHT WAS A night of the Great Marriage: when both Brightmoon and Greatmoon were full, dancing in the sky together, the blinding-bright white moon and the great blood-red one, so splendid together that they blocked out the stars. Here where the world was so much closer to the sky, the moons seemed near enough to touch. Near enough to knock out of the sky and shatter on the earth, and pour out their blood, white and red, in shining rivers.

Kimeri was dizzy with excitement. She had got out of the house as she had come through the Gate, by making herself a shadow. None of the Olenyai had followed her. Her mother and Vanyi were singing the rite of the moons' rising; the mages were with them, even Kadin. She should have been there, but she made sure to vanish before anyone could start looking for her.

By the time the Olenyai understood that she had escaped, she was deep in the palace, almost to the room at the end of the hidden passage, and Borti was running toward her, wrapped in a cloak and a hood. "Quickly," Borti said, catching Kimeri's hand as she ran past. "People will be following."

Kimeri lightened her feet to run faster, and kept up easily with the woman's long stride. They went by ways that Kimeri did not know, with many twists and turns and doublings-back. Borti knew the palace as well as Hani had ever pretended to: she never hesitated, and never paused when there was a turn to make. In almost no time at all, they had passed through a gate and found themselves in a dark and deserted street.

Greatmoon was up, casting a glow like fire into the sky. Brightmoon would follow in a little while: Kimeri could feel her below the mountain walls, climbing slowly, taking her time. The sun was still close to the horizon on the other side of the sky, staining it a different red than Greatmoon did, more rose-red, fading to palest green and then to purple as it sank. The stars were trying to come out, but tonight they would not last long, not with both moons to drown their light.

Borti paid no attention to the splendor in the sky. She was even more nervous than she had been in the morning, and her thoughts darted almost too quick to follow. More about the king, about the fight they had had, about people who smiled with their faces but who thought terrible things. She was thinking that she should have stayed in the palace, but that she had to come out, she had to get away, it was only for a little while, then she would go back before she was missed. Which did not make sense to Kimeri, since Borti had already been missed: or why had she wanted to run so fast?

She slowed down in the street, just a little, enough to seem purposeful instead of panicked. "You have to lead me now," she said. "I've never been to the house where the Gate is—was."

"Is," said Kimeri. She let her feet go heavy again, and turned where her dream told her to go. It was hard, because the dream, like a bird, flew the straight way, but the streets were not straight at all. They twisted and turned, went up and down, round and about, and stopped in blind walls or closed gates. She had to thread her way through them, less quickly or surely than Borti had come through the palace. But she did not get lost, and she only ran into one wall, and that turned out to have a door in it, which opened into another street. At the end of that was a stair, then yet another street, and then at last, when they were both winded and ready to rest, a house that looked from the outside like any other house. But no people lived in it. No lights hung in strings along its roof, and no lantern hung by its gate to welcome people as they went past.

This street had people in it, but only a few, and they were not paying attention to a cloaked and hooded woman leading a cloaked and hooded child by the hand. Kimeri decided to venture a light, since the moons' light shone too dim yet, with Brightmoon just up and Greatmoon keeping more light than it shed. Her left hand was clutched tight in Borti's. She freed the right from her cloak and unfolded her fingers from her palm.

The sun in it shone dazzling. She damped it quickly, till it was just bright enough to see by, like a shaded lantern. She felt Borti's start of surprise, the stab of fear that disappeared as quickly as it came. Borti was brave, to be so calm about magery, and without warning, too.

By the light of the *Kasar* they went up to the gate. It was latched but not locked. There was a warding on it, with a taste of Kadin and a hint of Vanyi. Kimeri slipped a bit of shadow-thought into it, until it was sure they were no one and nothing but a night wind and a glimmer of moonlight. Then she slipped through, pulling Borti after her.

The house was dark and cold, as if summer had never come inside. It smelled of dust and of old stone. Kimeri knew people had lived here, and not long ago, either: mages, Guardians, coming and going through the Gate and into the city. The house had forgotten them.

A spell was on it, a spell of dark and of forgetfulness. It tried to weave itself around Kimeri, but she was ready for it. She sent it running with a flash of the *Kasar*. In that clean bright light they walked through empty, dusty rooms. Furniture was as the Guardian had left it, a bed that had been slept in, a chair drawn back from a table, a scroll on it with weights on the corners, the page half written on. Kimeri could not read yet. She was saving that for when she had time to learn it properly.

There was a loaf of bread on the table beside the scroll, green with mold, and a knife beside it, and a withered wheel of cheese. The black wrinkled things in the blue bowl must be fruit.

Borti's hand was cold in Kimeri's. She was not afraid of a mageling with a handful of light, but ghosts made her bones shiver. She thought she saw them in every shadow, every flicker of light as they moved.

Kimeri could not think of a way to comfort her. There was a ghost in the house, after all, if only one. She felt him in the innermost room. It was like the room the mages had taken in the house in the palace, deep inside, walled all around and windowless, but larger—a good deal larger, to hold the Gate. It had been a shrine, Kimeri guessed: the walls were splendidly painted and the floor had tiles like the speaking god's shrine in the palace. There was no god here. Only a blank grey wall with the faintest suggestion of an outline drawn on it: posts and lintel, the shape of a gate.

There was a lamp-cluster here, with oil in the lamps, and flint and a striker hanging from the hook on the base. Kadin kept the lamps filled, Kimeri thought. She wondered if he ever used them. He could make magelight, even darkmages could do that; or he might like sitting in the dark.

He was not there now. He was singing the moons into the sky. Kimeri lit the lamps by thinking about it, because it seemed the right thing to do. Their light was warmer than the light of the *Kasar*, and gentler. The lines of the Gate were fainter in it, but the grey of the wall seemed more silvery, as if there were a Gate there still.

Borti's voice came soft, no more than a whisper. "Are there words one says? An invocation, a calling up of the dead?"

"He's not dead," Kimeri said. She hoped her voice was not too sharp. "Can you see where the Gate was?"

"I see a wall," Borti said.

"That was it," said Kimeri. "Does it look a little odd to you?"

"It's painted grey," said Borti. "Like rain."

"Like rain," said Kimeri. "Yes. See, it shimmers. The Gate is broken, but somehow it's still here. Like a ghost of a Gate. He's keeping it here by being in it."

Borti shivered, but she was strong. She did not run, or think about running. "I don't see anything."

There was nothing to see. But he was there, in the greyness that looked like a wall but was not. Kimeri wondered what would happen if she touched it with her hand. She was not sure she needed to know.

"Uruan," she said, which was the Guardian's name. Names had power, all the mages said so, and the priests, too. "Uruan, can you hear me calling?"

He was trapped in the Gate, drifting, dreaming. All he could see was grey, nothingness, no sight, no sound, no taste, no scent, no touch. Kimeri tried to push through the grey, to give him the touch of her mind's hand, the sound of her voice. "Uruan!"

Borti gasped. Kimeri, half in her body and half out of it, saw how the wall changed, how its grey turned silver. There was a shape in it. A body. A face. Uruan was a red Gileni: he was easy to see, dark bronze against the grey, with his bright mane.

"*Begone*, foul fiend from the hells below!"

The voice was a brass bellow. It rang in the empty space. It knocked Kimeri down and set Borti spinning, crying out. Uruan struggled in his prison, waking out of his dream into a madness of panic.

Kimeri scrambled to her feet. She was too furious to be afraid. A man stood in the doorway, a preposterous figure, shaved head and shaved face painted half black, half white, and the rest of him ordinary Shurakani brown, which was easy to see because he was naked. Maybe he thought he was dressed: he was hung everywhere with jangling ornaments, amulets, images, fetishes, things that smelled of black dark and things that smelled of bright light, all jumbled together and jangling against one another. He was dancing from foot to foot, a rattle in one hand, a long and dangerous-looking knife in the other.

"Oh, goddess," said Borti. She was laughing, though she sounded as if she wanted to cry.

Kimeri was not laughing at all. The man's jumble of amulets matched the jumble of his power, and it was power, magery all twisted and odd, half real, half pretended. He was aiming it at the Gate. At Uruan, who was a half-thing himself, half alive and half not, and like to become nothing if the man kept on.

"Stop it!" Kimeri yelled at him. "Stop it! You're killing him!"

The man turned the force of his power on her. It swayed her, and she could not see for a bit, but she was stronger than it was. He was dancing and hopping from foot to foot, waving his knife about as if he had the faintest idea how to use it. "Demon! Creature of darkness! Back to thy hells, and thy foul spirit with thee!"

"Oh, come," said Kimeri, too angry to be polite. "That's silly. I'm not a demon, and that's not a foul spirit, that's a man trapped in a Gate. What in the world are you?"

"He's an exorcist," Borti answered for him, since he seemed unable to speak. Demons, it was clear, were not supposed to talk back, still less tell him exactly what was what. Borti went on, "He sends demons back where they came from, and lays ghosts to rest."

"He's not much of an exorcist," Kimeri said tartly, "if he can't tell a demon from a Sunchild, or a trapped Guardian from a creature of the hells."

The exorcist blinked. His magic was in rags. Under it he

was not a bad man, simply ignorant. Kimeri was not inclined to be kind to him for that. Even when he said in a completely different voice than the one he had been using, soft and rather diffident, "Have I made a mistake? This isn't the haunting I came to be rid of?"

"Who sent you?" Kimeri demanded. "This is our house if it's anybody's. *We* certainly didn't want an exorcist."

"We send ourselves," the exorcist said. "Every night of great moment, when the moons are full or the moons are new, or one or both is in a position of power, somebody comes to dance the haunting away."

"It never works, does it?" Kimeri said. "It's not going to work now." She advanced on him and plucked the knife out of his hand. It made her fingers tingle. It had a black blade; at home it would have been a darkmage's instrument, and not a pleasant one, either. Usually its blade was poisoned.

This one was not. She broke it across her golden palm and flung the pieces away. "You shouldn't walk around waving darkblades as if they were kitchen knives. Don't you know they can drink souls?"

The exorcist opened and shut his mouth. "I don't—I didn't—"

"Obviously," said Kimeri. "So you people think there's a ghost here, and he walks when the moons are up. He doesn't, really. He's trapped in the Gate. It's just his fetch that walks, trying to find its way out. If you hadn't interrupted, we might have been able to help him."

The exorcist looked completely crestfallen. He was not very old, Kimeri saw, for grownfolk. He was maybe as old as her mother. He was full of himself, all fresh and newly initiate, and this was supposed to be his first great charge.

It served him right, she thought nastily, for being such an idiot.

He tried to scramble together his dignity, and his

crooked magery with it. "You are a demon," he said in as steady a voice as he could manage. "You were set here to test me."

"I am not," said Kimeri. "I told you that already. People look like this where I come from. Now will you go away? We're busy."

That was the wrong thing to say. He had his power all together, and his temper to make it stronger. He rolled it into a ball and threw the lot of it at her, so fast and so hard she could barely get out of the way, and even more barely see where it was going. Her own power lashed out desperately, all anyhow, and struck it sidewise.

There was a blinding flash, a clap of thunder. Kimeri was knocked down again. But her body did not matter. Her power was flying into the broken Gate, locked with the exorcist's, and Uruan was right in its path. Holding himself there. Seeing his death, wanting it, wanting to be gone, away, out of this agony of half-existence.

"No," said Kimeri. She said it in her ordinary voice. In the howling of Gatewinds, no one should have been able to hear it at all, but it was clear, its sound distinct.

The Gate was awake. It should not be—it was dead. But neither should Uruan be alive, and he was. Somehow he and the Gate together had kept it all from falling apart.

The bolt of power struck them both. Something ripped. Something else tore. It might be the inside of Kimeri's head. It might be the fabric of the Gate, or the thing that had bound the Gate, knocked it down and fallen on it. Through the gap, something fell—something large and breathing and bruised, that looked around, laughed once as a madman might, and crumpled to the floor.

So that was what Uruan really looked like. He was more like the people here than anybody else in the embassy, copper-bright hair and all. He looked like the prince in Han-Gilen, which was not surprising, since the prince was his elder brother. His face at the moment was grey, as if he had brought some of the nothingness with him, but that was only shock and unconsciousness. He was very much alive, and very much there, lying on the threshold of the new-waked Gate.

Kimeri scrambled to her bruised knees. Borti was struggling up, too, and the exorcist was starting to come to himself. They were both staring at the Gate. It was awake but not focused. On the other side of it was night, with stars; but no stars that shone on the world Kimeri knew.

They were quiet, and that was what mattered. Kimeri asked them to guard the Gate for her. They did not exactly agree, but she felt as if they had. They were inside of her somehow, as they were in the Gate. It was strange, but it felt right; they belonged there, they and the Gate both. Nothing would touch that Gate, or pass it, or hurt it, as long as they were there and she was there. She was content with that; she hoped that everyone else would be, too.

22

Kᴉᴍᴇʀɪ ꜱʜᴏᴜʟᴅ ʜᴀᴠᴇ known better than to expect that anybody would be reasonable about the new-waked Gate. Especially with Uruan back, as they all thought, from the
dead. Borti had to make the exorcist help her carry him,
since Kimeri was too small and too tired from everything
she had done; then they had to go by back ways, because a
naked exorcist and a hooded woman and a yellow-eyed
child carrying an unconscious man through the streets at
night was suspicious to say the least. Kimeri had enough
power left to cover them all with shadows, which helped.

Vanyi and Daruya both met them halfway to the house
in the palace, with Olenyai and mages behind. Kimeri could
have hidden from them, but she was too glad to see them,
even if she would get a right tanning when they had time to
think about it. At least she did not need to explain anything
to start with; Uruan was enough to engross them all, and
Borti and the exorcist rather faded into insignificance. They
were swept along whether they wanted it or not, but no one
asked questions, nor said or did anything but keep them
under guard.

The house was warm and welcoming, Olenyai in it to let
them in and bar the gate behind them, lamps lit in the dining-room, which was the biggest room and the one where
everyone could gather, but no servants anywhere. They had
all disappeared.

The Olenyai brought in a pallet and spread it for Uruan,
and he was laid on it. People tried not to crowd. Vanyi bent
over him, and Daruya, running their hands down his body,
tracing it in power.

"Alive," said Vanyi, saying what they all knew. "And well, except for shock. He'll sleep it off and wake sane."

Daruya sank to her heels, hands on thighs. Her eyes found Kimeri, who was trying to find a shadow to slip away inside of. "Merian," she said.

Her tone was mild, but she never called Kimeri by her grownfolk name unless Kimeri was in trouble. Kimeri came forward slowly, holding her courage in both hands. Just outside of her mother's reach, she stopped.

"Ki-Merian," said Daruya. "Can you explain this?"

Kimeri swallowed. They were all staring, mages, Olenyai, Borti and the exorcist too. "I told you he was in the Gate," she said. "You wouldn't listen."

Daruya's brows drew together. "You told me you were having nightmares. You didn't say what those nightmares were."

"I told Vanyi," Kimeri said.

Vanyi flushed, which was startling. "God and goddess. So she did. I thought she was babbling, or telling stories."

"Because I'm too young," Kimeri said. "I know. Nobody would listen."

Except Borti, but Kimeri did not think she wanted to say that. Not yet. Kimeri was in enough trouble by herself.

"Well then," Daruya said, "since we didn't listen, and that's our fault, suppose you tell us how you woke the Gate and got the Guardian out of it."

"I didn't mean to," said Kimeri, trying not to whine. "The exorcist was trying to lay the ghost and exorcise me, and I tried to stop him. The Gate woke up. Uruan fell out of it. The Gate's still there. But it's not opening on anything but stars."

"A blind Gate," Vanyi said. She sounded afraid. That, like her blush, was not like her at all. "We're warned in all the books of Gates, not to let that happen."

"Do they ever say why?" Daruya asked. Odd to see her the calm one, and Vanyi flustered.

"No," Vanyi said. "Only that they're dangerous; that they open on the living heart—whatever that means. They don't say."

Kimeri could feel the Gate in her. In her heart? Maybe. She was not going to tell Vanyi that. Vanyi might try to do something about it, and that would be dangerous. Kimeri knew that because the stars knew it: the stars in the Gate.

"Can we use the Gate?" Daruya asked. "Can we get back to Starios through it? If we can do that—"

"No," Vanyi said again. "That much I do know. A blind Gate leads nowhere. If you try to use it, you'll end up as Uruan did: trapped till something sets you free."

Daruya might not have left it at that, but someone started pounding on the gate, so loud that they heard it even this far back in the house. There was shouting, Olenyai voices, and another voice over it, deep and clear at once. "Damn you, you sons of the Pit! Let me in!"

"Let him in!" Daruya called in Asanian, rising so fast Kimeri hardly saw her move, and running toward the door; then stopping as if confused, blushing and going white, then blushing again.

Bundur ran in trailing hot-eyed Olenyai, ignoring them completely. He looked wild, his hair down out of its knot, his coat as short as a commoner's and torn besides, and a cut on his cheek that he seemed unaware of. He was talking before he had come all the way into the room. "You have to come, you mustn't stop, you've got to get out of here."

Now it was Daruya who was in a flutter and Vanyi who was calm: the order of the world was back in place again. "Stop babbling, take a deep breath, and start from the beginning," Vanyi said.

Bundur took the breath, and shut his mouth, too, but he still did not seem to see anything much but Daruya's face. When he spoke again he sounded much calmer. "The king is dead." Maybe only Kimeri heard Borti's gasp. Maybe not. "Do you remember the people I told you of, the ones who want to expel all foreigners and kill the mages? It seems my uncle was more difficult to bring round to their way of thinking than they thought he might be. They've killed him and set up their own king.''

"The queen?'' Vanyi asked.

"Dead,'' said Bundur. "As far as anyone knows. She hasn't been seen since the murderers broke into the palace. They'd have got rid of her first, even before they issued their ultimatum to the king. They're still dealing with resistance from the queen's people—but once they've broken that, they'll come here.''

Vanyi's eyes went vague: she was using her magery to see. "Not for a while yet, but yes. We'll be a fine symbol of the new reign, with our bodies spiked to the walls and our heads over the gate.''

Bundur shuddered. Somebody was retching—Aledi, with Miyaz holding her head. He looked as if he would have liked to join her. "Listen to me. There's one way I know of to keep you safe. Come back, all of you and all the belongings you can gather, to House Janabundur. I'll keep you there.''

"And die when they come for us,'' Daruya said.

Her eyes seemed to steady him, though they were burning gold. "No,'' he said. "Not my wife, and my wife's kin and servants.''

She shuddered as he had, but with less of a greensick look. "It can't be that easy.''

"Custom is strong,'' he said, "and it will confuse them—at least long enough for us to think of other ways to defend ourselves.''

Daruya raised her hands as if to push him away, then knotted them together and twisted them. "What if it doesn't work?''

"It will,'' he said. He was sure. He was also out of patience. "But you have to come now. They've closed the great gates—I just got in before the bars went down. They'll be securing the lesser ones soon."

"And we have seneldi to move." That, for some reason, seemed to calm Daruya down, get her thinking. "We'll go through the stable. Vanyi, Kadin, we'll move everything the fastest way, and keep a shadow over it."

Bundur had not expected that. Kimeri watched him think that he had not been planning to take in all their live-stock too, but nobody heard him when he tried to say it. Then it struck him what it meant. Daruya was going to marry him. Kimeri would have gone over and held him up if he would have let her.

As it was, his knees buckled, but he stiffened them somehow and ran with the rest of them, scrambling together everything they could. Not much from the house— clothes to change into, one or two of the packs of trade goods that Vanyi had brought in, weapons for the Olenyai; and Kimeri wondered what the guards of Shurakan would give to know how the bred-warriors had got their swords back again. From the stable they had to take more: grain for the seneldi, bales of cut fodder slung across unwilling backs, saddles and bridles and the rest.

By that time the tumult inside the palace was loud enough to hear with human ears. Kimeri kept a grip on Borti. Nobody had been taking particular notice of the woman—Kimeri helped them with that, and helped to think she was some kind of servant, or maybe the exorcist's assistant, until the exorcist saw the seneldi and bleated something incoherent and bolted. He would be safe. His magery was all tangled up, but it was good enough to hide him while he needed to be hidden, and when he found an open gate he would run back to his temple.

Borti had no such escape. Her brother-king was dead. The people in the palace were hunting her. She was safest where she was, with a hood hiding her face and a shadow hiding all of them, creeping along the wall toward a gate that might, with the gods' help, still be open and unguarded when they got to it. The seneldi came quietly, with a magery on them, but even that could not keep them from rolling their eyes and snorting at the sudden reek of death from inside the palace. Someone had opened a door and died in it. Several other people ran out, looking for enemies to kill, but they saw nothing but moonlight and darkness and an empty yard.

Borti stumbled. Kimeri kept her on her feet, using magery when bodily strength was not enough. She kept trying to run inside, as if it would do any good at all to die as her brother had. She was not thinking; something in her had gone blank and blind. Mages would have to mend that when they got to House Janabundur.

The gate had a guard, but Chakan killed him. It was almost too quick to see: one moment he was alive, the next he was not. His soul hung about, bewildered, till a gust of wind caught it and blew it away.

Once past the gate they mounted quickly. Rahai tossed Kimeri into the saddle of the starbrowed bay; she pulled Borti up behind her, with Rahai pushing, not asking questions. He was a wise man, was Rahai. Borti had no kind of seat on a senel, but she could balance herself, even tranced, and she clung to Kimeri.

Bundur was riding, too. He rode well—he wanted to gallop down the twisty street, but Daruya stopped him. There were people in the way. The shadow would not hold if they went too fast or ran into anyone. They had to walk, mostly, and trot in the few stretches where it was level enough and empty enough. They were still faster than if they had tried to go on foot, though Bundur did not like to admit it.

The city was quiet. It was only the palace that was in uproar. The people would wait till it was over, then decide what to do. Kings had died this way before, though not for a long while. Shurakan had got used to peace, but it had never forgotten the scent of blood in the air.

House Janabundur waited for them. It was remarkably like Kimeri's earlier homecoming: the same warm welcome, the same barred gates, the same gathering in the largest room. But there were differences. The seneldi had to be put somewhere and taken care of. The back garden did for that; Lady Nandi sighed for her flowers, even after Kadin assured her that these seneldi were civilized and would eat only what he gave them permission to eat. They liked having a space to roam in, even one as small as that, and settled happily enough to their fodder and the handful of grain that Kadin fed each one in turn.

He stayed with the seneldi. The rest of them went up to the hall where they had dined on festival night. It was only yesterday, Kimeri thought. It felt years gone.

They had to have tea and cakes—they could not be welcomed without them. Everybody choked down a sip and a bite, even Hani creeping out of bed to see what the commotion was. It seemed natural for him to set himself beside Kimeri and keep quiet while Bundur told his mother that her brother was dead.

Lady Nandi had expected it. "I knew," she said, "when the whispers grew so loud, and everyone so sure that he would yield. I knew he never would." Her eyes were dry, her voice steady. She kept all her tears inside until she should have time to be alone. Then she would weep. "He believed that the haters of foreigners were right, mind you, and that foreign presence could only destroy what we have built here. But he was also the king. The king is above the fears of simple men."

But not the queen, Kimeri thought, with Borti gripping her hand till it hurt, sitting on the other side of her from Hani. No one really saw her yet, though the shadow was wearing thin. Kimeri was tired, even with the Gate inside her to make her stronger. The queen had been afraid, and was becoming afraid again as she woke from the horror that had held her speechless. But she was brave, as always. She fought her way through the fear. Kimeri helped. She held the light where Borti could see it, and guided her out of the dark place.

All the while she did that, the others talked. Kimeri's mother was being stubborn again. "Did I say I'd agreed to marry you?" she was saying to Bundur. "Marry Vanyi. She'll take you."

"With all due respect to her ladyship," said Bundur, "I don't want her. I want you."

"Stop that," said Vanyi, so sharp and so sudden that they started and fell silent. "That will be enough out of you, Daruyani. You will do as your heart is bidding you do, so loud even I can hear it, and that will be that."

"Not tonight," Daruya said, obstinate still. "At least give me time to think about it."

"Time for the palace to discover and stop you? I think not." Vanyi was on her feet. She was not a tall woman and not usually imposing, but when she wanted to she could stand as tall as the mountain that guarded Shurakan.

Daruya stayed where she was, sitting at the table, but somehow she was as tall as Vanyi.

They all waited for Vanyi to say something devastating, something that would break Daruya down and trample on the shards. But Vanyi said nothing at all. Simply stared at her, long and long. Then turned her back on her in profound contempt.

The silence was deafening. Lady Nandi thought for a moment, then stood as Vanyi had, and turned her back, too. So did Chakan.

That cut Daruya to the bone: Kimeri heard her gasp of shock. After Chakan, the rest followed. They did not understand Shurakani, but they understood what had been happening, and this was what they thought of it. Even they, who should never have cared to wed their lady to a foreigner.

That left Kimeri and Hani, and Borti by now visible but ignored, and Bundur. Kimeri got up slowly, turned even more slowly. It hurt; it wrenched at the place where the Gate was. But she had to do it.

Behind her she heard her mother's breath catch. "Not you too?"

Bundur did not say anything. He was too much in love to be contemptuous, but he was hurt, hurt enough to want to wound. And he let her see it.

Daruya's anger was like a breath of fire, sudden and whitely hot. "Damn you! Damn you all! I'll do it!"

23

THE WORST BETRAYAL, absolutely the worst of all, was Chakan's. He tried to slip out of Daruya's sight, but she caught him and dragged him with her into the room she was given to dress for her wedding, and shut the door in the face of everyone who tried to follow. She did not notice what kind of room it was, except that it was small, lamplit, and seemed to lead to another, which would be a bath from the scent of warmed water and herbs that came from it.

She backed Chakan against the wall, well aware that he could have escaped if he had put his mind to it. He eyes were not contrite at all; they were laughing as they had not since he came to Shurakan.

"Why?" she demanded of him. "Why you? You were the one who warned me against him!"

"The emperor wants you to marry him," Chakan said.

His laughter, she realized, was as much at himself as at her. "You're not his slave," she snapped.

"I serve him," he said. "And he approves this match."

"Do you?"

"It doesn't matter."

"It matters profoundly."

He looked away, which was not easy as close as they were, eye to blazing golden eye. "You need this marriage to keep you safe. Your grandfather and the Guildmaster approve it. Whatever I may think, you have to marry this man or endanger the embassy."

"I don't matter to you, do I? Except as the heir to the throne you serve."

He would not look at her even then, even at such a blow. His voice was soft, without expression. "I was bred to serve. I can do no other."

"Chakan!"

The pain in her voice rocked him. She saw it. She also saw that his eyes were fixed on the floor beside her foot, and that his face, what she could see of it, was rigid.

She spun away. Her throat was tight, but she had no tears to shed. She never did for the things that truly hurt. "Go," she said.

He did not pause; did not speak. He simply went.

For a little while then she was alone. He did that—damn his hide, he told the others to let her be. She turned slowly. It was a small room indeed, very small, little more than a closet. There was a clothing-stand, and garments spread over it. Her eyes avoided them. Beyond, in a room no larger, was a basin full of water, steaming gently, and all the appurtenances of the bath.

Her anger was gone. It had left with Chakan. She took off what she was wearing, dropped it where it fell, lowered herself into the water. It was hot—almost too hot. She welcomed its nearness to pain.

She was wallowing. She knew that perfectly well. Her grandfather would have taxed her with it if he had been there. Her grandmother, too. Haliya had great compassion, but not for young things who, in her mind, were taking their fits of temper altogether too far.

Of course they were all perfectly right. This marriage would save the embassy, if only for a little while—long enough to find other expedients. It would confuse the faction that had killed the king, and confront it not with a defenseless party of foreigners but with a powerful, indeed royal, house and all its allies and dependents. It was supremely practical and quite devastating.

If she were the proper obedient creature that Chakan was, she would swallow her objections and submit. What difference did it make, after all? She would leave when she wished to leave. She did not have to take her husband with her, or even remember that he existed, except as a convenience, a name of respectability. Lovers would find it an added spice to bed another man's wife.

She sank down till the water lapped her chin. The trouble with all of that cold practicality was quite simple and quite inescapable and quite substantial. Bundur himself. He was not the kind of man one could forget. He had somehow, without her knowing precisely how, crept in under her skin and set up residence there.

No man had ever done this to her before. Those who adored her, worshipped her, fell breathless at her feet, she had always dealt with as gently as she could, and sent toward women who would indulge their follies. Those who had the sense to regard bed-play as the game it was, she took to her bed when she wished, eluded gracefully when she did not. She had never been thrown into such confusion, never so lost her temper with anyone except—god and goddess help her—her grandfather.

"Does that mean I love him?" she asked the ceiling. The ceiling, plain plastered surface, returned no answer. She slid completely beneath the water and stayed there, counting the heartbeats, till she had to breathe or burst.

People were staring at her. Some looked ready to bolt for help. Others—Vanyi foremost—knew her too well to think that she would ever take her life in such ignominious fashion. She stood up in the basin, water sheeting from her, and reached for a drying-cloth. Some of the people staring were servants; they scrambled to serve her.

They were all women, she noticed. Two of them were Bundur's sisters. They tried to pretend that they were not staring at her, how strange she was, the color of pale honey

all over, and curly golden patches under her arms and between her thighs as well as on her head. She was thinner
than they liked to see, lithe like a boy, with training scars
that she had never tried to hide, and a real scar taken in battle: the deep gouge of an arrow in her hip.

"It wouldn't have scarred," she said with careful amiability, "if I'd let the healers at it; but I had to keep riding,
you see, and fighting, and being too brave for belief."

The sisters regarded her without comprehension. She
tried a smile. They did not smile back. They disliked her,
and no wonder. This, soulbound to their beautiful brother.
This, accepting him with the strident opposite of grace,
needing to be dragged kicking and struggling into the arms
of a prince who could have had, willing, any Shurakani
bride he chose.

Daruya could have asked why he had not taken one of
those willing brides, except that she already had, and had
been answered. He wanted her. He had a strong streak of
the contrary in him, too.

"In that," said Vanyi, "the two of you are beautifully
matched."

Daruya's smile was very, very sweet. "Aren't we?"

"Ah, child," Vanyi said sighing. "Times are when I'm
glad your grandfather is as long-lived as he looks to be.
You'll need all those years to grow out of your crotchets."

That stung. Daruya kept her smile, but with an effort.
"Maybe I wasn't meant to inherit."

"You're not that fortunate," Vanyi said. She took the
ivory comb from the hand of the servant who wielded it,
struggling with hair that curled in most unnatural and
lively fashion. She did not make undue effort to be gentle,
but neither was she baffled by all the sudden knots and tangles. She made order out of them as competently as she did
all else, and with dispatch, too.

There was no time for braids. A cap had to do, of deep

blue silk embroidered with golden beads in a pattern much like the Sun in her hand. The garments that went with it were of like color and kind, fashion of her own country for once, but close to what the women wore here. Soft plain shirt of raw silk tucked into loose trousers the color of the sky at evening, but brocaded all over with golden suns. Shoes for her feet, silken slippers such as a lady would wear in her palace, deep blue, golden suns. And over them the coat, blue silk, brocaded suns round the edges, but sleeves and coat proper sewn of panels of silk the color of bronze and copper and gold, and each, again, sun-brocaded. She had not even known that Vanyi carried such a thing in her baggage, or that it would have been cut to Daruya's height and slimness.

She stood up in it while a servant clasped the amber necklace about her neck, and met Vanyi's calm ironic stare. "I had it made today," the Guildmaster said. "It's the same pattern as your riding clothes, more or less. Easy enough for a handful of good needlewomen to manage."

"It's very handsome," Daruya said.

"It suits you," said Vanyi. From her, that was high praise.

It was deep night by the time they all gathered again in the hall with its ancient hangings, in front of the dragon tapestry. There were a great number of them to Daruya's eyes, what with all the embassy that had survived the Gate, and the servants and the women of House Janabundur, but not—to Daruya's faint shock—Bundur.

She knew a moment's wild hope that he had turned coward and fled. But he would hardly do that now, after all he had done to win her. As she took the place she was pushed and prodded to, in front of the rest, Bundur appeared at the inner door. He was wearing the black-and-bronze splendor of the festival. The cut on his cheek had been stitched up neatly and washed clean. His chin was shaven, his mustaches brought to order, oiled and persuaded to hang politely on either side of his mouth. He had not, she noticed, succumbed to any urge to make his hair fashionable. It was sleeked smooth and clubbed at his nape as always, bound with cords of green and glimmering bronze.

He was really quite beautiful in his way, like a big sleek cat. He was not prostrate with nerves that she could see, though he was trembling around the edges of her magery—a trembling to match her own. He smiled as he came toward her and held out his hand. Her own hand had reached to clasp his before her mind came into it at all.

Lady Nandi stood in front of them with an air of solemn ceremony. She spoke words that Daruya did not afterward remember. Nor, she thought, did Bundur. Something about the gods; something about souls and bonds and women and men. Nothing about love, Daruya did notice that. Was it nothing they thought of here? Or did they so take it for granted that they saw no need to name it?

He had both her hands now, or she had his. *Damn,* she thought. *Damn, damn, damn.* But beneath that: *Yes, yes, yes.*

Bundur repeated the words his mother spoke. His mind was not thinking of them. Only of her face, of the golden shining thing that she was, for all her tempers and crotchets and follies.

But you don't know me, she tried to say. *You don't know me at all.*

I know what matters, he said deep inside of her. *I know what you fear.*

Her heart clenched. "What? What—"

"Say after me," Lady Nandi said with considerable patience: " 'Thy soul mine, my soul thine, from life unto life, to the worlds' ending.' "

Life unto life? But—

Bundur's eyes were dark, resting on her, driving sense, logic, even rebellion straight out of her head. She heard her voice speaking, faint and breathless but clear. " 'Thy soul mine, my soul thine, from life unto life, to the worlds' ending.' "

Nothing happened. It was not a spell, not a magery. It described, that was all; told the others what was true, or what they believed to be true. What Daruya believed . . .

No one cared. She had said all that she needed to say. The lady said the rest. Then not the lady. Someone else, a woman whose face Daruya had seen somewhere before, but she did not know where. A narrow face, stern, with eyes that cherished some deep anger and some deeper grief. But the voice was clear, level, deep for a woman's and firm. "I bless you both in the name of all the gods; I grant you the grace of heaven, and such protection as heaven may give. May you prosper and live long, and be reborn as children of the gods."

Daruya came out of her fog abruptly—as abruptly as Bundur had. No one was staring at them any longer, but at the woman in the dark plain cloak with its hood on her shoulders, and garments under it that might have been a servant's. She returned their stares with massive calm. Her hands rose—narrow hands, beautiful as her face was not, with slender elegant fingers—and came to rest on Daruya's head and on Bundur's. She was tall; she did not have to reach far, nor did she struggle to follow as he knelt, drawing Daruya with him whether she would or no. "May the gods protect you," she said, "and honor your marriage."

Bundur's head bowed under her hand, then came up. "I should think they would, now," he said. "Borti. Lady. How in the world—"

"She helped me wake the Gate," Kimeri said from beside the stranger. "*She* listened to me."

"Imp," said Vanyi, with mirth in it. "Oh, imp! Have you been hiding her all this time?"

"Yes," Kimeri said, keeping her chin up and her eyes level, not on Vanyi but on her mother. "She insisted she had to say the blessing. To make it stick."

"It will now," Bundur said. Laughter burst out of him, rich and infectious. "Borti! Thank all the gods. We were sure you were dead."

"I might have been," the woman said. The queen. Daruya read that in the minds around her, the queen's strongest of all. How like Kimeri, she thought, to find and befriend the person in Shurakan whom they needed most, and to produce her in the very nick of time, too, and never a word before then.

The queen said, "I fled, I thought, to distract myself from fear of what would happen—what did happen while I was gone. The gods were guiding me. Or this child of theirs was."

"Does that mean we're kin?" Kimeri asked. "I like that. Mother, can we be Borti's cousins? Avaryan must be her goddess' brother at least. Or maybe he *is* her goddess."

"In the end all gods are one," Daruya said. She rose from her knees, where she should not have been; no queen was equal to the princess-heir of the Sunborn's line. Borti was not indeed much shorter than she. "Lady," said Daruya, inclining her head. "I thank you for your blessing. It was generously given."

"It was my thank-offering for my escape," Borti said. "As little thankful as I feel now—I live, and that, I'm sure, no one expected. Nephew, half-sister, you have full freedom to cast me out. The king they've raised in the palace will be bringing in his sister to claim my place and my office; she'll want my life if she can get it, and the life of anyone who shelters me."

"I don't think so," Bundur said. "They were going to crown Shagyan, which would have brought in Mandi, but he developed a backbone when they murdered the king. They hacked it, and him, in two. Paltai took the crown from the king's hand and set it on his head before anyone else could move."

"And Paltai," said Borti, "has no sister." Her eyes closed; she drew a breath. "Goddess! And we thought his family cursed by heaven, because it begot only sons."

"Heaven curses the king who rules alone," said the Lady Nandi. "That was ill done, to let him take the crown and keep it."

"Not for us," said Bundur. "Not for many who may accept a deed done before they could prevent it, but who may be inclined to support us if we challenge it."

"Dare we challenge?" Lady Nandi demanded.

"Dare we not?" he shot back.

"I think," said Vanyi, "that this needs a council of war, and sustenance to help it along. Here's the wedding feast spread, and it looks splendid considering how hastily it was cobbled together. Shall we eat it while we talk?"

Everyone looked startled, but no one quarreled with her eminent good sense—Daruya least of all. The queen's presence here changed everything. It was no longer only a wedding in haste, an expedient adopted to save the lives of a mere foreign embassy. Now they were honestly at war with the faction in the palace.

And in war, even weddings could lose themselves to necessity.

They sat to a feast that, with Brightmoon setting and Greatmoon hanging low and dawn paling the eastern sky, could well do duty for an early breakfast. Hasty it might have been, but there was plenty of it, too much for most until they discovered a quite unexpected hunger. Even the Olenyai partook of it, as awkward as that could be for people whose honor forbade them to unveil before strangers.

For a while no one spoke except to call for another basket of bread, or to ask a neighbor to pass the wine. Borti ate, too, as they all did, reluctantly at first and then as if she were starving. No one stared, or waited on her with slavish adoration, or treated her otherwise than as a kinswoman of rank. Daruya might have expected more servility, as rigorously as these people had kept their rulers from the taint of foreign eyes, but the ruler in her own person stood no more on ceremony than Daruya herself did.

It was well, Daruya thought, filling a fold of bread with spiced meats and cheese and handing it to Borti while she prepared another for herself. She could almost ignore the man on her other side in considering this stranger who was a queen. A ruler who kept to the strictures of old Asanian royalty, or who believed too much in her own divinity, might be difficult to deal with. This plain sensible woman with her solid appetite and clear affection for Kimeri was much to Daruya's liking—and would be to Estarion's too, Daruya suspected.

Gods. She was thinking of what Estarion would like, and not sulking over it. Had she grown up so much? Or had she merely replaced Estarion-as-adversary with Bundur? Her husband, they were all thinking when their eyes fell on the two of them. Her protector from the king's murderers.

It made her ill to read such thoughts. She flung up her shields and rested in the quiet behind them, listening to voices that were only voices, watching faces that showed little of the minds behind.

"So then," said Vanyi, taking the lead as she always seemed to do, "we're best advised to wait, you think."

"Yes," said Lady Nandi. "Now that you have the protection of our name and kinship, no one from the palace will move directly against you, since that is also against us."

"And in any case," Bundur said, "the fighting isn't likely to get this far. Palace coups here always restrict themselves politely to the palace."

"Then I didn't need to marry you at all," Daruya burst out. "We could simply have come here and been safe."

"No," he said. "You would have been pursued—maybe not at once, but soon enough. Now that you are part of House Janabundur, that changes things. That gives you power in the kingdom; it equips you with allies and defenses, to all of which you're entitled, since as my wife you rule this house and everyone in it."

"I do not," Daruya said. "Nor would I displace the lady whose house it is."

"But that is the way of the world," Lady Nandi said. "If you wish me to continue, but in your name, then that's well, and sensible of you, too. But you rule. You are House Janabundur, as is your husband."

"You do see," Bundur said. "Don't you? Before, you were an outlander, nothing and no one, no matter what power you might hold in your own country. Now you hold the power of the second house in Su-Shaklan."

"You'll pardon me if I don't let it go to my head," Daruya said.

"I'd never forgive you if you did," he said. He was grinning at her again. His white teeth and his bright dark eyes could make her knees buckle. Damn them. Damn him.

"I see," said Borti beside her, "that these two are indeed soulbound. It's an old binding, and strong. I've never seen a stronger."

"Nor I," said Lady Nandi with the same air of resignation with which she had confirmed Daruya's sudden new rank. "And she fights it, which only adds to its strength."

"No." It escaped before Daruya could stop it. She bit her tongue before it betrayed her further.

"Unfortunately, yes," Vanyi said. "As far as I can tell, and mind you I've never thought of matings in quite this way, your kind of resistance simply encourages it."

"Then if I give in, it will go away?"

"It doesn't work like that," Vanyi said.

Daruya had thought not. She finished rolling meat and

cheese in bread, and bit into it. Her hunger did not care if
she was angry or happy or a mad mingling of both.

"So we wait," said Vanyi, taking up where they had left
off. "And see what the palace does."

"And watch, and keep Borti hidden," Bundur said.
"That, we have to do, I think. They'll be hunting her for a
goodly while, and wanting her dead."

"Luckily," said Borti, "very few people have any idea
what I really look like. They only ever see me in court, when
I'm robed to immobility and weighted with wig and crown,
and painted to look like a mask of the goddess. Who would
know a tall plain woman in a servant's coat, doing servant's
duties in Janabundur?"

"You can't do that," Bundur said, shocked.

She laughed at him. For a moment they looked very
much alike. "Of course I can! I do it more often than anyone
would want to know. It's a convenient way to learn what
people are saying, and it gives me something to do. It's mas-
sively dull on the throne and behind the screens that are
supposed to protect me from common eyes, with ministers
speaking for me, and making all my decisions, too."

"Not all of them," Vanyi said, "I don't think. If you
speak, you're listened to. When it suits you to speak."

"When I'm given knowledge enough to speak." Borti
sighed. "When I stop to think—now I have leisure for it—I
realize that we used to see much more of our common sub-
jects. We've been closed in, walled about, cut off. Cleverly
too, and imperceptibly, till it was too late for my brother
and almost for me."

"It was a common expedient once in our Golden Empire," Daruya said, "when a man wished to be emperor, to
do just as your traitors did, and cut off the emperor who
was, and destroy him."

"But not any longer?" asked Borti.

"The Golden Empire is gone," Daruya said. "I'm all

that's left of it, I and my daughter. Now we have assassins, though not of late, and the occasional rebellion. Our rulers walk out where anyone can see, and everyone knows their faces."

"That was true here, once," said Borti. She looked suddenly exhausted, hollow-eyed and pale under the bronze sheen of her skin. "I shall sleep, I think. Then think again, and consider what to do."

"So should we all," Lady Nandi said, rising. Her glance at Bundur was bright, suddenly, and full of mirth that echoed his own. "With possible exceptions."

No, thought Daruya. But her mouth was full of spiced meat and festival wine, and Bundur was pulling her to her feet, and the Shurakani were singing, out of nowhere and none too tunefully, what must be a wedding song. The sun was coming up—it was morning. How could there be a wedding night?

Bundur swung her up in his arms, swept her clean off her feet. He was laughing. They all were. Except Daruya, who was rigid with shock and resistance; too rigid to fight. Even when he carried her away, and no one followed, not one. Not even an Olenyas.

24

BUNDUR SET DARUYA on her feet. She was still stiff, still furious, but all too wide awake to the absurdity of resistance. Awake too to where she was. A room with tapestried walls, a broad hearth swept clean, a low table, cushions, and a curtained alcove. Behind the alcove was the bed.

He did not drag her to it. Once she was steady on her feet, he went to the hanging that bled light, and slid it aside from a window. Sun, topping the Worldwall, washed him in brightness. He stretched, yawned, pulled the cords out of his hair and shook it down. He turned, smiling.

God and goddess, Daruya thought. She was terrified—panicked. Her eyes darted without her willing it, looking for escape. The door was barred. Another door—a bath? Another portion of the suite?

She could not move at all. He wandered to the table where things were set for tea, including a little brazier and a copper pot full of water, singing as it came to the boil. He folded his legs under him and made tea, his big hands deft with the delicate pots, the bronze spoon, the dried leaves of the herbs and the pinch of flowers.

"The trouble," she said, out of nowhere in particular, "is that I can't—let—myself love a man. Not without fighting with him endlessly, trying to make him hate me and leave me, or at least let me be. It's so much easier to choose lovers as one chooses one's dress for the day, for its color or its style or its suitability to the weather. And come nightfall, one can take it off and forget it, and put on another."

He was listening, but not discomfiting her with his stare.

He lidded the teapot and set hands on knees and waited while the herbs and flowers steeped. Their fragrance wafted toward Daruya in a breeze from the window: sweet and pungent, with a faint green undertone.

"I've never felt this way before." She could not stop talking, filling the awful silence with a babble of words. "I've never wanted to be near anyone all the time—thought of him when he's not there—remembered his hands when I should be thinking about something else altogether. I'm losing myself. I don't want that. I hate it."

"Time makes it easier," he said.

"You know that?"

He raised his head and looked at her. His eyes were too bright to bear. "Not . . . from personal experience. I'm still rather lost myself. But I've been assured on excellent authority, one does grow accustomed; one learns to keep the self and the other, both, without losing either."

"You can't feel that for me. I'm all edges. I make a great deal of noise. I wound your pride with every word I speak."

"But not with every word you think," he said, "or every glance you turn on me. Fear makes you say all those words that wound."

"I wish," she said tightly, "that you would lose your temper. Just once. And stop being so bloody understanding. It makes me sick."

"Am I too much like your grandfather?"

She leaped. He caught her. He was stronger than she, and he had skills she had not expected. She could not fling him down and pummel him. "Who told you?" she gasped. "Who told you that?"

"The Lady Vanyi," he answered. "She says I well ought to drive you wild: I'm too damnably like him. But steadier, she says. I don't think she means it as a compliment."

"She's been desperately and hopelessly and unrequitedly in love with him for forty years," said Daruya.

"Not unrequited," he said. "Not the way she tells it. Though I suppose I'd have to ask him for his side of it. They do best as they are, that's all."

"Then can't we?"

He laughed. "Oh, you are clever! No, we can't. Do you want to? Really? In your heart?"

"In my heart," she said, "I want to be a child again, and never to have heard of what's between men and women at all. I'm afraid of you. Every time I look at you I feel as if I want to drown."

"Oh, that's only love," he said. It came out light, but she could sense the weight of fear beneath. He, too. He was afraid. Of her; of what she did to him, so close, with those hot-gold eyes of hers, and all that outrageous hair.

It was happening again. She was blurring into him. She wrenched away, body and soul, and backed against the wall. "I can't do it," she said. "There's no maiden-blood to show here, not with my daughter for proof that it's long since shed. Can't we just . . . not, and pretend we did? Aren't the words and the blessing enough, and the name of wife that the queen gave me?"

"Do you want it to be?"

"I want," she said. "I want—I don't—"

Oh, damn her traitor feet. They were taking her straight back to him, and her hands were seizing him, pulling him to her. They were exactly of a height. But he was much broader. She measured the span of his shoulders. He smelled of spices, of the herb they liked to sprinkle in the bath, of wine and tea-herbs and flowers. And under it, subtle but distinct, musk and maleness. It was different, a little, from other men she knew. Foreign. Sweeter, less sharply pungent. Or was that because he fit so well?

Horribly well. The skin of his face looked faintly weathered but felt smooth, molded tight to the proud bones. His eyes were shut—narrow eyes, but long, the lids folded as a plainsman's often were, so that they seemed to tilt upward. Open, they would be dark, almost black.

He was breathing shallowly. Breath that caught as she ran a finger down the line of his mustache, tugging it gently. His hands were fists at his sides. Every muscle in his body was bent on not seizing her as she had seized him; on not sending her back into panic flight.

"Too late for that," she said. "I did it already."

His eyes snapped open. "You can read my mind."

"I thought you knew." Fear, elation: she was a mage, he was sure of it now, he would thrust her away, shun her in horror of what she could do.

He did none of that. He shivered, yes, but he raised his hands, took her face between them, met her eyes. His thought-speech was clumsy but astonishingly clear in a man without training in magery. *I love you.*

It echoed down to the bottom of him, truth within truth within truth.

"You know nothing of me," she said. "How can you love what you don't know?"

"I know what the soul knows." Aloud, that, because she spoke aloud. "We believe that souls are eternal, but bodies come and go; souls are born and reborn, over and over, on the wheel of the gods."

"That is horrible."

"Beautiful," he said. "We were lovers before, but perhaps I treated you badly; perhaps you loved me too much, and cost us both that turn of the wheel. Now you flee and I pursue. But it's all one, do you see? We were bound before the wheel began, and will be again, until the wheel is gone."

"When I die," she said in a voice that tried not to shake, "I want to lie on the breast of Mother Night, in the god's peace, and never wake."

"But of course you want that—but only for a while. After night is dawn again. You'll be up and doing, loving and being loved, casting your bright soul on the wheel where it serves best. You're never one to be content with simply being."

"That's too easy," she said. "Too simple a wisdom. You prattle it like a child its lessons. I'd rather a round of honest bedplay, and a goodbye after, without the facile philosophy."

"It is not facile." Ah, at last: she had goaded his temper. But too briefly. He calmed himself again, and that was not easy with his banner flying as high as it was, urging him to seize her and rape her where she stood. "You don't understand. I can't expect you to. You're an outland woman who follows outland gods."

"Now you're talking down to me. Stop it."

He stiffened. "You *are*. Is the truth such an insult?"

"When you put it that way, it is."

"I don't know how to talk to you," he said. "All I know how to do is love you."

"I'd rather you talked more and loved less."

He saw the lie in her eyes. It brought his smile back, his wicked, innocent, brilliant smile. "You do love me," he said as if he had just discovered it. "You do. You did from the first. Didn't you?"

"Of course not!"

But he was exploring her face as she had explored his, with delicate fingers, tracing the arch of her brows, the shape of her eyes, so round and so shallow-set beside his, the curve of her cheekbone, the fullness of her lip. There was nothing in the world but that touch, so light it barely brushed her skin, so hot it burned.

"Honey," he murmured, "and gold. Why, you are beautiful."

He was surprised. She hated him for it, or tried. She was blurring into him again, feeling his wonder, his delight in her strangeness, in discovering beauty where he had never thought to find it.

"The Spear of Heaven in the morning, all fierce and

burning gold," he said. "The she-tiger in the wood, snarling defiance at the hunter. But a tall lily, too, in a queen's garden, soft as silk, soft as sleep."

"Poets have made love to me before," she said—gasping it, with none of the edge of viciousness that she had intended.

"I'm no poet," he said. "I'm telling you what I see. I didn't marry beauty. I married my soul's self. But to find it—oh, that's wonderful." He paused. "I suppose I'm quite ugly to you."

"Why, you're as vain as I am," she said. "Of course you're not ugly. You're not pretty, but then I never cared much for pretty men, even when I chose one to father my daughter. I like a solid man with substance to him, good bone, a bright eye—"

"Like one of your seneldi?"

She had flattened his poetry into plain practicality, but he had turned it to laughter. "—a thick mane," she carried it on, "long and glossy, and a fine slope of shoulder, a strong back, good haunches, a straight leg and a sturdy foot . . . "

"But I have no horns," he said as if he lamented it, "and my tail is not even a nubbin. I'll never make a stallion."

God and goddess help her, he had her giggling. And finding fastenings, and discovering that there was not much to his clothes, but enough if one were in a hurry to get him out of them. The coat fell easily. The shirt had buttons, which needed wrestling with. The trousers were held up by a belt, and a cord under that. He did not wear trews.

He was a goodly stallion. But—

"They scarred you! Who cut—who—"

He gaped. Stared, as if she had found some mutilation that he had never known he had.

Understanding dawned. He went scarlet under the bronze of his skin, from the peak of black hair on his forehead all the way down to his breastbone. "It's . . . something we have done to us when we're newborn. They consecrate us to the gods. It's only the foreskin. The rest of me is quite as it was made, and quite able to—to—"

Quite willing, too. And not so odd, maybe. Barbaric, but not ugly, not really. To cut a man *there*, even if he were too young to know what was being done to him . . .

"I *am* ugly to you," he said, wilting as he spoke, all over.

"No," she said. "Damn it, no." She got out of her clothes, not being too careful of fastenings, to set them level and give him something else to think about.

It succeeded; that much she could say for it. He had modesty like an Asanian, a body-shyness that she had never had; her grandfather had seen to that, brought her up with and around northerners who went naked as often as they went clothed. It had not kept Bundur from letting her undress him, but it did strange things to his composure to be seeing her as naked as he was, and so different.

The women had seen how tall and narrow and boyish she was. He saw as he had seen in the garden not so very long ago, that she was a woman; slender certainly but full-breasted enough, breasts that were still round and high and firm though she had suckled a child. Her skin was finer than he was used to, its texture softer, but the golden down on it was strange to him—he had little even between his thighs, was all smooth bronze. What he would have made of a true northerner, and a male at that, she could not imagine. Some of them were pelted like bears, with beards to their breasts.

"Am I ugly to you now?" she asked him.

"No," he said. "Oh, no."

"Nor are you to me." She took his shaft in her hand, warm heavy solid thing, coming alive to her touch. Beautiful, even so altered. As all of him was. As it had always been—yes, since first she saw him, sitting at a table in the teahouse, daring her to flay him with her tongue.

She could cut him to the bone now if she said but a word. Or two. Or three. She knew exactly which words they would be. And she said none of them.

He had skill. She had not expected otherwise. When she moved toward him he was there. There was a moment of hesitation; awkwardness, not-fitting. Then, as each found the rhythm of the dance, each fit to each, matched—

"Like riding a senel," he said. His voice was deep, full of laughter even in the midst of loving.

She locked legs about his haunches and drove him to a gallop: then back, slow and slow, grinning to match his grin.

Beautiful, his mind said. *So beautiful when you smile.*

"So ugly when I scowl?"

He laughed, outside and in. *Always beautiful. Always. And well you know it, too.*

"Then we are matched," she said. "Perfectly."

Haven't I always said so?

"Insufferable," she said. "Intolerable. Beloved."

URUAN THE GUARDIAN slept straight through the night and the day and the next night. When he woke with a raging thirst and a desperate lunge toward the privy, Kimeri was there. She helped him as she could, with him too caught up in his body's needs to be amazed that the golden power of his dream was a child, and a very young one at that, even if she was the Sunlady's heir.

Vanyi he knew better, and greeted with a recollection of his princely manners, though he nearly fell on his face trying to bow to her. She got him back into bed and saw him fed rich broth and strong tea, and answered the questions that babbled out of him. She was afraid that his mind had got scrambled in his long imprisonment, but Kimeri had no such fear. He was only weak, and having trouble understanding that he had been inside the Gate for more than a full cycle of Greatmoon—forty-nine days altogether, since he insisted on counting.

"It was no time at all," he kept insisting, "but it was an eon and then another. *She* was there," he said, tilting his chin at Kimeri. "She was the only light in that dark place."

Kimeri wanted to duck her head, embarrassed, but what he said was true, mostly. "That was the god who's in my blood. He kept making me dream about you."

"And so kept me alive and bound to the Gate." He could have been blaming her for it, but there was the beginning of a smile on his face, and in his eyes that had seen too much nothingness. He focused them on Vanyi, frowning. "What are you doing here? I was trying to get through before the Gate broke, to tell you not to come; it was getting too dangerous. The palace—"

"The palace was perfectly quiet when we arrived," she said, "but last night they killed the king and set up another."

He sat up, though his face went green and he reeled, trying to get to his feet. "Then where are we? We're not in the house of the Gate. I can feel it—it's somewhere else. Are we in prison? Has the faction that favors us won after all? They were all to be killed or silenced."

"We're in House Janabundur," said Vanyi, "and safe, for now. Stop trying to get up and gallop off."

"Janabundur? But that's—" Uruan went perfectly green but not unconscious, and folded up. The Olenyas on guard scooped him back into bed and laid a sheathed sword, very gently, across his chest.

He understood the message. His lips quirked wryly. "All right. I'll stay put. But, Vanyi, Janabundur is the king's—the old king's—clan-house. Not that its lord isn't disposed to be friendly; he is, and he's honest in it, but there would be better places to hide in plain sight."

"I don't think so," Vanyi said. "His lordship offered for the princess-heir and won her, with the emperor's consent, too. They married after we brought you here. Marriage in this place, it seems, can make a native out of a foreigner, and a power out of a nobody, and a proper noble lady out of a mage."

"The princess-heir? *Daruya?* Married to—" Uruan started to shake. It looked like convulsions. It was laughter.

Vanyi waited it out with more patience than she had ever shown Kimeri. Kimeri herself sat on the bed and tucked up her feet and watched him till he stopped giggling and wiped the tears away. "Really? Lord Shakabundur *married* her? She didn't throttle him for his presumption?"

"Really," said Kimeri. "She only tried to strangle somebody once. He was pushing her when she didn't want him to, and trying to get him to kiss her. Great-Grandfather said she should have gutted him instead." Since he could hardly argue with that, and did not seem inclined to, she went on, "She likes Bundur. She makes a great deal of noise pretending she doesn't, but that's because she's afraid. She's not used to liking men who want to marry her."

"Let alone marrying them." Uruan cradled his head in his hands, after assuring the Olenyas that that was all he wanted to do. The sword retreated but stayed within reach, poised to stop him if he tried to get up again. "God. Goddess. I gather the Gate's not passable?"

"It, and the whole chain of Gates from here to Starios," Vanyi said. "We had to walk in from Kianat, with a broken Gate behind us. Something here began it, but we've found nothing, except you."

"One redheaded fool trapped in a Gate." He closed his eyes, but he was not asleep. His mind was wide awake and very keen. Kimeri helped with that. The Gate inside her made it easy to run a thread of feeling-better through him, and keep it running till he had all he needed. He did not know what was happening, though if he had asked she would have answered. He thought it was something Vanyi was doing. "I'll do what I can," he said. "You can use another mage, yes? And I know people here. Some of those who were favorable to us might still be; and if Lord Shakabundur is with us, we're stronger than we've ever been."

"You're running no errands tonight," said Vanyi sternly. "Believe me, when I need you I'll use you. Until then, you'll rest and eat and make yourself strong."

He looked for a moment as rebellious as Daruya could ever be, but he was older, and better trained. He lowered his eyes and said, "Yes, Guildmaster."

* * *

Daruya woke toward sunset with every memory intact, Bundur beside her and a scowl on her face. He smiled back. "Good evening, madam," he said. "Are you always so cross when you wake?"

She snarled and went to the garderobe that was past the bath, and stopped to plunge her head into cold water in the basin, and came back a little brighter of eye. He sat up in bed, raking fingers through his thick straight hair.

She hunted, found a comb. He sat still while she plied it, finding it much easier to make order of hair so thick when it was straight and not curling everywhere at once. It was waist-long, cut level—if it had never been cut, she thought, it might have been as long as he was. Combing it was like combing silk, or a senel's mane.

When it was smooth she plaited it in a single braid as if he had been a priest. He did not protest, though she had never seen a man with a braid here. He liked the feel of it, less clumsy than a knot at the nape, more easily managed than a long tail bound with a bit of leather or ribbon.

Then he wanted to comb her hair, for which she pitied him. Each knot untangled only bred a new one. But he insisted, and it gave him pleasure, like playing in gold. "Do women cut their hair short in your country?" he asked. "Your Guildmaster and the woman with her wear the long braid, I notice. Your men, too, those whose hair I can see."

"Royalty never cut their hair at all," Daruya said, "nor priests once they take up their office. I was sick of knots and tangles and hours with combs and brushes. I hacked it off when Kimeri was born."

His brows lifted. "All of it?"

"Right to the skull," she said with remembered satisfaction. "It was wonderful. Cool; light; simple to keep clean. Everyone howled."

He took a curl in thumb and forefinger and stretched it straight. Left to itself it fell just below her shoulders.

Straightened, it was halfway to her waist. "Why did you let it grow again?"

"Laziness," she said. "Contrariness. I discovered I'd started a fashion; half the young idiots in the court were going about with heads cropped or even shaved bald, as if I'd ever intended to go that far. I think I'll be glad when it's long enough to make a decent braid. It gets in the way as it is."

"I can imagine," he said. "I remember when I came out of the temple to inherit Janabundur, how I regretted the simplicity of a bare skull. But I was glad, in the end, to leave that behind. It gets beastly cold in the winter."

Daruya tried to see him in a priest's robe, shaved clean. He would have been much younger; awkward, all angles, with big hands and feet, and a blade of a nose.

Charming, rather. She leaned back against him, because he was warm and solid and it seemed like something she should do. His arms settled about her. He nuzzled her hair. They did not kiss here; she remembered how odd she had thought it, but how little she had been moved to teach him the art. There had not seemed to be any need of it.

She was comfortable. That alarmed her, but not enough to move. Comfort had never been anything she expected to have with a man. Arguments, yes. Resistance. His will striving to bend hers. Not this calm accommodation, or this conviction that she would do what he wanted, because she too wanted it.

He had much to learn of what she was. But not now. Not . . . quite . . . yet.

Tradition in the empire would have given a newly wedded pair three days of solitary lovemaking. In Shurakan they were given two full hands of days, and kept strictly apart, too, which as Bundur pointed out, favored the cause of protecting Daruya and her companions from enemies in the palace.

"Unless of course they find Borti," he said. Seclusion did not prevent the family from communicating with bride and bridegroom; they could speak, even eat together, as they were doing, the third morning after the wedding.

Borti looked up from slicing a scarlet fruit and feeding bits to Kimeri and Hani. Her face was blandly innocent, her accent slightly but distinctly countrified. "Why, and what would the great ones want with a children's nurse?"

"Not, I hope, what they'd want with a queen," Daruya said. If anyone had expected marriage to smooth her edges, he was disappointed. She was still Daruya; still all prickles and sharp words, and she did not spare Bundur any more than the rest. But something was different. Some tension eased, and not only that of a woman who needed a man for her bed; some resistance softened. As if, thought Vanyi, she had stopped fighting the inevitable and faced the fact that she was a woman, and royal born at that.

It was a young change yet, and might not hold. But Vanyi decided to let it hearten her. Estarion would be gratified; he had hoped for such a result.

They did match well. The awkwardness of new lovers was missing, the fumbling, the distraction, the obsession with one another. The bond between them ran deeper than that. Daruya had been fighting it since she came to Shurakan; had fought it maybe lifelong, as if her soul knew where the other half of it was, but the rest of her had refused to listen.

She was still fighting, but not against that. She would always fight; that was in her blood. Now maybe she would choose more useful causes.

As Vanyi reached for the pot to refill her cup of tea, one of the servants glided in and bent toward her. "Lady, one asks for you. Are you at home to him?"

"Who is he?" Daruya, stretching her ears and making no effort to pretend otherwise.

"Lady," said the servant with a deeper bow than he had accorded Vanyi, "it is one from the palace, a man who comes quietly but walks with the gait of rank."

"The Minister of Protocol," said Daruya. She half-rose. "Should I—"

"I'll see him," Vanyi said. And at Daruya's frown: "You're in seclusion, remember. It suits us to keep you that way."

Daruya sat down again. It was not acquiescence. Bundur, Vanyi noticed, kept out of it. Wise man.

"Yes," Vanyi said as if Daruya had spoken. "As long as we can use the marriage-days as a shield against intruders, we gain time to think our way out."

"Little enough of that we've done so far," said Daruya.

"You think so?" Vanyi asked. "I'd say we were doing well. We're keeping Borti hidden, we've got Uruan back up to strength, and we have watchers in the house of the Gate in case someone comes there, thinking it deserted, and tries something. Now we have a visitor from the palace."

"Who, I hope, simply wants to exchange pleasantries with you, and not arrest you for high treason." Daruya gestured to the Olenyas who hovered nearest. "Chakan. Go with her."

Chakan bowed, scrupulously correct as he had been since his quarrel with his lady. That would take some smoothing over, thought Vanyi; but it was not her place to say so.

She could easily imagine what Daruya would say to that: When, pray tell, had Vanyi ever cared whether it was or was not her place to say whatever she had a mind to? But Vanyi could take refuge in proprieties when they served her purpose, or when it was simply practical.

The Minister of Protocol waited in an antechamber with

tea and cakes and carefully schooled patience. He was not accustomed, clearly, to wait on the convenience of others.

Vanyi found his presence and his continued good health interesting. Palace coups in Shurakan, she had been assured, were civilized; no one died except by strict necessity, and those who could continue to serve, did so. It reminded her in a way of the Olenyai and their honor, which was sworn to the throne and not to the one who sat in it.

She did not have to like it or him. She spoke abruptly, without greeting. "What do you want?"

He blinked at her discourtesy, but answered as he could. "You must understand, lady, that while I am utterly orthodox in my convictions, I am not in sympathy with those who would destroy all that even hints of magic."

"Is that what's happening in the palace?"

"It is what is going to happen soon. The new king has ordered the palace to his satisfaction. His followers are free to pursue the purposes for which they raised him to the throne."

"And those are?"

"To drive out all foreigners. To destroy all taint of magic in Su-Shaklan."

Vanyi considered that. It was nothing surprising, nothing unexpected. But to hear it spoken so baldly by this of all men—that brought it home, and forcefully. "How far are they thinking to go?"

"Far," he said. His hands, raising the cup to sip cooling tea, were not quite steady. "They seek even to suppress some of the odder cults and priesthoods among our own people: the exorcists, the spirit-speakers, the counters of the dead, even some of the oracles and prophets and the holy ones of the heights. All those, they say, are workers of magic."

"Some of them probably are," Vanyi observed.

"Only in the broadest sense," he said. "Too broad, in my mind. I mislike what it may lead to."

"Indeed," Vanyi said. "Broad interpretations can become very broad, until they include anyone whom one doesn't love, and any doctrine that one disapproves of."

The Minister of Protocol bobbed his head: Shurakani agreement. "Yes. Yes, that is what I see. Already they make lists, name names, reckon up their enemies and their unfriends."

"Are you telling me," Vanyi asked, "that I should get my people out before the whole palace falls on us with fire and sword?"

"No, lady," said the Minister of Protocol. "That would destroy you certainly. The guards of the borders have been instructed to slay you if they see you. In the city you are safe; in this house you are protected still by the name of Janabundur. No one yet is willing to challenge it or those who hold it."

"But for how long?"

"Lady, I do not know." A mighty admission, and a great abdication of pride. "I know only that you, through your kinswoman, are now of Janabundur, and Janabundur has great influence among those who might wish to avert what comes."

"The lord of the house is in seclusion," Vanyi said, "till the days of his wedding are over."

"His lady mother is not. And his sisters. Nor are you yourself."

Vanyi poured tea, to give her hands something to do while she pondered. His mind was as readable as ever—to the same point as ever, neither deep nor shallow, but beneath was a darkness she could not penetrate.

Did he know that the queen was here? His thoughts were innocent of such knowledge. They saw much amiss in the kingdom, a king whom he reckoned more puppet than ruler, weak and vain, and puppetmasters without let or scruple. They would trample the ancient orders and courtesies in the name of the gods and the ban against magic.

She held great weapons, she thought, sipping tea that she barely tasted. The queen. House Janabundur. Her own magery, and the power of all her mages. The Olenyai, warriors in a mode that was unknown here. Even Gates, if she could open them again.

But the palace ruled Shurakan. Its armed men might not be equal, man for man, to any Olenyas, but there were hundreds of them to her nine bred-warriors. Its power might—must—encompass a force that could break Gates.

Yes. It must. She had no proof, no certainty, but her bones knew. Whatever had broken Gates, its wielders had slain the old king and given the crown to one of its own.

The Minister of Protocol waited, silent, for her to finish pondering. She spoke abruptly; he started. "I'll speak to the Lady Nandi. More than that I can't promise."

"It will help," he said. "Not all of us in the palace are bound to the new lords. Those of us who can will assist you. Come or send to us discreetly, in my name. I will come at once, or my messenger if I am detained."

"What do you want?" Vanyi demanded of him. "The new king killed, his followers likewise? Yet another new order?"

"Lady," he said. "Lady, he who is king is king. But he should not permit his people to indulge in excess."

"Ah," said Vanyi. "You want us to sweep the rags and the gutter-leavings out of your palace. What do we gain in return?"

"You will not be hunted," he said, "nor expelled. And the haters of what you are will be constrained as before by the bounds of law and custom."

"That's not enough," she said. "Give us freedom of the kingdom—swear that we'll not be made prey to the hatred of the ignorant. Or," she added, catching his eye, "of those who fancy themselves wise. Allow us full status as ambassadors, with full respect and full privileges."

"If you succeed," he said, "that will be inevitable."

"Swear to it."

"By the gods and the goddess, and by the children of heaven," he said without hesitation. "Set us free of those who would run to mad extremes, and you will be accorded the rank and respect of friends. You are already possessed of privilege, as the kin of Janabundur."

Vanyi inclined her head. "We're allies, then. I'll send to you when I've spoken to Lady Nandi."

26

LADY NANDI WAS carding wool as women did here, with her daughters for company, and Borti with a spindle, spinning thread out of the wool. They made Vanyi think, with unexpected poignancy, of women in a fishermen's hut on Seiun isle, waiting for the men to come back from the boats.

Odd to think that these were royal ladies, and one a queen. Queens in the empire did not spin or weave. They led councils and commanded armies, and held regencies when they did not rule in their own right. If they indulged in any stolen leisure, they rode seneldi and hawked or hunted; embroidered tapestries, or made music, or read from books. Weaving was a guild and a craft, and not the province of a princess.

Here the women of the house, even if they were of high rank, spun and wove and sewed, and dressed their kin and servants in their looms' weaving. They did not weave rugs or embroider tapestries. That was an art, and practiced in the temples, which seemed here to do duty for guilds.

Vanyi could remember how to spin, if she thought about it. She had not done it in years out of count. She had never threaded a loom; that had been her mother's task, while her mother lived. After she died, Vanyi had turned rebel and sought the sun-god's temple and become a priestess. Novices of Avaryan's priesthood did what they were bidden to do; Vanyi's tasks had been the planting and harvesting of vegetables for the pot, and the mending of nets, and long hours of study in the arts of magecraft, for that was and had always been her great gift.

She sat on the stool that was nearest, while the women carded and spun. Sun slanted through tall windows, warming the room, making stronger the heavy scent of wool. Someone had begun to thread the loom, but stopped halfway; the threads were a deep crimson, nearly black unless the sun shone on it. The wool that Borti spun was dyed a soft green. Vanyi wondered if the two colors were meant to be woven together. It did not seem likely, but with weavers one never knew.

It was peaceful here, even with her presence to make the servants uneasy. The high ones were placid, unruffled, their hands deft in their tasks. Borti spun a fine thread, Vanyi noticed, of even thickness; yet she seemed hardly to be aware of what her hands were doing. Her eyes were on the windows, her gaze full of sunlight, but under the brightness the shadow ran deep.

She grieved for her brother and lover, her king who was dead. They had not agreed on policy, they had quarreled often, but Vanyi knew how little that could matter between two who were friends and lovers both. She withdrew delicately from the other's thoughts, save for the flicker of emotions across the surface. "The Minister of Protocol wants an alliance," she said.

The servants lowered their heads and made themselves invisible. Lady Nandi said, "I thought he might."

"Have you spoken with him?" Vanyi asked, a little sharply perhaps.

"I know him," Lady Nandi said. "He would hardly approve of all that the new king's counselors are doing. Does he wish us to appear in the court and listen to what people are saying there?"

"Would you want to do that?"

"I had thought of it," Lady Nandi said. "It might not be excessively wise after what was done to my brother—and no one has come to me, who am, in their knowledge, his only living kin, to offer me the death-scroll and bid me fetch his body."

"You might," said Borti quietly, "go to the palace as one who has the right, and ask for those things. They won't harm you, I don't think. There's another thing these hot-heads, most of whom are young, hold as truth revealed: that women are weak and must be indulged and protected."

"And I am old," said Lady Nandi, "and the old are weakest of all."

Surely, thought Vanyi. The lady was little smaller than her son, and he was a big man, rock-solid and built to last. But a young male, blinded by grey hair and a lined face, might be persuaded to see frailty where there was none. Vanyi would exploit it herself if she had the chance; though Nandi would do better in this, there was no denying.

Lady Nandi had no magery to read Vanyi's thoughts, but her wits were quick. She smiled at Vanyi. It was a wicked smile, much younger than the face it shone on; she had been a hoyden in her youth, or Vanyi was no judge of women. It might not be so surprising after all that the woman had let her beloved and only son take a wife as wild as Daruya.

"I think," Lady Nandi said, "that I may be driven to stumble to the palace on my ancient feet and beg weeping for my brother's remains. My daughters will follow, of course, with loosened hair and distraught faces. And servants with a bier."

"Pity is a powerful ally," Borti observed. "Our brother would laugh. He did love a scene well played."

Nandi bobbed her head. "Oh, he did indeed. Will you come? A servant's coat, a properly humble bearing . . . no one will know you."

"No," said Borti. Her voice was harsh; she softened it with a perceptible effort. "No, it's too chancy. If even one servant recognizes me, I've lost us everything."

"I would trust you not to be indiscreet," Nandi said.

Borti's hands faltered in their spinning. Her face was calm, even cold. "I thank you. Trust is no easy thing to earn. But I won't risk it. When you bring him back, with all such news as you can gather, and goodwill in the court, too, I'll perform the rites with you. If, of course, you permit."

"I permit it," said Nandi with formal precision. "I wish it."

"Make them pity you greatly," Borti said. "Win their hearts for us."

But before the Lady Nandi could risk herself on such an errand, before she could even finish preparing to go, a guest was brought to Vanyi as she tried to read in the library that was next to the hall. She never remembered afterward which book it had been, or even what kind of book it was. The man who stumbled and fell at her feet was a preposterous creature, naked but for festoons of charms and amulets; his face and body were painted, often garishly, but the bright scarlet and the livid blue were blood and bruises. He had been beaten, and badly; it was a wonder he was walking, let alone running ahead of the servant.

Vanyi abandoned her book with open relief and knelt to turn the fallen man onto his back. Her hands were as gentle as they could be. Even at that, he groaned and struggled, but stilled as he understood that she meant him no harm.

As she had expected, it was the odd creature who had helped to bring Uruan back from the house of the Gate: the exorcist, who appeared to have no name, or none that his sect would let him confess to. There was a scent of magery on him, weak but distinct.

His eyes opened in the bruised and swollen face. Much of the paint had rubbed away; the features under it were unremarkable except where they were swollen out of their wonted shape. His nose was broken, Vanyi noted, and he had lost a tooth or two.

"You were lucky," she said, "that they didn't break anything more vital."

He blinked at her, struggling to make sense of her. His magery, as ill-trained and twisted as it was, recognized hers, but he did not know what he was seeing; only that she seemed more real than the world about her. She made no effort to soften the effect. He would learn what it was that made him see her so; or he would not.

"Tell me why you came here," she said when he kept staring, blinking, poised on a thin edge of pain and panic. "Why here, and to me in particular?"

Her voice anchored him as she had hoped it would. "I ask you for sanctuary, lady of the mages," he said.

"Why?"

"Because," he said, "I'll be killed else. They've stripped my temple bare and burned it. They've beaten or killed the priests. They're doing it all through the city, wherever the whim strikes them. They say—" He had to stop and swallow bile. "They say that they're cleansing the city and the kingdom. Of—of—"

"Of evil magic?"

His head bobbed assent, unwisely: he gasped with pain and dizziness, and retched. But his stomach was empty. Those who beat him had seen to that.

"Why did you come here?" Vanyi asked. "You don't know us."

"But you are—that. What they said we were."

"What, mages? We're no more evil than any other mortals."

"Mages," he said. "M—mages. And strong. And they said—I heard them say—they can't touch you, not while Janabundur speaks for you."

"Not yet," Vanyi said.

"So I came to you," he said. "You can fight. You have light and dark in your hands like swords, and demons at your call. And gods; and the little goddess."

"What—" Vanyi laughed, but not with mirth. "I suppose you could call the imp that."

"I want to fight with you," he said. "I want to see them fall as my temple fell, in bloody ruin."

He was fierce as only the young can be, and muddled beyond belief. "I'm not going to kill anyone right at the moment," Vanyi said, "and never with magic, in any case. It's forbidden."

He did not understand. He said, "I want them to fall."

"From what I can gather," Vanyi said dryly, "your temple was sacked and burned by half the rabble in the city."

"They were led," he said. "Led from behind by those who called themselves pious and lovers of the gods. Lovers of their own greed, I call them. I saw how they took the best things for themselves, and stood back for the mob to scrape up the leavings." He scrambled himself erect, mustering a surprising degree of dignity. "I have no magic such as you have, but I can serve you and run errands for you and be your hands and feet."

Vanyi looked at him and sighed. She did not need servants; she had more than enough. But there was no graceful way to turn him out, not as battered as he was, and in such need of a bath and a physician.

"Ah well," she said. "What's one more mouth to feed? Go on, follow the servant, bathe yourself and rest. I'll send someone to look after your hurts."

"I don't need to rest," he said, though he was wobbling on his feet. "I want to serve you."

"Later," she said. "Now, off with you."

Kimeri heard the exorcist come in. She listened as he spoke to Vanyi, and was ahead of him when he went to the servants' wing, where they had a bathhouse and an extra room or two. In the big wooden tub, with his amulets off and his paint washed away, he was a perfectly ordinary, rather skinny and gangly person with a spectacular crop of bruises and cuts, and that poor broken nose.

"I'm sorry I can't mend your nose," she said, clambering up on the rim of the tub. He had been left to get himself clean, which was not very kind of the servants. They thought exorcists were as bad as mages, and smelled worse. It did make it easier to talk to him, since there was no one about to stop her, except her Olenyas; but it was Rahai again, and Rahai never got in the way unless she tried to leave the house.

The exorcist almost drowned himself trying to bow in the water while scrambling away from Rahai's shadow.

"Stop that," Kimeri said. "You'll hurt yourself. And stop thinking that I'm a goddess. I'm a god's get, but I'm nothing to fall at the feet of. I'm not even a beauty yet."

He was so confused that he obeyed her. By the time he thought about what she had said, he was safe on the ledge in the tub, scrubbing gingerly at the last of his paint. He kept looking at Rahai as if the Olenyas were something to be afraid of, but since Rahai was doing nothing more threatening than standing by the door, he at least stopped trying to hide under the water.

"I'm sorry about your temple," said Kimeri. "And about your nose. Vanyi's going to send Aledi to look at it. Aledi's got a little healing magic. You'll be afraid of her: she's Asanian, and her eyes are yellow. But she's very gentle."

"Your eyes are yellow," the exorcist said.

"That's because my father is Asanian, and my mother is mostly Asanian, and so were her mother and father. But I'll be taller, because my great-grandfather's mother was from the north, where everybody is as tall as a tree."

"North is the Spear of Heaven," said the exorcist. "There are no man-trees there."

"Not in your north," Kimeri said. "You should get out of the water now, before your bruises get stiff. Do you mind wearing clothes? Everybody seems to, here."

He did not mind wearing clothes. All the amulets and the paint were really only for formal occasions; his temple had been having one of its great exorcisms, when they tried to drive all the evil out of the kingdom for another turning of the moons. Evil had found them instead, and broken the temple. Kimeri watched him think about that as he climbed into the shirt and trousers and coat. He left his amulets in the box the servants had set out for them. He was not afraid that anyone would steal them. They all had curses on them, and everybody knew it.

All but one, which he put on. It was a leather cord with a stone on it, smooth and round and grey, with a hole worn in the middle. "To keep my soul safe," he said.

If he thought it would, then it might. Kimeri thought the stone was rather pretty.

Aledi came in then and chased Kimeri out, not meaning to be impolite, but she was thinking much too clearly that small children had no place in the middle of magic. Aledi did not understand Sunchildren at all. Kimeri could not expect her to. She was Asanian, and High Court Asanian at that. But it stung.

Hani could not play with her. He had lessons in a temple near the house, just for the morning but enough to keep him away when she needed him. She was too young for lessons, even if she had been Shurakani. She was supposed to do what young children did, which, as far as she could see, was nothing at all but be chased out of people's way.

If she could have gone outside of the house, she would have been able to find something to do. But the Olenyai would not let her. It was too dangerous, they said. People were hunting mages. They were burning temples and chasing people out of houses and beating up anybody who looked or sounded or acted different. The air, even in the house, had a foul smell, like blood mixed with the thing that men and women did, that her mother was doing with Bundur and not bothering to hide it.

Except that what her mother and Bundur did was a joyful thing, like singing. What the people were doing in the city was ugly. It made Kimeri want to scrub herself over and over, to take the stink away.

Kimeri went to where her mother was. She stayed outside while they finished what they were doing, then waited a little longer, in case they started again. They got up instead and put on their clothes, and talked about eating.

She went in. Bundur was sitting on the windowledge. Kimeri's mother was braiding his hair. Kimeri climbed up on his lap, not even asking him if he minded, and buried her face in his shirt. He smelled of clean man and clean wool and the thing that, in this place, was joy. He did not push her away but gathered her in, though he looked a question at Daruya.

"She's . . . what I am," Daruya said after a little while. "She knows what's happening in the city."

He was shocked. "All of it?"

"All that matters." Daruya's hand brushed Kimeri's head, bringing calm. "You should be flattered. She never goes to people she doesn't trust."

That was not exactly true, but Kimeri did not say it. He was warm and solid, and yes, she trusted him. He made her feel safe.

He kept on being solid and warm, and being glad that she was there. That must be what it was like to have a father. Great-Grandfather felt the same way about her, mostly, and he understood her, too, and Bundur did not, yet; but this was different somehow. This was nearer to her, with her mother in it, being part of it and part of him. While she was with them, the ugliness could not touch her, or make her afraid.

27

THAT NIGHT WAS full of fires and shouting, broken temples and shattered gods and mobs that raged from end to end of the city. House Janabundur was as safe as a house could be: it was high up on a hill, with no roofs overlooking it, and its walls were strong and its gates were barred. Olenyai guarded them, side by side with Janabundur's strongest servants. Daruya was not surprised to see how many of those there were, or how loyal. Janabundur had an army of its own if it chose to raise one. Many of its best men had been finding their way to the house over past days, coming from houses in the city, farmsteads in the valley, holdings along the mountain walls. They brought with them bundles that, when opened, revealed well-kept weapons and armor of leather plates strengthened with bronze.

It was not war, Bundur insisted. Fools in the palace had raised the mob, and would pay dearly for it, come the cold light of morning and the colder eye of the law. He had no comprehension of the discrepancy between a rule of law and a palace coup leading to rampage and riot. "The law has always banned magic," he said. "They've spread the net so broad that they're sweeping in innocents. Then, when every sane person recoils from what's been done in the name of law, another law will save us all: the law that protects the innocent, and the law of the human heart, which is always contrary. They'll be favoring mages, you'll see, out of pity and guilt. Out of that we'll make a new decree, one that softens the strictures against magic."

"It should remove them altogether," Daruya said.

"Someday," he said, "it may."

They could not sleep in one another's arms: Kimeri was between them, and Hani, who had crept in to have his own fears soothed away. It was peculiarly comfortable to lie all of them in a bed, demurely clothed, the children asleep in the circle of their parents' protection, lulled by their voices.

Morning came with crawling slowness and a sense as of a long debauch barely begun. Daruya had been in a siege once, in her grandfather's wars. She remembered this sense of being trapped in walls and yet sheltered by them, the determined cheerfulness, the refusal to consider what would happen if the enemy broke through their defenses.

Hani would not go to his lessons this morning. Bundur took both children to the kitchen, where a hound bitch had whelped in the night. Daruya was glad to be away from him, to be herself again for a little while, and yet she missed him keenly, the touch of his hand, the smell and the taste of him. She had not been out of his sight since she married him, nor he out of hers.

Truly, then, it was past time. She put on her riding clothes and went to see which of the seneldi would be amenable to a canter round the garden.

Daruya brought her dun mare to a neat halt precisely in the center of the circle that had marked the limits of her exercises. As she dismounted, Kadin came through the gap in the hedge. He too was in riding clothes, but no senel followed him.

It was not noble of her, but whenever she saw him she shivered. His grief seemed to shape all that he was; that, and the darkness that was his magery. She, bred of the Sun, could with utter ease have matched him, light to his shadow.

It was not the matching of souls that bound her to Bundur. It was another kind of twinning, one that by the laws of her inheritance she could not accept. She had never known exactly why, unless it had to do with her firstfather's conviction that light and only light must rule, or with Vanyi's refusal to submit the Mageguild to the emperor's will. The Guild served him when it could, which was often, but it remained distinct. All worlds were its concern; it would not bind itself to the lord of this one, however great a mage he might be.

And yet, faced with this darkmage whose power so craved the light that would complete it, Daruya suffered sore temptation. She was all edges and angles, shocked by the marriage that had been thrust on her, the murder of a king, the fall of Gates. One more shock surely could not matter, one more transgression, one more count against her in the minds of her people.

She was tired of being wild. It struck her as she stood there, loosening the saddlegirth and rubbing an itch out of the mare's neck. She was weary of resisting; of breaking law and discipline simply because they discommoded her.

The trouble, she thought, was that Bundur would not fight back. He yielded; he smiled; he slid smoothly round her and showed her her own face in the mirror of his mind. She was usually scowling. She was always rebelling. It was her art and her gift.

But here in the face of a rebellion that would put all the rest to shame, she sickened of it. Kadin did not know what he did, how his darkness lured her, how even his grief made it easy to succumb. He would not want her for a lover; twinned mages need not be bedmates, or even friends. They raised power together, that was all. They made each other complete.

No, she thought. Resistance again; she almost laughed at that—bitterly, again. She was a pattern of repetitions. Could she not vary it?

Kadin was oblivious to her maundering. He caught the

mare's bridle as Daruya began to lead her out of the hedged circle that had become the riding-ground. "Lady," he said, "wait."

Daruya paused. She had grown accustomed to men who were her own height or smaller; it was odd to have to look up. He was keeping his hair cropped short, she noticed, but letting his beard grow. That was like a northerner, as was the gold ring in his ear. Northerners felt naked without their beards and their gauds.

"Lady," Kadin said again. "Daruya. If I named a quarry, would you hunt with me?"

For all her noble intentions and her real weariness, her heart leaped. "A hunt? Where?"

"In this city," he answered. "For breakers of Gates."

"Yes," breathed Daruya. "Oh, yes." But— "Did the Guildmaster send you to me?"

"No," said Kadin. "I came to you first."

He was speaking the truth: he opened himself to let her see it. He also let her see why. Vanyi would wish him to be cautious, to be circumspect. Daruya, he thought, would be eager for a wild hunt, for the revenge that twisted like hunger in his belly.

He approved her wildness; admired it. She was not as flattered as she might once have been—and not long ago, either.

Still. A hunt, and a quarry. "Who is it?" she asked. "Where did you find him?"

"I'm not sure yet," said Kadin. "I know that my magic has found a place, a lair of . . . something, and a remembrance of fallen Gates."

"You really should have gone to Vanyi," Daruya said, but not as a rebuke. "If it's this uncertain still—you could be catching the death of the one who did it, killed in the confusion. Maybe he was the target of it all."

"I think not," Kadin said. "It's strong. The uproar

stripped its shields, I'll wager, and I was hunting just when the shields went down. It doesn't know they're down; it's made no effort to raise them again."

"A trap," said Daruya.

"Possibly," he said. His eyes were bright. His teeth flashed in his beard. "Will you hunt with me, Sunlady?"

She should not. She should go to Vanyi, speak to Bundur and his mother, talk it to death.

Then sit in this cage while the others pursued the hunt.

Ah well, she thought. He had asked; and he was strong, both mage and man. What danger in simply finding the quarry, so that he could bring sure word back to his Guildmaster?

Even the voice of temptation knew what folly that was. Kadin would not play scout in this. He hunted to kill.

All the more need of her to keep him from doing something rash. She unsaddled and rubbed down the mare and stabled her with the rest, took the hooded cloak Kadin offered her and hid her alien face in it, and drew shadows about her besides. He was a shadow beside her, following the scent that he had found.

28

THE CITY WAS quiet in the warm noon, as if it rested from its exertions of the night. A pall of smoke hung over it; some of the markets were shut, and some had suffered at the hands of rioters. There had been efforts to keep order: streets with guards strolling or standing, wearing the colors of one noble house or another, or else the shaved head and saffron tabard of a temple. Not one of the temples that had been attacked; those, Daruya suspected, were mostly the poorer or smaller, too weak to fight back.

Where guards were was greatest quiet, shops unlooted, houses or temples unburned. Even so, too much of the city had suffered, she saw as she ghosted through it with Kadin. Once or twice she saw desultory parties of looters behind broken gates, gutting temple or house and setting fire to what they left behind. They did not think that they were serving the gods or upholding the law. They were smashing and seizing, that was all, and taking pleasure in it.

She had been sheltered from it in House Janabundur. How much, she had not known till she passed through the middle of it. It was no consolation that everyone who could, had retreated behind walls and barred the door. Too many had not been able to, or had seen their walls breached and their door battered down.

The cold part of her, the part that was bred to rule, took note of who had been the targets. Smaller temples, temples of the odder or more exacting gods, particularly those without the numbers or the weapons to mount a defense. Houses of simple citizens, physicians, herb-healers, astrologers, diviners. Foreigners of any and every description.

None was as foreign as she: all were of Merukarion or of the mountains. They had been driven out of houses or hostelries, beaten, robbed, even killed.

And she had been safe. She had lain abed with her Shurakani prince, while people died.

Guilt was no alien thing to her. But guilt for being powerless and accepting it—that was new.

She was doing something now. It was dangerous, it was badly advised, but it was something. She was not idling in House Janabundur and letting the city rack itself to pieces.

Kadin led her with a hunter's speed, a hunter's quiet. Her magery touched his, found what he followed. It was more memory than present reality: a scent, a taste, a quiver in the air. As he drew closer to the source of it, he needed her to keep him hidden, to steer him round obstacles. He was blind, focused on the one thing alone, the thing that had an air, however faint, of magery.

He stopped abruptly. She nearly collided with him. His face turned from side to side. His eyes were shut, his nostrils flared. He turned till he faced straight away from the sun, and stopped, standing stiff, like a hound at gaze; but his eyes were closed still.

Daruya looked where his power was focused. It was a temple; she had learned to recognize the shape of the gate in the blank wall, and the fact that it was open, inviting strangers in. It could dare that: the street was guarded, the guards alert, armed with pikes. People passed, going to and from the market at the street's end, where the guards were thickest and trade was almost brisk. Daruya caught a scent of roasting meat, baking bread, spices, flowers. Ordinary scents of the Summer City, eerie now with the stink of smoke and blood beneath.

Her stomach growled. She quelled it, and a completely unexpected urge to laugh. The body always had its say, no matter what the mind might think.

Kadin moved away from her so suddenly that she was

left flatfooted. He had forgotten his cloak of shadows; he slipped along the wall, hunter-wise, but there was no mistaking his size or his foreignness. She darted after him, shadow-shrouded, before anyone could see and raise the alarm.

At the temple gate he paused. Daruya felt it with him: the faint hum of power, the skin-prickle of wards. Magic, in a place devoted to the destruction of mages?

It was not strong, not a Great Ward. It was set against a hostile mind, but not against a mage wrapped in shadow and shields. Both of them slipped through carefully, for such wards were delicate. Daruya did what she could to seem no more than a gust of air, a trick of the light.

Inside was a temple like many another: outer court, inner court, shrine and sanctuary, garden and cloister and dwellings for the priests behind. It was not a large temple, nor particularly small. Its god was more human-faced than most, but its body, though standing upright, was that of a mountain ox, and on its head were great sweeping horns. A white she-ox lay in a golden pen inside the shrine, chewing her cud. Devotees might purchase a twist of green fodder and offer it to her with bowings and prayers, and seek her consort's favor for their petitions.

If the ox saw the intruders, she did not betray them. Kadin ran soft-footed past her, round a knot of worshippers, through the god's shadow and into the deeper sanctuary. Daruya heard sounds from within, the ringing of bells, the echoing hum of a bronze gong, the sound of voices chanting. She could not make out the words, if words there were.

So were the gods worshipped here, ceaselessly, in a long drone of chants. She had felt before this the power that rode the chanting, the strength of focused will that came close to magery. But never so clear. Never so distinct.

The sense of it on her skin was strikingly familiar. She

had known just that brush as of wind, just that shiver beneath, as she approached a circle of mages in a lesser working. Guard-magic, she thought; a touch of wind-magic. Her own power woke to what it looked on: the swirl of winds in the upper air, a gathering of clouds above the mountains. Left unattended, they would swoop down into Shurakan in a storm of wind and hail, in a roll of summer thunder.

The inner chamber was open, unguarded save by the shimmer of wards. Daruya looked past Kadin to a circle of men—yes, all men, no women—in crimson tabards, each sitting on his heels, hands on thighs, head bent, eyes closed, chanting. The light of magic on them was as bright as a beacon to her inner eye.

And they did not know it. True mages—Guildmages, priest-mages—would have done their working behind a layering of wards, one for protection of their bodies, one for shielding of their minds from intrusion, and one for the working itself, to turn aside the unwary or the hostile. The warding here was weak, little more than a prayer for safety. The mind-shields were all but nonexistent. Thoughts babbled without direction and without focus, like a river beneath the ice that was the working.

They had no faintest conception of what they were doing. They were praying away a storm, they thought, and asking their god to guard the city, to defend their temple against the wrath of the mob. Here and there, like a spark on flint, was a thought of greater intensity: fear of mages, relief that they were nigh gone from the city, a wish that their kind had never been.

Suppose, thought Daruya, that the sparks found tinder: Gates open and vulnerable, mages passing through. Suppose that this and nothing else was the source of the Gates' fall.

No. It was too simple, the circle too weak. There was real magery in it, but feeble, undisciplined. What she had felt in the Gate had been greater—had been a real and present malice, directed at the Gate and at the mages within it. She did not sense it here.

Kadin, it seemed, did; or did not care that there was a difference. The drawing in of his power sucked at her, reaching for the light that was in her, seeking it to complete itself. Her power trembled in response.

She clamped it down, got a grip on Kadin, set her teeth and hauled him back out of the doorway. He was too surprised to fight, too intent on the circle and on the calling of his power. She struck him with her own magery, a swift, fierce blow that rocked him on his feet.

"What in the name of—" he began, making no effort to be quiet.

She clapped a hand over his mouth. "Shut *up*," she gritted, barely above a whisper.

He struggled. She held on. Her power was stronger, even holding together shields and shadows. If it did not give way to the seduction of his darkmagic—if the priests or their guards did not rouse to the presence of strangers in their temple—if she could get him out before he unleashed a blast of power upon the men who, he was certain, had killed his lightmage—

The chanting went on, endless, unvarying. Its magic spun and wove into a circle of dim light, stretching and elongating, curving up past the temple's roof. Weather-magic, and no awareness at all of the world's balance. Rain that did not fall here must fall elsewhere; that much a child knew. But these pious priests did not. Ignorant, blind, utter fools.

And Kadin wanted to blast them from the earth. "They're not worth it," she hissed in his ear.

They killed Jian.

Deprived of his mouth to speak, he resorted to mind-speech. That too was perilous—more so than a whisper.

Guards might not hear soft voices, but wards woke to the inner speech of mages.

"We don't know that," Daruya whispered as fiercely as she could. "Come out of here. We know there's magic working in Shurakan—that much you won for us. Now let's take it to the Guildmaster. She'll know what to do about it."

Kadin's resistance was beyond words, his body coiled to fling her aside, his power poised to leap, to destroy, to kill. That such use of magery would destroy him, he knew. He was glad.

"No," said Daruya, almost aloud. She caught a trailing edge of his magery and did a thing no Guildmage would ever stoop to: looped and bound him with it. He raged, he fought, but the harder he fought, the tighter the bond grew. Enough of that and he would strangle his power, turn it inward on itself. Then he would have the destruction he yearned for, but all within.

She had gambled rightly. He wanted to die, but not without purpose. Not unless he took his enemies with him.

They got out of the temple, though it cost Daruya high, sustaining shadows, shields, and mindbond, and dragging a large, reluctant, half-stunned darkmage bodily past the blind eyes of guards and the oblivious faces of worshippers. The white ox watched her, mildly curious. If she ever came back, she would bring the beast a gift of sweet fodder, in thanks for keeping her secret. She swore that as an oath in the silence of her mind, where only a god—or a god's white ox—could hear.

Kadin was nearly unconscious by the time he stumbled into House Janabundur. Daruya was in little better case. But she found Vanyi first, before her knees gave way: dropped the darkmage like a rolled carpet at the Guildmaster's feet and crumpled beside him, still awake, still aware, but no more strength in her than in a newborn baby.

There was someone else there. She could not see him at first; her power was too sorely strained. It came back slowly, feeding itself on her stillness. She was kneeling at Vanyi's feet, yes. Vanyi was standing face to face with one who was not here in body at all, and yet was visible: the more so, the longer she stared.

How dark he was, she thought, how bright a gold his eyes. And how young he seemed. He had always been ancient to her: her grandfather, her emperor, source and cause of her rebellions. He was not a young man, no; his hair was flecked with grey, his beard silvered. And yet he looked not much older in truth than Bundur.

If he had been any less meticulously and brutally trained, he would have been dancing with frustration. "You see?" he said. "*You see?* There *is* magery in this wretched little kingdom."

"They don't know that's what it is," Daruya said. Her voice was faint, breathless.

"They have little discipline," said Vanyi to Estarion, "except in the raising of wards. That's what deceived us for so long. But with the uproar in the city, they got careless. Or their wards weren't strong enough to hold against the force of hate and fear that was beating on them. Then they betrayed themselves."

"And lured yonder darkmage into a trap," said Estarion.

"They didn't mean that," Daruya said. "Can't you hear me? *They don't know.*"

"I hear you," he said, as maddening as ever, as if she were no older than Kimeri. "I commend you, too, for saving him from himself."

"How do you know what I did?"

"There now," said Vanyi, coming between them as she so often had before. "He's got eyes, and he knows Kadin. It's not hard to guess what you two were up to, considering the storms that have been shivering the Great Ward from end to end and shaking loose whole scores of lesser wards. This whole kingdom is infested with them. Every temple and shrine and holy man's hut must have at least a warding or two, if not more."

"It's prayer to them," said Daruya. "When they work magic, they think it a miracle, and the gift of a god."

"And isn't it exactly that?" Estarion sat on a cushion, for all the world as if he were there in the flesh. He looked comfortable but tired—as he would be, for it must be late night in Starios, and he did not look as if he had slept.

Daruya had no sympathy to spare for him. "But they don't know," she said, stubborn. "They don't see what they are or what they do. They just do it."

"And hate us, and pray their gods to destroy us—and so, in their minds, the gods do." Vanyi sighed. "They won't thank us for telling them what they're really doing."

"They won't believe it," said Estarion. "That kind never does."

"Unless we can prove it to them," Daruya said. "Somehow. Show them that they're as much mages as we."

"That's for later," said Vanyi. "Much later. Now we have a greater urgency to face: to be rid of the mages who broke the Gate."

"We don't know it's those mages," Daruya said. "It could be any circle of priests in Shurakan—any holy man, if it comes to that, who has reason to hate mages and Gates."

"It could," said Vanyi, "but I think not. Do you know what temple that is?"

"Should I? It has a god like an ox with a man's face, and a white she-ox for his consort."

"Yes," said Vanyi. "That is Matakan, whose father is the greater moon, and whose mother is the white moon-goddess, the mother goddess of Shurakan. The king and the queen are his kin. His chief power is the blessing of crops

and the fields, and the guidance of princes. His legend calls
him friend of the earth, brother of the children of heaven,
and destroyer of unclean magics."

"Magic," said Daruya in dawning comprehension. "Ox-
droppings. Excrement of Matakan—the evil that he casts
out when he consumes the fruits of the earth."

"Exactly," Vanyi said. "What would you like to wager
that Matakan's temple is the place where the new king's faction gathered before it seized the palace, where behind
wards they conceived their plots and broke the Gates?"

"I saw none of that," said Daruya. "I saw a circle of
priests turning aside a storm. They hate mages, yes, that's
underneath everything they do, but there's no clear intention in it. No malice."

"Not in the priests you saw," Estarion said. "But
wouldn't those be the lesser ones, the ones who aren't
needed to hold the palace? They perform the offices, keep
the storms at bay, while their masters go about the greater
business of their order."

That made too much sense. And it had to come from Estarion, at whose every *Yes* she shouted, by instinct, a vehe-
ment *No!*

Not now. She was too tired, there was that. And he
could not do anything here but talk, no matter how solid he
seemed.

"So," said Vanyi, "we find the masters. That should be
simple enough. They'll be in the palace, ruling it and its
king."

"And warded, guarded, and praying you'll fall into
their hands." Estarion reached but did not try to touch her.
"Prayer here is magery. Remember that."

"I'm hardly likely to forget it," Vanyi said. Her voice
was tart.

Kadin stirred suddenly at her feet, thrashed, flailed
at air. Daruya flung herself on him and wrestled him into
stillness.

The silence was much larger than it should have been. Much deeper. Much more . . . numerous.

Kadin was awake, but he was quiet, breathing hard, staring toward the door. Daruya followed the line of his gaze.

What Bundur must be seeing, she could well imagine. His wife on the floor with the black mage, in a posture she had more than once assumed in the marriage bed. The Guildmaster standing over them. And the stranger who sat by the wall, the dark man with the lion-eyes, whose like he could never have seen before, nor ever imagined.

Estarion looked both real and unreal. Solid, yet not quite there—as if he were more distant than he should be. His edges shimmered.

A demon, Bundur was thinking. A dark god. Both and neither.

"Grandfather," said Daruya steadily in Bundur's language, "this is my husband."

Estarion inclined his head. He had grace; he carried himself as one who had been emperor from his childhood.

Bundur saw it. Understood it. "Sir," he said, a little abrupt perhaps, but courteous. And to Daruya: "This is your emperor?"

"This is the Lord of Sun and Lion," she said. She rose carefully. Kadin sat up but offered no violence. She could forget him, she thought, until she had dealt with the rest of it.

They were measuring one another, her grandfather and her husband. Finding one another immensely strange, and very foreign. There was no leap of liking, no meeting of minds that she could discern. And yet somehow they agreed.

Maybe it was simply that they knew her and acknowledged her failings. Estarion had that look about him. So did Bundur—a quirk of the lip, a glint of the eye.

"And how," Estarion asked, "do you contend with the hottest temper in my empire?"

"As I do with all forces of nature, sir," Bundur answered: "swiftly, thoroughly, and with great respect."

"Is it worth the trouble?"

"I married it," Bundur said. "Sir."

"Ah," said Estarion, "but did you think you were going to tame it?"

"Of course not," said Bundur.

Estarion smiled his sudden brilliant smile. "You're a wise man, I see. And remarkably courageous."

"She's no danger to me," said Bundur.

"No? Then she must love you for a fact." Estarion settled more comfortably, stretched out on the cushions, propped on his elbow. "But I was thinking of your courage in standing here, talking to the most foreign of foreigners, and knowing that I'm not, strictly speaking, here at all."

"You're not here?" Bundur sounded puzzled. "I can see you, hear you."

"But I have no bodily substance. I'm a working of magic, a figment of your mind's eye."

"Grandfather—" Daruya began, half angry, half afraid.

He ignored her. So did Bundur. Bundur's vitals were knotted to the point of pain, but he was strong. He held his ground. She dared not touch him, still less ease the pain, for fear he would revolt.

"Tell me," he said, "O shape of air and darkness, if what I hear is true. Is it magic that they practice in the temples? Are the greatest haters of magic its most devoted practitioners?"

"I'm no oracle," said Estarion, "but from all I've heard and seen, it's true."

Bundur's knees gave way. There was a cushion close enough to fall to; he dropped onto it with something resembling grace, and sat for a moment, simply breathing. At length he said, "I thought I was stronger. I thought I knew what it was to live among mages."

"Even mages are never quite prepared for everything that can happen," said Estarion. "And you were taught from childhood to hate mages and to reverence priests. To discover that they're the same thing . . . that would break most men's minds."

Bundur laughed shakily. "I've married a demon's child, I've consorted with mages, I've seen a dark god in my own sitting room. What's another terrible truth, to that?"

"Not all priests are mages," Vanyi said, sharp and clear. They listened to her as they would not have done to Daruya: stopped their stallion-dance and stared. She glared back. "No, young Shakabundur, not even in our country, which isn't half as preposterous a place as you're coming to think it is. It's just a few priests and a particular form of prayer, and a fairly universal talent for raising wards. We would be a threat to that, we and our Gates, not least because we can name it for what it is."

"You think the leaders know," said Daruya.

"Know or suspect," Vanyi said, "and believe themselves righteous because their gods answer their prayers. Maybe they didn't know before they saw us. Who's to tell, till we can ask them?"

"You're not going to do that," Estarion said quickly.

Vanyi's brows went up. "And why not? Do you think we should cower here till they fall on us and destroy us?"

"I think you could let them come to you."

"I could," she conceded. "It's a decent stronghold, this. Well armed, well guarded; good walls, no easy way in. They'll come here, of course, before too long. Once their other quarry is hunted out and disposed of."

"Promise me you won't do something rash," said Estarion.

Vanyi looked at him. Simply looked. He withstood her

stare far better than Daruya could have, but even he could not find a grin to set against it. She said, "I won't do anything that isn't necessary."

"That's not what I asked," he said.

"That's what you'll get."

"Gods," muttered Bundur. "And he's her king?"

"More than king," Daruya said. "But she's the Master of Mages."

"My sorrow," said Estarion, flashing a glance at them, "that I ever let it be so. Damn you, Vanyi—"

"Damn you, Estarion," said Vanyi. "Go away and let me work."

"Not till you promise to be sensible."

"I'll be exactly as sensible as I need to be."

"If you get yourself killed," he said, low and fierce, "I'll haunt you till I die myself."

"The way you're haunting me now?" Vanyi wanted to know. "Avaryan help us. I'm like to die of it."

"Don't," he said.

"What, you care that much?"

It was mocking, but it was not. Estarion met it with sober certainty. "Always, Vanyi." He paused. "You didn't know?"

"I didn't dare." She rubbed her eyes. She looked as if she was suddenly, cripplingly exhausted. "Go home, Estarion."

This time he obeyed her—if anyone could call it obedience. It looked like the yielding of royal will to royal whim. Daruya herself could not have done it better.

29

Vanyi entered the palace without concealment, and with no particular care to be either nameless or faceless. She had had some difficulty escaping House Janabundur—everyone was determined to keep everyone else safe, and never mind how many of them had already rebelled against it—but after all she was the Guildmaster, and the oldest woman in the house besides, which mattered more to the Shurakani. She had her way. She also had a pair of Olenyai at her back, but that was more help than hindrance. They kept her from having to fret about attacks from behind.

The palace, like the city, was quiet, almost too much so. It was waiting for something, she thought. Her arrival? She would have laughed at herself, but there was cold in her bones.

The Minister of Protocol's workroom was empty, its table tidy, dusted and clean. He had not been there that day, or the night before, either. She followed the memory of him, brazening her way past guards and chamberlains, going invisible when she must. She was taking no great care to hoard her magery. This was her gamble, her last cast of the dice. That she knew who had cast down the Gates through the circle of priests. That that one was waiting for her as a spider waits for its prey, crouching in the center of its web.

Fear had no part in it. She had been considering this for a long while now, perhaps since she decided to come to Shurakan in spite of the Gate's fall. Someone would have to lure the enemy out. Her mere presence in the kingdom had not been enough. She must force the meeting, and the confrontation.

If she had guessed rightly. If the enemy was the one she thought, and not someone else, someone unexpected.

The palace was a warren. Not as much of one as the Golden Palace in Kundri'j Asan; nor was it as large as Estarion's palace in Starios. But there was a great deal of it, a great many doors and passages, staircases, rooms that were full of people and rooms that were echoingly empty.

Vanyi followed the thread of presence that was the Minister of Protocol. Either he had been wandering lost for long hours, or he liked to ramble. Or it was yet another aspect of the trap. If she gave in to tedium and retreated, the enemy had won a respite. If she persevered, she was caught. In either event, the enemy won.

Which was exactly what Vanyi hoped for. She pressed on past weary feet and aching head, staring strangers, guards who barred her way and found themselves confronted with the threat of Olenyai swords. Neither bluster nor insults swayed the veiled warriors. They spoke no Shurakani; only the common language of hand on sword-hilt and a few fingerbreadths of bared steel.

The trail led her into darker, narrower ways, perhaps older, certainly the province of servants and lesser ministers. Rooms were crowded together here, with larger ones at intervals, full of the scents of cooking and the clatter of plates and bowls. It was the hour for the daymeal. Vanyi had eaten, but not in a while. She regretted not thinking to bring at least a pouchful of fruit or a round of bread to nibble on. She had thought—hoped—to be seized at once and taken to the one she must see.

Foolish of her. An enemy clever enough to hide from mages who were actively hunting a destroyer of Gates, had more than enough sense to lead her on a merry chase before going to ground.

Indeed, and it was growing less merry by the heartbeat. She stopped abruptly. The Olenyai drifted past her, halted.

One circled round to guard her back. The other poised just ahead of her, alert, though the corridor was empty.

Think, she told herself. What was this for? Why a trail this long and this convoluted, if they both knew how it had to end?

Subtleties within subtleties. The enemy might be afraid of her. She was a master of mages, after all—and that one knew what the title meant.

Or she might be hunting the wrong quarry. Why then would he run? He should not even know she hunted him.

Unless he ran from someone else.

But who—

She began to run.

Back the way she came. Back through the twisting, turning passages. She forgot that she was a woman of venerable years, with stiff knees and shortening wind. She ran like the girl she had been.

The Minister of Protocol's workroom was no longer empty. The Minister of Protocol sat in it, upright at his worktable, smiling. And very dead.

The smile was rictus. Certain poisons induced just that expression, and just that blue cast to the lips. Vanyi was glad, at least, that he had had no pain. She had feared much worse.

She said so, taking a great deal too many breaths to do it, to the seemingly empty room.

"But, lady," said a gentle voice, "death is death."

"Some deaths are worse," she said. "And some, if your sages are to be believed, cast a man lower on the wheel of lives. Is it easier to die if you believe you'll be reborn?"

"One would think so," said Esakai the priest of Ushala temple. He had been using no magery to conceal himself, only a fold of curtain over an alcove. He came forward slowly, leaning on a staff.

He looked no different. Elderly, gentle, amiable. No hatred in him, no terror of what she was.

He regarded the Minister of Protocol with honest regret. "I do wish he could have lived," he said. "But he was obstinate. He would not see reason, even with the authority of the gods behind it."

"What reason was that, if it was too unreasonable for this of all men?"

"Why," said the priest, "that truly he was not well advised to ally himself with you. Your magery is difficulty enough. Your Gate is deadly. What is it after all but an instrument of conquest, conceived to destroy our kingdom?"

Vanyi gaped. Of all reasons she had expected, this was the last. Hastily she mustered wits and voice. "*That* was why you broke the Gate? Because you were afraid of armies invading through it?"

Esakai's thin white brows rose. "You expected any other reason?"

"It's too logical," Vanyi said.

"Lady," said Esakai sadly. "Oh, lady, how little you must think of us, if you believe that we can only fear you because you possess powers we were all bred to despise. That is no trivial thing, mind, but it's not all we can think of. We remember what you've told us of the empire you come from, how vast it is, how small we are, and how insignificant. It could consume us in an instant. And so it will, unless we resist it."

"No," said Vanyi. "That's not what I meant. You've let your mobs destroy half of Shurakan in the name of the gods' will against mages. If invasion were all you were afraid of, you'd have done none of that. You'd have marched on Janabundur—regardless of the power of the name or the house—and dragged us out and made examples of us."

"Yes," said Esakai, "and given your king-above-kings

all the cause he would ever need, to fall on us and destroy us."

"He can't come through the Gate," Vanyi pointed out. "It's broken."

"And so shall it stay, while we have the power of the gods to help us. But, lady, if he has armies of dragons as the tales say, he needs no Gate, and no long march overland, either. We won't chance that. We'll see to it that no mage can ever live safe in Su-Shaklan, and we'll wield you as we may, to gain your emperor's promise that he won't conquer us."

Vanyi had been aware of the armed men closing in behind her, the drawn swords, the pikes, the hum of chanting that bore magery in it. The Olenyai would have sprung to her defense. She held them back. "No," she said. "Hold; be quiet. Get away if you can. This is strategy, and planned for."

From the roll of their eyes, they knew it already. One might approve. The other might be thinking her a raving idiot. There was no telling; they were shielded against magery.

But they were quiet, which was what mattered. To Esakai she said, "It's very odd, you know. One of the first things I did when I began building Gates to span this world, was to inform the emperor that whatever he did, he was never to think that he could use my Gates to further his conquests. He'd do it the old way or none, foot-slog and senelback. My Gates are not his to use, nor are my mages his servants.

"He honored that agreement," she said, "though I gave him precious little to sweeten it: promise that he could use Gates himself, to see what was on the other side, and promise to share what we learned. He'd never bring his armies to overwhelm Shurakan."

"Unless," said the priest, "he were given what he considered reason. However slight. And his heir is here—the one who will rule after him, if the gods ordain. Might she not be the beginning of his invasion?"

"Believe me," said Vanyi, "Daruya would sooner die than be her grandfather's puppet."

The priest shrugged slightly, contemplating the dead man as before, with an expression of honest grief. "So would this man, and we gave him his wish. We cannot endanger our kingdom. Surely, lady, you understand that."

"I understand that you barely comprehend what you did in breaking the Gate. And your servants don't comprehend at all that the prayers they chant, the circles they dance in, are workings of magery. What will happen when they learn the truth?"

"The gods defend them," said Esakai, "and through them this kingdom."

"All priests are blind," said Vanyi, who was herself a priestess of the Sun.

He did not know that. He sighed, pitying her. "You thought to be a sacrifice. I name you hostage. Let your people pay the price to gain you back—let them depart from Su-Shaklan and never return."

"It's not going to be that easy," said Vanyi. She was feeling odd. Her breath had come back, but shallower than before. Her chest was tight. Her arm ached. Had she struck it against a wall somewhere, or strained it careening round a corner?

But she was where she needed to be. "Let me send these warriors as messengers," she said. "They're safer so; I don't know how many of yours it will take to subdue them if you let them stay, when your own guards try to carry me off."

Esakai believed in the Olenyai no more than any other Shurakani; he could only see their small size and their quiet bearing. But it served him to be rid of her guards, however weak they might seem. He agreed to it.

They did not, but she commanded them. "Tell Daruya," she said. "She's not to come galloping after me. There are subtler ways to win this war."

One of them, who was slightly the taller and rather the elder, inclined his head. "I'll tell her," he said. "She won't like it."

"Of course she won't," said Vanyi. "I expect her to control her temper and think, and do what's sensible. She can do it if she tries."

"Yes, lady," said the Olenyas. His voice was perfectly bland.

She was sorry to see them go. They had been like a wall at her back, visible and tangible protection against the dark. Without them she was utterly alone.

She was bait, and this was the trap: trap within trap. She could only pray that Daruya would understand the message and see what she must do. It was more trust than most would have given that wildest—and many would say least—of the Sun's brood. But Vanyi had never quite believed that Daruya was as feckless as she seemed.

It was a frail thing to rest her hopes on, but it was what she had. She smiled at Esakai. "So then. Am I to be shut up in a dungeon, or may I have dinner and a bed?"

"You are our guest," said Esakai, "until we are given reason to think otherwise."

She bowed, ironic. "My thanks, sir."

30

DAMN THAT WOMAN, thought Daruya, to all twenty-seven
hells.

They were all in the hall, even the children—happen-
stance, chiefly, since it was evening and the daymeal was
past. The women were sewing by lamplight, the children
playing on the floor, Bundur reading from a book of old stories. Daruya listened, wondering how any of them could be
so calm with Vanyi gone to the palace and not yet come
back, and no word from her, no message, nothing. The
mages, who should have been either fretting over their
Guildmaster or arming for the fight, were sitting on the
edge of the lamplight, Aledi and Miyaz close together,
Kadin well apart and utterly silent, and the Gileni Guardian, Uruan, seemingly asleep. Even the exorcist was there,
looking surprisingly ordinary, playing with the children.

Hunin and Rahai burst in with signal lack of ceremony,
and the rest of the Olenyai after them. The hall seemed suddenly full, and not only with bodies; the air had the scent
and the taste of a storm that was ready to break. Daruya
stood up with the swiftness of relief, and half-stepped toward the Olenyai. "Where is she?"

"In the palace," Hunin answered. "She sent a message.
You are not, lady, to gallop to her rescue. You are to remember that there are subtler ways; to think, to be sensible. And
then to do what you must."

"And you *let* her send you away?" demanded Daruya.

"She commanded us," said Rahai, and not happily, either. "She was captured and is being held hostage."

"In return for what?"

"She didn't say," said Rahai.

"You didn't ask?"

He met her ferocity without blinking. "She didn't tell us. They were speaking Shurakani. I caught the word for hostage, but the rest was babble."

"I think," said Uruan from the edge of the light, "that they were meant not to know, so that they couldn't tell us. She doesn't want us to surrender whatever it is they want." He faced the Olenyai. "Did you know the men who captured her?"

"It was one man," Hunin said. "He came here more than once: a priest of the palace temple. Esakai, his name was."

"What is this?" Bundur demanded suddenly, his Shurakani voice running swift on the heels of Hunin's Asanian. "What are you saying? What is this about Esakai the priest?"

"He is saying," said Daruya, reining her patience tight, "that Vanyi has been captured and held hostage, and that she doesn't want a rescue. He doesn't know what she's hostage for. He thinks she doesn't want him, or us, to know."

"I can guess," Uruan said in Shurakani. "All foreigners out of the kingdom, and all mages dead or exiled."

"It might be more than that," Daruya said. She clenched her fists. "*Damn* her! I knew she'd do something like this. What is she trying for? To get herself killed and make a martyr, and bring down the wrath of the whole Mageguild, and the empire, too?"

The Olenyai did not understand her. The Shurakani, who did, did not know what to say. She started to stamp in frustration; caught herself. "Damn," she said, but much more mildly. "Uruan, come here. We're wasting time, talking in two languages and getting nothing said. Translate for us."

He was willing, even glad to oblige. He was still hag-gard and a little wild about the eyes, but he was in better case than Kadin. His ordeal inside the Gate seemed to be fading like a black dream; and he was strong as all his kin were, with a fierce resilience.

He would do. He rendered her outburst into Asanian, word for word. She could have done without quite so faith-ful a translation, but she had asked; she could hardly call back the asking.

Chakan responded at once and firmly. "The Guildmas-ter would do no such thing. She asked you to be sensible. To think."

"I am thinking," said Daruya. "I'm going to fetch her."

"You are not."

It came from both sides, in two voices, in two languages: Chakan, Bundur. They stared at each other in astonishment and swift anger—gods, even in that they were alike.

Suddenly they laughed. Chakan recovered first, and spoke in Daruya's furious silence. "She was not, whatever you may think, telling you not to do it so that you actually would. She has a better opinion of you than that."

"Not that I've ever noticed," Daruya muttered.

"I have." Bundur glanced at Chakan. "The warrior is right. She thinks she can accomplish something in the pal-ace, and safely enough to send her guards away."

"Or unsafely," said Daruya. "These aren't her warriors. They're my grandfather's and mine. It's not her place to get them killed."

"Daruya," said Chakan, "as logical as that might be, it's not like Vanyi. She's in the palace, yes. She knows who's been breaking Gates—he's holding her hostage." He turned toward Bundur. "My lord, do you know this priest?"

Even in a temper Daruya could note the enormity of the concession: Chakan the Olenyas had granted a foreigner his title.

Bundur could not be aware of the exact degree of the

honor, but he seemed to notice that he had been admitted to favor. "I know this priest," he said through Uruan. "He's one of the oldest of the old guard, well known to everyone, with no enemies that I've ever heard of. I'm amazed if what your warriors think is true, that he's been the mind behind the attacks on mages. It seems unlike him."

"Yet he is of the old way of thinking, yes?" Chakan inquired. "And he has the art of seeming less than he is— that's not uncommon. Who notices a harmless old creature doddering about, mumbling a word here, casting a smile there? What if the word were that mages were to be destroyed and the foreigners cast out, and the smile were directed at those who did so with utmost dispatch?"

"He needn't have done anything himself," said Daruya. "He could just suggest. And hint. And deplore. Oh, so many foreigners, so many mages, and that ghastly Gate of theirs . . ."

She stopped. They thought her finished: Bundur said something, but she was not listening.

Gate, she thought. That was how it had begun—not with mages killed or hunted out, or foreigners expelled. With a Gate, through which an embassy was known to be coming, an embassy from a great and distant empire.

Suppose . . .

"Suppose," she said, "that mages aren't what he fears most. He's afraid of them, there's no one in Shurakan who isn't, but they aren't his great fear. No; he dreads what their magic has made. Their Gate. Their door to other worlds, that opens on a particular city in a particular realm. Now suppose he's given word that an embassy has asked and been granted leave to use that Gate to enter Shurakan. The embassy is to be made up of mages—whom all Shurakani hate and fear—and of the heir to that foreign empire, which is ruled by mages who are also priests." She paused. They were all silent, staring at her.

"Don't you see?" she said. "We were thinking to honor

Shurakan by sending our best and highest: the Master of the Mageguild, the princess-heir of Sun and Lion. What if Shurakan didn't see the honor? What if it saw something else?''

"Conquest," said Chakan. "Yes."

"Not all of us saw that," Bundur said. "Not even most. We were honored, as far as we knew how to be."

"But a few saw the Gate, and saw armies riding through it," said Chakan. "So did the emperor, for the matter of that. Vanyi prevented him from doing more than think, but would Shurakan know or trust that she would do it?"

"I would wager," said Daruya slowly, "that she thinks she can convince her captor of that, and talk him round—or at least confuse him enough to let us escape."

"Not escape," Bundur said. "Or exile, either, I don't think. She wouldn't give up that easily. She thinks she can gain time somehow, maybe for us to bring back the queen."

"There is that," said Daruya. "Borti—majesty—what do you—?"

There was no answer. Borti's chair was empty. And Hani was alone on the floor in a wrack of scattered toys, looking dazed and somewhat sleepy. Daruya throttled an urge to seize him and shake the truth out of him.

His father spoke before she had mastered her voice. "Hani, where did Kimeri go?"

Hani blinked. "I don't know," he said. "She went away."

Bundur would have pressed, but Daruya forestalled him. "No, don't. The imp put a wishing on him. If he ever knew where she went, or even when, he's forgotten."

Bundur's eyes rolled like a startled senel's. She caught him, shook him till he looked her in the face. "There. There, stop it. You're supposed to be reining me in, not the other way about."

He gripped her arms hard enough to bruise, and sucked in a breath. But he was calmer; he was seeing sense again.

His hands loosened but did not let go. "I'll tan her hide," he said.

"You'll have to wait till I'm done first." Daruya glanced about. No one else was gone. If they were quick—if they raised a hunt—

"They might only have gone to the privy," said Chakan, "or the imp might be getting into perfectly reasonable mischief with the hounds or the seneldi."

Daruya did not believe it, much as she wanted to. But she let him send his hunters through the house, to discover what she had known already: that her daughter and the queen of Shurakan were gone. Together, she was sure. To the palace, most possibly. Where Daruya could not in good sense go—not while Vanyi was there and doing whatever she was doing to protect the embassy.

It was nothing different from what she had done since she arrived in Shurakan: waited, fretted, found nothing useful to do with herself.

And the queen, whom she barely knew, whom she did not truly trust, had taken her daughter and vanished. Another hostage; another prisoner. Another and most compelling reason to do as Vanyi forbade, and descend on the palace with fire and sword.

There was a hand on her. There were two. One was broad and bronze-dark, one smaller, narrower, ivory-pale. She met two pairs of eyes: narrow and black, wide and yellow-golden. Such unlikely allies. They did not know or like each other, or even speak the same language. And yet, when it came to Daruya, they agreed altogether too often.

"Wait," said Chakan.

"Be patient," said Bundur. "You'll have your gallop, I'm sure, and your cup of blood, too, that you seem so thirsty for. But wait a bit. Give Vanyi time to work."

"If she's not dead," said Daruya, "or too badly hurt to do anything at all."

"You'd know," Chakan said.

She would. Damn him for knowing it. And damn Vanyi for forcing her to think about sense. And damn Borti, and damn Kimeri, and damn her own self, because she could do nothing at all but wait and seethe and, when she had wits enough, pray.

BORTI IN HER plainest self seemed no more in the mind's eye than a servant. Kimeri being nobody in particular struck anyone who looked at her as simple child-shaped object moving in shadow of adult object, and therefore safe and not to be noticed. It was easier than wearing shadows, and harder for mages to track, though they would after a while.

They walked into the palace as if they belonged there, which in fact Borti did. Vanyi's traces were in front of them, clear to a mage's sight, like the track a star leaves when it falls. She was safe, Kimeri had made sure of that. She was eating a very good dinner and talking to the priest who thought he was her captor, and thinking about going to sleep. Her thoughts were very clear inside the palace; outside of it they had been blurred, shadowy, not quite there.

The palace was warded, of course. For people who insisted that they were not mages, Shurakani were very good at raising wards. Kimeri could only do mind-shields and shadows and nothing-in-particular, yet. She did not know how to protect a whole palace or a whole city.

She was shaking inside. Not because Vanyi was caught, or because she was in the palace and it was full of people who hated what she was. No; she was used to that. But she could see inside the priest's mind, and it was all gentle and pious and very determined, and he was going to make a magic in the night that would break every Gate in every world.

He did not really know that that was what he would do.

He thought he was going to pray to his gods to keep the Gate in Shurakan closed forever, and invaders on the other side of it.

As soon as she could do it without making anybody notice, she let Borti know that she was there. They were in a passage that was empty, with empty rooms opening out of it, and an empty stair at the end. There was no light in it, but Kimeri could take care of that.

Borti stopped when the clear yellow light welled out of Kimeri's burning hand, and stared, shocked to her bones. "Child! Where in the world did you come from?"

"I've been right beside you," Kimeri said. "You couldn't go away all by yourself. You could get caught. They'd kill you."

Borti paid no attention. "You must go back," she said.

"You're going the wrong way," Kimeri said. "You need to go where Vanyi is."

"I am going where the king is," Borti said.

"You can do that after. We have to find Vanyi first. And the priest. He doesn't know what he's going to do."

"Then I'm sure she'll keep him suitably confused," said Borti. She sighed. "Child, you should have stayed with your mother. I can't trust a guard to take you back. Unless one of your shadow-men came with you?"

"They're all with Mother," Kimeri said. "You don't understand. Esakai is going to sing a prayer, and he thinks he's going to keep anybody from ever opening the Gate again. He's really going to break Gates everywhere. All of them."

Borti blinked. "Gates? All? How many are there?"

"Millions," said Kimeri. "Mages only use a tiny bit of them, but they're everywhere, on all the worlds. And they'll all fall down if Esakai says his prayer."

"Is that so terrible?" asked Borti. "It would be inconvenient, I suppose, not to be able to go from end to end of the world in a step, but people weren't meant to do that in any case. Gates are unnatural. How can it hurt any world to be rid of them?"

Kimeri was glad she was used to grownfolk who were willfully stupid. If she had not been, she would have stamped her foot and screamed. Instead she said, "Gates aren't unnatural. They're part of the worlds. Mages find them where they are, that's all, and open them. If they all break, anything can happen. Worlds might—might fall in on themselves, and Things come off the worldroads." She was shuddering. She tried to stop. "Terrible Things, Borti. Things that nobody should ever want to see."

She was scaring Borti. She had to make that better, or Borti would not want to move at all. "It might not be that bad," she said. "It might only be, if enough Gates are broken, the rest won't be able to shut. And new Gates might open by themselves. Most of them probably will open here, because this is where the first Gate broke, and it's the weakest of them all."

Finally she had said something that Borti could understand, mostly. "If Esakai tries to shut the Gate, he'll not only fail, he'll open Gates all over Su-Shaklan?"

Kimeri bobbed her head the way people did here, to say yes.

"Oh, goddess," Borti sighed. "It's like an old story. The more they try to make things better, the worse things get."

"Well," said Kimeri, "maybe the prayer will fold this world in on itself, and we'll all fall off the wheel together and have nowhere to be born again. That's not so bad, is it? Being unborn is like not knowing you exist at all. Hani told me that."

Borti shivered. "It's . . . a little more complicated than that. You don't want that to happen, you really don't."

"But if it has to," Kimeri said, "it will. Can we go find Esakai now?"

Borti thought about it for much longer than Kimeri thought she needed to. But she was not a mage, though she had a bright and shining soul inside her; she did not know how to think about magery, except with fear wrapped around it. She had to cut through the fear first, then see what she had.

After a while she asked, "How long do we have before Esakai says his prayer?"

"A while," Kimeri admitted, not wanting to, but she hated to tell lies. "He'll wait till middle night, to make it stronger, with dreams in it."

"We have time, then," said Borti. "We'll go to the king first. He may be interested to know what his allies are doing, since they don't know it themselves."

"I don't think—" said Kimeri.

"Child," Borti said, and she sounded exactly like Kimeri's great-grandfather when he had made up his mind and that was that, "I would have time to take you back to Janabundur, too, if I pressed it close."

She did not. But Kimeri shut her mouth and kept it shut.

Borti bobbed her head, satisfied. "Come with me, then. How good can your manners be? Paltai was never a monster, but he is frightfully stiff about protocol. He'll be worse, now he calls himself king."

"I can be very polite," said Kimeri, "even when I have to go to the privy and I'm in High Court and I can't."

Borti gaped at her, then laughed, hardly more than a snort. "Yes, we'll stop at a garderobe, too, before we visit Paltai. Come, child."

Paltai the pretender king was a handsome man, like Bundur but not so big, and with a much more fashionable air. He grew his mustaches to his breastbone and wore his hair in a lacquered tower, even in bed. He looked rather ridiculous, except for his eyes. Those were cold and clever, and they did not look as if they had ever worried about hurting anyone.

Kimeri wondered how he got the crown on the edifice of his hair. At the moment the glittering thing was sitting on a cushion next to his bed, where he had been playing with a servant when Borti walked in through a door that maybe he had not known was there. The servant squawked and ran away. The king scrambled all the bedclothes together around his middle and glowered at Borti, who was all he could see; Kimeri was wearing shadows again. "Woman! Did I summon you? Out, and come back in the morning."

He thought Borti was a servant, and not a very bright one, either. Borti knew it. She smiled, not a pleasant smile at all, and said, "Paltai. I'm devastated. You don't recognize your last mistress but six?"

The black eyes blinked, reckoning names and connecting faces. None of them was a plain-faced servant of early middle years. But one had been a strong-faced queen whose maids had a particular talent with paint and perfumes.

Borti showed her teeth, which were not bad for a woman her age in Shurakan. "Not much to look at, am I, without a little help from my ladies. Still, I'd thought better of you. You claimed never to forget a face or a lover."

"I never forgot you—as I knew you then," he said. "You were magnificent. You look sadly fallen now."

"I always looked like this when I wasn't being beautiful for a bedmate." Borti sounded calmer than she was. "Do you think you can rule Su-Shaklan without a queen?"

He did. But he was not going to tell Borti that. "When I've had time to settle the kingdom, I'll take a bride."

"I'm sure," said Borti. She did not believe him. "Tell me, Paltai. Did you know that your mage-killers are working magery themselves?"

"Are they?" He was not shocked at all. He was amused. "Who told you that? Your pet mages?"

It sounded like "your pet ox-droppings." Kimeri wanted to giggle, but that would have given her away.

Borti was not even thinking about giggling. "I've seen what mages do. I've seen what the priests do. It's the same thing, Paltai."

"Except," he said, "that mages do it of their own will, in overweening pride, and priests do it of the gods' will, in fitting humility."

"Such humility as this?" Borti picked up a shimmer of folded silk. It slithered down into a coat twice as long as Borti was tall, and it was real silk, worth more in Borti's mind than Kimeri could easily imagine.

Kimeri realized something that she had been too busy to notice. Paltai was a priest. His hair was a wig and his mustaches were false. He was pretending to be beautiful as he thought of it, and enjoying looking the way he meant to look when he had been king for years and years. It made him feel more like a stallion.

It was a twisty feeling. She did not like it. She was much happier when he got up, taking his blankets with him, and took off his wig and his mustaches and looked like a priest again—peculiar with his bald head and shaven face, both of them starting to grow out in a furze of black down, but not as peculiar as he had in the wig. And she could see that the crown went on his head, and fit, too, though he only rested his hand on it and stroked its tall jeweled peaks.

He was telling Borti who was king now, and enjoying thinking about it. He was a little sorry to have had to kill Borti's brother in order to be king, but not very much. He had never liked the man—had found him stiff-necked and stubborn.

He liked Borti better. He liked her rather a great deal, in fact, which was good of him. But she was in his way, and he could see that she was going to be difficult. He edged his hand toward a cord that hung by the crown.

Kimeri tugged very lightly at Borti's coat and whispered, not even aloud, though Borti heard it that way. *Let's go now, quickly. He's ringing for the guards.*

Borti's face did not change, though she heard Kimeri. She did not move, either. "This magic that the priests work is dangerous. They're trying to close the foreigners' Gate beyond all opening; they'll open it instead, and open gates all over Su-Shaklan, with the gods know what waiting to come through."

"So your mages tell you," said Paltai, his mind tight shut. "You owe them gratitude for sheltering you, certainly, but credulity was never a flaw in your character. Have they bewitched you?"

"I believe that they know their own art and its failings," Borti said. "And that they have honor, as difficult as that is to believe." She steadied herself, and throttled the temper that had always got her in trouble. "Paltai. People who could kill one king can very easily kill another—and if they remove any thought of the queen, why not remove the king, too, and establish a rule of abbots and priests? Wouldn't that be logical? Do you want to be their proof that the line of kings has failed, and the children of heaven have been forsaken by their mother and by all the gods?"

She had not even ruffled the king's composure. It was too enormous for that. "The gods have chosen me. No priest will question that."

Borti drew breath to argue, but Kimeri could hear the guards coming. She caught at Borti's hand and pulled her, no matter how strange it might look to Paltai to see Borti being tugged away from him by a blur and a shadow.

Borti came, which was more than Kimeri had quite dared to hope for. She was sad and upset and furious, but she could see what was in front of her. And that was a fool who believed more in himself than in the gods.

The guards were at the door, hammering on it. The king

ran to open it. They would know where the passage was that had brought Borti here. Kimeri kicked herself for not thinking about that till it was too late. And if the guards caught Borti, Borti was dead, just as dead as her brother who had been the king before Paltai.

There was nowhere to go, nothing to do. Except one thing. Kimeri had not known she had it till she reached inside and it was there. It was in the Gate, and part of it. It showed her how to begin. She took a deep breath and did it.

Guards poured into the room, bristling with pikes and spears and swords. There was nobody there but the king. Nobody in the hidden passageway or hiding behind the curtains. Nobody anywhere near that room, not even wrapped in shadows.

32

VANYI HAD GOT rid of Esakai at last, but not through any doing of her own: he was going to the temple of Matakan, where the priests raised the circle that would bind the Gate. He left her under guard, in reasonable comfort, with food and drink and a bed. And he left her warded. It was an effective ward, not strong but strong enough, that tangled her gently and inextricably in strands like spidersilk when she tried to lay a wishing on the guards and walk out of the room.

Clever, clever working. It used her own strength against her. The harder she fought, the tighter she was bound.

She had outsmarted herself. Her brilliant plan to lull Esakai into thinking he held her hostage, then to trust Daruya to move against the priests in the temple while Vanyi escaped and sped to Daruya's aid, was no use at all if she could not get out of her prison.

And time ran on. The priests were gathering. She had no way of knowing what Daruya was doing—the tangle of wards robbed her of any useful magery. Her body at least was behaving itself. It was more tired than it should be, but the tightening in her chest was gone, lost somewhere in the wards.

Something plucked at them. They quivered and tightened. The touch came again, subtler this time, slipping through them like a thin sharp-bladed knife, pausing, then slashing, sudden and swift. In the instant of the wards' breaking, the power—for power it had to be—caught Vanyi in a vast but gentle hand, and lifted her as a woman might lift a fledgling from the nest.

* * *

The hand vanished with breathtaking suddenness. Vanyi, robbed of its strength, staggered and almost fell.

The floor under her had changed. She had been standing on rugs. Now she stood on patterned tiles. The walls had grown both higher and wider. Much higher. Rather wider. Where the bed had been stood a monstrosity of wood and paint and gilding, several times taller than a man.

She had companions. The Queen of Shurakan, drab as a servant and grey with shock, and ki-Merian regarding them both with a worried expression. It took a moment to realize that the child was glowing like a lamp at dusk, a pure golden light that neither blinded the eye or overwhelmed the mind: sunlight as it shone in the palace courts of Starios on a fine day in spring, just after the snows had gone but before the *ailith*-boughs burst into blossom.

Kimeri did not seem aware of the power that filled her full and overflowed. Nor did she wonder at what it had done: taken a master of mages out of a warded trap and set her down far from there, and the queen too from the look of her, reaching as if to touch walls that were no longer there.

Avaryan and Uveryen, thought Vanyi, too astonished for awe. *God and goddess. What that child can do, not even knowing it's impossible . . . she's a living Gate.*

Vanyi should have seen it long since. But she had been blind as they all were, looking at a child of three summers, almost four as the child herself insisted, and deluding themselves that she was anything like an ordinary young thing. Vanyi should have known better. She had heard the tales of what Estarion had been when he was a child, and she had seen his son and his granddaughter—mages born, with the Sun's fire in them even in the womb. None of them had been as purely mageborn as this one, she did not think. Unless they were better at hiding it, or had more determined guardianship.

None had been so surely bound to Gates. And none had

been caught in a Gate as it fell, not so young. Vanyi had seen what Daruya could do on the worldroad, the glorious blaze of her power that she raised in that place as easily as she breathed. Suppose that that power had roused her daughter's power as well. Then suppose that Kimeri's magery had begun to grow, fed by the Great Wards and by the troubles in Shurakan, and by the Gate she had awakened and left blind after the Guardian was rescued from it.

Suppose that the Gate was not blind. Suppose that it was part of the child. Suppose . . .

Vanyi was dizzy. She found herself sitting on the floor, with Borti slapping her face lightly and Kimeri clinging to her hand, pouring magery into her. "Your heart tried to stop," Kimeri said. "Don't let it do that again."

Vanyi felt very strange. She could not shape words at all, and yet her mind was dazzlingly clear. The pains in her body, in her arm—idiot. Of course. Any herb-healer knew what that meant.

Her heart was beating oddly. It was scarred, distended, as if it had tried to shake itself to pieces but been forestalled. But when—?

When she argued with Esakai. It had been happening for a long while, but quietly, as these things did. She had refused to notice. She was getting older, she tired more easily, how not? There was nothing wrong with her.

Kimeri was beginning to be frightened. "I can't make it better," she said, half in tears. "I don't know how."

"This is close enough," Vanyi said. Ah: words again. And breath that did not seem to tighten her chest every time she drew it in. She tried standing up. Dizziness hovered, but she drove it away. She could walk: she circled the place, which was a curtained sanctuary, she saw, in a larger temple.

"Vanyi," said Kimeri. Her voice trembled a little. "We have to go now, if you can. They've started the magic."

So they had. Vanyi found that the palace wards were not

as strong as they had been, or else and more likely the child's power pierced right through them. She heard the opening notes of the chant, felt in her bones the shifting of powers about the circle.

The outer sanctuary was empty. She strode toward it.

"By the time we could run there," Kimeri said behind her, "it would be all over. We have to go the other way."

"No," said Vanyi. "You're staying here, and I'm going there."

"You'll die," Kimeri said. "Your heart will burst if you run."

So it would. Damn the child's clear sight. But if she used the Gate—

She was, abruptly, elsewhere. It did not grow easier with use. The dizziness this time at least did not fell her, and her battered heart stumbled but steadied. She saw it with her mage's eyes as a great bruised fist.

She forced herself to understand where she was. Another temple, a god with an ox's body and human face and stance, a white ox drowsing in a pen heaped high with offerings. People staring—painted images, she would have thought, but they breathed. Their eyes were blank, bedazzled, lost in dreams of woven darkness and light.

The weavers of the magery stood together where the Gate-magic had set them, staring about as blankly as Vanyi must have the first time she was swept away by the Gate. One or both had had the presence of mind to catch and hold the priests in the sanctuary as soon as they all appeared out of air, but that might have been instinct, or magery wiser than its bearers.

Daruya came to herself before Kadin. Her face woke to an expression of pure, fierce glee—swiftly conquered as she guessed who must have brought her here. "Vanyi! So you needed me after all."

"Not I," said Vanyi. She tilted her chin. "That one."

Kimeri looked little enough like a child caught in mischief. She was urgent but polite, as she had been trained to be. "Mama, could you tan my hide later? They're breaking Gates in there."

"And if they break Gates," Vanyi said, "they'll very likely break her. Though I can't be sure. I've heard of a living Gate—it's supposed to have been possible, long ago, if a mage were powerful enough. But I've never seen one, or heard more than the mention."

She was babbling. Daruya did not not tax her with it, or silence her, either, but went straight to the point. "Kimeri. Shield yourself, and stay shielded. And stay close to me. It's you they'll break if they can—you've got the Gate inside you."

And how, Vanyi wondered, did she know that?

She was Sun-blood. They were all outside of ordinary human reckoning, no matter how human they seemed—no matter how young or wild or foolish.

Kimeri went to her mother as she had been commanded. She took the hand her mother held out: the burning hand, that flamed so bright as they touched, that it put every shadow to flight. The temple afterward seemed black dark despite the many lamps that were lit in it, and the light of the Sun's youngest child, as coolly golden as ever, and as steady. Daruya shed no light but what had been in her hand; she was shielded. "Kimeri," she said, warning, reminding.

Kimeri's light went out abruptly. She seemed shadowy without it, insubstantial, small gold-and-ivory child with wide yellow eyes, more like an owl's than a lion's.

A shadow shifted, startling them. Kadin glided toward the inner sanctuary, toward the sound of chanting that came clear now that Vanyi listened. There was nothing human in the way he moved. He was pure hunter, pure panther.

Grief stabbed Vanyi, sudden and unexpected, twisting

in her struggling heart. He had been a beautiful boy, quiet but brilliant, with a great gift for weaving shadows. Jian had cast light in his dark places, heart as well as power. Without her he was a shell of himself.

Vanyi had hoped that he could be healed; that he could find another lightmage and be, if not what he was before, then strong enough, and whole. It had happened before with twinned mages left alone by death of body or power. But not often. Not when they were bound in heart as in magery, as Kadin had been with Jian.

There was little left of him now but air and darkness and a great hate. She watched Daruya run after him—saw the brightness that yearned to fill the dark, and the dark that would have welcomed it. She thought briefly, wildly, that it was possible. That this darkmage could join power with the heir of the Sun—law, custom, compacts be damned. What did Daruya care for any of them?

But the dark was empty of aught but vengeance. The light was too searing bright, its bearer too much the child of Avaryan. Even as the two powers met, they recoiled. Kadin stumbled. Daruya nearly fell.

They recovered almost as one. Kadin flung himself toward the door of the inner sanctuary. Daruya caught at him, too late.

When Vanyi was in great extremity she was at her calmest, and at her coldest and most clearheaded. There was a way, she reflected, to break any ward ever raised, even a Great Ward. One had to be mad to try it, or so set on a goal that one took no notice of the wards at all. One leaped, body, power, and all, full into the center of the warding.

And, if one was fortunate, one died. If one was not, one suffered as Uruan had in the broken Gate: one was trapped and unable to escape.

Kadin was not fortunate. Nor was he trapped. As he touched the wards, as they flared to light and life, his power snatched at Daruya's and seized it. Kimeri's was woven in it, and in Kimeri's was the Gate.

All together they struck the wards. No such defense had been made to withstand the full power of Sun and dark, wielded by one who cared not at all whether it killed them. The light of the Sun seared the wards from end to end of their expanse. The darkness in Kadin opened wide to swallow them.

And they were through, into the sanctuary.

The circle in its actual presence looked like a gathering of priests about an elder. In magesight it was like one of the peaked round towers that were so common in Shurakan, its many pillars holding up a tall conical roof adorned with a glitter of ornaments, a spikiness of cupolas, a bristle of rods that called away the lightnings from the rest of the tower. The king's crown of Shurakan was very like it in shape and semblance.

This was a tower of prayer—of magic, many-pillared but rising to a common center. That was Esakai, anchoring the chant with his voice, thinned with age as it was, but true.

He faltered not at all as his wards were broken, his shrine invaded. His priests were rapt in the chant. Their minds were pure prayer, pure magic.

Mages never let themselves be so lost in their workings, not even when they raised the circle. It was dangerous: it could cost them power and sanity. But it was a mighty sacrifice. It left them all open to the wielding of the one who led them, the one who preserved will and awareness, and directed their power as he chose.

"As *you* choose," said a voice, clear and cold and seeming inhuman. But it was Daruya's, familiar enough yet unreachably strange. This was the Sunchild pure, stripped of passion and of petulance, speaking with the clarity of a god.

"You choose this, Esakai of Ushala temple. You work your will upon this edifice of magic. No god speaks through you or wields you. Only your own desire."

"You are blind and deaf to my gods," Esakai said—chanted, weaving through the drone of the priests. "You know nothing. You are nothing. You shall be nothing."

Nothing, nothing, nothing. The echoes throbbed in the heart of power, sapped it of strength, drained light away and made darkness dim and frail.

Vanyi's own power lashed out in pure denial. She would *not*. She refused.

She almost laughed. Daruya, great artist of refusal, wove power with Vanyi's and strengthened it immeasurably. She saw the humor in it, too: laughter, painful but true, and levity that turned the priests' chant to a shimmer of wry mirth.

Truly, Vanyi realized. The chant had faltered. Priests were giggling or grinning or simply looking surprised.

"Yes, laugh," said Daruya with sudden fierceness. "Laugh at this liar who bids you work magic in the name of his gods. No god speaks to him. He is a mage, no more, no less. A worker of his own will on the gods' creation."

"You are a demon," sang Esakai, "sent to tempt us. See, my holy ones! See how this child of the realms below has twisted and mocked all that you are."

"I am the Sun's child," said Daruya. "You are a mage, and a ruler of mages. Your kind drove the goddess' children to Su-Shaklan and taught them to hate the very name of magic. You defended yourselves with lies and deceptions. You named yourselves priests, hid in your temples, worked your magics in secret, under the name of prayer. But they are still magics. You are still mages. You cannot deny the truth of what you are."

There was more than conviction in her voice. There was power. She spoke truth as only a mage could speak it.

It swayed those priests who had fallen already out of the

chant, but the rest were bound still, held by the power of the one who led them. The circle was diminished, but it held.

Beyond the world of the senses, where magery came into its own, Vanyi felt the trembling of ground beneath her feet. Gates were woven with the substance of every world. This prayer, this working, sought to unweave it, thread by thread on the loom of the worlds, Gate by Gate. One by one, from Shurakan outward, through the place where its Gate had been, the Gate that was now a living thing.

Vanyi heard a child's voice, soft, frightened. "Mama. Mama, I'm all strange inside."

Daruya had Kimeri in her arms and such an expression on her face as no enemy should ever live to see. Kimeri was bleeding light. The swifter the chant, the swifter she bled. Her center was darkness, shot with stars: the Gate, and the focus of the working.

Shadow swept across the circle. Silence rode it. Kadin the darkmage wielded it, smiting it as he had smitten the wards on the door, with the same perfect heedlessness of the cost.

He had won through the wards. The circle was stronger. It took its strength from the toppling of Gates. The chant wavered, the Gates ceased to fall, but only for a moment. It rose again, mightier than before. Kadin fell reeling back.

He caught himself, sprang forward once more. He would do it again and yet again, till he destroyed himself.

Vanyi called in all the power she had. She felt the gathering of Daruya's magery, bright blazing thing, feeding Kadin's darkness, giving him all her temper, all her pettiness, all her rebellions both lesser and greater—all her weaknesses melded into one great strength.

She made of it not a weapon but a vision. Clarity. Truth unalloyed, driven straight and clean and true, direct to the heart of the circle. Full into the mind and soul of the one who led it, the priest who believed that he served his gods.

He could refuse it, but Daruya was a master of refusal.

She knew precisely how to force it past his resistance. He could blind himself to it, but she of all people knew the art of opening eyes and mind that were shut, locked in stubborn certainty. He could even try to run away from it—but she caught him and held him and made him see exactly what he had done, the good and the ill, the piety and the folly. Gates opened rather than broken, powers roused that had never known the name of Shurakan, worlds shivered on their foundations, that must break under the weight of his beloved kingdom.

He had fallen silent in shock and resistance. The chant went on without him. It had its own power now, its own will to completion. The magic wove itself, unweaving worlds.

Vanyi cut across it with her own strong force of truth, her dart of power into each separate mind, rapt, entranced, lost in the working, it did not matter. She spared nothing of her strength.

She met a force of darkness, darkmage striking with the same truth and the same vision. He too spared nothing, not even mercy. Minds shrank in horror from what they had done, from what they were trying to do. He showed them their folly bare. He turned them on themselves, and their working with them.

One by one and then together, they fell from the working.

But the working was too far advanced. It sustained itself. It fixed on the focus that was the youngest of all the Gates, the one that dwelt in living flesh. It poised to strike, and in striking to fell them all, Gates, worlds, whatever was woven in its substance and so must be unwoven.

One last time the darkmage sprang. He made himself a shield. He took the force of the working full in his center.

It pierced him through. It unmade him. It shattered him from center to farthest extent, body, mind, and power.

And it veered aside not a hair's breadth.

Kimeri could do nothing. She was in pain beyond anything Vanyi could imagine, rent from within and without, and that only by the beginning of the working. Her mother held her in silence more terrible than if she had raged or wept.

Estarion would have Vanyi's hide if she let both his heirs be destroyed by a mageworking gone mad. She thrust her sluggish body toward them, with its stumbling heart, its blurring sight, its cold feet. She was dying, that was perfectly obvious. She would do her best to take the working with her.

Kimeri gasped. It was loud in the silence. She struggled in her mother's arms. Daruya, taken off guard, dropped her.

She stumbled as her feet struck the floor, but she did not fall. Her whole body shook. Her face was stark white, her eyes white-rimmed. She raised her hand, the one that flashed gold. "No," she said remarkably clearly, remarkably steadily. "I don't want to. I won't."

The working had no awareness to know what she said, or how she resisted. It struck her hand.

And stopped. She did not pause to be amazed. She pushed against it—only the one hand, only the *Kasar*, with wisdom that must be instinct—and it gave way. It yielded. It flinched, even, before that palmful of burning gold.

She braced her body and leaned into the working as if it had been a vast unwieldy creature, an ox that stood in her way and sought to trample her. She pushed it back and back.

Just as she began to waver, as the working began to resist, Daruya set her hand above Kimeri's. Gold as bright, but larger, woman-large, with strong power behind it, and the force of the god. Between the two of them they drove the working inward toward the place where it was born, the circle's center, the man standing alone there, with his priests fallen or stunned or fled. It shrank as it retreated. Sun's power withered it, Sunchildren's will overwhelmed it.

They might have tried to bend it aside from the man in the circle. Or they might not. Vanyi had loved the Sun's brood for forty years and more, served them, protected them, been as kin to them. But she had never understood them; never been part of them.

Whatever they willed, whatever they intended, the working, shrunk now to the breadth of a javelin and as sharply deadly, pierced straight through the priest's heart.

He made no effort to escape it. Vanyi hoped she would never see such despair again, such perfect awareness of what, all unwitting, he had done. Even before the spear struck, he willed himself out of life, casting his soul upon the wheel, seeking life on life of expiation.

Not in truth because he had tried to unmake the worlds. Because he had failed, and in failing brought both magic and ruin to Shurakan.

33

THE POWER WAS fallen that had ruled so short a time in Shurakan. The people of the Summer City, both city and palace, woke as from a dream to find their city half in ruins. In the palace, lords and servants wandered as if lost.

All of them had seen the vision that Daruya forced upon the priests in Matakan's temple. All had known exactly what it was that they followed, and exactly what it was that they feared.

She had never meant it to spread so far. The priests' working had woven it into the fabric of the realm. They had the truth now, whether they wanted it or no.

Most of them forgot it soon enough, either because their minds could not absorb it or because they refused to accept it. Some few died of it—her fault, and her grief forever after. The rest had learned something, if only that magery was indeed something to fear.

The queen, who had seen and known it all, was strongest, too. It was she who saw to the tending of the fallen priests, both the dead and the living, and the cleansing of the temple. Inevitably, people discovered who she was. They began to trickle in as the night reeled into dawn, to look on her face that had gained nothing of beauty in the long hours since she slept. None offered to speak to her, still less to denounce her or to sink a dagger in her heart.

Word spread, soft on the morning wind. *The queen lives. She sits in the temple of the ox-god who defended White Moon-Goddess and led her into Su-Shaklan. Now he defends her child. He blesses her; he protects her as his own.*

The king came in the evening. He did not come will-
ingly, not he whose pride deafened his ears to the gods'
voices. His allies were humbler or more sincerely afraid.
They understood that their leader was dead, his body laid
before the god, and his priests dead or vanquished. Their
alliance was broken. They looked about them and saw lords
who had come out of their houses with armed men at their
backs, and the lord of Janabundur foremost. They saw a
court diminished to nothing, its ministers suddenly and nu-
merously indisposed, and its Minister of Protocol dead,
who would have had the power to impose order on confusion.

They came to the queen one by one, mute, as suppliants
to a goddess, or transgressors to a ruler from whom they
could not expect forgiveness. She forgave them—how
could she not? Without them she had no court and no kingdom. And she was fond of them, as one is of one's erring
children, one's foolish servants.

Last and most lonely and most stiffly proud came the
king. He had been left all alone in his splendid new palace,
without even a bodyservant to wait on him. They were all
gone. All fled, or huddled in and about the temple in which
the queen sat.

When he came, she was sitting at a table in the abbot's
workroom, trying to eat a roast fowl. Kimeri, none the
worse for her night's terrors, was up from sleeping the day
away, and nibbling a wing. The others were still asleep or
pretending to be, in priests' cells that had been emptied for
them, with Olenyai come from House Janabundur to guard
them—except Rahai, who insisted that he was going to
guard Kimeri and nobody else.

People kept looking at her strangely and muttering
about her being a Gate. She was not, not exactly. She was a
mage and a Sunchild who happened to have a Gate inside

of her, along with the Sun's fire and her magery. Vanyi wanted to pummel her with questions, but Vanyi was not going to be pummeling anybody for a while. Aledi had got there just before she fell over, and kept her heart beating when it tried again and determinedly to stop.

Vanyi was still alive, but it had been a near thing. She should have told Aledi long ago that she was having trouble with her heart; it was nothing a healer-mage could not mend, not if she knew about it soon enough. As it was, Vanyi was going to be well, but it would take her a long time, and she would have to be very careful. No mage-battles. No arguments, even, most of all with Aledi, who stopped being gentle when she had to contend with difficult invalids.

So Vanyi was in bed trying to get better, and Daruya was asleep, and Kimeri was with Borti, who did not seem to mind that Kimeri was a living Gate. Borti was tired almost to tears, and fighting it, which made her look stiffer and more queenly than ever. She could persuade the priests to keep people out while she got a little rest, but they would not stop lingering and staring and offering her reverence.

"You'd think I'd be used to it," she said crossly round a bite of roast fowl, "but it's downright embarrassing to have them groveling as if I were Moon Goddess herself, and not just the least of her children. If I'm not careful she'll take offense, and I'll be worse off than I was before."

"She won't mind, I don't think," said Kimeri. "They're scared. They don't know what you'll do to them. They helped the others kill your brother, after all, and they would have helped kill you, if they could have caught you."

"They thought they were doing the gods' will," Borti said. "Don't they think I understand that? They were preeminently wrongheaded, but they meant well. And I need them. They prove that I've a right to my title."

The king came just then. Hunin brought him, because

Miyaz the darkmage had insisted. Miyaz had been a prince of five robes in the High Courts of Asanion: he knew how to tell when a queen would want to be left alone, and when she would want to have a visitor.

The king looked ruffled and surly. His extraordinarily long coat was dirty all along its trailing hem, and somebody had thrown a basket of ancient vegetables at him. He had wiped the worst of it off his face, but his coat was sadly stained.

He had not worn the crown, at least, to come over to the temple. That would have got him killed. He was not much loved in the Summer City. He was a false king, and no son of heaven.

The daughter of heaven, plain tired blunt-spoken Borti with her dinner in front of her half-eaten, looked at him and sighed. Particularly when he said nastily, "So now you accept the service of demons."

He meant Hunin, who was laughing behind his eyes. Hunin did not think much of this poor shift for a king.

Borti could see that. She said to Kimeri, "Tell your warrior that I apologize for this my kinsman. He's not so ill a man, not when he's getting his own way."

Hunin approved when Kimeri told him that in Asanian. He said, and Kimeri said for him to Borti, "That is the way of princes, lady." He bowed as low as he would for a princess of seven robes in Asanion—not quite as he would for a nine-robe princess, which was what Kimeri was, and certainly not as for an empress, but from an Olenyas to a foreign queen it was a great honor. Kimeri said so.

Borti smiled at him. "Thank you," she said. He bowed again and made it clear that he was part of the wall, since she had to be polite to the king.

She bit her lip. She was trying not to laugh. "Such a prince of servants!"

She was learning to understand Olenyai in spite of their

yellow eyes and their black veils and never being able to see their faces. She barely even thought of them as demons any longer. Kimeri was proud of her for that.

The king was getting impatient, but he was too scared to show much of it. Borti looked him up and down. "Paltai," she said, "you idiot. You should have come here in a priest's robe. No one would have noticed you then."

He stood stiffly, reeking of ancient bloodroot and defunct ox-garlic. "I came in what was on my back. The servants are gone, and have taken the keys to the wardrobe with them."

"But there's another key in the—" Borti stopped, then started again. "The king would know where to find his own key. And how to convince a priest of Ushala temple that it would be to his best advantage to lend a robe for a good cause."

"There are no priests in Ushala temple," said Paltai. "They're all gone, and the doors are locked. Every door in the palace is locked, except those that lead from the king's chambers to the gate."

Borti's face stayed calm, but inside she was exultant. She had not dared to hope for that, not even in her heart, where no one else—except Kimeri, but she did not know that—could know. A lord's servants could tell him that they were no longer serving him. They did it by locking everything but the way out, and leaving him to find it before he froze or starved, since he could not get at his clothes or his dinner. It was a very rare thing, but it had happened before, if not to a king.

Paltai had to tell Borti that it had happened to him. That cost him a great deal of pride. But he was not too proud to do it. Real pride would have stayed in the palace till someone came to drag him out, or else slunk away to hide and brood and work mischief later. Paltai was more honest than that.

He also thought Borti was soft in the heart. He was gambling on it, that she would not have him killed or sent to exile in the mountains. He had earned that, and would have had it if Kimeri had been the one to decide, but it was Borti's place to say what she would do with him.

She thought about it for a long while, while he stood stiffer and stiffer, till he started to tremble. He had been too angry and arrogant to be afraid. Now, in front of Borti, as ordinary as she looked and as indecisive as she seemed, he was suddenly terrified. Something about her reminded him at long last that she was the daughter of heaven, and his allies had killed her brother, who was also her husband and her king.

After a long while she said, "There are many who would say that this upheaval in the kingdom is my fault and my brother's, not only for letting foreigners in but for failing in our duty to the gods. Since we had no heirs—since the goddess never granted us children of our bodies." She paused. That was an old pain, and one that went deep. "I am not so old yet that I cannot bear a child. I may be barren—"

"You aren't," said Kimeri. It was neither wise nor polite, but she hated to see Borti hurting. "It wasn't you. It was the king. His seed was weak."

They both stared at her. She stopped herself before she started to fidget. "I can see," she said. "I can't help it."

"Child," said Borti. "Oh, child." Kimeri could not tell if she wanted to laugh or cry. She did not know which, herself. She made herself look back at Paltai, who was looking at Kimeri with wild speculation, seeing in her a power he could use. Borti said, "No, Paltai, don't think of it. This child is my kin, if somewhat distant. She too is a daughter of heaven."

"And an heir?" Paltai asked with a twist of the lip.

"Not to this kingdom," said Borti. "And since I may not after all be barren, and my brother-king is dead, I'll be needing a consort, to do my duty to the goddess. It would have to be someone of known ability to beget children, of high family, of the blood of heaven.''

''It is a pity,'' said Paltai, ''that Lord Shakabundur is so recently unavailable.''

''Yes, it is, isn't it?'' said Borti. ''I blessed his wedding, too. They're soulbound beyond any doubt, and beyond any hope of changing it.''

''What's to prevent him from doing stud-service in the palace for the kingdom's sake?''

''Why, little, I suppose.'' Borti sighed again. ''Paltai, you do have a terrible tongue on you. Hasn't anybody ever taught you to be sparing with it?''

He started as if she had slapped him. In a way she had. He was not used to that: it made him angry. But he bit his tongue and did not say any of the things he was thinking.

Borti saw. She smiled. ''I could ask Bundur to favor me, of course. It's been done before. His lady might even allow it—one never knows. But there is another way. You've been king already. Would you return to the palace if I sanctioned you before the people?''

She had astonished him. He had been thinking that she was playing with him, taunting him with his failure, asking him to help choose his supplanter. He was really quite fool-ish, Kimeri thought, and he did not know Borti very well at all.

''There is a certain logic in it,'' Borti said. ''Granted, you saw my brother killed by your allies, and seized the crown before anyone else could move. You made no effort to pre-vent the sack of the city, nor were you able to hold your place once it was known that I was alive. You were a very poor king, taking all in all.

''But,'' she said, ''within your limits, you're not a bad choice. Your family is royal kin. You have children but no wife, which proves your ability to beget heirs to the crown, and offers no impediment to your taking the place of consort."

"Not king?" Paltai asked. He had come back to himself, sharp, wary, and beginning to believe she meant it.

"The king is dead," said Borti. "The queen has need of a consort. You were a wretched king, Paltai, but you would make a reasonable husband, all things considered."

He looked away. His tongue wanted to cut her till she bled, but the rest of him was telling it to be sensible. "I . . . don't know if that's wise," he said finally, which was not what he had started to say at all.

"Probably not," Borti said. "I don't think I care. I've always been inexplicably fond of you, and you're a pleasant bedmate. You would have to be oathbound, of course, and purified before the kingdom."

He shivered. Purification in Shurakan was not an easy thing, not for sins as great as his. He would have to shed blood and endure a great deal of pain if he wanted to be soul-clean by his people's reckoning. Even so he said, "It would be worth the trouble, to father the next children of heaven."

"I thought you might think so," said Borti.

They understood one another. Liked one another, too, better than they would ever admit. Borti would not forgive her brother's death. This was her revenge, and very clever, making Paltai give up the crown but live always in sight of it—but there was more to it than that. Someday maybe Kimeri would understand.

Paltai was ready to say yes, but he was not quite willing to let Borti know it. "What about them?" he demanded, with a stab of his chin at Kimeri. "We'll never be rid of them now, since they've won your crown back for you."

"We would never have been rid of them in any case," Borti said, not looking at Kimeri but very much aware of her. "Once they had come, they were going to keep coming, no matter what we did. I'm going to treat them like people of honor, and if necessary shame them into doing the same for us."

"Will you let them build their Gate again?"

"I don't think I can stop them," said Borti. "I may be able to control them, to a degree. After all, we know now that our priests can break Gates. If we allow the one, and set limits on who and how many may pass it, we'll give them what they want but keep them aware that we can take it away."

"We never did want to invade you," Kimeri said. "Really we didn't. We just wanted to see what was here."

"So would a child say," said Paltai.

Kimeri looked at him hard, till he flushed even darker than he was already, and ducked his head. "We aren't all perfectly honorable," she said, "but we are honest. When we say we'll do something, we do it. We keep our word. We're very simple people, I suppose."

"Or else," mused Borti, "with mages to keep everybody honest, honesty is easier." She shook herself. "No, Paltai, I won't be filling my court with mages and turning this into a realm of magic. But we do have to discover our own honesty, and our own magics. Since we've lied to ourselves for so long."

"You didn't know," Kimeri said.

"Now we do." Borti stood, wiping her fingers where they were greasy from her dinner. "Go and bathe, Paltai. When you've done that, and have rested, we'll let the kingdom know that it has a queen again in truth, and that the queen has a consort."

Paltai did not like being told what to do, but he had wits enough to know that he was outmatched. Borti's smile was warm, but it was absolutely implacable. He would do as she said, or he would be disposed of.

They would get on well together, all in all. He knew that; it made him smile after a while, wry and rather pained, but real enough. "Yes, divine lady," he said, and only about half of it was mocking.

34

VANYI WAS THOROUGHLY annoyed with herself. She had had to be carried from the sanctuary like a blasted invalid, and she had not been allowed to do so much as raise her head. If she wanted anything she asked for it, and Aledi gave it to her, or Miyaz while Aledi rested, or, the past hour or two, the youngest of the Olenyai. It was not pleasant to have to ask him to carry her to the privy. She was years past anything resembling prudery, but damn it, she was a grown woman; why in the hells did she have to be packed about like a baby?

"Because," said a warm deep voice, "you had no more sense than one, carrying on while your body was trying to kill itself. This is fair punishment; you can't dispute it."

Vanyi would have snapped erect if a pair of all too familiar hands had not held her down. An all too familiar brush of magery soothed her hammering heart and brought, if not calm, then a kind of resignation. Another came in behind it, less familiar but in its way immeasurably stronger.

She looked from Estarion to the priest-mage who had come in behind him. The latter could have been a Shurakani in a Sun-priest's torque; he was a plainsman from Iban in the Hundred Realms, and he was chief of the healer-priests in Starios. He was neither ghost nor sending; he was very solidly there.

So was Estarion. "You're not supposed to be here," Vanyi said. She was half in a fog already, what with the healer's working, and not even a by-your-leave, either. But she kept enough of her mind alert to focus on Estarion.

"I'm not here," he said. "I'm in Starios, being emperor. You're being visited by a simple citizen of the empire who offered to try the Gate now it's open again."

"The Gate's open?" She stretched out a finger of magery, but the healer slapped it back. She snarled and subsided. "We haven't done anything to rebuild it. It's a blind Gate—and Estarion, about that—"

"It's open," he said. "All Gates are open as they always were, though there are cracks in the walls in the Heart of the World. Mages are mending those. The Gate in Starios is up and strong, and when I told it to open on Shurakan, it did. Your Guardian met me on this side. I brought two pairs of mages to give what aid they could—the twins from the Lakes of the Moon, and your Guardian's cousin Iyeris and her lightmage. They're in the house of the Gate, making it habitable again with help from the people of Janabundur. Did you know that exorcist of yours has Gate-sense? He might be worth training as a Guardian. Imagine," he said, entranced with his own vision. "A Shurakani born, being Guardian of its Gate."

Somewhere far down below the fog of healing, Vanyi was furious. She was the Master of the Guild. She was the ruler of the Gates. How dared he order her mages about? How *dared* he meddle with her Gates?

He sat on the edge of the bed, perfectly pleased with himself, having broken every pact they had ever made. He only made it worse by saying, "All of this, of course, is by your leave. The Guild was struck hard when the Gates started to fall—it was all they could do to hold themselves together. They cried out for any help they could get. I happened to be nearest. I tried to do everything as you would wish."

"You came here," Vanyi said. "Do you have the least idea in any of the worlds, what will happen if people here discover what you are? They're already certain that we mean to conquer them out of hand. Your presence will only confirm it."

"Then we had better not let them know who I am," said Estarion placidly. "Later, of course, we should propose an exchange of state visits, here and in Starios, and an alliance of goodwill between our nations. At the moment I'm a messenger from your Guild, guard and escort to the healer whom you so badly need. You can receive messengers, surely? That's not forbidden?"

Vanyi closed her eyes. "Hells," she said, but without force. "Esakai was right. None of us will ever be rid of you."

"Not even if you die," he said. "Remember that." He took her hand. He was warm, sun-warm, and strong. "Haliya sends her love and her sympathies."

"And her I-told-you-sos?"

"She saves those for people who can argue with them."

She looked at him. Her mind was empty. She was healing, being healed. Slowly; Aledi had been right, it could not be quick, not as foolish as she had been.

He smoothed her hair back from her brow, easily, tenderly, as if she had been one of his children. Now that he was quiet, she could see how worn he looked. It had not been easy in Starios, either, when the Gates began to fall.

"And when you began to die," he said.

"Stop reading my mind," said Vanyi.

"I can't help it." Nor could he, since he did not want to.

She sighed. It was good to have him here, and never mind the difficulties, the politics, all the rest of the nonsense that hovered on the other side of the healer's magery. He bent over her. His face was all the world; and she could not touch it. She could not reach so high.

"You will be well," he said. It was a prayer, and an emperor's will.

* * *

Daruya had not meant to sleep till evening. There was so much to do—the Gate to look after, the mages, Vanyi—and she had dreamed straight through the day and into the night. Troubled dreams, most of them, full of shouting and confusion. Gates falling, walls tumbling in the Heart of the World, mages dying or being caught in Gates as Uruan had been. She kept trying to hold it all together with her two hands. Both of them in the dream were branded and burning with the *Kasar*, a living fire that ate at flesh but never consumed it.

She woke with relief to lamplight and quiet and the blessing of memory. The Gates were safe. She and Kimeri between them had seen to that.

Kimeri was with the queen, and content. Vanyi was asleep and very much alive. They had brought in a new healer—Daruya knew the mark of a healer-priest's power, as distinct in the mind as the *Kasar* itself. The Gate was up, then, and open, and letting people pass.

Bundur was not thinking about her at all. He was in the palace. It had been locked tight, which seemed to be the Shurakani way of telling its king that he was not welcome. The king was gone. Bundur was finding everyone who had keys, and seeing that those keys were set to the locks and the palace opened up again. The queen was coming back to it; she would find it waiting, all cleansed and opened and giving her welcome.

Daruya should not mind that he was occupied in doing his duty—she had done the same in following Kadin through Kimeri's Gate. But he was not thinking of her, either, or missing her presence. That stung.

She rose, washed the sleep from her eyes and her face, and put on her clothes. They were clean, a little damp about the edges. Her hair was a hopeless tangle. She did not even try the comb that was laid on the table beside the bed; she raked fingers through instead, tugging out the least of the knots, and gave up the rest for lost.

Someone had left her a basket with bread in it, a bit of cheese wrapped in a cloth, and a bowl of spiced fruit. She ate, and drank from the bottle beside the basket—water, nothing more.

Up, awake, dressed and fed, she ventured forth into the temple. It was dark, save where once in a great while a lamp was lit, and seemed echoingly empty. The white ox was not in her pen; she had a stable to rest in at night, out past the priests' cloister. The god did not appear to notice her absence.

"How like a man," said Daruya. Her voice woke echoes in the shrine and sent something fluttering and squeaking through the rafters.

She paused by the white ox's enclosure. Someone had cleaned it and washed it, as must be done every night, and taken away the heaps of offerings—food to the kitchens, fodder to the stable, valuables to the treasury. A faint scent of ox remained, a suggestion of ox-droppings—like magic, it could never quite be denied. The gilded bars were cool, and just high enough to fold her arms on and to prop her chin. The god's image glimmered above her.

She felt light and oddly empty, as she always did after a battle. She was not startled to hear a step behind her, soft but making no attempt at stealth. It was not Chakan: him she would not have heard at all.

She turned, prepared to greet a priest, or maybe someone from Janabundur.

Priest indeed, but not of any god in Shurakan. He was here in the flesh: she could feel the warmth of him and catch his scent, which was different from that of the men here, sharper, with a suggestion of seneldi, a hint of ul-cats. He leaned on the bars of the ox's pen, chin on folded arms as hers had been, and studied the god who loomed above them. "Fascinating," he said.

"Does the queen know you're here?" Daruya asked.

Estarion slid a glance at her. "Vanyi asked me much the

same thing. The answer is no, and will continue to be no. I brought Lurian to look after Vanyi, and mages to tend the Gate. I'm going back, and quickly, too."

Why, she thought, he was defending himself—as if he thought he had any need to do any such thing. Estarion the emperor never stood in need of defense. He did as he willed, and that was that.

Estarion in the temple of Matakan seemed no older than Bundur. He was not the emperor here. He was simply Estarion.

"Grandfather," said Daruya in sudden comprehension. "You've run away."

He raised a brow. "What, you didn't think I could?"

"What if the Gate falls again? We'll all three of us be trapped on this side."

"That would be interesting, wouldn't it?" He yawned and stretched like one of his enormous cats, from nose to nonexistent tail, and stood grinning at her.

"You look," she said, stumbling over the word she wanted. Damn it, then. She would say it. "You look bloody irresponsible."

"That's exactly how I feel." He was still grinning. "I've shocked you. Imagine that. Maybe it's time I did the running away and you did the ruling in Starios. You're old enough, more or less, and steady enough, no matter what you want people to think."

"That," said Daruya through gritted teeth, "is exactly what drives me wild. You never see me as anything but good, loyal, solid, dependable, dull—"

"—despite all evidence to the contrary," he finished for her. "Not dull, no. Not you. You're a golden splendor of a child. But underneath all the sparks and the temper is a right worthy queen. You show it when you have to, you know. In Gates as they break. In temples when priests are praying the worlds to pieces."

"I had to do it," she said. "Nobody else would."

"Nobody else could."

"Except Kimeri."

"Kimeri is not quite four years old. You are what she will be when she's grown to a woman—crotchets and all, though if she's as like you as I think, she'll be utterly dutiful and obedient and quiet, because you've always made so much noise about being a rebel."

Daruya flushed. "And she'll despise me for it. That's what you're telling me, isn't it?"

He regarded her in honest surprise. "Of course not. Children will do the opposite of what their parents either want or expect. It's the way the world is."

"I don't want her to be like me."

"Nor do you want to be like you. Do you?"

Temper flared as she unraveled that. She bit back the angry words. He was waiting for them, ready to smile at them, and say something that would make her look a perfect idiot.

No. Not this time. Not either of them—not she with her outbursts, or he with his maddening calm.

God and goddess. He was exactly like Bundur. So complacent. So perfect in his superior wisdom.

With Bundur it was a pretense, a prince's mask. With Estarion—

The very same. It was easier to see here, without the dazzle of his rank to blind her. And, she admitted with creeping shame, the flare of her temper whenever she saw him or thought of him.

It had not always been this way. When she was as young as Kimeri, she had adored him. She had followed him everywhere, got underfoot in everything. And he had allowed it. Only when he fought in battles did he forbid her to follow—and she obeyed, because he showed her exactly how terrible battles were.

Somehow as she grew older it had changed. She had begun to resist him, at first to prove that she was herself, apart from him, and could do as she chose and not as he expected. Until rebellion became the expected, and she was trapped in it. And he was always the one whom she resisted most strenuously, and the one who seemed least perturbed by it.

She could never crack the polished surface of his composure. No, not even when she drove him to a rage. It was always a calm, reasonable, rational rage. He always forgave her. He never seemed to hate or scorn her, no matter what she did or said.

She did not want to tell him so. He would only tell her that his own youthful sins were far worse than her own. For all she knew, they had been. Even in that she was never his equal. She could only follow, and be the lesser.

That was foolish, too. It was wallowing, and a ripe rotten sea of self-pity it was, too.

She tried something. She said as calmly as she could, "I suppose you expect me to go home with you when you go."

"Actually," he said, "I don't. You're a lady of this kingdom now. You have duties here."

She was gaping. She shut her mouth. "Responsibilities. But I have them in the empire, too."

"None that can't wait," he said, "or be done through Gates, by messengers."

She did her best to comprehend what he was saying. "You . . . want . . . me to stay here? On the other side of the world? With people who know how to break Gates?"

"You may not want to stay," he said. "There is that."

Her eyes narrowed. "You're going to take Kimeri back, then. Aren't you?"

"Only if you ask. And if she consents."

"I won't—" She broke off. "You can't mean you're letting me decide for myself."

"Why not? You've been doing just that for rather a while now."

"But I don't want—" She stopped again.

This time he spoke before she could go on. "Do you want to go back?"

"Bundur wouldn't come. Kimeri might not. She likes it here."

"Child," he said with all the gentleness in the world. "I'm not asking you what they want, or what I want. I'm asking you, Do you want to go back to Starios?"

"Yes," she said at once. Then: "No. No, I can't. Vanyi can't travel, there's the embassy, there's Kimeri—she likes having a brother, and I—"

"And you like having a husband." He smiled. "It's pleasant, isn't it? Even if you went into it screaming denials."

She nearly screamed denial of that, but that would have been too easy. "You didn't want to marry Haliya, did you?"

"Not at all," he answered. "Not at first. I wanted Vanyi or no one. Least of all a yellow woman. Who was sure that I was going to marry all eight of her fellow concubines, that being the absolute smallest number of women an emperor in Asanion could possibly have in his harem. Even when I convinced her that I wanted only her, she was still certain that I'd take other wives later."

"Ziana," said Daruya.

"The beautiful sister, yes. But she didn't want to marry, not really. She preferred the princedom I gave her, and the daughter she adopted, and the freedom that she'd hardly dared to dream of inside an Asanian harem."

Daruya knew that very well. She had spent summers with Ziana before that lady died. But it sounded different coming from Estarion, who had taken the lady as his second wife in Asanian law, then sent her to be ruling princess in Halion. People whispered that he had put her aside in all but name, but Ziana had never thought so. Nor, it seemed, had Estarion. He had given her what she wanted most.

"You give too much," said Daruya. "You don't take enough."

"Why, what should I do?" he asked with all apparent honesty. "Run away? Leave you the regency?"

"If you have to," she said steadily.

"Maybe," he said. "In a while. Once matters are settled in Shurakan. Would your lord like to see the world beyond his mountains?"

"He intends to," said Daruya. Her heart had quickened a little. "Would you—really—?"

He held out his hand. The *Kasar* glittered. "Shall we swear a pact? When Shurakan is settled—in a year and a day, perhaps?—you'll come to Starios with your lord, and take the regency."

She kept her own hands on the bars of the ox's pen. "And you? What will you do?"

He shrugged, smiled. "I don't know. Wander. Be nobody in particular. Explore the worlds beyond the Gates."

Yearning struck her so hard that her knees buckled. To do that—of all things one could dream of, that, she wanted most.

He saw. His smile widened. "And when I come back, as I give you my solemn word I shall, then you have your freedom to go where you will. A full priestess-Journey, seven years long, if that's your wish."

"I've wished for that . . . " Her voice died. She flogged it to life again. "I could even run away to sea?"

"Even that," he said.

And his hand was still up, still waiting. She clasped it, *Kasar* to *Kasar*. No bond was stronger than that, no pact more potent. "A year and a day," she said, "until I come to Starios. And while you journey—a hand of years?"

"Not so long, I think. Another year and a day. Or two."

"You never had your priest-Journey either," she said. "A hand of years. And then I go on my own way." And what Bundur would say to that—if he thought he had any say in it—

He would lead the way through every Gate. He had it too, that eagerness rigidly curbed, that longing to fly free.

"God and goddess," said Daruya. "I married my grand-father's image."

"And your own," Estarion said. He pulled her into his embrace. She startled him, nigh hugged the breath from him. He laughed with what little he had left, and kissed her forehead, and left her there, blinking, astonished at them both.

35

WHEN THE QUEEN had returned to the palace and taken her consort, and the mages had rendered the house of the Gate fit to live in, and Vanyi was up and walking and doing her best to outwit the healer-priest who stood watch on her, Daruya climbed with Bundur and the children and two of the Olenyai, up the Spear of Heaven. It was a full day's journey to the mountain, even on senelback; the seneldi waited in camp on the mountain's knees, with Yrias to guard them and keep them from straying.

Daruya had seen little of Bundur in the days of the queen's return. For all her magery and for all her resolve to be a woman and not a petulant child, she could not help feeling as if a distance had grown between them.

He seemed oblivious to it. And yet it was he who said to her as they woke of a morning and he prepared to go yet again to the palace and the court, "If I asked you to run away with me, would you go?"

Her heart leaped, but she was wary. "Where would you run?"

"Not to your empire," he said, reading it in her eyes. "Not yet. But there's yonder mountain my namesake, and it's calling me. I've a mind to climb it."

"Even to the snows?" she asked.

"Even so far, if you like," he said.

"I would like," said Daruya.

Which was why they were here, scrambling up the steep stony track, still well below the line of the snow. It would have been only the two of them, but Kimeri was not to be denied, and Hani refused to be left out. They would go as far as a place Bundur knew, and share the daymeal; then they would go back down with their Olenyai, and Bundur and Daruya would go on till they met the snow. The summit they could not reach, or so Bundur thought. The air was too thin.

But he had never climbed a mountain with a mage. Daruya meant to stand on the Spear's very tip and greet her forefather the sun, and see all the world spread out below her.

This was a more earthly pleasure, much like the journey into Shurakan, climbing the side of a mountain with a pack on her back, for they would not come to the snow till nearly sunset, and would have to camp there, up against the sky. It was still almost warm here below. Her boots felt hot and unwieldy; her coat was rolled and fastened to her pack, and she climbed in her shirt, and would have shed even that if it had been a little warmer. The Olenyai, wrapped in robes and veils, must have been sweltering.

From the mountain's side she could see little of what was ahead, but if she looked back she saw the whole of Shurakan, deep green goblet of a kingdom, rimmed with snow. Clouds ran swift below, and broke like breakers against the mountain walls. The Summer City on its terrace seemed far away and yet very clear, a circle of walls enclosing roofs and turrets.

One tower flew a streamer of scarlet, a minute flash of gold: House Janabundur with its banner that Chakan had raised, golden sun on scarlet silk. It was the custom, he insisted, when a Sunchild was in residence and making no secret of it; therefore he would have it here in this foreign country. Some of the court already had admired the fashion and considered flying banners of their own, oblivious as all Shurakani were to the distinction between an imperial heir and a mere and minor lordling of the court.

Daruya smiled at the banner and at the one who had insisted on it. He was carrying Kimeri on his back, making nothing of the child's light weight; his eyes returned her smile. The grim guardsman of the first days in Shurakan was gone. He was the Chakan she remembered, on guard always but willing to ease into laughter. And he seemed to have decided, if not to trust Bundur, then at least to regard him with less suspicion.

They scrambled up a last and nigh impossible slope, slippery with stones and scree, and teetered on a sudden narrow rim, and descended into a ring of startling green. It was like an island in a sea of clouds, a tiny valley, even a forest in miniature, a grove of gnarled and knotted trees that bore sweet fruit. A little stream ran through it from the living rock, a cavern overhung by the arch of a tree.

Daruya stood on the valley's edge, struggling for breath yet trying to laugh. When at last she could speak, she said, "Bundur! This is just like the dragon's cave in the tapestry."

"This is the dragon's cave," he said, and very pleased he was with it, too. "This is where the Warrior Sage fought with the dragon, and won by losing, and the dragon taught him to brew tea from the leaves of the cloudfruit bush." He gestured toward a tangle of low thicket. "There, see. Cloudfruit."

"And water, and mountain apples, and grass to sit on," said Kimeri, standing on her own feet again and running toward the stream. Daruya reached by instinct to catch her, but Bundur had no fear; nor did her power. There was no dragon in the cave, and no cave-bear either, though she heard the squeaking of cavewings deep within.

The Olenyai paused in following the children toward the water. They exchanged glances. Chakan dropped veils, headcloth, outer robe. He folded them, tucked them under his arm, and grinned at Bundur, who was struggling not to stare and failing miserably. "No fangs," he said in atrociously accented Shurakani. And trotted after the children, lithe in shirt and trousers, with his swords slung behind him. Rahai strode in his wake.

"Gods," said Bundur. "They're no more than children."

"Rahai is older than you," Daruya said. "And he won't live as long." She paused. "An Olenyas' face is his honor. Who sees it, unless he be friend and kin, must die."

Bundur went very still. "And what am I? Friend or prey?"

"Both," said Daruya. "It's an honor—and a warning."

"Ah," he said. "I serve you well, or I return to the wheel of souls on the blade of an Olenyas' sword." His eyes followed the bred-warriors where they dipped water from the stream, forbidding the children to drink until they had proved it safe. They did look like children themselves, as small as they were and seeming slight, with their cropped yellow curls and their smooth ivory faces. But the scars of rank on their cheeks—Chakan's five, Rahai's four—betrayed the truth; and the twin swords, and the way they moved, light and supple, like hunting cats.

"I suppose," mused Bundur, "they took the veils at first because no one reckoned them dangerous. Are they beautiful in your country?"

"Very," said Daruya.

"They're pretty," Bundur said. "You are beautiful."

She widened her eyes at him. "What? I thought I was ugly but interesting. Now that I'm beautiful, am I dull, too?"

She was only half laughing. He caught at her, pack and all, and turned her round to face him fully. "Is that what you think? That I've grown bored with you?"

"No," she said, but slowly. "I think you've been too busy to be bored."

"Too busy to notice you, or to see that you're fretting as if in a cage." She would have spoken to deny it, to say that she had enough to do among the mages, looking after her daughter, tending Vanyi, standing guard on the Gate. But he laid a finger on her lips, silencing her. "You were bred to rule over princes, and we keep you locked up like a novice in a temple. If it's in your heart to go back to your empire, go."

Her eyes blinked against sudden tears. Foolishness: her courses were coming on, that was all. "Do you want me to go? Have I become an inconvenience?"

"No!" He had spoken too strongly, or so he was thinking—idiot man. He softened his voice. "Lady, I would keep you here your whole life long, and love you every moment of it. But you were never born for a realm so small. It stifles you."

Guilt stabbed. She had not told Bundur of her pact with the emperor. There had been no time, and no suitable occasion.

If she did it now, he would think she mocked him. If she did not, she truly would be making a fool of him, who had never done her aught but honor.

She bit her lip. "Bundur—"

"You'll leave when your time comes," he said. "I know that. I expect it. But if you think you have to endure until then, out of loyalty or honor or even pity—"

"Bundur!" He stared at her. "Bundur," she said, less sharply. "I will leave, yes. I gave the emperor an oath that in a year and a day I'd go back to his city and take his place while he rested. He's been emperor for half a hundred years—it's horrible, when I think of it. I wonder that he didn't run away long since." She was babbling. She made herself stop. "I also promised him . . . you'd come, too. I wasn't thinking at the time, I wasn't remembering—you can be so proud, and I—"

"Daruyani," he said. He had loved the full form of her name ever since he first heard it; but he kept it for great occasions. It was too beautiful, he said, to dull with use.

Her eyes were blurring again. Loving a man was nothing like bedding him. It was awkward; it was difficult. It kept reducing her to tears.

"Daruyani," said Bundur, "I told you long ago that when you went to your own country I would go with you, if you asked. But if you only think to ask for fear of offending me, then I refuse. I won't burden you with unwanted presence."

"I want you," she said. Her voice was rough. "You'll have to learn our language; you'll be needing it, to be my consort. You'll have to learn our laws and our customs, and all our ways."

"Am I such a barbarian as that?" he asked, trying to be light, but his eyes were glittering.

"You are exquisitely civilized," she said, "and very foreign. The courts will find you exotic, and call you beautiful."

His cheeks flushed darkly. It was one thing to know himself a handsome man. Beauty—that was difficult, if one were a man, and possessed of a certain kind of pride.

She linked arms about his neck. They fit well, they two; they were eye to eye, standing on the edge of the grassy level. She thought briefly, mischievously, of plucking loose the cords that bound his hair and letting it fall straight and shining. But that would embarrass him in front of the children and the Olenyai.

Later, she thought. Tonight, under the stars, on the edge of the snow. "They'll call you beautiful," she said, "but none of them will lay a hand on you. Unless of course," she added after a moment, "you want it."

"And will you kill them then?"

"I might."

"Am I allowed to ask what I can do to a man who lays a hand on you?"

"You can kill him," said Daruya.

He began to smile, long and slow. "I like your country, I

think. Here, you could take another husband, and I would have to suffer it."

"And in some parts of my empire," said Daruya, "you could take other wives, and I would be expected to smile and be kind to them, and share your gracious favors."

He knew her well. He heard the edge in her voice. It widened and deepened his smile. "You like our country, too, then, where no man takes more than one wife."

"I suppose that means we're well matched."

"Very well," said Bundur. He sounded enormously complacent, much pleased with himself and his world. She would slap him out of that. But later. When he was not so charmingly entranced with her.

"Yes," he said, with his eyes full of her face, and his mind full of wonder that it should, after all, be beautiful. "We are matched." His brows drew together. "It doesn't make you angry still. Does it?"

She did slap him for that, but lightly, barely hard enough to sting. "Idiot," she said. "Of course it does. But only when you ask."

She caught at his hand and tugged him forward. The Olenyai were well ahead, with water-bottles full, carrying them up to the cave. Kimeri was carrying something taken from Chakan's pack; Hani had something else, balancing it gingerly as he picked his way through the grass.

As Daruya realized what they carried, she burst out laughing. Kimeri had the little brazier with its lidded jar of coals, Hani the pot and the cups for brewing tea; and that would be the packet of the herb that rested so precariously on top of the heap of cups. They were going to brew tea in the dragon's cave, for luck and for friendship, and because no one could ever do anything in Shurakan without a cup of tea.

She looked back at Bundur, who was following slowly. His somber expression had vanished. He grinned at her, and a fine set of white teeth he had, too.

"And what," she wondered aloud, "would a dragon look like, if he were flesh and not myth? Might he look like a prince of Shurakan?"

"He might," said Bundur. "Or she might look like a princess of Sun and Lion, from the other side of the world."

She stopped, briefly outraged. Dared he liken her to a ravening beast, however prettily subdued?

Indeed. And rightly, too. She shrugged, sighed, smiled, and went to drink tea in the dragon's hall.